19/04/22

PUSHKIN PRESS

"A born storyteller"
Guardian

"Germany's answer to J.K. Rowling"
Telegraph

"A master"
Independent

"A highly distinctive imagination"
Daily Mail

The Reckless Series

Cornelia Funke

RECKLESS IV
The Silver Tracks

With Illustrations by the Author

Translated by Oliver Latsch

PUSHKIN PRESS

MIRRORWORLD was originally a collaboration between Cornelia Funke and Lionel Wigram.

Pushkin Press
71–75 Shelton Street
London WC2H 9JQ

Original text and illustrations © 2021 Cornelia Funke
English translation © 2021 Oliver Latsch

The Silver Tracks was first published as *Auf silberner Fährte* by Dressler in Hamburg, 2020

First published by Pushkin Press in 2021

9 8 7 6 5 4 3 2 1

ISBN 13: 978-1-78269-329-1

Typeset by Tetragon, London
Printed and bound by CPI Group (UK) Ltd, Croydon, CR0 4YY

www.pushkinpress.com

FOR GARCIA

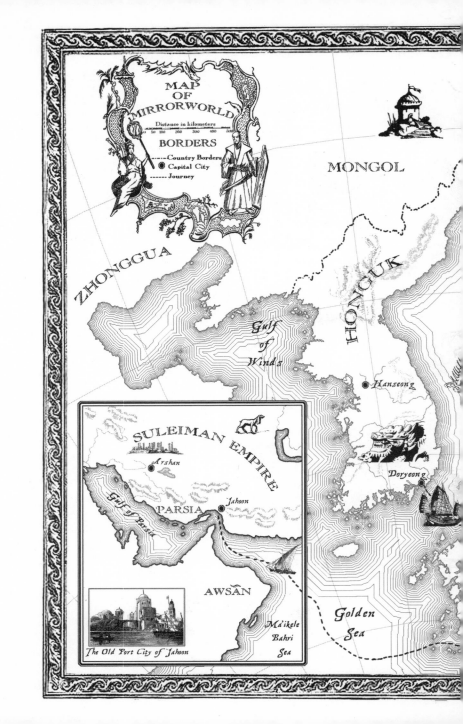

MAP
OF
MIRRORWORLD

Distance in kilometers
0 50 100 200 300 400 500

BORDERS

---- Country Borders
● Capital City
----- Journey

MONGOL

ZHONGGUA

HONGUK

Gulf of Winds

● *Hanseong*

SULEIMAN EMPIRE

● *Arshan*

Gulf of Parsa

PARSIA

● *Jahoon*

● *Doryeong*

AWSĀN

Golden Sea

Ma'ikele Bahri Sea

The Old Port City of Jahoon

SAKHA

Great
Serpent
Sea

Toyohira

Ezochi

Sea
of
Silence

Shu

Shinano

NIHON

Edo

Miyako

Kannai

Fushi

Naniwa

Karatsu

Futana-shima

Hodogaya

Kyukoku

1

TOGETHER

Fox felt Jacob's breath on her neck, warm and familiar. He was sleeping so soundly that he didn't wake up when she gently eased out of his embrace. Whatever he was encountering in his dreams made him smile, and Fox ran her fingers over his lips as if she could read what he was dreaming. The two moons that shone on her world dappled his forehead with rusty red and pale silver, and birds whose names she didn't know cried outside the inn.

Doryeong... Her tongue could barely pronounce the name of the port city where they had arrived the day before. They had given up. Maybe that was why Jacob was sleeping so deeply. After all the months in which they had lost his brother's trail and picked it up again countless times. A time or two, they had almost caught up with Will. But by

9

now they had been searching in vain for weeks for any sign of him, and yesterday, as the sun had set over a strange sea, they had finally decided to call it off. Even Jacob believed that his brother did not want to be found after all that had happened, and that it was time to go their separate ways. So why could she still not sleep? Was it because she wasn't used to being so blissfully happy?

Fox pulled the quilt over Jacob's shoulder. Their own path. Finally. A sprig of white blossoms filled the room they were sleeping in with lush, sweet fragrance. Two more travelers were sleeping on the mats the landlady had word-lessly rolled out for them. The ferry to Aotearoa ran out of Doryeong. An old friend of Jacob's, Robert Dunbar, kept sending enthusiastic telegrams from there, which told of three-eyed lizards, of enchanted whale bones, and of wild kings who had the fern forests of their homeland tattooed on their skin.

Their own path. Fox kissed the moonlight off Jacob's face and carefully slipped out from under the quilt that warmed them both. The night lured the vixen outside. Maybe if she wore the fur, all this human happiness wouldn't make her heart overflow so much.

She stole past the two stone dragons that guarded the entrance to the modest inn, and under trees that swayed their branches in the breeze from the nearby sea, she changed. The inn stood on an unpaved road, and the flat wooden houses that lined it wore their roofs like wooden cowls. Doryeong was nothing like the seaside village where Fox had grown up. Even the fishing boats on the dark waves that lined the harbor just a few houses away seemed to come from a fairy tale she had never heard of before.

The vixen looked up at the stars, and in their constellations she found images of all the roads she had traveled with Jacob these past months. Varangia, Kasakh, Mongol, Zhonggua... A year ago, all these names had meant nothing. Now they were tied to unforgettable memories — of the time when she no longer had to hide her love. They had soon lost count of how many weeks they had traveled farther and farther southeast. At some point, they had even almost forgotten that they were searching for Jacob's brother. Perhaps, in the end, they had simply wanted to leave everything behind them that might cast a shadow on their newfound happiness: the renewed treachery of Jacob's father, the death of the Dark Fairy and the role Will had played in it — and the Alderelf who wanted their child and sent hunters of glass and silver after them. In a foreign land, all of this was so much easier to brush aside.

The vixen paused. Sniffing, she raised her nose. Even the sea smelled different from that of her homeland. The wind carried the biting scent of pepper from the ships and coaxed a gentle chime from the little bells that hung in the branches everywhere. Like the inn, the empty square in front of the ship docks was guarded by stone dragons. They crouched everywhere, between the harbor barracks and in front of the jetties. Most of them were garlanded with flowers. In the past few months, they had seen many dragons: made of stone, of wood, of clay, so small that they could be carried around for good luck, and so large that you had to crane your neck to look at them. But even in Zhonggua, where swarms of Dragons had once darkened the sky, they had only encountered their lifeless effigies. 'Somewhere,' Jacob had whispered to her as they'd made love in the shadow of a stone dragon looking down on them with eyes of lapis lazuli, 'there must be a magic thing that brings statues to life. And when we find it, we'll come back and wake them all up.'

Fox took human form and stroked the scales of one of the dragons. He wore a wreath of red and yellow flowers. A petal clung to the gold yarn that snaked around her wrist. So much in the world was lost for all time. The Dragons, the Giants, and now the Fairies. She had found the golden thread next to the motionless body of the Dark One. Fox had hated and feared her so much. But now, it seemed that without her and her sisters, the world suddenly lacked rain.

As Fox crossed the empty dock to study the ferries' departure times, the moons gave her two shadows. Very fitting for a shapeshifter. Aotearoa... Yes, she was looking forward to meeting three-eyed lizards and searching for carved whale bones that gave one the shape of a fish. She wanted to continue traveling like this with Jacob for all time, searching for magical things that they fantasized about during long nights of lying side by side.

The first ferry, whose passenger list hung by the first jetty, departed for Tasmania. The second one sailed to Nihon. The Islands of the Foxes... Maybe that's what made her stop and glance at the passenger list.

Will's name was the third on the list. He had also entered a wife. The Goyl had put "The Bastard" after his name.

Fox stepped out onto the empty dock. The ferry to Aotearoa was leaving from the next pier. There was a flag flying on the shack where tickets were bought, showing the giant ferns that grew only there.

Nihon's flag showed a flying crane against a red sun.

What if she didn't tell Jacob about the names she had seen on the passenger list? Surely there was a ferry to Aotearoa that left later than the one to Nihon, and the list would be long gone by the time they got to the port. Stop it, Fox. Who was she kidding? Jacob could read any lie from her face, and this one he would not forgive, even if she told it to protect him.

She made her way back to the inn in human form. Not even the fur would have made her heart any lighter. *It will make Jacob happy to see his brother, Fox.* Yes, it probably would, but what about the Goyl? The Bastard hated Jacob. And the wife Will had put on the list... was that Sixteen, Spieler's glass and silver assassin? As far as Fox knew, Will's girlfriend Clara was in the other world, and Jacob's brother had slain the most powerful of all the fairies for the Alderelf. What if Will was still doing his bidding?

Spieler... His name nestled in the chime of the bells moving on the wind. It whispered in the wind, in the rustle of the trees and the murmur of the sea.

No, they had not escaped the shadows.

Fox climbed the shallow steps in front of the inn, past the dragons and the trees whose branches whispered Spieler's name. *You have to tell Jacob, Fox. You have to wipe the smile from his lips.*

She slipped off her shoes, as her landlady demanded, and opened the sliding wall of wood and milk-white paper through which lay the bedroom. The two other guests were a man and a woman. When they stirred behind the partition the landlady had put up, they looked like figures in a shadow play.

Jacob was still sleeping as soundly as when Fox had left him. She stroked his sleeping face. She liked to read his

13

familiar features with her fingers as much as with her eyes. Why had she gone to the harbor?

He woke as she lay down beside him.

"The vixen went wandering." He reached for her hand. "Didn't you hear what the landlady said? There are undead out there that look like humans, and—"

Fox closed his mouth with a kiss. "And Bulyeowoos, fox demons who like to pretend they're women. I feel right at home!"

It still felt like something deliciously forbidden to her when she kissed him. He was so happy. Why didn't she just keep quiet, and they could simply forget about his brother and instead go back to doing what they were so good at together—treasure hunting? All the magical artifacts they still wanted to find, all the places they hadn't seen yet... Aotearoa... There, no one knew anything about Elves and Fairies, did they?

"What is it?"

No. He knew her too well.

He sat up and stroked her fingers, one by one. Love could manifest itself in such inconspicuous gestures.

"I was down at the docks. I wanted to see when the ferries were leaving for Aotearoa. Your brother is registered to sail for Nihon tomorrow morning."

Yes, for a moment, she could see that he was thinking the same thing she had thought at the harbor: if only she hadn't spotted Will's name, if only they could have finally given up the search. Of course, he was ashamed of the thought. Older brothers probably never stopped feeling responsible, especially when they had left their little brothers alone for years. And yes, there was joy too, the relief that Will was alive—even though he had gotten caught up in the war of immortals.

"What about the Bastard and the Mirror Girl? Are they still with him?"

"Will is traveling with a woman. And yes, the Bastard is with him."

Jacob stared into the alien night. Yes, the smile was gone. He was probably asking himself the same question that had haunted Fox on the way back to the inn. Was his brother now on Spieler's side?

During their search, they had passed through villages where they heard stories about a man whose skin turned into pale green stone. It seemed to happen only when Will was angry, but there was no doubt. He was the Jade Goyl again, though Jacob had risked his life to save him from becoming that. And he was traveling with two of their fiercest enemies.

"When does the ferry leave?"

"In six hours. Just after daybreak."

They made love, but the peace she had felt so often in the past months was gone. They lay awake next to each other afterward, listening to each other's silence. It would all be all right. Fox simply would not allow any other thought. And no matter how Jacob's encounter with his brother turned out, hopefully it would finally absolve him of the responsibility of being Will's keeper. She wrapped her arms around him and felt his warmth ease her to sleep. But Will was waiting in her dreams. He had a face of jade, and by his side was not the girl made of glass or the Goyl who had sworn revenge on Jacob. The man at Will's side had no face. It was an empty mirror, and Fox whispered his name in her sleep.

Spieler…

2

Brothers

The first thing Jacob glimpsed when he and Fox made their way through the waiting crowd outside the ferry dock was the Bastard. No wonder. Everyone kept their distance from the Goyl. Even the Dokraebi avoided him, pixie-like creatures, some one-legged, some two-legged, who fought the gulls for scraps. No one in Doryeong Harbor had ever seen a man with stone skin and golden eyes.

Who was the most successful treasure hunter in the world? Likely, Jacob Reckless would have been the most commonly heard answer. But the Bastard was a fierce competitor, and he was never going to forgive Jacob for depriving him of the most precious magic weapon in existence behind the mirrors: the crossbow that had killed entire armies with one bolt and, by his brother's hand, had killed the Dark Fairy

16

as well. Is that why the Bastard was at Will's side? Because the crossbow was still in his possession?

The Bastard did not try to hide how much he enjoyed the almost reverential shudder he elicited from the bystanders. He owed his name to the malachite that dappled his dark onyx skin. The onyx lords usually drowned their bastards, but Nerron, as he was in fact called, had survived his childhood and was now spying for the onyxes' worst enemy—Kami'en, the King of the Goyl.

Most who stared at the Bastard probably thought he was a foreign demon, but even on this side of the world, people had heard of the Goyl and their invincible king.

THE KING OF THE GOYL HAS BROKEN OFF PEACE TALKS WITH HIS HUMAN ENEMIES. BAVARIA AND WALLACHIA CAPITULATE. THERESE OF AUSTRY EXECUTED FOR KIDNAPPING KAMI'EN'S SON.

Such had been the headlines they had seen even in the remotest villages. The Dark Fairy was dead, but her former lover proved every day that he didn't need Fairy magic to defeat human armies.

Jacob hid behind a cart as the Bastard's golden gaze wandered in his direction. The merchants loading their wares, the mercenaries guarding a lord's palanquin, the overly made-up women offering company with a red smile to the sailors arriving in a foreign land—the golden gaze touched them all. The sea had long set damp limits to the Goyl's conquests. They feared the open water, but Jacob was certain that the lords to the east were nevertheless scanning the horizon with alarm, for the more than ten thousand human Goyl who now

17

fought for Kami'en knew no such fear. Jacob had learned this firsthand. After all, his brother had been one of them. He still was, presumably.

Jacob slipped out from behind the cart. *Forget the Bastard, Jacob.* Was he really hiding from the Goyl, or was he afraid of meeting his brother? Would Will's eyes be golden? Jacob was surprised to find that there was something else he feared more now: that his brother was in Spieler's service.

Fox made a sign to him and pointed to a palanquin that the porters had set down just beside the jetty. Will stood beside it. There was no trace of Jade in his face, even though to Jacob, he appeared taller and stronger than when they had last met in the other world. Will had leaned forward and was talking to the occupant of the palanquin. Sixteen hid behind curtains of orange silk. Had her mirror skin healed, or was it covered in bark like her brother's who had frozen into a tree in the mountains of Kasakh? Will looked around as if he had heard the question. Yes, his little brother had changed. He was all grown up. *What did you expect, Jacob? After all, he killed the most powerful of all the Fairies.*

"Shall I distract the Bastard?" Fox stepped to his side.

Jacob shook his head. What was hiding behind the orange-red curtains was far more dangerous than the Goyl. "Stay away from the palanquin. Promise?"

She just gave him a bemused look. Love was doing odd things to him. He worried about her all the time, or maybe he'd just been afraid for her too many times in the last few years.

"Go to him. The ferry is leaving soon."

Yes, what are you waiting for, Jacob? Go. Even if you have no idea what to say to your brother. How are you doing, Will? Your traveling companions both tried to kill me already?

18

A group of Ronin was waiting a few steps away, masterless samurai from the islands that were the ship's destination. Nihon. One of the most powerful magic swords in the world was there: the Sword of Murokamo, with a blade that commanded the wind. Nihon held so many magical things that the Bastard's mouth was probably watering with excitement. But what was there for his brother? There was also a caterpillar in Nihon that spun a cocoon, which stopped the rapid aging of shapeshifters. Spieler had told Jacob about it. Of course. The Elf not only read mortals' most secret wishes from their foreheads but also their most secret fears. And then... he played with that fear.

Someone grabbed him by the shoulder.

"On the lookout for new enemies, Reckless?" The Bastard's smile was as wolfish as ever. "How about them?" He motioned to the Ronin. "I hear they fight even in their sleep."

The last time they had met, the Goyl had shot an arrow into Jacob's chest, and in return, Jacob had stolen from him. They had no reason to trust each other.

"What do you want with my brother? Let me guess. He has the crossbow."

"Oh yes? Then I would have taken him to Kami'en long ago, along with the crossbow, wouldn't I?" the Bastard spat out. "Imagine, he even let me have it because he was so distraught over what he had done with it. For three days, I was the most powerful mortal in this world. Three days. They were good days. And then... that damn crossbow dissolved into silver smoke. Like all magic things that were created for one purpose only and had fulfilled that purpose. I'm sure it's happened to you too, so spare me the incredulous stare!"

19

Yes, it had happened to Jacob. More than once. He believed the Goyl, as much as he hated to admit it to himself. The most powerful magic weapon in this world had been made to kill a Fairy, and it had done just that. Jacob had to admit he was glad the crossbow was gone.

"Then what is it?" He glanced at his brother. "Still harboring dreams of Will making your king invincible?"

"Sure." The Bastard enjoyed making Jacob feel his dislike. "That's his destiny. Your brother doesn't doubt it any more than I do, but all in good time. I have his promise that he will come with me as soon as he gets a few more things settled. And your brother keeps his promises."

Jacob didn't get to answer that.

"Well, well, the Bastard." Fox emerged from behind the Goyl as silently as if she were wearing her fur.

The Bastard eyed her with the same distaste he had shown for Jacob. "The vixen. Dressed in men's clothes, as usual? In these latitudes, that is easily rewarded with death."

Fox did not dignify that with an answer. She didn't take her eyes off the Goyl as she stepped closer to Jacob's side. "The ferry leaves in half an hour," she murmured to him.

Go, Jacob.

Will was still standing by the palanquin. He turned only when he heard footsteps behind him. Oh yes, he had changed. But this time, Will hadn't forgotten who he was, unlike when the Jade had first grown on him — as a result of the Dark Fairy's curse. Had he perhaps killed her in retribution for that, too?

He hesitated for an incredulous moment as he realized who was coming toward him. Then he walked up to Jacob and hugged him as tightly and as long as he had as a child.

"How did you find me? I can't believe you're here!"

20

He let go of Jacob and then hugged him again.

"She found you."

Fox approached hesitantly, but Will hugged her almost as warmly as Jacob. The two hadn't always gotten along so well, but now they were united by the fact that they both shifted forms at times.

The Goyl stepped to his brother's side as if he had always stood there. *Don't be fooled, Jacob Reckless*, his gaze mocked. *He's one of us*. Will, too, seemed to trust the Bastard completely. Was he more Goyl than human now, though it didn't show? What had his brother experienced since Jacob had last seen him, aside from becoming the doom of a Fairy? Whatever it was—it was the Goyl, not Jacob, who had been at his side.

Ask him. Ask Will how he feels about Spieler, Jacob. But they'd both always been really good at not talking about what was truly on their minds, and Jacob didn't want to talk about the Elf in front of the Goyl. The Bastard might hear how much he feared Spieler. So he pointed to the ferry instead.

"Why Nihon?"

Will glanced at the palanquin. Could what Jacob saw on his brother's face be love? Love for what? A thing made of mirror glass and silver?

"Her skin is lignifying. The curse continues to work, though..." His brother didn't have to finish the sentence. Though he had killed the Fairy. He hadn't done it for Sixteen, or had he?

The curtains moved subtly as Jacob glanced over at the palanquin. That the curse still worked was good news. If it was defacing Spieler's creatures, then maybe it was still doing the same to him, keeping him in the other world.

Will grabbed Jacob's arm and pulled him along. The Bastard wanted to follow them, but like Fox, he stayed at the ferry dock. Still, he didn't take his eyes off them.

Will stopped among the crates piled between the jetties. "Sixteen says there's another mirror in Nihon," he murmured to Jacob. "She says she can sense them all."

"Well, sure, she's made out of the same glass." Jacob couldn't hide his disgust. He remembered all too well Fox's figure frozen into silver after Sixteen's brother had touched her.

"It's not her fault!"

Heavens. His brother was actually in love.

"I have to go back to our world to check on Clara. It's a long story. Spieler lied to me. But I will find him and demand that he help Sixteen."

Demand? Help? Should he explain to him that Spieler's help cost dearly? Jacob was relieved nonetheless. Sixteen seemed to resent her master for sending her to this world, and Will must have realized that he couldn't trust the Elf. *Spieler lied to me.* Of course.

The sailors waved the first passengers onto the ferry. The litter bearers looked around searchingly for Will.

"Sixteen says the mirror belongs to another Elf. An old enemy of Spieler's. He calls himself Krieger, and right after…"

Right after… He avoided speaking of what he had done as if saying it out loud would make it happen all over again.

"Will." Jacob reached for his arm. "The Fairy had thousands on her conscience."

Will just nodded.

"Tell me about the other Elf. Does that mean he's already in this world?"

"Yes. Sixteen says they're all coming back."

This was bad news. As long as Spieler had been in the other world, Jacob had at least been able to fool himself into thinking that he and Fox could hide from him. And even Spieler's joy over the end of his exile certainly wouldn't make the Alderelf forget the debt Fox and Jacob owed him.

Will stared out to sea, lost in images Jacob could not see. One day he would ask him how he had killed the Fairy. But not now. No. Jacob could tell by the look on his brother's face that he had no words for what he had done — and that Will wished he could undo it. No wonder. Spieler had seduced him into it. His help always carried the silver hook, like bait on a pole.

"Sixteen thinks the other Elf will let us use his mirror if she promises him some information about Spieler in exchange. I guess those two have been enemies for a long time."

This wasn't a plan. This was madness.

"Didn't Sixteen tell you about her maker? Spieler is just as dangerous as the Fairy. And a lot more devious. I'm sure this Krieger is no better! If he helps you, it will cost you dearly!"

That sounded very much like a big brother. *Shut up, Jacob. Just shut up!* Will's look said the same thing.

"He lied to me! He sent Clara a Sleeping Beauty spell and made me think it was the Dark Fairy."

Ah, of course. All you had to do was fool Will into thinking he was saving the world or his girlfriend, and off he went. Spieler read mortal hearts more effortlessly than an instruction manual.

"Trust me!" This time Will's embrace felt a little cooler. "I know what I'm doing. I'm an adult, brother! I'll see you around. Here or in the other world."

23

Jacob wanted to reach for his arm, as he had done so often when they were children. *Wait, Will.* He hadn't even told him he'd met their father… But his brother was already walking toward the ferry. The porters hoisted the litter onto their shoulders, and Will followed. 'Take care of Will, Jacob.' How he had hated it when his mother had said that. And then he'd usually done it anyway.

I'm an adult. Yes, he was, and had been for a long time now. Jacob no longer had to tell him stories of this world. Will was writing his own story behind the mirrors, and as far as their father was concerned, it was better to just forget about him anyway, the way he'd forgotten about them.

You can take your time with the payment. But you will pay. Jacob thought he heard Spieler's voice as clearly as if the Elf were crouching inside him. *Today I bake, tomorrow brew, the next I'll have the young Queen's firstborn child.* What if Sixteen still served her creator after all? What if she let Spieler know that she had seen them? So often, he thought of the Elf when he made love to her. Was it the same for Fox? He was glad that years ago she had had a witch show her how not to get pregnant.

The Ronin boarded the ship.

Your vixen will make beautiful children. I hope you don't take too long. Absurd, how the memory quickened his heartbeat. As if the Elf was standing behind him, whispering the words in his ear.

"I hear there are very powerful foxes in Nihon."

Jacob winced, even though it was Fox, not Spieler, standing behind him. Powerful foxes and butterfly cocoons that extended the lives of shapeshifters. *No. Spieler told you that, Jacob.* Reason enough never to travel to Nihon. He pulled

Fox to him and buried his face in her hair. *Your vixen will make beautiful children.*

She raised her hand. The reddish-brown henna stamp on the back of it showed a crane in the circle of the sun's disk.

"You get your stamp there."

She pointed to the shack next to the dock. "I already paid for our passage."

She pressed her hand over Jacob's mouth when he tried to protest. "The Goyl told me that your brother is looking for an Elf who is an old enemy of Spieler. Perhaps he will tell us how to break our bargain with him."

Jacob thought he detected a dread in her eyes that he had not seen there before. She wasn't pregnant, was she? He didn't dare ask. *Your vixen will make beautiful children.*

"No," she whispered to him. "I'm not pregnant, but I want to be one day, so let's take the chance. You have to know your enemies as well as you know your friends. Isn't that what you always say?"

Yes, but knowing an immortal enemy all too well had almost cost him his neck once.

Will stood behind the railing, looking over at them.

"They also call Nihon the Islands of the Foxes." She actually thought it was a good idea. And he had thought he was the only one who kept thinking of Spieler.

"The Elf calls himself Krieger." He stroked her red hair. "Does that sound like someone to meet willingly?"

She laughed. And kissed him.

"You actually want to run away, Jacob Reckless," she murmured to him. "I never thought I'd live to see this. You want to hide from the Elf, like a rabbit!"

"No, like a clever fox."

Her face became serious. She looked toward the mountains from which they had come to the old port city, as if recalling the long journey and all the days and nights that had brought them here. Then she looked to the ship.

"I think Krieger sounds promising." She grabbed a Dokraebi that was about to crawl into her jacket pocket and shooed it away. "Go get the stamp. They'll be casting off soon. Or do I need to tell you about all the magic things they have in Nihon?"

3

JUST ONE DEAD

The porters had set the palanquin down by one of the ship's masts. Fox could not take her eyes off it. She remembered well the muddy pond to which she had fled with Jacob after Sixteen had chased them like rabbits before her. 'You won't be fast enough, fox-sister.' How she had spread her deadly fingers. Like a cat looking forward to sinking its claws into the mouse. Would Fox have believed then that one day they would follow Spieler's assassin, hoping to learn what protected her from him? No. And yet, Fox still felt that getting on the ferry had been the right thing to do.

Jacob was leaning against the railing with Will, even though the sight of waves made him seasick. Did he trust his brother, even though Will was traveling with Sixteen and the Bastard? They had talked since the ferry had sailed. Was Jacob telling Will how John Reckless had made off with the Flying Carpet they had stolen from the Czar? Was he admitting to Will how it had broken his heart to once again have been merely used and then abandoned? No, Jacob found it hard to talk about such pain, and the two kept falling into silence as if there was too much they couldn't bring themselves to say. Had Sixteen told Will things about Spieler that could help them? And had Jacob told him that they owed the Elf their firstborn child? No. He also didn't talk about what scared him, and didn't she feel the same way?

The moonlit night had been followed by a hazy, cold morning. Wisps of fog hung over the waves, and the mainland of Honguk had long since disappeared. 'South Korea,' Jacob had replied when she had asked him what name the ancient kingdom had in his world. 'Another country I've now only traveled to behind the mirrors. I know your world so much better than mine.'

One of the sailors had climbed the mast soon after they had cast off, but he kept the spyglass pointed not at the horizon but at the waves. Fox didn't have to wonder long why he was scanning the water with such a worried face.

"Funayùreiiii!"

Fox would have liked to know what creature inspired such fear that the passengers immediately jumped back from the railing. But all that emerged from the morning haze was a fishing boat, and the lookout gave the all-clear. The crossing from Honguk to Nihon seemed to be considered a dangerous affair. The lookout sounded the alarm several

28

more times. Still, they encountered nothing more threatening than a school of flying fish. The Ronin remained so calm amid all the clamor from the mast that Fox finally decided to look only at them when the sailor thought he saw something frightening again. *The most dangerous creature sits in that palanquin there!* she wanted to call out to the lookout at one point. Even as the silvery body of a giant sea serpent rose from the waves in the distance and most of the passengers forgot their fear in the face of its beauty, Fox thought she could feel only the silver into which Sixteen's brother had once transformed her.

The sea serpent wriggled away without paying any attention to the ship, and the litter bearers recovered from the fright by queuing up for an old man who was serving warm soup at the bow on the captain's orders. This was the opportunity Fox had been waiting for.

The curtains covering the palanquin looked precious only from a distance. The silk was soiled and torn in some places. *Do you have to eat when you are made of glass?* Fox wondered as she ambled toward the palanquin. She remembered Sixteen's eyes, so unaffected by the fear of her prey, almost amused. Spieler's silver dagger. Which of her stolen faces had she shown Will, or had he fallen in love with them all? Fox kept some distance between herself and the palanquin as she stopped in front of it, just enough so that the occupant could not touch her.

"The vixen. Have you come to feast on my misery?" Of course, she had recognized Fox. Faces were Sixteen's specialty.

"Why should I? I hear we're on the same side now. Even if that's hard to believe. I haven't forgotten who made you."

29

A hand pushed back the curtains just enough for Fox to catch a glimpse inside. Sixteen's face was wood and glass. Tree bark grew on her cheeks and neck.

"The one who made me also did this to me. My left arm is wood, and my brother is dead."

Brother... You have no brothers, Fox wanted to say. But who decided what the word meant? She loathed her two oldest brothers, even if they all shared the same mother.

Will had noticed that Fox was standing by the palanquin. He didn't take his eyes off her, but he stayed with his brother.

Ask her, Fox.

"Is Spieler still in the other world, or is he back as well, like the Elf you told Will about?"

Sixteen didn't get to answer. The lookout shouted again, but this time he pointed not to the sea but to the ferry deck.

Something took shape beside the mainmast as if the haze that was still drifting up from the water was taking the silhouette of a human being. Even the sailors stumbled back in such horror that one almost fell over the railing.

The Bastard seemed to know who was showing himself. He shoved everyone who stood between him and Will out of the way and drew his saber as he planted himself protectively in front of Will. But weapons could not hurt the handsome young man who, paler than the mist, suddenly stood beside the mast. The turban and tunic he wore were from a time long past.

"Why the shouting?" asked Sixteen.

"It's just a ghost." Fox had encountered too many dead people to find them any more troubling than the living. The Ronin didn't stir either, but their faces were rigid with respect — for death and those who came back from its realm.

The Bastard had been right to stand in front of Will. The ghost had eyes only for Jacob's brother. He walked slowly toward him—with soundless and weightless steps. Jacob had drawn his saber, like the Goyl, but Will needed no help. He had pushed the Bastard aside and faced the Shadow unmoving. The jade came as naturally as skin tans in the sun, and Will's stiffening face showed no trace of fear. Just guilt. And pain.

"How do you like the world without my dark mistress, Fairy killer?" The shadowy young man stopped in front of him. The words did not seem to come from his lips. They were whispered by the wind, salty and wet, and they were made of rage. "Tell those for whom you murdered her that she is not forgotten! And hear Chithira's promise that you will never again have joy in life, for I will be waiting for you in your dreams."

Fox could not read the look with which the spirit eyed her as she stepped to Jacob's side. The yarn on her wrist grew cool as dew, and the anger on the hazy face gave way to a smile. The dead man bowed so low to her that she almost returned the bow. Then his form dissolved with a sigh, and a black moth the size of Fox's hand, with skull-white spots on its frayed wings, fluttered away and lost itself among the sails.

The jade in Will's skin disappeared as quickly as it had come, and the Goyl snapped so gruffly at all those who continued to stare at him in bewilderment that they retreated to the other side of the ferry to discuss what had happened in hushed voices. Had anyone understood who the dead man meant when he spoke of his dark mistress? Probably not.

The Ronin had watched the ghost's appearance as unmoved as when they had heard the lookout's cries of alarm, but Will's transformation had clearly impressed them. They did not take their eyes off him and seemed to wonder what kinship he had with the Goyl. How did Will see himself now, as Goyl or human?

The Bastard was not as unaffected by ghosts as the Ronin were. As he slid the saber back into its scabbard, he did so with an unsteady hand.

"I take it you recognized him?"

Will nodded.

How do you like the world without my dark mistress, Fairy killer?

He turned and walked to the palanquin as if the only thing keeping him steady waited there.

Jacob leaned his back against the railing. He was certainly seasick by now. He hated sea voyages, but his pallor was surely also to do with the dead man.

"Whose ghost was it?" he asked the Bastard. "Tell me. You're dying to talk about it, aren't you?"

The Bastard shoved something into his mouth. He also avoided looking at the waves. It was said that the Goyl grew mushrooms that alleviated their fear of the water. "That? That was the Dark Fairy's coachman. I guess when he was alive, he was also her lover. He tried to protect her, but your brother has good aim."

Fox closed her eyes. The yarn on her wrist was still cool as frost, and for an instant, she thought she felt the crossbow's bolt drive into her chest. Had the Dark One found no remedy to save herself because she had trusted Will to the end? Her coachman probably knew the answer. She was so cold!

The wind freshened as if the spirit had left its wrath behind. Jacob cursed as the ship dove bow-first into the waves. *Damn it, Fox*, his gaze said. *I didn't want to go to Nihon.*

"I thought the moths died with the Dark One," he said.

They had been her deadly companions and were supposedly the souls of her dead lovers.

"Maybe the coachman was her favorite, and she gave him some more protection before your brother..." The Bastard motioned the firing of a crossbow.

Jacob's gaze sought Fox as if she could shield him from the images summoned by the Goyl's gesture. She had not told him that, since she had picked up the yarn from beside the dead Fairy, she had often seen these images herself. She found them waiting in pools and streams, even in the dirty harbor water that had washed around the ferry's dock. She didn't just see the end of the Fairy. Sometimes she saw the lake with the lilies and the island where the Dark One had lived with her sisters before leaving them for Kami'en. Kami'en. Sometimes the water showed Fox the King of the Goyl so clearly that she looked around for him. Why didn't she tell Jacob about the images? Or how sometimes she thought she could feel the crossbow's bolt in her own chest? Because she knew what he would have said. *Throw away the golden thread, Fox!* But she couldn't just throw it away. She ran her fingers along it while Jacob argued with the Bastard about how they could protect Will from the ghost. She often caught herself tracing the golden thread with her fingers. She felt life in it, beauty, strength, and love. More than anything else, love. And sometimes she felt—Jacob would have laughed at her—as if the golden thread left behind by the Dark Fairy was protecting all the love in the world. Including the love between her and him.

The lookout called something down from the mast again, but this time his voice sounded relieved. Several islands had

33

appeared on the horizon. They floated on the sea like a chain of green jade.

The Islands of the Foxes. Fox felt curiosity, hope, and the shadows of coming danger.

4

YANAGITA HIDEO

When, by the stench of all the lava lizards, was the Pup finally going to tell his big brother to go to hell? Nerron had thought several times about pushing him discreetly over the railing, but the Pup would probably have jumped after his big brother. And so, when they docked, all five of them went ashore.

Why? Had he and the Pup not been doing just fine without the fabulous Jacob Reckless? "Happy" was not a word Nerron usually used to describe himself. It was, in his eyes, an emotional state only possible when paired with stupidity. But in the last few months, he had come perilously close to that emotional state. The Pup just had a way of stealing into your heart, even if your heart was made of stone. His unreserved trust, the friendship he draped around his onyx

35

shoulders like a warm blanket, the esteem Nerron hardly even had to earn. All of them were very suspicious and unfamiliar sensations that made the Bastard shudder, and at the same time, filled him with—yes, damn it, he just couldn't call it anything else!—happiness. The only living creature that had ever granted him such unconditional affection had been his mother, and what choice did a mother have?

The Bastard and the Pup... It sounded like they had always been meant to be together. Even the malachite in his onyx skin no longer seemed like a blemish but an echo of the jade that made Will Reckless his equal in rage. Yet despite all this Nerron could not forget that the Pup was first and foremost the hero of his childhood fairy tales, the Jade Goyl who would make his king invincible. True, Kami'en was conquering one country after another, but the good times never lasted long. Other times would come, dark times, all signs pointed to that because every victory also increased their enemies' number. And then? Then Kami'en would need the Jade Goyl; until then, the Bastard would take good care of him.

It wasn't going to be easy. The glass viper was very good at making the Pup forget what he had been born to do. Sixteen... Too bad the Fairy hadn't killed her. Oh, what a sad spectacle to see how much the Pup adored her. Nerron, of course, pretended that he understood this adoration. He didn't know much about friendship, but he knew that if he had told the Pup what he really thought of Sixteen, he probably would have been sent packing. It was a mystery what he saw in her. The bark disfigured her so badly that one might as well have been caressing a tree. Offset with a few shards of mirror. But—as Nerron kept telling himself, to keep his patience—it was better to let some more time pass before he took Will to Kami'en. After all, the Jade Goyl had killed his king's lover. On the other hand—what could dead love weigh against the promise of invincibility?

Yes, better to let a few more months pass, Nerron reassured himself as he disembarked behind the palanquin. Perhaps it was even better not to return the Jade Goyl to Kami'en until he was in need. That would also allow him to follow the Pup to the other world if they did indeed find the mirror. After all, he had to make sure the fool came back. Yes, of course, he had to follow him. A new world... Since childhood, he had dreamed of finding a new world behind some enchanted door! But in his dreams, he had done it alone, not side by side with a friend.

Side by side with a friend... Just listen to yourself, Bastard!

Nerron almost laughed out loud. The ferry had docked in a bay surrounded by green mountains and a cluster of houses that looked like a sleepy village rather than a port city. No matter. It felt so good to finally have solid ground under his boots again, even if Jacob Reckless was trudging ashore just behind him. Surely he would soon see to it that the Bastard's happiness was dimmed.

None of them spoke the local language. But waiting at the docks, along with white-painted prostitutes and obsequiously smiling porters, were men who offered their services as guides and translators. Some were Ronin, like the warriors who had traveled with them on the ferry. But most wore the patched garments worn the world over by those who had not been born to princes or warriors.

Jacob Reckless walked up to the same man the Bastard would have chosen as a guide: a hulking young giant who

37

tried to keep an attentive expression on his face, though he was visibly bored with waiting at the docks. Boredom came only to those who had a good measure of cleverness and imagination. Nerron saw the beginnings of a tattoo on the fleshy neck and the powerful forearms. The rest of the massive body disappeared under an unadorned dark tunic and wide pants, like those worn by most of the waiting men. Even the Ronin had worn such wide, shapeless pants on the ferry, very unbecoming of warriors, Nerron thought, compared to his tight lizard-skin garments. But though their clothes did not imply it, the fighting skills of Nihon's inhabitants were legendary.

The young giant seemed to have no trouble conversing with a Westling. The dove-eyed hulk did his best not to stare at Nerron as Reckless pointed first to the palanquin and then to the rest of their traveling party. The sight of the vixen, on the other hand, had an undeniably dramatic effect on the mountain of flesh. He could hardly take his eyes off her, but finally, he nodded several times and followed Reckless eagerly to the palanquin, watched by the envious glances of his guildmates. When Nerron joined them, the hulk was explaining to Reckless in fluent Albian where they could buy horses and donkeys. Then he greeted Fox in Lorrainian with a bow that was noticeably deeper than he'd given to the others, and finally, he addressed Nerron with the correct Goyl salutation.

"Last but not least, may I introduce myself? My name is Yanagita Hideo," he explained with a smile that was at once friendly and as guarded as the vaults of an onyx lord.

"Your very esteemed brother," he said to the Pup, as he ever so scrupulously avoided looking toward the palanquin

38

as if to demonstrate his respect for the drawn curtains, "has informed me that your destination is Kakeya. This is usually a journey of five days, but we must regrettably make a detour. In the vicinity of Ómi, the Mizuno and Ikeda clans are fighting each other, as the former supports the Shogun and the latter supports the Imperial House. Sorry to bore you with the political squabbles of my country, but our empress is old and ill, and the crown prince is still very young..."

Yanagita Hideo did not elaborate on his last words. He rightly assumed that the foreigners knew the dangers it brought to a country when a veteran ruler departed.

"May I further ask what business brings you to Kakeya?" He bowed his head as if apologizing for the rude inquiry. "I am obliged to report to the imperial authorities your reasons for traveling our lands."

Nerron saw the Pup seek his older brother's gaze. Old habits died slowly, even with a skin of jade.

"We want to take my brother's wife to one of your sacred shrines," Reckless said. "Even in our distant homeland, people know of their healing power."

Ah, of course. Jacob was a fabulous liar. A pinch of truth and the whole soup tasted of it. Yanagita Hideo swallowed it without hesitation, but he glanced at the palanquin with slight concern.

"It's not contagious," the Pup assured him, disregarding his brother's warning look. "Someone cursed her."

The wrong word.

"A holy curse!" added Nerron quickly. "She touched a sacred tree, and now she is turning into its likeness. We've heard that the gods of Nihon dwell in trees, mountains, and rivers, so we're hoping one of them can return her to human form."

It was probably better not to mention that she was actually made of glass.

The relief on their guide's face proved that Nerron had judged him correctly. How convenient that years ago, he had casually quizzed a monk from Nihon about his islands while stealing some magic amulets from him.

"A sacred tree!" Yanagita Hideo lowered his voice reverently. "Which one was it? A sakaki?"

"It was a Silver-Alder," came the voice from the palanquin.

"Ah." Yanagita Hideo nodded as if that explained everything. "I take it that is your name for hannoki. I've heard it's better not to get too close to these trees, despite their beauty."

He nodded again as if all his questions were answered to his complete satisfaction. "Our path will take us through the Misasa mountains," he continued. "There are many yōkai there: karasu-tengu, mujina, kitsune," he gave Fox a quick glance, "and many yùrei... angry spirits of the dead."

Reckless reached into his coat pocket. The coins he held out to their guide were, as far as Nerron could see, not the gold talers he used to pull out of his pockets in inexplicable quantities, but Russian silver ducats.

"Reckless-san, please do not insult me," Yanagita Hideo said with a dismissive gesture. "I am in no way outlining these dangers to increase the fee for my services. I admit that such dishonorable behavior," he looked to the other guides, "is quite common on these islands, but my motivation was different. You are strangers in my homeland, and I must make you aware of the dangers before you entrust yourself

40

to me. I am no warrior, but I will protect you as best I can and guide you by safe paths to your destination."

The giant emphasized his honesty too much for Nerron's taste, but the other candidates didn't necessarily look any more trustworthy. As for all the dangers Yanagita Hideo had so carefully enumerated—well, they would have to be on their guard. So? The only reason Nerron was alive was that he had been doing precisely that since he'd been able to walk.

Yanagita Hideo was still trying hard not to stare at him. But after the customs guards waved them through, at last, Nerron finally caught him at it.

"What?" he snapped at him. "No, I have not touched any of your sacred stones. I was born with this skin. But if it reassures your countrymen, tell them it was your stones."

The monk had also told him about those. Supposedly, they were all over the roadsides. Yanagita Hideo surely found it disrespectful the way he talked about the sacred objects of Yanagita's islands. But his face remained expressionless.

"You are not mistaken, Nerron-san. You are the first of your kind I have met," he replied in a dignified, controlled voice. "But even in Nihon, one has heard of the great Kami'en who has brought Austry to its knees and made Albion and Lorraine forget their old enmity. Our newspapers have told of his campaigns in Wallachia and Bavaria, two conquests in only five months. On the battlefield, no one can match the King of the Goyl. Many of our samurai admire him, and only last month a hundred Ronin set out for Vena to offer him their services."

This speech from so strange a mouth filled Nerron with the unpleasant feeling that he had not served his king very

41

well in recent months. But after all, he was guarding the Jade Goyl and with him the embodied assurance of Kami'en's invincibility.

The Pup had averted his eyes. Was he thinking of the Blood Wedding and how he had defended Kami'en with his own life? Nerron had Will's promise that he would return with him to Kami'en, but his gaze was already back on the palanquin.

"We should be on our way, Jacob. She desperately needs an inn and a bed!"

The look Reckless exchanged with the vixen was lost on Will, but not on the Bastard, and for a fleeting moment, Nerron almost felt something like sympathy for the glass viper. *Soulless thing,* said Reckless's look. *My brother is a lovelorn fool.*

They left it to Hideo to choose the provisions, as they were unfamiliar with most of the foods that could be bought in the port town. The shaggy horses they acquired on their guide's advice were stout but hardly larger than the donkey Hideo mounted himself. The gray mule made their guide seem even bulkier, but his rider seemed very fond of him, and the donkey trotted along as light-footed as if it were carrying a sack of feathers on its back.

As they left the harbor behind, a few of those who had offered their services in vain called out a nickname to their guide.

"Nuppeppō... why are they shouting that?" asked Nerron as they took a narrow, unpaved road that led into the green mountains encircling the bay.

"It is the name of a yo-kai found in ruined temples. They like to say he looks like me. I prefer the name my parents gave me." Yanagita Hideo gave Nerron a look that did not hide how hurt he felt. "Humans are often cruel to each other. Is the same true of your kind, Nerron-san?"

"In my youth, they called me mold-skin," the Bastard replied. "Does that answer the question?"

5
In Foreign Woods

Fox was surprised at how dense and extensive the mountain forest was through which they had been following Yanagita Hideo and his donkey for hours. She had not expected to find woods like this on an island. The leaves above were damp from the rain, and pads of moss muffled the hoofbeats of her horse. Every stone was covered with the dark, furry green, every tree root, even the branches above their heads, and Fox soon found it hard to believe that this was her first time in Nihon. Her heart said otherwise. The forest Yanagita Hideo traversed in respectful silence seemed as familiar to Fox as if she had roamed it countless times. It felt like she had dreamed this forest into existence. The paths were so narrow that they rode single file, and they often had to skirt giant trees that lay where they had fallen, surrounded by saplings that had been planted not by man but by the forest itself. This did not make the litter bearers' task any easier, but they only expressed their exhaustion with hushed voices as if they did not want to disturb the silence surrounding them. It was not the oppressive silence Fox knew from her homeland's enchanted forests but one of strangely peaceful enchantment. No one seemed to be cutting down these trees to build ships or houses or to burn them for firewood, and many were familiar to her, but among the oaks, beeches, and pines grew trees she had never seen before. The same was true of the animals they encountered. Beavers, squirrels, badgers, even the deer looked like the animals of her homeland at first glance, but each time she looked more closely, the fur was a slightly different color or the shape a little more delicate.

"Yanagita-san?" Fox addressed her guide at one point in a hushed voice (a sailor on the ferry had explained to her that the family name was first in Nihon). "Whose forest is this? It looks like there's no one here to cut down the trees."

"Oh, this is a Talking Forest, mistress," Hideo replied with a smile that forgave Fox for her ignorance. "It belongs only to itself. The trees are their own masters and very powerful. Even when old age cuts them down, they remain part of the forest, nourishing young trees with their decaying wood. Many are older than Nihon's most venerable families, even older than our imperial house. It would be extremely foolish and very reckless to treat them disrespectfully, let alone cut them down, for the others would strike you dead with their branches!"

Then he lapsed once more into the thoughtful silence in which he had been riding in front of them for hours. Fox

45

would have liked to ask why his islands were also called the Islands of the Foxes, but the question finally answered itself.

The fox, who suddenly stood on the narrow path they were following, only at first glance resembled the she-fox to whom Fox owed her coat—as a gift for protecting her pups from her brothers. This one had a much darker pelt and, to Fox's amazement, three magnificent bushy tails.

Yanagita Hideo hastily reined in his donkey and bowed his head reverently, while the fox eyed them all with a serene look and finally disappeared into the forest. When Will asked for a short rest for Sixteen, Fox could not restrain her curiosity any longer; she followed Hideo as he watered his donkey by a stream that ran lazily over the moss-green stones.

"You greeted the fox we encountered with a bow, Yanagita-san," she said as she let her horse drink alongside the donkey. "In my homeland, they are hunted and killed. Is that why they call your islands the Islands of Foxes? Because you worship them here?"

The smile their guide gave her was very mysterious. It seemed almost conspiratorial—as if they both shared a secret.

"Oh, yes. Nihon's foxes are very powerful," he said. "We revere them and fear them, especially when they put themselves in the service of a lord or seek revenge for a wrong committed against their kind. I'm sure the foxes of your homeland also possess great power. Surely that's why they're hunted!" He pulled a small clay figurine from his donkey's saddlebag. The figure resembled a sitting fox, but its fur was black, and its eyes were red. "Our foxes are messengers of the gods. Some even believe they are gods themselves. We

46

call them kitsune, and there are many sacred shrines where they are worshipped. You would probably call these shrines temples, but they are often very small. Our gods prefer to be worshipped and summoned in nature. They don't like to be indoors like yours. This kitsune," he ran his hand over the clay figure's head, "is from the Oba shrine. The monks there always keep a few dozen on hand for supplicants."

He placed the small figurine in Fox's hand. "You take him home and make your wish. Then you feed him fried tofu every morning, honor him with a red kerchief, and delight him with a lit candle in the evening until the kitsune grants your wish—and you return him to his shrine."

Fox stroked the tiny figure's black fur. "Do you have to keep the wish a secret?" She returned the little fox reluctantly.

"Absolutely," Yanagita Hideo said, shoving it back into his saddlebag. "It's best not to anger a kitsune. They are certainly not always friendly, and often show themselves in human form."

He again looked at Fox as if they shared a secret.

She brushed her red hair from her forehead. "Is that so?"

"Oh yes. However, they grow much older than humans. The most powerful ones have nine tails and can fly and make themselves invisible!"

Fox felt an almost irresistible urge to transform on the spot, even though it might disappoint Yanagita Hideo that she had only one tail in fox form. There was something in his face, longing for wonder, for a world where wishes were granted and people understood each other. There was so much selfless goodness in his boyish features that Fox wanted to protect Yanagita Hideo, even though he was almost a head taller than her and certainly twice as strong.

47

"I hope we meet many more foxes," she said, "with lots and lots of tails, and that they mean us only well."

For a moment, Yanagita Hideo looked at her searchingly, as if he were not sure of her words' real meaning.

"I have a confession to make, mistress," he said, as his face flushed almost as red as the blossoms that had opened behind him on the branches of a bush. "I've never seen hair as fox-red as yours before, and I... oh, it's too foolish! I was sure you were a kitsune too! Forgive my foolishness!" He bowed deeply. "Can you remind me of your name? I'm sure Reckless-san told me, but it must have slipped my mind."

He must not have heard what Jacob called her, and Fox decided to keep her secret for the time being. "Celeste Auger," she said. After all, that was the name her parents had given her. "I'm from Lorraine."

"Enchanté, Auger-san." Yanagita Hideo bowed again. "Please call me Hideo. It's so much easier. In Nihon, one sees many of your countrymen. The Empress had a military advisor from Lorraine. Neither the Shogun nor her son liked that, but..." He fell abruptly silent.

Will helped Sixteen out of the palanquin. The robes she wore hid her disfigured skin, but her left arm was stiff and immobile, and her every movement betrayed that she was not well.

"This stream," Will stepped to Hideo's side, "perhaps it flows into a pond or lake nearby?"

Hideo pointed toward the trees to their left. "It feeds a small but deep pond. Just beyond the firs there."

Sixteen seemed relieved at the prospect of bathing her aching limbs in cool water. She leaned heavily on Will's arm, and as Fox watched the two of them go, she felt a twinge of sympathy for the first time, but her distrust returned quickly. What if Spieler had Sixteen watching her and Jacob?

What if… no, he was far, far away. It was better to believe that.

6

The Fortress of the Moons

Kakeya did not look like the kind of place an immortal would choose as a residence. But the same could have been said about the overgrown island where Spieler lived in Jacob's world, or about Schwanstein, the sleepy little Austryn town where the ruined castle contained the mirror through which Jacob had changed worlds for years.

Kakeya, like Schwanstein, was surrounded by densely forested mountains. The steepest of these cast a shadow over the village. The fortress, which could be seen high up its slope, spoke of a past in which Kakeya had been more than just a shabby, forgotten village. The complex was massive, that much Jacob could see even from a distance. Behind its black walls, there would have been room for a dozen castles like the one whose tower had so often welcomed him into

50

this world. But the fortress looked dilapidated. As it pleased immortals…

"This is Tsuki no Yousai," Hideo explained. "The Fortress of Moons. Time and wind have eaten away the silver and bronze that gave it the appearance of the light of both moons playing on its stones. The walls are as black as a moonless night."

The houses in the shadow of the fortress hill were the same plain houses they had seen in all the villages they had passed through, with walls of wooden slats covered with milky paper, roofs with shingles of cypress bark, and low entrance doors guarded by carved dragons and demons. Cherry trees and weathered street lamps lined the unpaved main street, which was wet from the recent rain, and on some houses, ornate carvings gave a hint of how beautiful Kakeya had been in its heyday. Among the dwellings were a few workshops open to the street, where potters and basket makers practiced their craft. At the end of the village, surrounded by ancient trees, a four-story temple pagoda evoked lost prosperity and influence almost as impressively as the fortress high above its roofs.

"What drove the lords of the fortress away?" asked Jacob, as Hideo stopped in front of an inn where the wilting leaves of a maple tree stained the roof in all the colors of autumn. "The walls look dilapidated but undestroyed."

"Oh yes, the Fortress of Moons was never conquered. But the last lord who inhabited it made the mistake of insulting an even more powerful lord, which resulted not only in his ruin but that of his entire family, even though he committed seppuku to protect them."

Seppuku… The same ritual suicide was known in the Japan of Jacob's world. The vanquished restored their honor

51

by drawing their sword through their guts, if possible, without flinching. Yes. Jacob looked up at the black fortress. This was undoubtedly a story that would appeal to an immortal who called himself Krieger. Jacob's Japan had opened up to the West in the late nineteenth century, but Nihon still seemed a world apart, where the warrior caste of samurai was unchallenged and powerful.

Fox glanced after three men walking down the main street. They carried swords on their backs like the Ronin on the ferry. "If the fortress is uninhabited, what are the warriors doing here?"

"They are here because the fortress is inhabited again," came the voice through the curtains of the palanquin. "We are in the right place."

Hideo cast a worried look at the palanquin. Jacob had the impression that their guide still feared that the occupant's illness might be contagious after all. Will didn't take his eyes off the black walls above them while Hideo disappeared into the inn to find out if there were enough sleeping mats for them all and where Kakeya's healing shrine was located. Jacob was already figuring out an explanation in case there was no such shrine. But their guide came back telling them that there were actually three in the Kakeya area—one dedicated to a war god and two dedicated to the kami, the local guardian spirits.

"Reckless-san," Hideo murmured to Jacob as he looked warily down the street. "Your brother's wife is right. A wealthy nobleman with ties to the Mifune family, one of our most powerful clans, bought the fortress a few months ago. For three hundred baskets filled to the brim with silver, according to the innkeeper. The renovation has brought work

52

to all the village craftsmen, so at first, the people were pleased about the arrival… even if it irked them that he dresses like a samurai despite not coming from any of the old families. He brought not only work, but powerful friends to Kakeya, and with them dreams of a future as glorious as the past."

It was not hard to guess who the new owner was. Jacob was starting to get curious about the Elf who called himself Krieger.

"You say 'were'? Is the new master not so popular anymore?"

Their guide looked around guardedly, but the street was once again deserted. Only a few chickens were scratching in the autumn leaves under the trees.

"Two months ago," Hideo said in a lowered voice, "the new lord challenged all the men in the area to beat him in hand-to-hand combat. He promised a princely reward to anyone who could defeat him. Since then, there has hardly been a night when there are no fights up there. And now the challengers come from all over Nihon. They climb the mountain at sunset, but no one comes back. Our landlady says the graves now surround the walls of Tsuki no Yousai like a second forest. A nephew of hers lies up there, too."

"Why the scaffolding?"

"The new lord is having the battlements and roofs clad in fresh silver. The villagers whisper that he derives his wealth from a demon. Or from the god of war whose shrine lies behind the village."

That wasn't all that far from the truth. The Elves were very similar to the old gods, and not just in terms of their immortality. Jacob wondered what guise Krieger had adopted to play the samurai lord in Nihon. He no doubt kept his real face as secret as Spieler did. On their journey, they had discussed whether they could risk asking Spieler's old enemy for help outright. Will had spoken in favor of it. But Jacob believed, as did the Bastard, that it was better to get a feel for the Elf first. Even Sixteen knew only that Spieler both feared and despised him—which was certainly not to say that he would make a good ally.

As Hideo and the litter bearers went in search of a meal, the Bastard offered to sneak up to the fortress. The Goyl was an excellent spy, and not only thanks to his onyx skin. Jacob was willing to forget his suspicions to get a first report on what was going on inside the fortress before nightfall. But Fox was not at all pleased that the Bastard would be their first scout.

"I'm going to go into the fortress, too," she announced to Jacob as they brought their horses into the inn's stable. "Will and the Goyl are only concerned with the mirror. But we need to learn more about the Elves and get out of the bargain with Spieler. I'm sure he'll be back soon, and I want to know his weaknesses before he finds us and reminds us of his price."

Jacob didn't know what to say in response. Fox had not yet met the Elf, but he remembered all too well how painfully helpless he had been when he had been caught in Spieler's web. He didn't want Fox to get too close to any of them, and he already regretted that they had come here. She was the most precious thing he would ever hold, more precious than all the magic things he had ever found, but he had to keep reminding himself that one reason he loved her so much was that she didn't want a protector and always followed her own path.

Fox reached for his hands. "Trust me," she whispered, kissing him gently. "You know I'll be careful."

"Fine, but I'm coming with you."

"No. Not unless you can turn into a fox."

He wanted to kiss, kiss, kiss her and ride away with her. But of course, she was right. They couldn't outrun Spieler. They had both been caught in his web ever since Jacob had been foolish enough to make a deal with the Elf. Stupid and desperate. Without that trade, Fox would have died in the Bluebeard's Red Chamber, and Jacob knew he would make the same deal again to save her, even though he now knew the price. Fox was right. They needed to learn more about Spieler to protect themselves from him.

Your vixen will make beautiful children. I hope you don't take too long.

7

FOX AND GOYL

Of course. The vixen didn't trust him. Why else was she going up to the fortress as well? It was no use pointing out that two spies were more easily caught than one or that the Bastard had decades more experience in espionage than her. Damn. His last forced collaboration had given him nothing but regular nightmares of the bloated, elven-dusted Crown Prince of Lorraine! No. Only alone was he invisible. More silent than an amber fly! Faster than a spiny salamander! Would he have taken the Pup with him? Of course not.

Nerron was still ranting to himself when the vixen set off without warning. She did it in human form, perhaps so as not to feed the kitsune cult their guide had been rambling about. She was still on two legs when Nerron caught up with her in the damp, thick forest that sprawled on the slope below the fortress like an army of moss-bearded sentinels. Goyl were excellent climbers, but she advanced as lightly as if she weighed no more than her fur despite the steep climb. Shapeshifters... Nerron had never liked them. He had a theory that they were two people in one, and you could never be sure which one you were looking at. That the vixen was also a woman didn't help matters. Nerron had only half trusted one woman in his life, and that had been his mother.

Of course, she had heard him long before he caught up with her.

"I've had to sneak onto an Elf's property before," she said without turning around. "They use traps you can't see to protect themselves from unwelcome visitors. I'm sure we'll run into them before we reach the main walls."

"Traps you can't see? You spend too much time with the slug skins. You're talking to a Goyl. We see a lot more than you."

How condescendingly she eyed him. Jacob Reckless's pet. That's what she was. Nothing more.

"In case it escaped your notice, Goyl, I don't have human eyes either."

Oh, he wanted to make a collar out of her fur! Only with her help had Reckless been able to steal the crossbow from him — the one treasure that would have made him the most famous treasure hunter of all, a legend despite his grained bastard skin. He would have brought the crossbow to Kami'en, who would have had a better use for it than killing Fairies, and the crossbow would not have dissolved so complacently into silver smoke. *Stop it, Nerron! Smoke is smoke, and the vixen couldn't care less what you think of her.* Damn, she was way ahead again. When she transformed, it happened so fast that he could hardly believe his own eyes. There were no shapeshifters among the Goyl. Stone remained stone, even in death.

The fortress was still high above them when they came upon the first wall. The gate through it was thick with rust and mildew, but there had been some makeshift repairs. There were no guards to be seen, and Nerron was still climbing over the wall when the vixen slipped under the gate like a furry snake and was once again ahead of him.

It was a cold day, but the sky was cloudless, and the damned sunlight was bleaching craters in his skin despite the oil he rubbed himself with in the morning.

However she had done it, Nerron soon saw the vixen high above him, and he cursed her with all the curse words his language had for her kind. When he finally caught up with her, she was sitting on a weathered statue that looked a lot like one of the demons their guide kept rambling on about, licking her fur with tantalizing composure.

"Alderelves love places like this," she said. "I understand Fairies and their love of valleys and lakes, but what is it about ruins left by mortals that appeals to immortals? Do they like the feeling of being immune to such decay?"

"I didn't know we were here to philosophize." Nerron eyed the walls above him. He could see the top floors of the main building beyond, each shaded by a pagoda roof. It was an impressive sight. The walls to the left suggested that the stables and other outbuildings were located there.

"There you go, I was right," the vixen murmured. "Do you see them?"

What was that? A trick question? Nerron peeked out from behind the stone demon. A dirt road led toward the main

58

gate, carts of building materials, a dozen workers anchoring scaffolding to the ancient walls... The fortress looked menacing with its black walls, but it resembled a warrior in hibernation, had it not been for the tombstones that drew wide circles around the fortress walls to the left and right of the road—and the guards just above the gate. Sunlight caught on the tips of their lances.

"I count four guards. But I'm sure there are more."

"I'm not talking about the guards. Don't you wonder why there are so few? Do you see the silvery blossoms?"

Silvery? Nerron saw yellow ones and white ones. Was she trying to fool him so she and Reckless could laugh at the simple-minded Bastard later?

"What about the threads? Like cobwebs of metal."

Nerron wasn't sure what annoyed him more: that he believed her or that he couldn't see what she was describing.

"If you touch the flowers and threads, the Elf will know you're here. Let Jacob tell you how it feels to be an Elf's prisoner. Spieler stuck a silver needle in his temple and stored him like fresh meat in one of his dungeons. But maybe this Krieger also has a couple of Mirrorlings like Sixteen who can turn you into silver."

"All right!" Nerron snapped at her. "I'm not a damn shapeshifter. I can't see any of the things you describe, so what?"

"Follow my lead." She leaped from the weathered statue so lithely that the grass at her feet barely swished. "The traps aren't everywhere. We're lucky the Elf hasn't been here long. If you don't stray from my trail, you'll be safe."

So silent. Rusty red in all that green, yet she knew how to make herself invisible. She ducked and crept toward the distant walls.

Nerron was sorely tempted to defy her instructions and make his own way, but he could sense the magic the vixen was describing, even though he couldn't see it. So, grudgingly, he took all the seemingly useless turns she led him on until she stopped between the last of the graves and ducked behind one of the gray stones. Nerron still counted four guards above the gate and three more in front of it. It was not easy to focus on them among all the graves. There must have been more than a hundred headstones, and some of them looked fresh.

The gate was open, and the three guards in front of it looked fatigued and bored. When they turned in response to someone calling out to them from inside the fortress, the vixen scurried to one of the man-sized stone lanterns that stood not far from the gate on the edge of the road leading up from Kakeya. Nerron followed her, and one of the guards looked round, but the lantern hid him from view in time. The fresh soot on the gray stone suggested that it had burned the previous night.

"Wait here," the vixen whispered to him. "I'll help you get past the guards." Her voice was like a nettle leaf when she wore the fur. "After that, it's everyone for themselves."

Fine. I'm thoroughly tired of your twists and turns. Nerron already had the words on his tongue, but she took human form before he could get them past his lips. Then she stepped out from behind the lantern and, before he could ask what in all the devils in the bosom of the earth she was up to, she strode toward the open gate.

The guards were dressed like samurai, with helmets that cut menacing grimaces, leather breastplates, and red-and-black patterned shirts and pants—tradesmen of war.

Nonetheless.

It was child's play for the vixen to get past them. She transformed as soon as one of the three gruffly asked her to stop in broken Albian.

"Kitsuneee!!!"

Faces contorted in fear like the metal grimaces their helmets made. Even the workers had dropped their tools and were staring down from their bamboo scaffolds, terrified.

The vixen was past the guards before they had their swords out of their scabbards. While the three stumbled after her after a frightened hesitation, Nerron darted through the gate and caught his first glimpse of the full splendor of the main building. It was a massive palace with four stories tapering upward, each topped by a sweeping pagoda roof supported by silvered dragons. The guards Nerron had seen on top of the wall were all staring at where the vixen had disappeared. No one stood in Nerron's way. The silence behind the walls still tasted of decay, despite the scaffolding, and the fortress garrison did not seem large at all. Nerron looked around for the vixen as he ducked under one of the scaffolds, but she had disappeared as if she were indeed an evil spirit in fox form. Many claimed that Jacob Reckless was only successful because of the vixen. For a fleeting moment, Nerron caught himself wishing for a similar shadow, albeit not with rust-colored fox fur, but with iridescent scales like the lizards that many Goyl kept like dogs.

The vixen had turned to the left, where the stables and outbuildings made it easier for her to throw off the guards. This gave him a good head start exploring the main building, and if he was lucky, the Elf was as stingy with his servants as he was with his guards.

61

Up close, the four pagoda roofs floating overhead looked like they could be scaled to the heavens, and the treasure hunter inside Nerron stirred vigorously when he saw the freshly silvered dragons supporting them. Oh, it was going to be fun to explore this building! And the Bastard would find the mirror before the vixen.

8

Very Old Enemies

Fox wasn't looking for a mirror. She had never liked them, those crystal doors between worlds, even though they had brought Jacob to her. They had also taken him from her again and again with their hungry glass. No, she wanted to find the Elf Sixteen had told her about. She had caught his scent before the gate, as clearly as when she had sought Jacob on Spieler's forgotten island, in the other world. The silver trail led her past stables and workshops to a courtyard, which granted a sweeping view of the surrounding mountains. Two voices reached her from the freshly silvered battlements, men's voices that tasted of silver like the trail. The vixen followed them down steep steps into a garden enclosed by high walls, the beauty of which momentarily made her forget what she had come for. It surprised her to

63

find, in a place where death was celebrated every night, a garden where everything sang of life and growth. But the wilting flowers she passed quickly reminded her that death was present here, too.

From stone to stone she crept, seeking cover among carefully trimmed azalea bushes, under bamboo rustling gently in the wind. Fox felt cedar roots under her paws, peony leaves in her fur. The two men whose voices she had followed knew nothing of death or withering. Their hands betrayed them, six-fingered as with all immortals. They knelt in the shade of a cherry tree before a little black lacquered table. An old servant was filling the clay tea bowls that stood before them with pale gold tea as Fox crept closer. The scent of jasmine drifted into Fox's nose as she ducked under a chrysanthemum bush growing among carefully arranged stones just a few steps away from the little table.

Yes. They were indeed back. Fox ducked low under the branches bedecked with white blossoms. Not even the birds pecking for insects in the cracks of a stone a few paces away noticed her, so silently did she blend into the shadows, ears pricked, amber eyes fixed on the two immortals sitting opposite each other. They spoke Albian to each other, even though the elder wore a golden kimono and looked as if he had been born on these islands.

"I still don't know why you're here," Fox heard him say. "So you can remind me again that without your mirrors, we would never have escaped? You've never missed an opportunity to remind us in all these centuries, and we've all paid for it one way or another." He was of stocky build, close to fifty if one was so careless as to believe his appearance, with short-cropped gray hair, narrow, colorless lips, and eyes that watched his counterpart from under half-closed lids. "I thought you were busy growing magic plants on some plantation in Alberica and renovating your old palace after being forced to leave it to the spiders for eight hundred years. You like to be secretive about its location, but I'm pretty sure I know where it is, and it's a long way from there to these islands."

"Believe it or not, Nihon was on the way." The other Elf looked much younger. He was dressed in western clothes, and his voice was as beautiful as his face. "I am on my way to the plantation. The climate there is ideal for the plants that interest me. But you are right. There is definitely a purpose to my visit. The others are worried that you will once again live up to your name and start a big war. They have asked me to tell you that they wish for a quiet return to their old world."

That you will once again live up to your name. So the older one was Krieger. He eyed the younger one with undisguised distaste. And no, he did not look like a trustworthy ally.

"I really wonder how you always manage to get the others to make you their mouthpiece," he said. "They can't be so stupid as to trust you. This world is already at war, in case that has escaped your notice, and only I will decide whether or not to take part in it."

His counterpart gave him such an indulgent smile that Krieger's face reddened a touch. "I'll pass that on. But there is something else. Several Silver-Alders have been felled in recent weeks before our unfortunate brethren could free themselves from their tree prisons. Apaullo has suggested that this is how you get rid of old enemies?"

This time Krieger eyed the younger man with undisguised derision. "Fallen Silver-Alders… I'm sure you know as much about that as I do, don't you?"

His counterpart reached for the tea bowl that stood before him and sipped the contents. "I don't know what you're talking about. But speaking of old enemies..." He took a sip and smiled conspiratorially at the elder. "What about Toshiró? I suppose you'd prefer he didn't come back, too?"

"My golems have cut down every Alder on his former lands. Toshiró will not return."

"What if he wasn't on his lands when the curse was cast?"

"Spieler, the pessimist? That's new."

No. The vixen pressed her chest against the cool earth. She felt her heart beating so fast that she thought she would choke on her own pulse. She must have misheard. Why would Sixteen lie to her about Spieler's enmity with Krieger? *Because she is his creature, Fox!* But Sixteen hadn't lied. The two of them *were* enemies. Their dislike for each other was as tangible as the gentle wind that brushed through the garden.

"You have far more reason to fear Toshiró than I do." Krieger rubbed the back of his hand. Fox thought she saw a trace of tree bark on it. "After all, it was thanks to you that the Fairies thought he was the traitor who got us past their unicorns."

"How could I resist? Toshiró was such a plausible scapegoat." Spieler seemed to remember it fondly. "It's still absurd how resentful they were of us stealing a few barrels of lake water, but in the end, they punished themselves. If they had been a little less vengeful, they could have passed the rest of eternity with their mortal lovers, but no. The Fairies and their curses..."

"If I remember correctly, they were convinced that the mirrors you made from their water would one day destroy both worlds."

Spieler wiped a withered leaf from his shoulder. "So, did that happen? There's nothing more tiresome than obscure old prophecies. We—"

He abruptly fell silent, staring at the black moth fluttering toward the table. Krieger swatted at it with a fan, but all he hit was his tea bowl. The glazed clay shattered, and the old servant hurried over and wiped the hot tea from the tabletop.

Something inside Fox began to whisper. It sounded like the trickle of water, and she thought she smelled the scent of the lilies that bloomed on the Fairies' lakes.

Spieler looked around. But the chrysanthemum bush kept the vixen hidden from him.

"How long will the sight of a moth keep us on edge?" Krieger angrily flung the fan on the table. "My skin still itches. Occasionally I even grow some tree bark on my arms. Didn't you say you'd take care of those pesky after-effects?"

"There's a lot I need to take care of. We've been gone eight hundred years. We began some things in another world that have now followed us here. Even your wars don't have just one theater, do they?"

Spieler stood up.

Fox didn't dare breathe as he stepped toward the bush under which she was crouched. *Today I bake, tomorrow brew, the next I'll have the young Queen's firstborn child.* She thought she felt him reaching into her womb and tearing out her love for Jacob, like a fruit he would savor between his perfect lips. Her heart was filled with the same helpless mixture of rage and hatred her stepfather had awakened in her with his beatings. At the time, she had only been able to escape her own hatred and the punches by running away. Perhaps

Jacob was right after all, and escape was also their only chance with Spieler?

The Elf had turned around. He looked toward the steps that led down into the garden. A young woman was coming down them. Clara wore a dress of the kind rich women in Lutis or Vena had tailored. It certainly did not come from the other world as she did.

Spieler went to meet her. She gave him a smile like someone she was familiar with. He helped her down the last few steps and kissed her hand.

"Let's continue this conversation later," he said to Krieger. "I promised Clara I'd show her your garden. And I'm expecting a visitor. I hope you don't mind her coming through your mirror?"

Krieger stood up and tugged his golden kimono into place. "Sure. My mirror is your mirror—even if I am no friend of your creatures. I prefer any beast over your creatures of silver and glass."

Clara looked questioningly at Spieler. He offered her his arm.

"Oh, this visitor is just an old acquaintance," he said. "I'm sure my guest here," he smiled at Clara, "knows her from the fairy tales of her childhood."

The servant cleared away the bowls, and Krieger led Spieler and Clara along his carefully raked garden paths.

What was Clara doing here?

Fox stayed hidden among the chrysanthemums until they had all disappeared through a door at the end of the garden. And her heart finally slowed down a bit.

Will didn't need Krieger's mirror anymore.

They had found Spieler and Clara.

9

GURASU

The landlady of the hostel spoke hardly a word. She did not seem particularly fond of strangers. Her guests slept in one room, on straw mats that were dappled by pale squares of light falling through the rice paper walls. When Hideo had asked if she could let Will and his wife have their own room, she had at first just shaken her head, but then she had partitioned off a small area at the end of the sleeping room with a sliding wall and brought them two mats and a little flat table for their tea. Will liked Nihon's sparsely furnished houses. It was as if their inhabitants wanted to make sure that no superfluous things came between them and the world — or between them and their gods, which seemed to be innumerable.

Outside, the mountain peaks, just visible behind the autumn-red trees, were white with snow, but the only source of heat in their quarters was a basin of charcoal. Sixteen didn't take off the veils until Will had the coals glowing. She hid behind all the layers of fabric like a caterpillar, hoping to emerge as a butterfly, but the bark disappeared only agonizingly slowly, and her left arm was still entirely wood. Will was glad she hid her body from him, but not because the disfigurement repelled him. The bark on Sixteen's skin seemed to him like a final scream from the Fairy. He kept seeing her raise her hands pleadingly as her moths swarmed toward him. *What did they promise you?* He had not looked at her when he had made the shot. She had given him the skin of jade, and he had killed her. *What did they promise you?* That everything would be as it should be. Whatever that meant. Will hadn't been sure of anything since he'd fired that crossbow — neither right nor wrong, neither good nor evil. Spieler had lied to him. But he had also made Sixteen. Sixteen...

Will stroked the back of her neck. "Trust me, it really will get better!"

Where the bark disappeared, the skin remained blank as mirror glass, and for a moment, he caught himself imagining Spieler's smile there. He had gone over the encounter with him again and again in his mind. On that bench in front of the hospital in the other world. Looking for what? For an apology for what he had done? An excuse for having trusted him? He would find him and confront him. He would demand that he wake Clara and cure Sixteen. And then?

Could Spieler turn back time? But wouldn't Will have shot again every time instead of watching the Fairy's spell slowly kill Sixteen?

The word for glass in Nihon was *gurasu*. Will had had Hideo repeat it to him three times to get it right. *Gurasu.*

Maybe he should call Sixteen that. He had tried several times to give her a new name. They pleased her for a few days, but then she was Sixteen again—the girl who didn't deserve a real name because she was a thing of glass and silver.

"I shouldn't have brought you here." She knelt beside the brazier and rubbed her wooden hand. "I feel something. Terrible darkness. The mirror is here, but there's more." She shook her head. "I can't see it. Everything inside me is fogged up. Wooden. I'm good for nothing. A wooden mirror!"

Will knelt beside her and enveloped her stiffened hand with his. "We will go back to my world and leave all this behind. There's no Fairy magic there. Why shouldn't the bark go away? It will be all right! I promised you it would! We will find a way."

Back. He hid from her that the thought made him shudder. He had gone back once before. Just one step through the dark glass. He had regretted it the very next night, lying there sleepless in Clara's arms, longing for the jade in his skin, the gold in his eyes. Only the Bastard understood that yearning and who he was when the jade grew.

Sixteen tried to pull her hand away, but Will held it tightly. It was so beautiful, even if it was made of wood. He had never loved in this way before. The admission, of course, immediately brought back the guilt. He couldn't tell what he was more afraid of: that he would find Clara and his kiss wouldn't wake her this time either, or that she would wake up and he'd have to confess to her that he now loved someone else.

What did they promise you?
That everything would be as it should be.

71

The dead coachman kept his promise. Chithira's pale figure stood beside the Fairy every night in his dreams, staring accusingly at him as he cocked his crossbow. Sometimes he tried not to shoot, but then the moths swarmed toward Sixteen, and Spieler handed him the bolt with a smile.

Sixteen fell asleep beside the brazier. Will covered her with her veils and kissed her face, which could be so many faces.

"Will?" Jacob was silhouetted against the milky paper of the partition.

"What?" Will heard himself, how cool his voice sounded. Jacob had never made a secret of what he thought or felt, and he let Sixteen feel very clearly how much he loathed her.

"Fox is back from the fortress. I need to talk to you."

Will bent over Sixteen's sleeping form and carried her to her mat. *Gurasu.*

He saw the look Jacob gave Sixteen as he pushed back the partition. She was a thing to them all, nothing but a deadly thing.

10

No Time

The poor houses along the dirt road, the woman returning from the old temple pagoda hand in hand with a child, the colorful paper lanterns in the maple tree in front of their inn... Will seemed more interested in all this than in the news Fox had brought back from the fortress. But Jacob knew this attitude from his brother. The more shocked Will was by a piece of information, the more expressionless his face became when he received it.

Why didn't he also finally tell him what Spieler had revealed to him when he had been his prisoner? *Your mother never noticed the difference. I was very attached to her. All too much, I must admit...* No, Spieler was a master at deceit and deception. It meant nothing that he claimed to have been their mother's lover for years—and by that, perhaps, their father.

An Elf for a father... As if they had not already been punished enough with their human one! Nevertheless, his words were like thistle seed. They took root and grew in the dark, prickly and irrepressible.

"All right." It was the first time Will had looked at him since he had listened to his report in silence. "Clara's here, and so is Spieler. Does that mean the Elf woke her with a kiss? And that he made her fall in love with him?"

Was that jealousy in his voice? Even though he loved someone else? Sure, and what did that matter? Jealousy often outlived love.

"What will you do now?"

A young woman steered a donkey cart down the street. One saw many more women than men in Kakeya. Fox had told them how many graves there were up by the fortress.

"I'm glad I don't have to go back. I would have only done it for Clara and Sixteen." Will actually sounded relieved. "I'll find out if Clara is with him willingly. And demand that he heals Sixteen. He owes it to me."

He owes it to me. Did he need to be told that Spieler made no debts but merely collected them? Perhaps Will should also ask the Elf to take away the guilt he had caused him.

Will turned around. Jacob knew he would never forgive himself for killing the Fairy. Even without her dead coachman to remind him.

"I'll go tonight. I'll pretend to be there for the fighting."

"Will!" Jacob reached for his arm. "We don't know anything about Spieler! If he hexed Clara, we should find out how before we walk into yet another fortress owned by another Alderelf, right? Well, maybe this Krieger is Spieler's enemy, but he's an immortal as well. You're nothing but

74

amusing toys to him! We need time! We need to find out what their weaknesses and goals are. We—"

"Sixteen doesn't have time," Will interrupted him. "And Clara? Should I just leave her up there?" He broke away. "But don't worry. I don't need an older brother to fight my battles for me anymore. If I need help, I'll ask Nerron. He understands me. Better than all of you. He understands the jade and knows more about this world than you do. If it weren't for him, I would have lost my mind in the last few months. Go and find treasure with Fox! That's all you've ever really cared about."

Will disappeared into the inn without looking back, and Jacob stood there, his mouth filled with words he hadn't said. *Yes, go take on Spieler, little brother. After all, you've already killed one immortal! The Bastard is your best friend, and you love a creature that almost killed Fox and me? Why not?* It was a useless, angry lather of words that filled his brain and heart.

He had to find Fox. She was the only one who could stop him from ripping his brother's jade head off! The Goyl had not returned yet, and she was on her way back to the fortress to find out if he had been captured. Of course, that wasn't the real reason. She couldn't get it out of her mind that Spieler was up there.

If I need help, I'll ask Nerron. Well, the Bastard certainly wouldn't like Will's idea of confronting the Elf either. That wouldn't give the fairy tale of Jade Goyl a happy ending.

11

THE OTHER MIRROR

The Fortress of Moons reeked of ghosts and fresh paint, and the servants Nerron encountered were so over-tired that they barely lifted their heads when he gave himself away by making a careless noise. Their master's duels apparently made for sleepless nights. The overhanging pagoda roofs made spying even easier. Most rooms were so dark that his onyx skin made him a living shadow as he crept from floor to floor.

Nerron had skipped the kitchen and women's quarters. The Elf would hardly keep his precious mirror there, even if the idea of cooks, servants, and concubines suddenly finding themselves in another world was amusing. Their mountain of a guide had explained to them with an authoritative air that each floor of the pagoda palaces of his homeland embodied an element: the lower one was earth, then water, fire, and

76

finally heaven. Where did a mirror belong? Nerron hoped for water, but he braced himself for having to creep all the way up to heaven.

Earth, water, fire, sky — Nerron almost felt at home on the first floor because the black-painted walls reminded him of the underground homes where he'd grown up. Right in the first room, a servant almost caught him. He had a strangely shapeless face. Another, into whom he almost stumbled before reaching the stairs to the next floor, had the same featureless, clay-like features. The Goyl had a myth about creatures that rose from the mud of their underground lakes. Nerron imagined them looking very much like that.

The water floor had pale green ceilings and walls painted with wave patterns. Three of the clay-faces crossed Nerron's path there, and though they didn't notice him, he was glad when their slow footsteps faded away. There was something about them that made him shudder. Perhaps they were to blame for his mounting sensation that he was not alone. Instead of doors, there were only the sliding walls that, like in their hostel, turned everything into a shadow theater, and usually, one glance was enough to grasp what was behind them. Even the largest rooms often contained only a few masks on the wall or a meaningfully placed vase. The treasure hunters in Nihon had to be bored to death! Still, Nerron increasingly thought he sensed someone or something behind him. Was this some Elf magic? It had been said of the Dark Fairy that her presence could be felt for miles.

The mirror. Where was the cursed mirror?

If only he could have snatched at least a few magic trinkets! He had initially hoped that the vases and masks held some magic. Yet when he found them in multiple rooms, he gave up the idea—and thanked the god of treasure hunters that not all palaces were as sparsely furnished as the Fortress of Moons.

In the final room on the water floor, things finally got a little more interesting. The samurai suits of armor that lined the walls probably held no magic, but they were an impressive sight. They looked like stuffed warriors with their padded vests and leggings, and beneath their helmets were masks with wide-open eyes and bared teeth. Nerron would have liked to steal at least one, but the room seemed even more filled with dark magic than the others.

On the stairs leading up to the fire floor, the feeling of an invisible threat became so acute that the Bastard almost wished he could encounter some flesh-and-blood guards. But all he heard was the sound of his own footsteps on the red lacquered steps, and when he stopped at a window and made the mistake of looking out, he saw below him the graves that surrounded the fortress. From this high, the number was even more unsettling. What if Sixteen had fooled them all and lured them here to ensnare them in her immortal creator's net? The Bastard was amazed by how convincingly he had fooled the Pup into thinking he trusted his beloved.

The walls that welcomed him to the floor of fire were as red as if the Elf had painted them with fresh blood. The sense of lurking doom grew so strong that the desire to turn around and stumble down the damned stairs became more and more irresistible. *Sure! Run away!* Nerron taunted himself, though he felt the fear like sweat on his stony skin. *The Bastard runs away from fresh paint and empty rooms. Reckless and the vixen will love that story!* Of course, there was nothing there but a protection spell. Damn immortals! The world

78

was better off without them. And why, by the stench of all the dead buried out there, was he so eager to make an enemy of one of them? It was the Pup's fault. He had turned him into a sentimental fool! *Nonsense!* Nerron snapped at himself, while the fear that lurked in the walls around him made his chest tight. *You want to find the mirror for yourself, too, Bastard!* Another world to escape this one. He'd been looking for it even before Jacob Reckless and the vixen had escaped right before his eyes through a pane of dark glass. They had smashed the mirror before he could follow them, and he had spent endless months looking for another. Ironic that he and Jacob Reckless were now searching for one together. Yes, he wanted to find that damned mirror for himself, too. For himself and for all Goyl. Had anyone ever laid an entire world at the feet of his king? What if the Bastard was the first?

There. His persistence was finally rewarded.

He stepped into the room with ceiling beams as red as the marks of lizard claws, and the chests that lined the walls made Nerron's treasure-hunting senses sing. In the first lay the most perfect sword he had ever seen. The one in the second was even more perfect. The third dazzled him with the magic that had been forged into the flawless blade, and this time he could not resist. But no sooner did he close his onyx fingers around the silver handle than he heard a rustling behind him as if from a thousand blossoms opening at once, and as he wheeled around, a thousand eyes stared at him from the red wall he had thought so unsuspiciously blank.

The eyes were in pairs and as different as if each pair had once belonged to a human. They continued to stare at Nerron even as he hastily dropped the sword back into the chest. *The walls have eyes*. Why hadn't anyone told him that this was actually true in this cursed fortress?

Think, Bastard! he snapped at himself, but the thousandfold stares paralyzed his mind. The black silence that surrounded him became filled with voices and heavy footsteps. They came from above from the celestial floor. Of course. Nothing good ever came from there. There were at least ten of them, if not more. He heard them already on the stairs. And what was the one thing he worried about? That the vixen would mock him for his recklessness!

There was a way out, but it was not a pleasant one. No, indeed not… Maybe the Elf would let him talk. Wasn't that what the Pup was going to do anyway? *His eyes saw that you wanted to steal his sword, Bastard. He'll treat you like a dirty thief, and those get their hands chopped off or get turned into some insect that can be quickly squashed.* No. It didn't help. He slipped his finger into the hem of his left sleeve, even though his guts were already protesting against what he was about to do. He had bought the barely cherry-sized hand he shook out of the hem of his sleeve from a traveling bone carver in Zhonggua (with his last red moonstone, after trying in vain to steal the thing). The hand was carved from the bone of a giant. In Zhonggua, they could be found in almost every rice field. The mother of pearl fingernails and the marks on the perfectly reproduced back of the hand were some sinister magic that the bone carver had awkwardly tried to explain to him. But what did it matter how the thing worked? He had tried it right behind the carver's cart, with impressive and absurdly painful results. Nerron stared at the little hand. Damn it! He was going to feel for hours as if the lizards of the onyx had chewed his guts out.

80

Come on, Bastard, or would you rather jump from the third floor? The vixen would surely like to watch you try to fly.

He pulled the tiny fingers of the bone hand so firmly across his forearm that they left bloody welts even on his stony skin. But the spell worked quickly. When the guards leaped into the room with swords drawn, Nerron was already looking at them from the perspective of a mouse. They looked around in irritation, and one threatened the eyewalls with his sword, angrily shouting, "Moku!" Whatever that meant.

The eyes in the wall were wide open, and their pupils wandered back and forth in search of the stone-skinned intruder who had suddenly vanished into thin air. Clearly, headless eyes weren't too bright. However, in fairness, the lowest of them stared out of the wall at knee level, while Nerron could have barely reached an ankle. One of the guards pushed open the sliding partition to the next room. Good! He almost got trampled as he dashed among all the boots. But since he'd gotten this far, he simply had to take a look at what all those eyes were guarding.

The guard nearly crushed Nerron as he slammed the partition shut again with an angry curse the moment Nerron stole past him. But when he'd recovered from the shock, Nerron found himself standing unharmed in the room beyond— gazing at the mirror he'd been searching for.

It was huge, and not just because he saw it from a mouse's perspective. The silver frame that held the glass was much less ornate than the mirror through which Reckless had escaped him with the crossbow. But in the spartan empty space in which it stood, the silver flowers that opened at the four corners of the frame seemed almost lavishly luxuriant.

Nerron could still hear the guards in the next room. They seemed to be arguing with the eyes. *Get out of here!* he thought, as he once again shook the bone hand out of his sleeve. They were taking their time. But at last, he heard them stomp back up the stairs, leaving him alone with the mirror.

The room in which he stood had no windows and was so immaculate it was as if no one was allowed to enter it. The sacred shrines of Nihon had forbidden rooms where offerings of white rice or savory soy cheese were placed to convince any of the countless gods to make the shrine their home. Nerron could discover neither such offerings nor any god, and since the walls remained eyeless, he finally pulled his bone hand over his arm again.

He grew so fast that the pain threw him to his knees, and he almost threw up in his own hands. It was as if someone was pummeling his insides until they were a muddy, burning mush. No, this method could not be healthy. He barely made it back to his feet, and like the first time, he suspected he had lost a couple of inches. His knees were still shaking as he stepped toward the mirror.

The glass was dark as the night sky.

Come on, Bastard! it seemed to murmur. *Take the world I give you. It is yours. I promise you: it's even better than you dreamed.*

Of course, he remembered how Reckless had done it. He had covered his mirrored face with his hand as if one had to forget who one was before changing worlds — that made sense.

A new world... Nerron raised his hand. And lowered it again. What if what Reckless had told him was true — that there were no Goyl in his world? Only soft-skinned creatures who would flock together and slay him — or stuff him, as the

82

emperors of Austry had done for centuries with his kind. Not that the Goyl were strangers to such behavior. The saurian who had strayed into one of their subterranean cities from the lava depths of Earth centuries ago could still be viewed in the royal palace, next to a human spy cast in amber.

What a coward you are, Bastard! he thought he heard the mirror mock. Had Jacob Reckless known what was in store for him when he first passed through the glass? And he had been just a child then.

His reflection showed all too clearly the envy he felt for his competitor. His face distorted more and more, as if the mirror had robbed him of the ability to hide his feelings behind his stony skin. Only when Nerron saw a tremor run across the glass did he realize that the distorted image was caused by reasons other than his anger at Jacob Reckless.

The glass made ripples as if someone had thrown a stone into the still waters of a pond.

Get out of here, Bastard!

Nerron backed away.

A face slid out of the mirror. The face of an old woman. It slid out of the glass with its eyes closed as if emerging from water.

Nerron did not wait for the eyes to open. This time even the shrinking hurt, but when the face was followed by a body, he was small enough to hide behind the mirror frame. The woman who stepped out of the mirror was hunched with age. She looked around with eyes that singed Nerron's stony heart. Oh, he knew such eyes. They were not from another world. Their terror belonged to his world, like man-eaters and Bluebeards, Loreleis and water sprites, but even they would have feared the old woman who had risen from the

83

mirror. Her shadow had nothing to do with her skinny figure. It was the shadow of a forest, dark and inescapable. It followed her like black smoke as she turned and stepped in front of the mirror.

"Look at yourself, Giovanna," Nerron heard her whisper in a hoarse voice. "Withered like a shriveled thistle. Consumed by the hunger you have awakened."

She stepped into the center of the room and stretched out her scrawny arms. They became wings, and a crow soared into the air. Its shadow grew and filled the room as if sinister trees were poking out of the ground. Strangler berries twined thornily up the walls, and every poisonous plant Nerron knew opened its blossoms among the shady trees. A vine crept toward the mirror, spiked with thorns that would have effortlessly impaled it despite its size. But before it could do so, the crow flapped its wings, cawing, and it dissolved into dirty smoke along with its murderous shadow.

Silence. And darkness. It was as if the forest shadows still clung to the walls when Nerron finally dared to sit up and crawl out of his hiding place. His shrunken legs were so numb they barely supported him, and the glass loomed over him like an icy lake that held other monsters. Nerron was sorely tempted to smash it, but that might call back the crow. *Find the mirror, Bastard!* No one had told him that dark witches hatched from them! He thought he tasted cinnamon on his tongue as he crept back to the partition behind which a thousand eyes watched, cinnamon and sweet cakes. He cut a path for his mouse body through the rice paper with his knife. Who had brought a gingerbread baker to Nihon?

12

The Necessity of Lies

Jacob found Fox not far from the graves surrounding the fortress, hidden in the crown of an old tree that autumn had dyed as rusty red as her coat of fur. She could not have found a better lookout. Jacob would have chosen the same tree. Of course. After all these years, they did almost everything the same way. That they were also a couple now didn't always make their partnership easier. Love was so much more complicated than friendship. Some days—there weren't many, but there were some—Jacob almost missed the unfulfilled desire, the longing for each other. Did Fox feel the same way? Maybe. Sometimes he saw in her eyes the question that followed so quickly when love was fulfilled: Will the happiness last or will it inevitably be lost? *Well, Jacob Reckless*, he thought he heard Fox mock him, *you really have changed for the better. In the old days, you wouldn't have asked yourself such questions.*

She acted composed as he joined her up in the tree, but Jacob saw the tension in her face. Until now, to Fox, Spieler had just been a threat he'd told her about, faceless and as abstract as a storm in a faraway land you'd never set foot in. Now she had seen his face—even if it was not his true one—heard his voice and perhaps even felt the magic with which he caught mortals so effortlessly in his web. Still, she did not want to run away. Jacob saw that in her face, too. No, now more than ever. He loved her so much. Even if her courage had never frightened him more.

The outer walls of the fortress and the pagoda roofs reliably hid what was going on inside. But on the north side, parts of the wall had collapsed, and with a good telescope, one could see the outer courtyards and part of the main building, despite the renovations. The telescope that Fox had trained on the fortress was excellent. It came from Jacob's world—one of the few things he had allowed himself to bring through the mirrors. Fox handed it to him as soon as he swung onto the branch below.

"On the left. The third-floor balcony."

Clara was standing behind the balustrade with Spieler.

She seemed to be fine. She even laughed. Spieler looked a little younger than the last time Jacob had met him. How absurdly fast his heart pounded at the sight of him. Fox felt no different, no doubt, but she was hiding behind the vixen. Oh yes, she could do that even in human form. Her features sharpened slightly, her lips narrowed a little, her back straightened.

"They look very familiar with each other."

Yes, they did. What would Will have thought, seeing the two of them together like this? *The same as you, Jacob.* He would assume that Spieler had enchanted Clara somehow and that he had to save her from the Elf. She looked truly happy. And Spieler—Jacob kept the spyglass pointed at his face—actually looked at Clara as if he were in love with her. *Think of the name he gave himself, Jacob. It's a game. Everything is a game to him.*

"Any sign of the Bastard?"

"No. But look at all that fresh silver. Who knows what treasures the main building holds. Treasure hunting could easily have led him astray." Fox took the spyglass from Jacob's hand. "Why is Clara with him?" she whispered as she pointed it at the fortress. "What if she's just one of Spieler's creatures—with Clara's face?"

Possible. Sixteen had used Clara's face when she'd pushed him in front of a car in his world. But the young woman standing beside Spieler smiled and moved like the Clara Jacob was so familiar with from the many evenings he'd spent with her and his brother.

"So, what should we do?" Fox lowered the spyglass. She took a deep breath, as she always did when she was about to say something he wouldn't like. "I think Will and I should go to see Spieler. What's the worst that can happen? Your brother killed the Fairy like Spieler wanted him to, and I could make him think we'll pay his price if he leaves us alone. We can find out if Clara is with him of her own free will, and…"

"And what? What then? Do you want to end up with a needle in your head like I did the last time I met him? Or as a silver statue if he turns one of his creatures on you? We

87

don't know anything about him! I've already tried to explain that to Will."

He could tell from Fox's face that she agreed with him. But she still shook her head.

"Your brother won't wait."

"Wait for what?"

The voice that drifted up to them sounded familiar. But Jacob could see no one under the tree, even though the words were clearly coming from there. The vixen's eyes found the Goyl immediately, of course, even though he was barely bigger than a mouse.

By the time they had climbed down to him, the Bastard had already started to grow again. Shrinking and invisibility spells very often had unpleasant side effects. This one was apparently no exception. The Goyl writhed in pain as he grew to his normal size.

"What are you two doing here?" he demanded. "I've been spying since I was five years old, and even then, I didn't need a nanny!"

He leaned, groaning against the tree. He was already back to his normal size. That had been quick. Was it a witch's potion? Or a ring that allowed its wearer to assume any size, depending on which way you turned it on your finger? Fox gave Jacob an amused look. Of course, she knew what went on in his head. Any unknown spell brought back the boy who had listened with bated breath to his old teacher, Albert Chanute, as he told of seven-league boots or crow's combs.

The Bastard gave him a sardonic smile. *You'll never guess what it is, Reckless*, it taunted him.

"That fortress up there is sticky with dark magic," he panted as he doubled over in pain again.

"Yes, I saw the two Elves," Fox said. "Spieler is here, too."

"Oh yeah? I haven't run into any of them, but I did run into one of their guests." He glanced up worriedly at the crows circling over the graves. "Let's get out of here."

The Bastard didn't stop until the rooftops of Kakeya were coming into view among the trees. It was evident that he was still in pain as he crouched down in the grass between the trees.

"Impressively effective shrinking spell, right?" He winked at Jacob. "Still, I can't recommend it."

He reached into his pocket and held something out to Jacob.

"Here. To make you stop staring at me like I'm a riddle you have to solve."

Jacob accepted the object the Goyl held out to him, almost with reverence. A bone hand. These were supposedly found only in Zhonggua and among some Indian tribes of western Alberica.

"I thought it would tear me apart," the Bastard spat. "I'm almost tempted to give you the damn thing. But only almost!" he added as he took the tiny hand back from Jacob.

"Did you find the mirror?"

"Oh yes." The Goyl shoved the bone hand into the hem of his sleeve. "I have some things to report."

"Fox, too. Clara's here with Spieler."

The Bastard frowned stonily. "You didn't tell your brother that, I hope?"

He shook his head incredulously as he read the answer off Jacob's face. "What's wrong with you, Reckless? And don't try to tell me lying is hard for you! A few good lies would have been the only thing that would have kept your brother away from that cursed fortress up there. Damn it! You can cut the magic there with a knife! I had an encounter with a wall that had eyes and a gingerbread baker!"

"Here?" Fox exchanged an unbelieving look with Jacob. Child-eating witches were a terror she knew only from the forests of her homeland.

"How could you tell him his former sweetheart is here?" The Bastard thrust his fist at Jacob's chest. "Must I explain to you what your brother is like?"

Well, did he have to? *If I need help, I'll ask Nerron. He understands me. Better than all of you.*

The Goyl stepped toward Jacob. "I'll try to make him understand that even the Jade Goyl can't just barge in up there. But your little brother isn't exactly the best at taking advice. You went to a lot of trouble to exorcise the stone from his skin back then. Maybe soon you'll be thankful you failed."

Fox gave Jacob a warning look, but there was nothing he could say to the Bastard anyway. The Goyl was right. He shouldn't have told Will about Clara. Not until they had a plan. *He understands me. Better than any of you. He understands the jade and knows more about this world than you do.*

The Goyl disappeared among the trees, and Jacob wondered if it was possible that his brother had found a friend in the Bastard—and that he envied the Goyl for that?

13

LIKE THEN AGAIN

Spieler had to admit it: he really liked her a lot. Clara Ferber…
She had immediately reminded him of Rosamund, with her
pale face that had the waxy beauty of a tulip. How old was
she? Twenty-three, twenty-four? Rosamund had been only
two years older when he had first met her.

Probably that was why he had visited Clara in the hospital
after her sweetheart had proved to be such a perfect tool of
his long-planned revenge. Yes, the hospital… it was there
that he had sensed how dangerous she could become to him.
When he had seen her lying there so pale and asleep, she'd
had the same vulnerability that had filled him with absurd
desire once before. He had introduced himself to the nurses
as a friend of Will's, checking on Clara while Will visited
her gravely ill mother, who was very worried about her
daughter. Mortals were so easily fooled if only they were
fed some sentimental yarn. He had worn the same face with

91

which he had seduced Rosamund, and all the nurses had pitied the handsome stranger who so selflessly cared for his friend's girlfriend.

Of course, he had made sure he was alone with Clara before he had awakened her: with a kiss that most certainly had been so much better than any kiss Rosamund's youngest son had ever given her. Oh, it had been divine—as befitted the kiss of an immortal. Regrettably, he'd had to arrange it so that she would not remember it. Love was not to be rushed, and Clara believed in fidelity and that there was only One… all the foolish ideas mortals associated with romantic love because they so longed for something that had no end.

She had been very disappointed at first that it was a stranger, not Will sitting by her bedside when she had awakened. But Spieler had quickly convinced her that he was a very good friend of his. That he had known Will's mother had been very helpful. Clara had probably estimated him to be in his mid-thirties, old enough to seem trustworthy, young enough to become her lover. She hadn't doubted for one breath that Will had gone through the mirror in search of an antidote for the Sleeping Beauty spell. Even if she may have wondered why her lover hadn't simply woken her with a kiss. Spieler had comforted her with the secret that, contrary to what the fairy tales told, the kiss rarely worked. Spieler hadn't mentioned that he had made sure Will's kiss wouldn't wake her, but he had confessed to her that he knew spells like Sleeping Beauty because he was from the other world. She had listened to him in disbelief but visibly fascinated, and when he had offered to help her find Will, that had surprised even him. As she had followed him through the mirror, he had begun to wonder if perhaps he would have done better not to kiss her. But alas, he often asked himself such questions too late.

"The headache is back. Do you have any more of those drops?" She stood in the doorway in the silk kimono he'd had tailored for her, painted with flowering cherry trees by the great Maruya Seijiro. "They really do help a lot. You must tell me the active ingredients."

Oh no, she'd better know nothing about them. Despite her light hair and her posture from another century, the kimono suited her very well. Nihon's restraint was something she knew and carried within her.

"I hope you feel better soon." Spieler rose from the high western writing desk that Krieger had placed in his room at his request. Krieger had, of course, mocked him for this as much as he had derided him for his young companion. One day—and Spieler looked forward to that day with great anticipation—he would put an end to Krieger just as he had put an end to the Fairies.

Clara smiled at him as he approached her. Was she beginning to fall in love with him? He wasn't sure, even though the drops he stirred into her water glass were laced with an aphrodisiac, of course. Even for immortals, playing with love and desire was not without danger. After his affair with Rosamund, he had actually vowed never to permit himself to have similar feelings for a mortal again. He had found other ways to enjoy the drug of love safely. But this time, he simply could not resist. Was it the hope that the girlfriend of Rosamund's youngest would finally make him forget the old love? Maybe.

Clara drank the water with confidence. She continued to believe that he stayed by her side only to help her find Will

Reckless, and she was not entirely wrong. He had always followed the fate of Rosamund's sons with great interest. There was a prophecy to blame for that. Spieler abhorred prophecies, quite unlike Krieger, who constantly had his future read out of someone's innards. But there had been one that had troubled him for more than two millennia, though he had tried to forget it. One of his mirrors had revealed it to him. He had smashed it at some point because it had developed an inclination for dark prophecies. He had not, however, been able to shatter the words that the glass had whispered with perfectly formed lips:

> *There will come a girl, Elf, when nine hundred winters have frozen the soil of this world, who will scare away all your silver mists with a laugh. She will have a vixen for a mother and a father from another world and rightly bears the name Reckless. All your mirrors will shatter, and she will know your true face.*

The chronology had been absurdly vague, as with all prophecies. Did the frostless winters count? However… Eight hundred and ninety-four winters had passed since then —yes, he had counted— so still enough time to worry about other things. At least those nebulous words had inspired him to invent mirrors that opened other worlds, and he had tracked down Rosamund Reckless only because he had intended to kill her son before he fathered any unwanted daughters. But instead, he had fallen in love and Jacob was still alive. It was an unedifying story. He observed Jacob's brother Will for much more gratifying reasons, and who knows, maybe he would have revealed to him long ago who his father really was if his girlfriend hadn't proved so desirable. Why did love keep getting in his way?

So yes, Clara was right: he wanted to find Will Reckless. And yet he didn't want to find him at all. How tediously complicated were the threads that fate spun.

Clara had stepped out onto the balcony that surrounded her chambers. Two bedrooms—Krieger had mocked that request as well, of course, in his humorless way. The old butcher was always anxious to prove his manhood in some fight or bed. How tired he was of them all! He caught himself more and more often fantasizing about being the only survivor of his kind. Why not? The mortals gladly believed in only one God, after all. Who knows, maybe... one day...

Clara brushed her ash-blonde hair from her forehead. Tulip petals.

Even her scent resembled Rosamund's.

14

A Drop of Glass

Sixteen had promised that one drop of her glassy blood would be enough. They would all be fast asleep when he stole away. It was the only way. Even Nerron had tried to convince Will to wait. Wait for what? No, the Jade Goyl would go up to the fortress tonight, with all the others who went to face the Elf in combat. And he would come back with Clara. *Really, Will? Will you introduce Sixteen to her?* Well, he didn't know what was going to happen up there yet, but he knew it was the only way to finish the story that had started in front of a hospital in another world.

Sixteen vowed that no one would be harmed, and if he didn't trust her, who could he trust? She pricked the thumb of her right hand. There, her skin was still perfect. The drop of blood actually looked like liquid glass, colorless and tough, a perfect pearl.

Will was surprised that Jacob had not been more suspicious when he had promised him and Nerron that he would not do anything for the time being. Had his big brother forgotten that he had wasted no energy on fights he couldn't win even as a child? Jacob had argued with their mother when she forbade something. On the other hand, Will had gone to his room and later had done whatever she had forbidden undetected. Will had to admit that he would have liked to have Nerron with him that night, but the Bastard had taken Jacob's side with all too much conviction. When he had described the witch and all the sinister magic he had encountered while searching for the mirror, Will had finally realized that he had to go alone if he didn't want to risk one of the others possibly dying because of him. He was already carrying enough guilt.

Sixteen had advised stirring the drop of blood into the tea the landlady brought them in the evening, on her soundless rice sandals, her head lowered, a smile on her lips that was as much a mystery to Will as the taciturn manner of their guide. It was a cold night, and the warm tea was welcome to all. Nerron's mouth twisted at the first sip, but eventually, he drank, as did Fox and Jacob. There wasn't enough tea to offer their guide and porters as well, but if they woke up, they probably wouldn't want to stop him. To them, he would be just one more who was crazy enough to climb up to the fortress.

Sixteen's blood worked quickly.

Before long, Nerron lay there as if he were actually made of stone, and Jacob and Fox slept so motionless in each other's arms that Will feared for a moment Sixteen might have downplayed the dangerousness of her blood. Still, as he leaned anxiously over his brother, he felt Jacob's breath on his face. Jacob had stolen away so many times while he and their mother slept, and Will would stand in his brother's empty room in the morning, disappointed, wondering how long Jacob was going to be gone. Will was amazed at how good it felt that this time it was he who was stealing away.

Will stepped out of the inn into a cloudy night. The two moons were nothing but a pale hint of light, and barely a star was visible as he took the road which all those climbed who had come to Kakeya that night for Krieger's duels. The stumps of freshly felled trees lined the road, proof that it had only recently been widened. Man-sized stone lanterns colored the pavement with reddish light, and Will wondered if it came from Fire Elves trapped inside the lanterns. Jacob had often told him about the men who stole honey from the tiny Elves to tame the flames. Fire dancers…

He didn't want to go back.

But what about Clara? She had never liked this world. Why was she here? To search for him? Or had Spieler cast a spell on her? He had to convince Spieler to help Sixteen. Who else was going to do it?

The light of countless torches sketched the outline of the fortress in the night, and Will thought he could feel the jade calling at the mere sight of it. Good. It would protect him. It always had so far. Maybe that was why Sixteen hadn't tried to stop him. Or was she hoping he would see Clara and know he loved her many faces more?

His pace slowed so much that two other challengers overtook him. One was a Ronin; the other looked like a young peasant. He carried a crude sword which he had probably forged from the blades of a plow. *John has a wandering heart.*

That was how his mother had liked to explain his father's disloyalty.

Will had told Clara so many times that he loved her. He had told her he wanted to spend the rest of his life with her. And believed it. A wandering heart...

Will walked on so briskly that he soon caught up with the Ronin and the farmer.

They had not been able to find out much about the duels, for Jacob had wanted Hideo to believe that they had come to Kakeya for the sacred shrines. A potter in Kakeya, who had once been at sea and therefore spoke Albian, had told Jacob that Krieger fought all the matches himself, often killing a dozen men in one night. There was a rumor that the Elf possessed a sword that made him invincible. Be that as it may. Maybe he wouldn't have to fight at all. It all depended on when Spieler was going to show himself. Will put his hand on the sword Nerron had gotten for him at a street market in Zhonggua. It was not as terrible as the young farmer's, but nothing compared to the Goyl sword he had guarded Kami'en with. The gate of the fortress stood wide open. Will made out more than a dozen figures striding toward it. Torches burned in front of and on top of the outer walls. The interior was also brightly lit. Would Clara be watching the fighting? Probably not. She hated any form of violence, and Will had never dared to confess to her how much he had enjoyed being Kami'en's bodyguard.

The guards beside the gate made no move to stop the men who were streaming toward it. When Will stepped into the courtyard beyond, the challengers were already crowding there. Most seemed to be from Nihon, but Will made out a few Westerners as well. Few wore the traditional samurai

99

armor, but hardly anyone had come without any protective gear at all, as he had. Even the young peasant who had overtaken him wore a leather doublet over his shirt, but he had no skin of stone.

Everyone was pushing toward a gate that led to a court-yard just below the pagoda building. There the guards turned away some men. Perhaps some seemed too old to them, and they probably sent away the young farmer because of his homemade sword. They also blocked Will's path as he approached the gate. He didn't understand a word of what they were barking in his face. Maybe it was about the lack of protective clothing, or they just didn't like his face. The stone came immediately. One of the guards drew his sword in alarm. The others followed suit.

Jade Goyl.

15

Death Makes Keen Eyes

The coachman was back. Sixteen noticed because her skin misted up. Death had a damp breath. *Chithira!* She thought she heard the walls of the inn whisper it.

Why had he come? Wasn't it enough that he stole into Will's dreams? He could not frighten her, the dead lover of a dead Fairy. Yet, she felt a strange curiosity about the ghost. Spieler had made it clear to her that she, like all his creatures, had no soul and could at best hope to eventually be melted down and become part of a new creature. But maybe he had lied? Maybe there was an existence after death for her, too?

She rose from the hard mat, which only made her limbs ache more, and peered through the sliding wall with which the landlady had separated her from the others.

101

The damp film on her skin had not fooled her. There he was: so beautiful, even in death. Or had it made him even more beautiful? Was he now all that had ever been good about him? No, he was angry, out for revenge, driven... So what exactly was that which mortals called soul?

He stood among the sleepers whom Sixteen's blood had stunned. They were the only guests left in the inn. Chithira... He must have been a powerful prince once. You could see it in his gestures and the haughtiness on his face. To Sixteen's surprise, he seemed interested only in the vixen. He bent over her sleeping form and touched her arm. It looked like he was trying to reach for something, but finally, he straightened up with an irritated cry.

"Why did you choose her?" Sixteen heard him whisper. "No one serves you more faithfully than I. Why the vixen? Do you need the protection of a living woman? Can she hear you? Can she hear you in the wind and in the water? In every flower and in the light of the stars? No." He stepped back and looked down disapprovingly at the sleeping woman.

Sixteen pushed the partition aside. With each step she took toward the dead man, her skin fogged more and walking hurt as if her bare feet were taking root.

Chithira did not seem surprised to see her. Perhaps death sharpened the senses.

"What do you want, mirror thing?"

Thing? How dare that pale shadow? Sixteen wanted to freeze him into silver, but she couldn't even do that anymore. She had tried it on a bird.

"Oh, have I offended you?" Chithira's voice came from everywhere and nowhere. "I guess you think you're more than just a thing because my mistress's murderer lost his heart to you. So? People lose their hearts to many things. Believe me, I had one once. His love can't give you a soul."

"Do you call that pale something that is left of you a soul?"

"Whatever it is, you don't possess it." He left her standing and stepped to the mat where their guide slept. Stepped, floated, glided… Sixteen did not know how to describe his movements. He resembled smoke, similarly fleeting, similarly toxic.

Their guide muttered something in his sleep. He had been drinking with the porters, but rice wine did not work as reliably as her blood.

"You there!" Chithira breathed his cold breath into his face. "Wake up!"

Yanagita Hideo rubbed the sleep from his eyes and hastily got to his feet when he saw the ghost. Sixteen had noticed that he was cloaking his body almost as carefully as she was. As he hurriedly tugged the clothes that had slipped in his sleep, she saw why. He was tattooed all over.

"Wake up!" he shouted to the others as he tightened his belt. "A yùrei! A yùrei is here! He wants to eat our souls!"

The porters opened their eyes in fright, but they quickly feigned sleep again when they saw the spirit. Yanagita Hideo tried to shake Jacob and the Goyl awake. Only then did he notice Sixteen.

"What does he want with your soul?" she said. "He's just a dead man. But you can give it to me."

He only stared at her, as horrified by her as he was by the ghost.

"Forget about her!" Chithira snapped at him. "I need your help. I need you to carry the vixen. We have to get her away from here."

103

Yanagita Hideo tore himself away from Sixteen's gaze and looked down at the vixen. Her hand was on Jacob's chest as if holding his heart.

"Take her away?" He clenched his mighty fists. "Where to? To the land of the dead?"

"Nonsense. No living person can go there. I was told to take her to safety. That's all you need to know. And if you waste any more time asking questions, someone you don't want to meet will soon come for her."

Someone... Sixteen listened into the night. Of course, Will had told her about the witch-crow. She did not fear her, but she feared the one who had called her, and he would be here soon.

Yanagita Hideo, however, seemed determined to be the vixen's protector. He stood in front of the mat on which she slept and raised his fists. "Don't look at him, Hideo!" he muttered. "Never trust a yùrei. That's what your mother taught you. All dead men lie!"

The spirit grew like smoke over a fire, but the smoke was cold. It covered Hideo's clothes and face with frost until he looked as if his flesh was moldy. "Now, do as I say! All is lost if he finds her!"

"Who are you talking of?" Hideo did not move aside.

Chithira pointed to Sixteen. "Of the one who made her. Of the one who killed the Fairies. He will kill you, too. And her, for she has something he seeks." His voice became soft. "You are devoted to her. I can see it in your face. I know the feeling. So—do you want to save her or not?"

Yanagita Hideo still hesitated, but finally, he lowered his fists. "Where are we going to take her? I'm not making a move until I know! I—"

"To someone who can protect her from him. Hurry!"

Yanagita Hideo still hesitated. But then he bent over the vixen. He lifted her as effortlessly as if she weighed no more than the mat on which she lay sleeping.

The ghost turned to Sixteen. The eyes with which he looked at her knew of a world that no mirror had yet shown her. "You cannot come with us. He made you."

Sixteen felt the same horror that had last filled her at the sight of her frozen brother.

"Please!" she stammered. "You have to hide me from him! He will know that I led the others here. He will know that I shared his secrets with a mortal!"

She thought she saw pity in the ghost's face, but he still paralyzed her limbs with his breath so she couldn't follow him. *How empty you are!* she thought she heard the dead whisper while Yanagita Hideo carried the vixen out into the night. *No soul behind all the faces. What will remain of you? Nothing, mirror thing...*

Chithira's breath paralyzed her even after they were long gone.

What will remain of you? Nothing.

She let her limbs become shadows, rice paper, and black lacquered wood, but her heart was sore with fear. She had asked Spieler why he had given her a heart when he and his kind were as heartless as the Fairies. 'To make you mortal, why else?' he had replied with a smile. How often that smile had stung and cut, seduced and destroyed her.

She pressed her aching back so hard against the thin wall behind her that she felt the wind and the night through the wood.

You can't come with us. He made you.

105

16

THE PRODIGAL SON

Blood. The blood of mortals everywhere. Spieler suspected that Krieger deliberately thrust the sword where it splattered most copiously. He was acting like one of the pompous old gods who had to be appeased with human sacrifices. Krieger's golem servants shoveled sand onto the blood and dragged the bodies away. The still surviving challengers grew paler and paler, but there was always one who stepped onto the bloody sand with a sword in his fist and the delusion that these fights could be won.

There, the next fool… He looked so young, as if he did not even shave. Krieger cut off his sword hand before slashing his chest with the next blow. He had played very similar games in the other world as well. One of his golems had revealed to Spieler that his master firmly believed that he had to kill at least five hundred mortals every year to keep himself young. Young… They all had that fear that one day old age would catch up with them despite their immortality. There were poisons that weakened their life force, curses like the one the Fairies had used to punish them. Who could say how much that spell had weakened them and whether the long exile in another world might have cost them their immortality? Being faced with losing infinity made one paranoid.

The next challenger took a while to die, and Krieger refreshed himself with rice wine while watching his opponent's death throes with a blank expression. He liked to claim that a Fairy had given birth to him on a battlefield, but none of them really remembered where they came from. Spieler found it impossible, even after a thousand years of living, to distinguish real memories from invented ones. He took pleasure in spreading the story that he had neither father nor mother and had been born through the song of a nightingale.

There was no end to the cries of pain in the square below him, and Spieler turned his back to the window.

The bee searches for the bloom, the Elf for the pain.

He had forgotten who had said that. It was undoubtedly true, but there had always been two factions among them — those who enjoyed mortal pain and those who sought to heal it. Toshiró had belonged to the latter. No. He didn't want to think about him. He no longer existed. Neither did the Fairies. Spieler stroked the shawl Clara had left on a stool. She was pinning flowers with Krieger's concubines. She had only watched the duels the first night.

The bee searches for the bloom, the Elf for the pain.

Below him, all was suddenly very quiet.

Spieler stepped back to the window and looked down at the battlefield.

A new challenger stood in the center of the courtyard. Everyone was staring at him — Krieger's samurai, the golems, the other challengers — as if they knew he was not from this world. But of course, all they saw was the stone.

The skin of jade looked perfect on Rosamund's youngest. So much better than the human skin, red from screaming, in which Spieler had once seen him in his mother's arms.

Oh, he hated surprises like this.

The sword he carried was little better than a kitchen knife. What was he doing here? He couldn't possibly know Clara was here, could he? Spieler backed away until the dark wooden struts framing the window hid him.

Krieger stared at the challenger as incredulously as all the others. Even in the other world, he had been continuously told about the Goyl and their invincible king, and of course, he knew about Kami'en's legendary bodyguard. As the Dark Fairy's executioner, he had impressed him less: 'Just one arrow? And she didn't even fight back?' he had commented with contempt. 'Is that a fitting revenge for eight hundred years of exile? You should have left it to me.'

Yes, that would undoubtedly have been bloodier.

Ah, Krieger had caught himself. You could always tell by the way he jutted his chin.

"Welcome to the Fortress of the Moons!" he shouted. "The Jade Goyl! I am pleased to see that even the stone faces have heard of my nightly duels by now! I greatly admire your king's warfare. So much so that I intend to face him on the battle-field one not too distant day. But what is that sword you are holding? People will say I defeated you just because of that."

One of his samurai approached Rosamund's youngest and held out his sword to him. Will ignored him.

"I'm not here to fight you!" he shouted to Krieger. "I came for the other Alderelf, Spieler. I hear he's your guest."

How did he know?

"Alderelf?" Krieger was clearly irritated that his challenger realized who he was dealing with. "What is this?"

Rosamund's youngest eyed him with a wariness that revealed he had once been a king's bodyguard. Yes, he had come a long way since he had lain as a screaming bundle in his mother's arms.

"He has a human woman with him. I am a friend of hers. I want to see her. I'm not leaving until I know she's all right."

Was the jade giving him that confidence, or was it the fact that he had killed an immortal? He had really come at the wrong time! Just a few more weeks and Spieler would have manipulated Clara to the point where she forgot her beloved and was hopelessly in love with an immortal!

Krieger wiped the blade of his sword and let it pass through the empty air as if he wanted to slice the night.

"The only way to leave this fortress is by defeating me in battle, and that goes for challengers with stone skin as well." He looked at his samurai imperiously. "How many challengers have tried to defeat me so far?"

"Five hundred and thirty-eight, sir," one called back.

Krieger stroked his sword tenderly as if congratulating it on its rich harvest. "You see, your story will end here, Jade Goyl. Despite your admittedly impressive skin. I'm glad you came here. Who knows, maybe there's some truth to the stories that it's you who makes your king invincible."

He didn't bother with opening poses. He tried, as he often did, to open his opponent's chest with one blow so that they could watch their own heart take its final beats. The Jade

Goyl easily fended off Krieger's oh-so-precious sword and, in return, dealt him a wound to the shoulder.

Oh, this night was turning out to be truly surprising.

A hot, dirty feeling stirred in Spieler, intoxicating like strong wine. He and Krieger had been enemies for as long as they could remember, even if they sometimes joined forces when it served them both. Still, he would never have dared to face Krieger in single combat. But when Rosamund's youngest son humiliated his old enemy like a novice under his window, Spieler enjoyed it almost as much as if he were standing down there himself.

Ah yes, another thrust, controlled and delivered with the will to wound. Krieger stumbled back and looked in disbelief at the deep cut in his side. The blood soaking his embroidered clothes was blue, of course. His samurai seemed surprised by this. Had they never wondered about their master's twelve fingers?

Spieler heard a rustling behind him.

A crow landed on the stand with the samurai armor that Krieger had imposed on him as decoration. Giovanna. That had once been her name. Her darkness filled the room like the smoke that rose from her gingerbread chimneys. With her, he had summoned dirty old magic to his aid, but what was left for him? All his new creatures had proved so useless that they had only earned him the ridicule of the others: his fabulous bloodhounds with teeth of glass, the silver dragonflies, larger than griffins, terrible huntresses… useless! None of them had found what it was that still made his and his kind's skin itch. Well, at least they were not frozen nor had found themselves in the barky skin of an Alder tree. What was left of the Fairies caused only an annoying rash. But it showed that there was

110

a remnant of their magic somewhere, and the helper he had summoned hopefully would prove to have a more delicate nose than any of the creatures he had crafted from glass and silver. After all, she smelled innocence for many miles, and the gingerbread bakers had hated the Fairies because they knew the darkest spells in this world without having to pay the price that eventually ruined them all.

The crow pecked at a spider spinning its web in the samurai robes. Yes, as he had said to Krieger—they were old acquaintances. Giovanna Massimo had once been Spieler's lover, long ago, when she had been young and very beautiful. But the hunger that stirred in them as soon as they lured the first child into their cake house had consumed her beauty and youth. It was a hunger that was insatiable no matter how many times they killed. Still, all that killing taught her many dark spells. No one knew more about the plants that brought madness or awakened dark lusts, and every now and then, Spieler paid for Giovanna's services with a few irresistible ingredients for the cakes at her sugary house. Or with a firstborn.

"For that bit of Fairy magic, that's what you called me for?" The voice that came from the crooked beak had once been very beguiling. Now it was that of an old woman. She paid a high price for eavesdropping on the world's darkest secrets. *Take it as a warning, Spieler.* Nonsense. Giovanna was mortal. He wasn't.

"So you found Fairy magic? Where?"

She was afraid of him, but not very much. Gingerbread bakers were afraid primarily of themselves.

"In this fortress, in the forest that surrounds it, at the foot of this mountain. That's where the trail fades."

In this fortress? Impossible. Was Krieger hiding something from him?

"It's the trail of a vixen. Does that tell you anything?"

Oh, the eight centuries of exile had dulled his mind. He should have known when Will Reckless had appeared on Krieger's fighting square. Where one brother was, the other would soon inevitably appear—and with him, the vixen. Could the Dark Fairy have found a more suitable caretaker? Hardly.

"She was here in the fortress? You must be mistaken."

The crow spread its wings. They became bony arms, and her body stretched. A few black feathers still clung to the withered skin of the old woman who now strode toward Spieler. She stopped so close to him that he could taste the cinnamon on his tongue.

Withered beauty. Lost youth. Mortality could be so very repulsive.

"Where in the fortress?"

"Everywhere. All the way down to the garden."

The garden? The vixen hadn't been there when he'd been talking to Krieger, had she? If so, she had come fatally close to him. No. *Don't jump to conclusions, Spieler. Or soon you'll have convinced yourself that the Dark Fairy is far from defeated and is still plotting your downfall!*

The clang of swords came from outside. And Krieger's curses.

He had to hurry. Krieger would not long forgive Rosamund's youngest for making a helpless fool of him in front of his men. He liked to pretend that he believed in fair duels. But that was only true as long as he was the victor. But first the troublesome Fairy spell! He was tired

112

of itching skin. He finally wanted to devote himself to more important things.

The vixen...

What had brought her here?

Or should he better ask: *Who?*

17

CREATOR

A silver tremor filled the inn, and Sixteen turned to fear. To fear and hate and helpless love for the one who had created her.

The crow that appeared out of nowhere with Spieler had the eyes of an old woman. As she flapped her wings, her shadow began to grow. Plants sprouted from the darkness, tendrils crawling across the ground and twisting around the mats as Spieler looked around searchingly. The litter bearers had probably thought themselves safe after the ghost had disappeared with the vixen. They tried to flee as the vines snaked gropingly around their bodies, but no matter how much they struggled, soon the sinister leaves and blossoms had smothered them. The death their creator sent out this time was not made of silver. He probably preferred older spells once more. Would he melt her down or smash her and her kind because they became useless so quickly in this world? Was he tired of them, his artificially created children? Spieler had made her believe that love was always linked to fear. Only Will had shown her that was a lie.

Spieler followed the crow to the empty mat where the vixen had lain. Chithira had been right. He was looking for her.

Where had her resolve gone to demand redress for her brother? Where was her strength, her fearlessness? Sixteen searched her heart in vain. All she found was the memory of the moment when Spieler had pulled her from the glass of a mirror, grabbed her under the chin, and christened her with a smile, Sixteen. A thing he had made and which had proved useless. She had even turned on him. Of course, he would kill her. Like all the others he'd fed to the smelters or had shattered like faulty wine glasses because they weren't as perfect as he liked.

"I wonder how the Dark One made the vixen her savior? She must have been long dead." Spieler stood in front of the empty mat where the vixen had lain. He liked to talk to himself. Sixteen had often listened to him doing so. His voice might be silver or velvet, but underneath it was always the glass. Or the edge of a silver knife.

"I knew a Fairy who saved her last spark of life in a willow leaf." The crow's voice was like her eyes, dark as a forest with no return. She spread her wings and transformed. The old woman squatting beside the empty mat was naked and haggard as if she had come back from death like Chithira.

She stroked the mat of straw. "She is with child."

Spieler closed his eyes as if she had announced something he had feared.

"It's still very early. Is it yours?"

115

"No." Spieler turned his back to the mat. "But it's still mine. And it's too early. Way too early. She must have gotten very close to me. What an unfortunate coincidence. Or is it more than that?"

He rubbed his neck. A trail of tree bark spread across his skin like a scar. The Fairy spell was still working on him, too. Why? Sixteen had thought her disfigurement had come from getting too close to the Fairy.

"What now?" he muttered. "What's your next move, Spieler? Too many pieces are lining up on the board. On the other hand," he stretched the white hand into the shadows that the crow had brought, "the game will be more interesting that way. And I will win it. I always win." He watched the shadows draw dark leaves on his hand and looked down at Will's brother, barely visible among the vines. "Your vixen now carries two things I need, yet she has left her most precious possession behind. How foolish of her."

"Take him with you!" he said to the crow woman. "Take him to the golem who travels with me."

Jacob disappeared under the dark leaves, as did the Goyl, as the old woman rose and stepped toward Spieler.

"I can't see the vixen anymore. A dead man is with her. He's blinding me."

Spieler frowned. "Find her. Bring me what the Fairy entrusted to her before it falls into the wrong hands. And not only that. Bring me the vixen."

"That's more than we had agreed." The old woman stroked her lean arms as if remembering the time when her flesh hadn't been like wilted leaves. "You're afraid of her. You're afraid of the child she carries. More than of what the Fairy left her? Why?"

"Bring her to me," Spieler repeated. "I will pay you well."

The old woman brushed the thinning gray hair from her forehead. "Free me from the hunger," she said, "and I'll bring her to you. Her and the child, wherever she is hiding."

Spieler wanted to say something back. But he changed his mind. He edged away from the shadows surrounding the crow woman, wiping his sleeve as if too much of her darkness had clung to the light fabric.

"Why not? Bring me the vixen, and I'll drive the hunger from you. Or shall we say, I'll try?"

"That's not enough!" the old woman snapped at him.

"That's all you get."

With a caw, she turned into the crow again, and the thorny thicket that had grown from her shadows took her in. It turned to smoke when she was gone, along with the Goyl and Will's brother. Only Spieler still stood among the empty mats as the smoke cleared.

"Show yourself, Sixteen," he said.

Everything inside her turned to glass. Fragile, splintering glass.

She stepped forward from behind the sliding wall where she had been hiding, with her useless, wooden arm and her skin disfigured by tree bark.

Her creator eyed her with disgust. His eyes were as blue as frozen river water. He usually showed himself with blue eyes.

"You look terrible. And why, by all the forgotten gods, are you wearing that face of all things? I gave you so many prettier ones."

Look at him, Sixteen. But it was so hard not to lower her eyes, as she had done whenever he had spoken to her in the past. She recalled the horror in her brother's features as they

117

had turned to wood — and the love on Will's face. The love helped more than the anger.

"I like this one more than the others," she brought to her lips.

"You do?" Spieler smiled as amused as if one of his dogs had contradicted him. "Where's the vixen? Who is the dead man with her?"

"He served the Fairy. He was her coachman."

"Where is he taking her?" He stepped toward her and stroked her disfigured cheek. "Is this how you thank me for the life I gave you? By bringing my enemies to me?"

She waited for him to clap his hands and crack her skin. She had seen him do it to others, shattering their faces like cheap china. But Spieler just rubbed the back of her hand in irritation. There was a hint of bark there, too. *I knew a Fairy who saved her last spark of life in a willow leaf.*

"You've always been very fearless, Sixteen." His voice rang with extra menace when he made it sound soft. "But I advise you never to betray me again. Fearlessness can have devastating consequences. Especially if you're made of glass."

He reached for her hand. The one she could still move.

"I'll let you live for now. Even if you don't deserve it. Tell me about the jade boy. Did you make him fall in love with you like I told you to?"

"Yes." It was little more than a whisper that passed her lips. She wanted to scream: *I didn't do it for you! I love him.*

"Good," said Spieler. "You're going to make sure it stays that way. Because I'm going to steal his girlfriend."

118

18

FOUND

On that night, three musicians played for Krieger's wives while they practiced the art of flower arranging. Krieger's wives… Clara was both frightened and fascinated by the fact that she accepted things behind the mirrors that she would have harshly condemned in the other world. Did she stay quiet because she was only a guest, a stranger who wanted to enjoy the otherness of this world rather than see its flaws? Krieger had five wives. 'Quite common among the rich and powerful of Nihon,' Spieler had replied when she had asked him if it was the custom in his world for a man to have several wives. 'But it's not much different in your world, is it?'

The answer had disturbed her, and as Krieger's main wife showed her how to pin almond blossoms, she wondered if she knew as little about her own world as she did about this

119

one. The three musicians were very adept at smothering the sounds that drifted in from the battlefield with harmony. Their instruments were as strange as the sounds they elicited from them so masterfully, but Clara could not have said whether there were similar instruments in the Japan of her world. Was she a stranger everywhere except in the corridors of a hospital? Her mother had once accused her of that during one of the loud arguments they'd had so often.

Next to her sat Krieger's youngest lover. Etsuko was certainly not yet twenty. She smiled at Clara as she added a chrysanthemum blossom to her arrangement. Clara had initially found the elaborate arrangements of flowers and leaves too absurd a contrast to what went on almost every night at the fortress. But Mego, Krieger's first wife, had reminded her that nothing epitomized mortality better than a blossom. 'The almond blossom honors all those who die young,' she had explained to her as she'd arranged a sprig of the pale pink blooms in a vase of dark clay. 'For it falls from the tree unwilted.' Beauty that spoke of terror — Krieger's women transformed his battles into blooming images every night, as wordless as the music that drowned out the clashing of swords.

Nihon... When Clara had followed Spieler through the mirror, she had expected to find herself once again in the ruins in Schwanstein. Instead, the fairy-tale version of a long-lost Japan had awaited her on the other side, with rooms filled with nothing but beauty and silence, and people who met her with shyness and touching kindness, even if they did not hide how strange she seemed to them. But fairy tales were always cruel too. The first night they had watched the fighting from Spieler's window, even though Krieger forbade all women in the fortress to observe. How she had jumped up in horror when Krieger had thrust his sword into the chest of the first challenger. Spieler had pulled her away from the window and held her comfortingly in his arms. 'Remember, they all come here willingly,' he had whispered to her. 'I'm sorry I brought you here. I thought Krieger had given up his barbaric games and that he might know where Will is. We'll be leaving soon.' The following day she had gone down to the graves, perhaps because she had already seen the dead come back in this world. The pale figure of a young man had indeed risen from one of the mounds, and Clara had reluctantly admitted to herself that she was still curious about Spieler's world. She hated that death was invincible in her world.

Etsuko was not the only one to drop her blossoms when screams reached them that were so loud the musicians could not drown them out. Krieger's wives hastily gathered the petals from their laps as they smiled anxiously at each other. Like on every other night, most had painted their faces white, even though Clara had warned them about the lead in the paint. White fingers, white faces, only their teeth were sometimes dyed black. What did all that white stand for? For innocence? Death?

The musicians struck up their tune again, but the shouting grew louder until they gave up and listened as anxiously as the women. Mego directed a servant to find out what was going on. The women had risen from the mats on which they had been kneeling. They were staring at the curtained windows. One began to cry in fear. But in Clara's case, she felt the composure she used to know from the hospital when she confronted pain and death. She had first felt this composure

121

when, at fourteen, she had stood at the bedside of her dead sister. It was then that the desire she guarded like a forbidden secret had been forged: the desire to be able to cure death, to make it nothing but a sleep from which she could wake anyone. Spieler was the first to discover it in her heart... He understood her so well. He recognized so much in her that others had never discovered — even Will. Perhaps that was why she had followed him so willingly when he had offered to help her, even though she knew little about him.

The servant returned. The lady of the house listened to him unmoving, but Etsuko's eyes widened. She reached for Clara's hand as Mego followed the servant outside, and the others rushed after her. Clara let herself be pulled along, even if she wasn't sure she wanted to find out what was causing the shouting. The servant hurried ahead of his mistress to a balcony overlooking the combat area.

It was gone. A sinister thicket of thorny vines and dark trees had engulfed the yard. The cries came from there, choked and lost. A crow circled over the sprawling darkness. One of the women cried out as three small children ran toward the thicket. Krieger's samurai ran after them and dragged them back, though they resisted. The crow cried out as they carried the children away — a sound of disappointment.

What did all this mean?

Spieler would know the answer. Clara looked searchingly toward the chambers Krieger had assigned them, but they were dark. Where was he?

Downstairs, a whole crowd of children was running toward the dark shadow forest. Clara saw by their clothes that most of them were servants' children. Among the sobbing women who were running after them, she recognized the servant who cleaned their rooms. Only two children wore more elegant clothes, and one of Krieger's wives cried out and hurried toward the nearby stairs. Before following her, Clara took one last look at the forest that had grown from the night. In a clearing in the center stood a man. He appeared to be one of Krieger's challengers, for he still held a sword in his hand. But he had Will's face.

Oh, how yearning could fool you. Clara backed away from the balcony parapet. But the stranger still had Will's face, and it was made of jade.

No. All the pain the stone had brought when it had first grown in Will's skin—she didn't want to feel it again. The memories came back as if the thorny thicket enclosing Will was reaching for her.

She ran to the stairs and stumbled down. Servants and guards were everywhere. They even poured out of the kitchen, many surely for the same reason as Clara—to get to someone they loved, worried that the forest that had grown from nothing would devour them. Men, women... Krieger's prohibition against them watching the duels seemed forgotten, and no one stopped the commotion that swept through the fortress. Only when Clara reached the gate behind which the combat area lay did the guards push her back. They did so roughly, and she fell. She barely managed to get back on her feet in all the panic that surrounded her. Her hand was bleeding from the tread of a shoe and one of the guards was yelling at her, pointing to the women's chambers. But then, suddenly, he bowed his head and dropped to his knees.

The hand that pulled her to her feet had six fingers.

"I'm sure you want to welcome Krieger's unexpected challenger as much as I do." Spieler smiled at her. "See? I promised you we'd find him."

The guard was still kneeling when Spieler led her through the gate. The first thing she caught sight of as she stepped through were witch trees, the kind she'd last seen when they'd ridden with Jacob to a gingerbread house. Their branches had impaled two of Krieger's samurai. They hung lifeless in the boughs, and their blood dripped onto waxy white blossoms that had appeared at the edge of the thicket.

"Spieler!" Krieger screamed to them as Spieler pushed aside a couple of vines that were turning toward them and headed for the forest that seemed to have grown out of the fairy tales of her childhood. "Call her back! Call back your damned witch-crow!"

His priceless clothes were red with blood, but his ran pale blue from his wounds. Clara had seen the colorless blood of the Goyl, and she wondered what kind of creature Krieger was as she watched his wounds close and disappear without a trace. The mysteries of this world... The night seemed to choke on them.

But Will was here. *See? I promised you we would find him.* Nothing else mattered.

"Are you declaring war on me?" shouted Krieger when Spieler didn't stop. "In my own fortress?"

Spieler raised his hand. The crow settled on it. Clara backed away when she saw its eyes. They were the eyes of an old woman.

Spieler grasped her arm reassuringly. "Everything will be as it should be," he whispered to her. "And you have no reason to be afraid."

"Twelve of your samurai you set upon him!" he shouted to Krieger. "Twelve! And those were just the ones he was fighting when I came back. Did you not proclaim that you would pay the man who defeats you his weight in silver? I'm just making sure you stick to your own rules!"

Clara stared at the thicket from which screams were still coming. She thought she smelled cinnamon. Cinnamon and sugar. Will. She stepped toward the trees, but Spieler pulled her back.

"He's safe. All this is for his protection. Stay close to me." The vines backed away from him, and a narrow path opened between the trees. Flowers of silver and glass bloomed at its edge.

"Bring me one of the children." The crow had not only the eyes but also the voice of an old woman. "They want to come to me."

"Not here and not now!" Spieler shooed her off his shoulder. A tendril wrapped around Clara's ankle, but it turned to silver as he pushed it away.

"Slake your hunger on the ones Krieger slew," he shouted to the crow. "Most of them were almost children."

The crow fluttered into one of the trees with a hoarse human cry. What was the meaning of all this? She would ask Spieler later. He would explain it all to her. The trees backed away from him as he pulled her along. And there was Will—as Clara had seen him from the balcony. He turned his back on her.

Had he forgotten her through the jade? For a moment, she wanted to run away, away from the pain she remembered all too well, the revulsion against the stone... But she was so happy to see him. So terribly happy.

125

Look at me! her heart whispered. *Will! Where were you? Do you recognize me?*

He turned as if he sensed her presence. The jade became human skin as soon as he saw her—as if a mask he wore only for the others was melting. No, he hadn't forgotten anything, neither her nor himself, but Clara wasn't sure if what she saw on his face was love. Relief, even an inkling of triumph—not necessarily a feeling she knew from Will—and... why that? Guilt.

Around her, the forest turned to smoke. It blew away, taking with it those it had engulfed. But the crow was still there. Perched on the gate through which one entered the square, she watched Krieger as he limped toward Spieler, followed by two samurai.

"You summoned the Jade Goyl!" Krieger looked around as if expecting the trees to grow out of his combat yard's pavement once again at any moment. "You called him here to make a fool of me!" He stopped in front of Spieler. "And the Witch Crow? The woods she comes from are only found on the other side of this world. That is a long journey even for her shadow wings, and I saw the silver flowers on her trees. Did you have her come through my mirror, perhaps, so that its magic might give her some of our power?"

"Your mirror? May I remind you that I was the one who made it?"

"How could I forget? I'll smash it before another old friend of yours crawls out, and you feed her some Elf magic! I'm going to smash all the mirrors you so generously gave me, and I'll make my own from now on. You will have to find your way home like a mortal. By daybreak, I don't want to see you here anymore! And you can tell the others that they

126

had better watch out for you rather than me. Yes, Krieger has big plans, but from now on, it's every man for himself. That's the way I've always liked it best."

He turned and limped away, but after a few steps, he turned again.

"He's Rosamund's son, right?" he called out to Spieler. "I knew he reminded me of someone. And her?" He pointed to Clara. "Don't think I missed that she looks like your old love. If he offers to make you immortal," he called to Clara, "say no."

Will's eyes lingered on Spieler. He didn't even look at her.

He's Rosamund's son, right? Don't think I missed that she looks like your old love. Secrets — Clara thought she felt them settle around her neck like the thorny tendrils of the crow. At the mention of Will's mother's name, Spieler's fingers had closed a little tighter around her arm.

"We are glad to see you so well!" he said to Will. "We've been looking for you for a long time." He gently pushed her toward him. "You gave me back my world. The least I could do was bring you your girlfriend!"

Will hesitated but finally reached for Clara's hand and pulled her to his side. "You lied to me. Used me and lied to me!"

"You were our only chance! We were desperate! The Fairies had cursed us for a few barrels of water. Do you know how many times we had begged them for it? But they despised our curiosity, our desire for knowledge. They thought we were too much like you mortals, and they abhorred change. Their punishment was terrible! Eight hundred years! Separated from all that was familiar to us!"

Will shook his head as if to get rid of Spieler's words. "It was you who sent Clara the brooch. Sixteen told me everything."

"To protect Clara! The Dark Fairy had much worse plans for you!"

"Liar." A hint of jade appeared on Will's forehead.

"Will!" Clara released her hand from his and backed away from him. "I thought you two were old friends." How she hated the stone. Spieler's face suddenly seemed so much more familiar to her. "He helped me find you," she snapped at Will. "He was there when I woke up."

Spieler smiled at her reassuringly. "He's been through a lot. Give him time. He has freed this world from a terrible curse. And he survived fighting Krieger. Krieger will never forgive him for that, and we should make sure we get away while he's willing to let him go."

Will stared at him as if trying not to hear what Spieler was saying. The jade stained his forehead and cheeks, and Clara felt the same shiver as the day she had first touched the stone.

"How does the other Elf know my mother?"

"I introduced her to him. A long time ago. There's a lot you don't know about her, but I'll tell you everything. And explain everything."

Will shook his head again. The gold was in his eyes, and his skin resembled pale green porcelain. "I don't want to hear anything. Clara!" He held out his hand to her. "I'll take you back. We'll find another mirror. I promise!"

He spoke to her as if she were a child he had to lead out of a dark forest. But she had gone into the forest only because of him. And Spieler had shown her the way out.

Spieler smiled at her, and Clara thought she felt her heart crack in two. One half wanted to go to Will. But the other wanted to go to Spieler. She saw in his eyes that he knew that.

128

"I have another suggestion." His words settled around her shoulders like velvet. "I'll take you both to a place where we'll be much safer than here. Sixteen is already waiting for us there. I was dismayed to see how badly she was doing."

Sixteen? Clara didn't understand what she saw on Will's face. Who was Sixteen?

"You've already met her, my dear," she heard Spieler say. "She gave you the brooch I used to protect you from the Fairy. She is sick, but I will heal her. Everything will be all right."

Sixteen. Clara looked at Will questioningly, but he avoided her gaze.

"You're going to cure her?" For the first time, he didn't look at Spieler like an enemy.

"But of course." Spieler snapped his fingers. "Crow!"

Crow fluttered onto his shoulder.

"Take us away!"

Clara smelled cinnamon and sweet cakes. She saw Will's face disappear among black leaves, and then she knew nothing more.

19

Taken

It was not like waking up. The vixen felt as if she were emerging from liquid glass with bursting lungs. *No, Fox, you are not the vixen.* She felt hands, even if she couldn't move them, fingers interlocking helplessly. She was shackled.

Jacob! She turned her head. It was so dark she could only make out outlines, but she was sure she was no longer in the inn. "Jacob?"

There was no answer.

The room in which she lay seemed windowless. But that could have been the darkness of night. It was night, wasn't it? Judging from the echo of her voice, the room wasn't too big. She tried to sit up, but her arms were strapped to her body so tightly that she couldn't support herself with her hands, and there was a noose around her neck that tightened as soon as she lifted her shoulders off the floor.

"Forgive me, Kitsune."

The voice was as familiar as the silhouette that approached her with a lantern. Fox saw red pillars in the light it cast, a bell, candles, dried flowers—and Yanagita Hideo's face. He looked very guilty.

"Chithira says that an immortal Elf named Spieler is looking for you," he murmured as he knelt beside her. "He says that if he finds you, he will kill you and that you must be tied up, so you don't turn and run back to the inn to check on the others."

"He's right about that!" Fox snapped at him. "Where are we?"

"In a sacred shrine dedicated to the kami of a waterfall. In your homeland, I think they would call him a god. Hopefully, he will forgive us for seeking refuge here. Dead people don't worry about such things."

Hideo bowed so low that his forehead touched the ground. "I was not mistaken. You are one of them, Kitsune! Forgive me."

Good. She'd better not talk him out of that.

"I'll forgive you if you untie me!"

Hideo shook his head. "Chithira says he'll take you to someone just as powerful as that Spieler and hopefully protect you from him."

"You and what you carry." Chithira's form seemed made of smoke, catching the glow of Hideo's torch. "Is it not strange? The Golden Yarn from which she sought to free herself is now all that remains of my dark mistress. It guards her last spark of life. But surely I don't have to explain that to you, do I, vixen?"

Fox felt no touch as he leaned over her and stroked the dull gold thread on her wrist, but the yarn began to shimmer

131

as if welcoming Chithira's touch. The last spark of life from the Dark Fairy... Her coachman was right. Something inside her had known it since she had begun to see the images, images of all that the Fairy feared and loved. But she had simply not wanted to think about it. She and Jacob had been too happy, and the war between Elves and Fairies was not hers.

"Take it!" Fox tried to squeeze her fingers under the restraints, but Hideo had done his job well. "Take the yarn and let me go! I have to go back! Jacob and I have our own war with the Elf, and if Spieler is really looking for me, then Jacob's in danger too!"

"What would the Elf care about him? No." Chithira was still looking at the gold on her arm. "He just wants the yarn. Do not be concerned. If Spieler finds your beloved, he will find him asleep, almost as deeply and soundly as a dead man thanks to the potion the Jade Goyl gave you so he could climb up to the fortress. I hope the other Elf slays him. Then I can make eternity hell for him."

Asleep? As deeply and soundly as a dead man? That meant Jacob was helpless if Spieler found him. Fox yanked so desperately at her bonds that they cut her skin. Spieler would be enraged by her disappearance if he really was looking for her, and he would take his anger out on Jacob.

"Take it!" she snapped at Chithira again. "Come on now! What are you waiting for? I'm sure the Fairy just made me pick it up so I could bring the yarn to you!"

But Chithira shook his head. "No. Death can call me back at any time. She knew she needed the protection of a living being. Don't worry. Soon someone else will be her protector, someone as powerful as her enemy, who will help

132

her regain physical form. She has explained to me where to find him."

The amazement on Hideo's face told Fox that this plan was also new to him.

"Take off her shackles," Chithira said. "But only on her feet, so she can walk on her own. We're leaving."

20

THE ALDERELF WHO STAYED

"Kitsune, you must eat!" Hideo suffered badly from his guilty conscience. Good. Fox was not ready to forgive him. The only reason she gulped down the dried fish he slipped between her lips was Jacob's voice inside her. *Eat, Fox! What good are you to me if you're dead? Of course, I'll find you. Or you'll find me. We're both good at that, have you forgotten?* She felt sick with longing when she recalled the teasing that lent feathers to his voice.

They had been traveling for the second day since they had set out from the shrine of the waterfall god. Fox had tried to escape once, but she had only managed a few steps. Chithira's cold breath had paralyzed her limbs, and she had hung over Hideo's shoulders like a dead fish for hours.

'I'll help you find Reckless-san,' he had whispered to her. 'I swear it, Kitsune! Chithira says we'll be there soon!'

Hideo never tired of pointing out that the only reason they remained unmolested on the deserted forest paths the coachman took was because of him. There was no end to the list of fearsome creatures he described to her in a hushed voice. But as dark as the forest Chithira led them through became at times, Nihon's forests still seemed far more peaceful to Fox than those of her homeland, healing instead of hungry and devoid of the fury she had so often encountered there.

It was already dawn, and Fox was bracing herself for another sleepless night when the wind brushing through the branches above her suddenly tasted of silver, and there was a glassy tinkle in the sound of the streams. A wide clearing opened up at the end of the path. In its center grew an ancient Alder tree. The forest floor around it was littered with offerings of silver, large and small.

Chithira had led them to another Alderelf.

Fox felt the vixen in her turn to flee, but Chithira gave her a warning look, and Hideo, at a hint from the ghost, put his hands on her shoulders.

There were such sinister things heard about Silver-Alders that neither she nor Jacob had ever felt the temptation to find one, and their acquaintance with Spieler had only served to reinforce that. How many there were, no one seemed to know, and from the conversation she had overheard in Krieger's garden, she had gathered that even the other Elves did not know where all the trees were that the Fairy's curse had turned into prisons for their kind. All the silver under the tree to which Chithira had brought her proved that there were still enough supplicants who tracked down the Alders,

135

even if they grew as far away from any human settlement as this one.

They had paid with rings and amulets, with coffers, coins, and robes whose silver-twined fabric had been so worn away by the years that the wishes they had paid for were surely long forgotten. The broad canopy that shaded all this was supported by a trunk that twisted and bent as if the Elf it had held captive had tried again and again to break free. Supposedly, one could discover their faces in the bark. But the trunk of this Alder was so furrowed that Fox saw a thousand faces in it.

She thought she could sense Hideo's fear of the tree as his hands closed tighter around her shoulders, but Chithira approached the Alder without hesitation. The trees around rustled as if outraged by the dead man's disrespect.

"Toshiró!" cried Chithira.

Toshiró... Fox's heart beat faster. Of course, she remembered the name. She heard Krieger's voice again. *My golems have cut down every Alder on his former lands. Toshiró will not return.* Who was wrong, the Elf or the Dark Fairy's coachman?

"Are you silent because I bring you no silver?" Chithira stepped even closer to the tree and looked up into the crown. "You should hurry and wake up! I am here to warn you. Of old enemies."

The Alder rustled as if invisible hands were brushing through the branches. From a silver casket that lay among the roots, a silver-scaled serpent writhed, and from behind a thorny bush that grew in the Alder's shadow, a fox slunk forth. With nine tails.

Hideo fell to his knees and pressed his forehead to the damp forest floor in awe. But the kitsune had eyes only for Fox. He lowered his muzzle with mock respect and transformed. His fur turned to fox red robes as he rose to his feet. The pointed ears disappeared under long black hair, and a young man crossed his arms in front of his chest with a mischievous smile.

"What are you doing in the company of a dead man, vixen? It's very unhealthy. They rarely have intentions that serve the living."

Fox held up her bound hands. "I did not choose the company."

"Ah." The kitsune brushed his hair behind his still somewhat pointed ears and eyed Chithira's pale form. "You seem to be a powerful dead man."

"My power is that of my mistress," Chithira replied. "And she was the most powerful of all. She sent me to find the Elf her sisters' curse had banished to this tree."

The kitsune's gaze drifted to Fox—and the yarn on her wrist. "The great Toshiró has left his prison. But he will receive you—if the vixen wishes it."

Fox exchanged a glance with Chithira. Did he see the gratitude mixed in with her anger at him? Toshiró... Perhaps he would tell her how to protect herself from Spieler? If it wasn't already too late. *No, Fox. It will be all right.*

"The vixen wishes it," she said.

The kitsune loosened her restraints with a touch.

"The Golden Yarn," he said. "So this is how the most powerful of all Fairies saved herself. With the yarn of love."

Hideo kept a respectful distance as the kitsune beckoned Fox and Chithira along, but he did follow them. The wooded slope the kitsune led them down smelled of death, and soon they came upon the skeleton of a giant ape. There were more of them lying everywhere.

"Fairy guardians," the kitsune explained, and Fox understood when the trees cleared, and she saw the water of a lake shimmering beyond them. The Fairy lake she had visited with Jacob had also had animal guardians, but there they had been unicorns. When they reached the foot of the wooded slope, Fox saw that this lake also had an island. Its silhouette resembled the one from where the Dark Fairy and her sisters had come. But the trees that surrounded the lake were not evergreen as there. They were bare as if in an eternal winter. And the lilies that floated on the water were withered and dead. Fox involuntarily closed her hand protectively around the yarn on her wrist. What she saw made her painfully aware that the thin thread she had wrapped around her wrist actually carried all that was left of the Fairies. They were really gone. Everywhere, even in the distant mountains of Nihon.

As they emerged with the kitsune from among the dead trees, Fox saw, standing in the waters of the lake, a mythical creature she had always wanted to meet. It was a centaur with a black hide and the torso of a man. Around him, the dead lilies had sprouted fresh buds, and Fox sensed that they were not looking at an ordinary centaur. When he saw them, he began to wade to shore. His hooves were silver, and where they sank into the muddy ground, it began to green up.

Toshiró's face resembled that of the samurai Fox had seen at Krieger's fortress, but he probably had as many faces as Spieler. The fact that, unlike him and Krieger, he did not show himself in human form made him almost likable to Fox—even if she scoffed at herself for the sentiment. He was an Elf, and there was nothing to suggest that he was less dangerous than those she had encountered so far.

"These are interesting visitors you bring, Kaze." The centaur shook the water off his human and horse body. His voice revealed what he really was. All the Elves had voices of velvet and silver. "A dead man, a vixen, and a man whose skin tells fables…"

Hideo lowered his head at his description as if caught.

The eyes with which the centaur regarded Fox were as black as his long hair, which he wore pinned up like the Ronin on the ferry. He made no effort to hide how much he enjoyed looking at her, but his gaze flattered without threatening.

"My mistress never believed Spieler's lies about you, oh Toshiró." Chithira was barely visible in the gathering dusk. "But she could not convince her sisters to spare you. This has always pained her. It is only for this reason that I dare to ask for your help today. Under your protection and with your help, perhaps she can take shape again and stand by you when…"

"Stand by?" The trees on the lake's shore began to blossom as Toshiró laughed. "Oh, you're lucky you came to the right Elf, dead prince." His voice grew softer than the vixen's fur. "I know your mistress very well. From a time when Fairies still took only immortal lovers. I admit that was a long time ago, even by a dead man's sense of time, but one does not easily forget, as you know."

"You were her lover?" The expression on Chithira's face proved that even the dead still feel jealousy. "But Fairies and Elves are mortal enemies."

"Only for scarcely more than eight hundred years. What is that compared to eternity?" scoffed Toshiró.

Silver hooves sank deep into the damp bank as he strode toward Fox. Man and beast seemed perfectly united in him,

139

and what she felt in his presence was so different from what she had felt in Krieger's fortress. This Elf seemed to bring joy into the world, and light. Like an early morning. Or a new spring.

"Ah, now I understand." Toshiró ran his hand through the air as if stroking along a thread that stretched from Fox's heart to another's. "You know it, too. That's why she chose you. Few know of the golden happiness and the golden pain. But now she needs a more powerful keeper."

The yarn came loose as if by itself when Toshiró touched it. It slipped into his hand as if it had been waiting for him.

"I'm glad you came to me," he whispered to it. "I will hide you from him until it is time for you to return. Spieler has betrayed us both, and he will regret it."

Chithira was barely visible.

"What about you, coachman?" Toshiró looped the yarn around his finger like a ring. "I have practice keeping secrets from Spieler, millennia of practice, but your mistress will take much time to grow again. Will you help me hide her from him?"

Chithira smiled.

"Nothing would make me happier."

Fox, however, glanced at the pale line on her wrist as the Fairy's coachman stepped up to Toshiró's side. What had she done? How had she been able to give the yarn away so easily? What if Spieler had found Jacob, and what if he demanded it as a price for his life?

Toshiró read the fear from her face, of course.

"I will let Spieler know that what he seeks has a new protector. But he won't give up the child you owe him, and you won't be willing to give it to him — not even in exchange for your lover, will you?"

He thrust his hoof into the earth. The buds that burst forth were silvery white. "Take care, vixen. Spieler fears this child even more than the Fairies. And he will soon learn that you are pregnant. Maybe he already knows."

No. What was he talking about? It couldn't be.

"Have you met Spieler lately?" Toshiró clapped his hands, and cranes flew up from the trees on the shore as if their budding branches had given birth to them. "If you owe an Elf your firstborn, you must never come too close. His nearness calls the child you owe him."

His nearness... Fox clutched at her body. She saw the garden in the fortress before her and the flat table where the two men knelt.

"Owe?" Hideo was still respectfully keeping his distance from Toshiró. "Why do you owe the Elf your child, Kitsune?"

"The father made a deal with Spieler." Toshiró waded into the waters of the lake again. Fish sprang from the waves as he dipped his hands in. "Very foolish, vixen."

"I'd be dead without his deal."

"Ah. How did Spieler make you believe that?"

It was still hard to talk about those days. "He helped Jacob free me," *say it, Fox!* "from the Red Chamber of a Bluebeard."

Hideo's horrified face proved he knew what that was.

Toshiró, however, laughed as he wet his human skin with the cool water. "Oh, Spieler. It wouldn't be the first time he used one of them to make a deal. Bluebeards, man-eaters... He's good at hiding it, but he's the slyest of us all."

Impossible. Fox recalled the inn where she had first met Bluebeard. Coincidence, nothing but coincidence.

"What does Spieler do with the children?" Her voice sounded hoarse from all the helpless fear she felt. *And he will soon learn that you are pregnant. Maybe he already knows.* The look Toshiró gave her was a warning. *Don't ask, vixen.* But she had to know.

"Sometimes he gives them to the dark witches." Toshiró glanced across the water. "But most of them he has taken to his palace. Look for your child there when he takes it. And for your beloved, too, if Spieler grabs him. The tallest towers, the most beautiful halls, the most precious paintings on silver walls and so deep underground you can hear their hearts beating underneath... He was always very proud of that palace, but only one of us has ever been there. Grunico. Even Spieler had to admit to himself at some point that Grunico was someone you could come to with desires even more sinister than his. Grunico probably didn't escape the curse any more than I did. At that time, he lived like a hermit near a town that feared him so much that it named itself after him."

Birds began to sing in the budding trees. Even the opposite shore began to green up. New life, a new morning... *You are carrying Jacob's child, Fox!*

If only she hadn't been so nauseous with fear.

"How can I protect her from him, tentei?" Hideo sounded respectful but determined. "Please! Tell me."

Toshiró looked at Fox for a long moment.

"Yes," he finally said. "Yes, she will need protection. Her and the child."

He raised his hand as if throwing something in Hideo's direction.

The latter uttered a silent cry and stared at his palm. The symbol that reddened his skin looked as if someone had just tattooed it there.

"Hogo-sha," Hideo whispered.

142

He looked up questioningly. But Toshiró had disappeared. And Chithira with him. Only the kitsune was still standing there.

"Come," he said. "I have orders to fill both of your pockets with silver."

21

Joy

Sixteen felt Spieler's displeasure in every cell of her body. She hated how connected she was to him, helpless as a hand puppet that he could manipulate and put aside. *Bad news!* whispered the corridors of the great house to which the witch's shadows had brought her. Its walls and pillars were as white as the freshly fallen snow she had loved so much in the other world, but outside it was hot and humid, the way only plants loved it. Sixteen hated the place.

Why had he summoned her to him? As usual, he was in no hurry to tell her. He loved to make her wait, like one of his statues, while he gave instructions to a golem to hang some pictures that Sixteen recognized from the house in the other world. Most of the things in the library where he had had them brought looked familiar to Sixteen: the silver vases, the busts of moonstone, the books bound in silvery leather… Was he planning to live in this place and not in the

144

underground palace about which the clay-faces raved with reverently hushed voices?

They were on the same continent where they had lived in the other world. Alberica. If Spieler had told her the truth. Sometimes he did. But who cared about the location? She was always merely a mirror of what surrounded her.

There were three others like her in the house, but Spieler had given her a room of her own, next to Will's. Sixteen had never had a room to herself before. She would have preferred it if Spieler had locked her in with her own kind, in one of the rooms where they learned to know and summon all their faces, with hundreds of little mirrors on the silver-gray walls. Even the tiles on the floor were glass, so they slept on mirrors. Yes, Sixteen would have preferred to be with the others, but what would they have said to the bark in her skin? Clara's room was just across the hall. Clara... Sixteen envied her name. It would have suited her, too, wouldn't it?

"Drink!"

The golem he called Beta was holding out a silver cup to her. The colorless liquid in it was bitter, but Sixteen obeyed and drank. She felt better. He seemed to actually want to heal her. Perhaps he didn't realize how great her betrayal had been.

"I'm always surprised at how easily you get lost in your thoughts." Spieler eyed her with his usual self-satisfied pride. He gazed at his paintings and sculptures in the same way. "Maybe all those faces I gave you are to blame. Just a few more weeks, and you'll be almost as good as new. Only you'll probably lose the arm. It's woody to the core, but I'll make you a new one."

145

She still didn't understand why he didn't smash her for bringing Will to Krieger.

"You've proven yourself very useful, Sixteen." He went over to the buffet the golems had set out for him on a table under the window. Edible flowers drizzled with honey, the leg of a newborn lamb on a bed of rose petals, figs filled with elven dust. Perfect fingers reached for one of the blossoms. "I admit I felt a little differently about this when you didn't come back, but you did your part. Will is no doubt in love with you, head over heels, as his kind would put it. And you're going to make sure it stays that way."

Her part... What did she care about his assignment? He believed everything was happening the way he wanted it to. But she had loved Will ever since she had first seen him, in that dirty cabin in the filthy woods. And he loved her, not because Spieler wanted it that way, but because it was meant to be. Because they were made for each other. How he would have laughed at her for thinking that. Of course, he hadn't made her for Will. And yet, to her, it seemed that way. Sometimes she even dreamed that love might give her a body of flesh and blood, even if she wasn't sure what skin she wanted. Just as long as it wasn't glass or silver.

She felt Spieler's gaze. She thought she felt him searching her face for all the things that filled his heartless chest: helpless longing, unfulfilled desire, consuming jealousy... pain.

"Remember. I want you to drive him crazy with love. And I want Clara to see it."

Clara. His voice changed when he spoke her name. Sixteen remembered how it had felt to have her face. She still carried it, but it was one of the ones she no longer showed Will, any more than she showed him his mother's. It had been a wicked joke of Spieler's to give her the face of Rosamund Reckless without telling her whose it was. Will had pushed her back and yelled, 'Why are you doing this?' Because it was one of her faces, and she had thought he would like it. His mother's face had a strange magic to it. It was a silent face, full of longing and love. Sixteen could understand falling in love with the woman who owned it. And with a girl like Clara. Will swore he had never loved Clara the way he loved her. How could one love in different ways? Sixteen knew only the one way. Her heart was a sightless mirror when she didn't have Will by her side. The world was so quiet and loud at the same time without his voice.

"Kiss him in Clara's presence." Spieler wiped honey from his fingers with a napkin. "I want her to lose all hope of winning him back."

"Why?" Her tongue had always had a mind of its own.

Spieler frowned. *Careful, Sixteen.* He turned and came toward her, step by step savoring the fear his annoyance aroused in her. There was still some honey on his fingers as he stroked her face.

"Sixteen." He made sure to touch her only where her skin was unblemished again. "You've had this penchant for inappropriate questions from the start." His voice sounded both mocking and amused. "You're lucky I have a weakness for rebellion. In moderation, of course."

He did not really understand his creatures, neither the Mirrorlings nor the golems. The Witch Crow was much more like him in her insatiable hunger. Spieler was also never satisfied. There was always something he wanted.

"How can I make him so in love with this body? Only desire turns love into madness."

He raised his eyebrows in amusement. He had the golems dust them with silver. "Is that wisdom yours?"

Sixteen wasn't sure. She rarely knew where what she said or knew came from. Too many faces.

"Let him see you in pain. Pity can nurture love, too."

"And if it never quite goes away?" The bark on his hand and neck was barely visible, but it was there. He eyed her until silence settled around her neck. He did not at all appreciate being found weak.

"The Fairies are gone, Sixteen. I had them wiped out. All that is left of them is a last whiff of poison in the air of this world. It will soon be gone."

He walked back to the table with the food. "Krieger thinks I should melt you all down. Don't give me any reason to think he might be right. Go. Find Will and make eyes at him."

He took a slice of the lamb. Born to be slain. Sixteen shuddered.

She glanced at the sculpture that stood on a small table in front of the shelves. She had looked at it often in the other world, too: a face, contorted in fear, frozen in the bark of a tree. Sometimes she had imagined it was Spieler's.

"My brother," she said, "I really miss him. Can you find him and bring him back to life?"

He turned and eyed her with amusement. "Brother? Are you talking about Seventeen? Fabbro warned me that with all the faces, we'd give you human feelings too. Seventeen doesn't exist anymore, Sixteen. We found him and burned him, like all your predecessors who were lost in this world. You are the only one who has been more fortunate."

Fortunate… He certainly hadn't made her feel fortunate. She wasn't even sure she knew what fortunate felt like.

148

22

So Many Stories

Will still felt the shadows that had brought them here. No forest had ever been darker, and he had looked in vain among the trees for Clara and Sixteen. Silver thorns on branches and bark, pale, waxy blossoms smelled of cinnamon and turned all thoughts to damp mist...

"So, where did you first meet Sixteen?"

Had Clara really asked that? No, she merely smiled sheepishly at him. The clothes of this world suited her, but her face reminded him of the other world, of all the months he'd spent trying to convince himself he didn't miss the jade and what it gave him: the feeling of finally knowing who he was.

One of Spieler's clay-faced servants had led them here, into the wood-paneled library that smelled of the jasmine branches blooming in a silver vase on the windowsill. The round table that stood between the shelves was set for only two. The tablecloth was as white as the jasmine flowers, and the plates were silver. Of course.

"Is your master not dining with us?"

The servant shook his head. "He asked us to set the table just for you and Miss Faerber."

Clara sat down and spread the white napkin over her pale yellow dress. "Aren't you hungry, too, Will?"

Yes, he was. Even if he didn't know where they were or how the forest that smelled of cinnamon and silver had brought them here.

He sat down on the chair that stood invitingly empty opposite Clara's and watched the servant fill their plates.

"Are you in love with her?"

So there it was. Clara still got right to the point. She hated secrets. Did she have thoughts she was ashamed of, deeds she wanted to forget? None that he knew of. But neither had he expected to see her on the arm of another man one day. An immortal at that, one who, with every glance, made him feel like he was just a clueless boy.

"Will! Do you love Sixteen?"

He glanced down at his plate. His body was still numb with exhaustion from the seemingly endless bout with the other Elf. That had happened, hadn't it? How many of Krieger's samurai had he killed? He couldn't remember. Many. It had been almost as bloody as when he had defended the King of the Goyl at his wedding. No. Kami'en and the Jade Goyl. Two sides of the same coin. Had he ever been so happy again? No. What had happened? He had gone back with Clara.

"I see the way she looks at you. And you at her."

What could he say? *Yes, I love Sixteen. I don't know why?* He reached for the silver fork waiting beside the silver plate.

"Spieler should never have brought you here. You hate this world. I'm going to take you back. Like I promised." He heard how absurd that sounded. And it wasn't really an answer.

"Whether I stay or go should be up to me, don't you think?"

The wine the servant poured for them was red and heavy, and the suit he wore was so black against the white tablecloth. White, red, black... fairy tale colors.

Clara wiped her lips with her napkin.

"She's not human, is she? She changed her face. She thought I didn't see it. Spieler says she's related to the Fairies and that it's not your fault. That every man falls in love with her."

Related to the Fairies? The Fairies were gone. But how could he explain that to her without telling her everything? That he had murdered because Spieler had made him do it. *We were desperate.* Where did the truth end and the lie begin? Will thought he could hear the books whispering on the shelves. *There are a thousand stories, Will Reckless. How will you decide which is the true one? What if they are all true?*

Clara put the napkin aside.

"This world has different rules, Will. Hasn't it been that way from the beginning? Everything we think we know—it doesn't apply here. We went back once before to forget what happened here. But it has happened. You have a skin of stone again, and you love another."

She stood up.

"Spieler helped me when you were gone. He was there for me without asking anything for his help. He's smart and wise, and I can learn a lot from him. I'm not going back."

The servant opened the door for her.

She turned around once more before she stepped out into the corridor. "You should talk to him about your mother. He says wonderful things about her. It's crazy. It was only then I remembered that I saw him sitting by her bedside a couple of times at the hospital. He says he tried to heal her but that she never got over the fact that your father cheated on her. And that ultimately killed her."

She was gone before Will could say anything in reply.

23

A Cell of Silver

Oh, they were rough with Reckless, yet the torturer hardly left a mark. The onyx lords would have admired his crafts- manship. They always allowed him a few hours of rest before coming for him again; they wanted to keep him alive. But even then, Nerron couldn't get much out of him.

"They want to know where Fox is."

"Why?"

"You think they'd tell me? They don't know where she is. That's all I care about."

"What about your brother? Is he here too? Did they catch him?"

Shaking his head. "I don't think so. None of the others are here."

Excellent. Nerron tried to convince himself that this was definitely a good thing, but he didn't like imagining the

Pup alone in the wild, wide world, and he liked the idea of Sixteen by his side even less. At least she didn't seem to have turned him over to her maker because there was no doubt that it was he who had carried him and Reckless off. Not that they remembered anything, but the golem who brought them the food—yes, it was undoubtedly a golem—was so impressed with his silver master that he talked of nothing else. Spieler. It was a wonder he hadn't carved his name on his clay forehead! They were all golems: the overseers, the guards... *Well, well!* their gaze seemed to say as they eyed Nerron with undisguised curiosity. *You're not so different from us, Goyl. Stone, clay, what's the difference?* He would have liked to explain the difference to them by slamming his stone fist into their plaster faces, but he was too grateful that they had only let him stew in the cell so far. One of the golems claimed that he had just ended up here by mistake. The Witch Crow and her shadow forest probably had something to do with it. Golems... The onyx had experimented with making clay slaves for a while, but they had all been uselessly stupid. These ones didn't give that impression, though their faces looked even cruder and more unfinished when reflected in the blank silver walls of their cell.

Nerron had not seen anything more than these walls so far, and Reckless told him only of endless corridors and another windowless room made of silver. When the guards brought him back, the metal opened like a curtain and melted back together when they left. Nerron had brushed over it a thousand times, tapped it, struck it, muttered opening spells in so many languages that his tongue had blisters from them... The wall remained closed, and what was most irritating about it: everything reflected on the silver remained there almost endlessly. Nerron had seen his own face a hundred times on the walls by now… a diabolical way to wear down prisoners. All his anger, exhaustion, every tinge of fear stared out from the gleaming metal and dissolved very reluctantly. His only consolation was that Reckless was much worse off than he was.

Spieler must have taken them to his old palace. They agreed on that, and it looked very different from the fortress where the other Elf played at being a samurai. Nerron wondered if it was one of the abandoned silver palaces that every Goyl knew about and which lay even deeper underground than their own cities. He had tried to find one years ago but had been unable to discover anything except sulfur lakes and petrified forests, as well as a blind monitor lizard that had nearly eaten him. If they really were that far underground, it would make escape even more difficult. But a way would be found. There was always a way to be found. The only question was—should he take Reckless with him or not?

They had probably been stuck in the cell for two days and nights (Nerron counted meals so as not to lose his sense of time) when Reckless started spitting up blood. That settled the question. He would escape alone. Battered as he was, Jacob Reckless would be of no help; on the contrary. Nerron worried for a fleeting moment about what to tell the Pup, but some touching story about his big brother's demise would surely come to him. Will Reckless was so easy to lie to. Wherever he was. And if he was still alive… Nerron avoided the thought as much as he avoided looking at his myriad mirror images. It was idiotic how attached he had become to the milksop—more than idiotic.

Reckless himself provided him with the opportunity. He didn't make it easy for the guards when they came for him again. Maybe he wanted to prove to himself that he wasn't quite finished yet. Either way, he resisted so successfully that the guards forgot about Nerron for a few precious seconds. Of course, they had taken everything he and Jacob had on them, but they hadn't found the bone hand any more than they had found his decoy pouches. Whoever had trained the golems knew nothing about lizard-skin clothes or how the Goyl kept their little secrets.

Reckless still kept the clay-faces busy in the corridor, and they didn't notice a mouse-sized Goyl scurrying past them, nor did they notice that they were leaving an empty cell behind.

Nerron glared after his old competitor as the guards finally managed to drag him away. There he went, the famous Jacob Reckless. Lost in an underground palace, leaving to the Bastard the title of best treasure hunter in this world. Could he now forgive Jacob for depriving him of the crossbow and beating him to loot so many times? No.

The corridor proved to be as endless as Reckless had described it. But at least, to Nerron's relief, it was made of refreshing gray stone. Since the guards had dragged Reckless to the left, Nerron decided to turn right. At some point, he came across two more guards who, thanks to his mouse size, did not notice him and were kind enough to demonstrate how to open the silver cells. They breathed against them. Three times. Ridiculously easy. Now it just had to work with Goyl breath in case they caught him again. *Why so pessimistic, Bastard?* No, he would get some weapons and then disappear, never to be seen again!

They usually brought Reckless back after three hours. That didn't give him much time before they would discover the empty cell—especially on mouse legs. Nerron estimated that half an hour had already passed when a barred gate appeared at the end of the corridor. The wide staircase leading up behind it looked promising. The two golems guarding the gate were arguing with a young man who looked suspiciously like a Mirrorface. Often, quarreling between bored guards had granted Nerron escape or access to places that were considered well-guarded. Only a few steps away from the squabblers, he saw an open door. Behind it, as he had hoped, lay a guardroom with weapons, but to steal them he had to risk assuming his normal size, though the guards could surprise him at any moment. No matter. He had no choice. He wouldn't be able to hunt on the run without a weapon, not to mention the blind monitor lizards, which he wouldn't have dreamed of encountering unarmed.

He was just reaching for the bone hand when the voice of the mirrored one gave him pause. Oh yes, he was clearly one of Sixteen's kind. They still sent shivers down Nerron's stony skin.

The Bastard wasn't sure if he believed that there was such a thing as fate for him, too. For the Pup, yes. But for the Bastard? No, but still… The conversation he was listening to, small as a mouse, among knives, crossbows, and shotguns in an immortal's dungeon, smacked very much of it. Someone seemed to want to protect his king. Maybe it was his mother's goddess. Perhaps it was some god who was not sympathetic towards the Elves. Whatever it was, it had sent the Bastard to the right place.

The Mirrorling was describing to the golems how their silver lord would exterminate the Goyl like rats in their burrows because their ever-growing warrens were getting too close to his palace. The stinking, ugly stone skins... His lord had never liked them. And what did their king imagine himself to be, the lord of this world? They would soon give him proof of his mortality. Words of silver, uttered with the haughtiness Nerron knew so well from Sixteen, and he felt the rage that stirred so quickly in every Goyl. Nerron felt it red and hot. They were coming, the dark times the old stories had spoken of! He had to find the Pup! The Jade Goyl would protect Kami'en! He would make him invincible, even against a band of immortals. But the mirror boy wasn't done yet.

He told of a bounty so princely that all the world, above and below ground, spoke of it: the King of the Goyl had promised it to the one who brought him the Dark Fairy's killer. He wanted to execute his legendary bodyguard with his own hands to avenge his lover. And who had orchestrated this? Spieler, the cunning one, Spieler, the master of silver and glass, creator of incredible creatures, with patience, cunning, and unbeatable guile. Oh, this Mirrorling was an insufferable braggart! The King of the Goyl, that clueless fool, would relinquish his own invincibility without suspecting whose game he was playing.

Oh, how the wrath shook the Bastard. How it burned his brain and heart. His shrunken body could barely contain it.

One of the golems trudged into the chamber to fill his shotgun with fresh ammunition. Outside, the other laughed with the Mirrorling. All quarrel was forgotten. Why should they fight each other when there were Goyl to crush?

Think, Nerron. Think.

158

He had to report to Kami'en what he had heard. But that would not be enough. The king would want his revenge. No Goyl could be talked out of that, certainly not their king. Was there anything he could do to make Kami'en merciful?

The Mirrorling was still rambling on outside about the age of silver that was dawning when Nerron had an idea... It wasn't a very good one, but it was an idea all the same. His dark childhood gave it to him, and a memory of his father. The golems stomped off to make their rounds, and Nerron heard the Mirrorling unlock the latticed gate and climb the stairs whose steps whispered *Escape!* so auspiciously. But the Bastard did not sneak after him.

He drew his bone hand across his arm, and, as soon as the pain that the waxing brought permitted, he stuffed two revolvers and a knife into his decoy pouches. His body burned as if someone was skinning him alive as he stumbled down the endless corridor and back to the cell. The silver actually opened as he breathed against it, and when the golems brought Reckless back, nothing revealed that the Bastard had been gone.

Reckless was unconscious, as he usually was when they were done with him. Nerron stared at the motionless figure and heard the Mirrorling mocking in his head. What would the Pup have said to what Nerron had heard about Kami'en and the Goyl from a voice that was as glassy as Sixteen's? Stone skins... They had grown accustomed to the hostility of men, but now they would have immortal enemies. Nerron felt the anger inside him like a cancer. The fury of the Goyl was legendary. The Pup knew it too. It ate away all fear and filled the body with fire, the fire that melted stone into lava and burned in Kami'en's skin.

Nerron closed his eyes so that instead of silver he could see the young Goyl his father had executed when he couldn't find his older brother. How he had screamed and protested his innocence. But that counted for nothing against one of the oldest laws of the Goyl, which said that one brother could take the blame of the other. His father had often used the law to punish enemies he couldn't catch. Nerron had rarely had cause to be grateful to his father, but in the silver cell of the Alderelf, he was. Jacob Reckless would pay the Jade Goyl's debt. He certainly would not scream and sob like the young Goyl. Shooting him in the chest and head would surely ease Kami'en's pain for the Fairy somewhat. Whether it was enough to save the Jade Goyl remained to be seen.

The Bastard would teach the Mirrorlings that it was better not to gamble with the Goyl.

Now he just had to get Reckless on his feet.

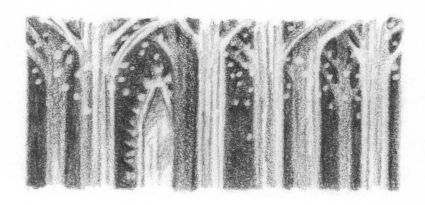

24

TREASURE HUNTERS

Fabbro. The golem lowered their voices to a nervous whisper when they spoke of Jacob's torturer. He was apparently also an Elf, but unlike Spieler, he showed himself in such ugly form that compared to him, even the one-eyed forest goblins of Lorraine who bit off the noses of unsuspecting travelers were beauties. When he reached into Jacob's chest with his twelve fingers, it felt like he was searching for the right thread in a sewing box. No, Jacob was not in good shape when he finally had the strength to open his eyes.

"I was beginning to think you were trying to escape to the realm of the dead," the Bastard murmured. "Our hosts are really not treating you well. I suggest we take our leave."

"Oh yeah, and how are we going to do that?" Jacob made it to his feet by pushing himself up against the silver wall.

The Bastard opened his hand. Their captors weren't as smart as they'd made out. He still had the bone hand. Spieler would strip them of their clay skin if he ever found out about it.

"Wait." This was too good to be true. After all, it was the Bastard he was facing, his old enemy. "Why don't you escape on your own? I'll be of little help."

"The Pup would kill me if I left his big brother in a silver cell." He had hesitated to answer, but perhaps the Bastard was simply embarrassed that he cared about his brother's opinion.

Jacob searched the mottled features for the lie, but he still couldn't read Goyl faces. Not even Will's.

"How is it my brother melted your stony heart?"

"He's different from you. Is that enough?"

Jacob was too exhausted to ask further. And too relieved that there was suddenly such a thing as hope, even if his pain-addled brain could barely grasp it.

The Bastard actually managed to open the cell, and they shrank as soon as they were out in the corridor. Just as the Goyl had predicted, it barely hurt, but Jacob remembered how badly the waxing had pained the Bastard. Anyway. The prospect of escaping Spieler's dungeons made up even for the loathsome feeling of suddenly being as small as a rat. *A rat, Jacob? You're no bigger than a mouse!* Only a few hours ever went by before the guards came for him for another session with Fabbro. This gave them horribly little time, but their clay guards were not the fastest, which gave them hope that they would be slow even when chasing escaped prisoners.

The Bastard led them to a gate, the bars of which were no obstacle given their new size. Unfortunately, the same

162

could not be said of the stairs beyond. Jacob climbed onto the Goyl's shoulders at the first step and then pulled him up to him, but after two more steps, they switched roles as Jacob's limbs were trembling with exertion. No, he really was no help, and Jacob braced himself at every step for the Bastard to change his mind and leave him behind. But they made it to the top of the stairs, even if it took them a painful eternity. The portal waiting for them at the top was unadorned and heavy. Nerron was just pulling out his bone hand, cursing because they couldn't reach the doorknob with their mouse size, when it opened, and a Mirrorling stepped out. He looked so much like Seventeen that Jacob thought for a moment that Sixteen's brother was back — until he remembered that Spieler probably often gave his glass-and-silver children the same faces. The Bastard dragged him along as soon as the Mirrorling was past them, and they barely made it through the door before it slammed shut.

Luck. They were indeed lucky. If only he had been stronger.

The portal had opened to a vast hall with white marble tiles stretching out before them like an icy lake. The noise of hammers and crowbars rang out toward them, and the air was thick with dust. It hung in veils between columns that ended in crystal-encrusted branches supporting a ceiling of glass. Spieler apparently no longer enjoyed this splendor. On the scaffolding that stretched along the high walls, dozens of workers, clay-faces like the dungeon guards, were knocking the plaster off the walls. The noise reliably drowned out any sound their mouse boots made, but the chipped plaster splattering onto the tiles in front and behind them made them take shelter under the scaffolding a few times.

163

There were three doors at the end of the hall. The looks the Bastard and Jacob exchanged revealed the same curiosity that the sight of locked doors inevitably aroused in them. Oh yes, they were made of similar stuff, even if they couldn't stand each other.

"The one in the middle," the Bastard murmured. "Studded with silver roses. Petrified wood. Promising."

He certainly wasn't talking about the shortest escape route. But how could you not think of treasure hunting in a hall like this?

"I'm for the one on the right. Mirrors in the corners. Spieler's 'S' in the middle."

The Bastard shrugged and pulled his bone hand out of his pocket. "I take it you don't want to wait for someone to open it for us?"

No.

Treasure hunters.

25

A Familiar Face

There were many doors in Spieler's palace, and with each hall they stole into, Jacob missed having Fox by his side more painfully. *She's safe as long as Spieler is torturing you to find out where she is, Jacob.* He kept repeating it to himself. If only he could have believed it.

Fabbro had weakened every part of his body. Yet, despite having to lean against a pillar all too often to wait for the pain to subside, he could no more ignore the treasures that surrounded them than the Bastard could when they should have been looking for the quickest escape route.

The Goyl took great advantage of the fact that the after-effects of torture had made Jacob's hands slow. He would have sacrificed a finger for some of the objects the Bastard stuffed into his decoy pouches, but there was plenty left over.

They passed through a few halls that were being remodeled, but there were also dangerously many where they could rummage undisturbed among sheet-covered furniture in the chests, boxes, and baskets that the golems had filled with Spieler's treasures.

Jacob, you're on the run! Forget about the treasures.

But there was always one last corridor they wanted to steal into, even though the few hours between torture sessions had surely long since elapsed. Were they both waiting for the other to urge caution? Was it the absence of day and night that made them forget time? The entire palace was illuminated by phosphorescent stone. The windows were closed with silver shutters, making it seem as if there was no outside world, and all they could hear, other than the hammering of the workmen, were their own footsteps. Perhaps Spieler had cast a spell on the palace, and no one who entered ever left? Perhaps. The silver apple the Bastard pulled from a box, the candles that ignited at a clap, the peacock feather that, when Jacob stroked his sleeve with it, turned the fabric into blue-green feathers... irresistible.

Finally, the lack of strength Fabbro's six-fingered hands had left him with made Jacob come to his senses. As he leaned longer and longer against the pillars, his treasure-fogged mind finally realized that they had to escape the palace at once if they didn't want to end up back in its dungeons.

As Jacob pried open one of the silver shutters, it became all too clear how difficult this would be. The view actually took his breath away. A forest of silver towers rose to the ceiling of a seemingly endless cavern studded with glass stalactites. Deep below, the palace walls disappeared into the dark waters of a lake —if it was a lake and not an underground ocean. Jacob could detect no shore. Pale yellow wisps of mist hung over the surface of the water, and there was no sign of a bridge.

"We call them the Carnivorous Lakes." The Bastard had stepped to his side. "They're often found at this depth. I suppose I don't have to elaborate on the name?"

The Bastard left no doubt that they were now in his territory, and Jacob became all too aware, as he gazed across the sulfur-shrouded water, that without the Goyl, he had not the slightest chance of ever making it back to the surface.

"Any Goyl lord would make a palace such as this accessible only from above: a tunnel in the cave ceiling, hidden by the stalactites, a retractable bridge leading up there from the highest tower…" The Bastard pushed open the window and leaned out. The air that rushed in was hot and smelled of sulfur. "I'm sure there is such a way up," he muttered. "But I can't see all the towers from here. Usually, the bridge is so well hidden that you don't discover it until you get close."

He was leaning farther forward when Jacob yanked him back and slammed the window shut. The guards had been even slower than expected, but now they were coming. The hammering of the workmen had drowned out their footsteps for a dangerously long time. Jacob heard their voices, shouting something to each other. He and the Goyl had certainly left tracks.

They took the next door. No choice this time. The hallway beyond was so plain that it was probably meant for servants. Soon they came upon a narrow stairway leading upward.

"The highest tower is to our left," the Bastard murmured as they hurried up the steps. Heavens, Jacob's legs were those of an old man, and after only five steps he was already gasping. The Goyl tugged him along. "Even if we don't find the access, we can get to one of the stalactites from there."

"And how's that?" wheezed Jacob. "Have you grown wings lately?"

The small box the Goyl pulled from one of his hidden pouches contained a magic thing that was very familiar to Jacob. A Rapunzel Hair. Yes, that would get them over any precipice. He had lost his in the Goyl king's stronghold. He would have laughed at anyone who told him then that one of them would one day free him from a dungeon.

"Yes, the Bastard has mastered the art of opening the right drawers." The Goyl shoved the tin back into the bag. "If we make it out of here, I say we compare our spoils. Shall we bet on who will be the winner?"

No, the Bastard had won that contest. The Goyl had to help Jacob along the steep stairs so many times it made him sick with shame. They had seen through the window that many of the towers were connected to the main palace by covered bridges. The stairs led to one of them. It was all glass, and it offered little cover but a far better view over the lake that surrounded Spieler's palace. Yes, it was a lake. This time they could make out a shore in the distance, but no bridges or boats to take them there.

The tower to which the bridge led showed no signs of remodeling, and its splendor was not tucked away in boxes or draped by sheets. Jacob had never seen anything like it. Its beauty was almost baffling. Walls and ceilings were covered with a shimmering crust of wrought gold and silver. Leaves, flowers, fruits, animals, as perfectly replicated as the roses that bloomed on the frame of Spieler's mirror. The treasure hunter in Jacob once again forgot that he was on the run. He spotted mythical creatures among the silver branches, faces peering out from between the shimmering leaves. And then...

Jacob stopped so suddenly that the Goyl looked around in irritation.

Hung on the curving walls of the tower were more than two dozen paintings. Spieler's memories? One painting showed Venice, presumably in this world, one showed New York, the New York Jacob had grown up in. There were paintings filled with dark forests and waves from which mermaids gazed back at the observer. Most, however, were portraits. It was not just the often faded colors but also the clothes of the depicted that revealed these to be the memories of an immortal. Two pictures had particularly precious silver frames, covered with leaves, blossoms, and twigs in which nightingales sang. One showed Will, aged seven or eight. The second was a portrait of their mother. Her face was thoughtful, as Jacob remembered it, but not yet as sad as it had been in her later years. Their clothes didn't match the lush frames any more than they matched the palace they were hung in: Will wore a T-shirt with the logo of a basketball team, their mother had on black jeans and the blue blouse on which Jacob had so often left fingerprints and lip marks as a child.

"Reckless! Are you growing roots?" The Bastard waved him on impatiently, but Jacob's limbs just wouldn't move.

So Spieler hadn't been lying. His mother and the Alderelf...

"Strange clothes." The Bastard stepped up to his side. "Let me guess. She reminds you of a past lover. If you ask me, the vixen is decidedly more attractive."

"She's my mother."

169

Well, well. The word softened the Bastard's stony features. His grained face spoke of tenderness and love—not of the guilt Jacob immediately felt when he heard the word mother. It was the first time he had ever envied the Goyl. No, it wasn't true. He also envied the Bastard's closeness to his brother.

The Goyl had only now noticed Will's portrait. "What in the hell! Is that?..."

"Yeah."

Jacob thought he heard something behind him.

When he wheeled around, there was a golem standing in the doorway they had come through. It was amazing how silently they moved, despite their hulking bodies. This one towered over them by almost a head and was as muscular as the rest of them. Their faces, so childishly unformed, were deceiving. They were anything but gentle. The dungeon guards had done nasty things to each other when they quarreled.

"I am Zeta, the guardian of this tower. I assume I'm addressing the treasure hunter my master captured? And the stone man who wound up in our cells as an unexpected addition?" The golem eyed the Bastard's skin with great interest. "I've been wondering what you looked like. My master should give us a skin like yours. It looks much more durable. But you are of no consequence." He turned to Jacob. "The guards will pay for your escape with at least one finger. Fabbro cut these off me for breaking one of his mirrors. He was very fond of it." The golem raised its left hand. It had only a thumb and forefinger; the other fingers were stumps. He smiled. "It displeases Fabbro that my master would allow a golem to enter this tower, but not him. Fabbro is so proud of his wickedness. Yet he fears my lord's magic."

His mouth was a lipless slit in the clay skin.

170

"Who knows what my master will do to him when he hears of your escape," he added. "I admit, I can't wait. And all I have to do is show you how to escape from this palace. This day has brought unexpected joys."

The Bastard gave Jacob a skeptical look. Yes, this seemed too good to be true—a golem who had a score to settle with Fabbro. Jacob could easily understand that, but they couldn't trust the golem, could they? The Bastard seemed as unsure of the answer as he was.

Zeta released the door leading back to the bridge and stepped toward the portrait of Jacob's mother. "Rosamund. That was her name... Rosamund Reckless, née Semmelweis. My master was very much in love with her. He still is."

The Bastard glanced toward the door. But the golem seemed to know that the portraits made Jacob forget any thought of escape.

"You're her oldest son, aren't you?" Zeta wiped a speck of dust from the frame from which Rosamund Reckless gazed. "We've met before, on the island where my master lived in the other world. You don't remember, of course. To your eyes, we all look alike."

Jacob tried to remember his face, but Zeta was right. Golem, that was all he saw when he looked at Spieler's servants. He had never considered that they might be different from each other.

"My master was pleased when your brother was born. He always hoped that the son he fathered with your mother would one day end his exile. And that's exactly how it happened. He loves it when things go according to plan. However, it was a surprise even to him that an ancestor of your mother had come from this world."

171

The son he fathered with your mother. Jacob stared at the picture of his brother. *That an ancestor of your mother had come from this world.* The golem's words turned Jacob's whole life into clay and remolded it into a new shape.

"Do you know why my master doesn't like you?" asked Zeta. "You look too much like his competitor, John Reckless, the mortal whom Rosamund could never forget. My lord was very jealous of him. But then your brother was born, and he had Rosamund's face — and his immortal blood in his veins. Not even Fabbro could have forged him a better weapon against the Fairies."

Zeta stepped toward Jacob. He had to peer up at the golem when he stopped in front of him. He was that tall.

"My lord has high hopes for your brother. But you... you have always been a pebble in his shoe. I think the only reason you are still alive is that you are also her son." He turned. "Come on. Eventually, they'll come looking for you in this tower, too."

He waved at them invitingly. But Jacob still could not move.

My lord has high hopes for your brother. Will was very well captured in the portrait. The toy he held had been a gift Jacob had brought him, from the world he had discovered behind their father's mirror. Their father? His father. And it had been Spieler's mirror... *That an ancestor of your mother had come from this world.* Is that why he had felt so at home right away? No. No, it was all a lie. He was in Spieler's palace! What did he expect? But why did his heart believe the golem? Believed every word he said.

Jacob felt the Bastard reach for his arm.

"Come on!" he said. "You can think about all this later! The news is not so bad after all! All right, your mother didn't

172

have a lucky hand when it came to her lovers, and don't you ever dare tell your brother that the Elf is his father! He is the Jade Goyl! That's all he needs to know about himself! Damn, it makes so much sense now that you two are so different."

Then he pulled Jacob along with him.

After the golem.

26

A Messenger for Spieler

Sixteen's skin healed faster than Spieler had anticipated, and the smile Clara gave him grew warmer with each passing day. It was a strange time. Krieger and the others seemed far away. The fact that his skin continued to itch was of little interest to him anymore. Yes, even the slight panic that gripped him at times because the crow still hadn't found the vixen's trail was easily calmed by remembering the length of a human pregnancy. All he cared about was Clara.

It was indeed like that time, and no, he didn't want to think about how that had ended. But the face of Rosamund's son would not let him forget. Will was still silent when they had dinner together, and Spieler often caught him eyeing him warily. But he could now sometimes be persuaded to ride out with him, and Will could not deny how grateful he was for Sixteen's skin healing. Rosamund's youngest, like his mother, could hide little of what was going on inside him—except when he had a skin of jade; and Spieler had the golems mix a herb into his food that had so far reliably prevented this. It helped against many kinds of Fairy magic. Why not this one?

Yes, perhaps it was time to let him look into the mirror he had passed by so many times by now, unaware of who he would encounter behind the cloth that covered it. Perhaps.

"My lord." Theta stood in the doorway. "I am sorry to disturb you."

Theta hesitated to enter. They all knew he wanted to be alone when he went to the greenhouse, where he grew some of his rarest plants. Besides, they had all surely heard that he had had the guards who had let Jacob escape thrown into the lake. They had dissolved in it like soap. Theta had probably known some of them.

Rosamund's eldest had escaped. Of course. How often had he had to listen to the arguments between his mother and him! Spieler had sent a few of the Mirrorlings in search of him, but they were still all too susceptible to the spells of this world, and God knows the golems were not very good sleuths. No, the crow would find the vixen. That was the only thing that mattered. It would put an end to everything—the Fairy magic, the Fairies, and the child that wasn't supposed to be. Let the monitor lizards eat Jacob! Maybe the Goyl would slay him. The two were supposed to be enemies, after all. Goyl… At least on that front, everything was going according to plan. Kami'en would never tolerate the Jade Goyl at his side again after Spieler had tricked him into killing his lover. And there went the fairy tale of his invincibility.

Oh yes, no one played with worlds with as much virtuosity as he did.

"You have a visitor, Silver Lord." Theta kept his head down, as they all did when they addressed him. "He says he comes from far away. As an emissary from… sorry, he has a strange name." He glanced at the note he held in his hand. "To-shí-ro?"

Spieler felt himself lose face for a split second. Literally. Beneath the one he was so fond of wearing, another became visible. But Spieler had regained his composure before the golem could see it.

"Toshiró," he corrected. "The emphasis is on the last syllable of his name. What are you waiting for? Let his emissary in."

Theta had only opened the greenhouse door a crack when something scurried past him. For a moment, Spieler thought the vixen had come to him willingly, not yet knowing that her beloved had escaped him. But then he saw the nine tails.

The kitsune straightened up. He stood on his hind legs as if there was no more natural posture for his kind. Then he transformed into a young man from Nihon.

He bowed to Spieler, but the respectful gesture was laced with mockery. He was not afraid of him. He didn't seem afraid of anything, not necessarily an expression of cleverness, although his visitor looked anything but stupid.

"Toshiró the Eternally Young, has the following message for Spieler, the Insatiable: *I know of the lies you have told about me. Rest assured, I will not forgive them. The vixen has left what you seek in my protection. Play your last game.*"

There went the peace—the illusion of new beginnings, the hope that all the old ghosts were dead.

176

"Interesting." At least his voice sounded controlled. "Tell your lord —"

"A kitsune has no lord," the fox-man interrupted him. "I am Toshiró's messenger because I like his scent. Yours, Alderelf, does not please me."

His fox magic filled the room like the rusty moonlight Spieler had not missed in the other world.

"Where is he?"

"Not where he was, and not where you will be looking for him."

The kitsune transformed so quickly that Spieler did not realize what he was about to do until the pointed fox teeth dug deep into his left hand. Then he burst through the glass of the greenhouse, as if the panes were nothing but solidified air, and disappeared beneath the trees that grew behind the greenhouses.

Spieler stared at his bleeding hand.

It had only five fingers left.

The kitsune had given him the hand of a mortal.

27

THE ESSENCE OF LOVE

Spieler's tower was high, but Jacob was too agitated to feel his exhaustion as he followed the golem up the endlessly winding stairs. Who was he? He no longer knew. Or did he understand better now? Never had he yearned more to be able to talk to Fox, but Spieler had made sure that he had lost even her. He had silvered all his memories, every fight he'd had with his mother, all the tears, his anger, and every inscrutable look Will had given him. *He's still your brother, Jacob, even if he has a different father.* Sure, but even the mother they had in common was no longer who he'd believed her to be.

The golem led them up to the roof of the tower. To a door made of silver. Zeta instructed them to wait a few steps below, so the metal only caught his reflection.

178

"Let Zeta in!"

The door swung open with a soft chime. The golem beckoned them into the dark room, which was round — like the tower chamber where Jacob had first stepped out of a mirror. But this room was much larger. The floor was tiled with silver and gold, and the tall windows, one for each cardinal direction, were closed with silver shutters, just as in the main palace. The golem lit two gas lanterns next to the entrance door, but much of the room remained filled with shadows that outlined the silhouettes of tables, chests, and statues. A sofa and armchair were from Jacob's world, the style of the twenty-first century, among things which the light of a lightbulb had never touched. Which world did Spieler like more? The tower room wasn't telling.

"Every item in this room is connected to a memory precious to my Silver Lord." Zeta lit another lamp.

Silver candlesticks and bowls, a rainbow velvet jacket, a ruby-studded comb, two glass daggers — the eagerness with which the Bastard eyed all these things seemed to amuse Zeta greatly. On the other hand, Jacob had to force himself to look more closely at Spieler's possessions. His mind was far away in another tower, in the apartment in the other world. Will and his mother — even in his memories, they suddenly looked at him like strangers.

Search, Jacob. There must be something in this room that tells you more about Spieler. But all that came to his mind was the image of his mother and Will's painted gaze.

The golem opened the silver shades in front of one of the windows. The light that fell into the tower room resembled that of a setting sun. Did Elves detest bright light as much as the Goyl? He didn't even know that about them, while

179

Spieler knew him better than he knew himself. Damn. The old, helpless anger stirred in him, the same anger that had filled him when his father had left them. His father. Not Will's.

"Of all this, what is dearest to your master?"

Zeta gave him a mocking smile. "The dearest thing? My master knows all about desire, but not much about love, treasure hunter. It frightens him."

And yet Spieler had loved his mother. Her picture was not a portrait that spoke only of desire. Probably the Elf even loved his brother. At least that would protect Will from him. Maybe.

Jacob's mother's favorite fairy tale had been the one about the six swans. Next to the sofa from Jacob's world stood a round table made of magic wood. Inlays covered the tabletop. Above a forest of malachite, six swans of moonstone soared into a night sky of obsidian. At the center of the table stood a box of chiseled silver. Jacob stepped up to it and opened it. It was filled with crystal vials, each shaped like a human figure. The liquid behind the cut glass was colorless, but it warmed Jacob's fingers as he touched one of the vials.

"You know your trade, treasure hunter," the golem said.

The Bastard gave him an irritated look.

"What is this liquid?"

Zeta looked at him as if he wasn't sure if he should tell.

"It is the essence of love," he finally said. "My master likes to grant mortals their most hidden desires, but the price they pay for his help is high."

The vials clinked like chimes as Jacob reached for one. *Tell him you don't want to know more, Jacob.* But he needed to know for himself and Fox. Zeta interpreted his silence correctly.

"If a child is the fruit of a great love," he said, "it is made of that love. That is why my lord demands as a prize their firstborn child. He does not devour them like the gingerbread bakers. He transforms them into vials of glass."

The golem came to Jacob's side. He took the vial from his hand and placed it back in the casket.

"The elixir he extracts in this way lets him feel love without having to feel the pain it usually brings. *'I am lost in a landscape of eternal ice, Zeta,'* he once said to me, *'and only love can warm my heartless chest.'* He has always found human women who made him feel love. But mortal love is so easily lost, and while my lord searches for the next woman, he warms the emptiness of his immortal heart with the tincture these vials contain. Since the liaison with your mother, he has needed it more and more often."

Jacob could not take his eyes off the casket. How was he supposed to tell Fox about this? No. She could never know about it. He wanted to smash the vials, but that would have been like finally killing the children whose love they contained. What if there was a spell that could bring them back?

The golem seemed to know what he was thinking about. "The stone man has already taken a lot," he murmured to him. "It seems you've found something you like, too?"

The Bastard was busy rummaging through the drawers of a dresser. Jacob still turned his back on him before he pulled out a feather from a hidden leather compartment under his belt buckle. It was a man-swan feather. Fox had found it and given it to him. Whatever you touched with it disappeared and only reappeared where you called it back with the feather.

Zeta did not stop him when he touched the casket with the feather. What would he say to Spieler when he discovered it was gone? Jacob did not ask him.

"You also have a debt with my lord, am I right, treasure hunter?" Zeta stroked the swans soaring on the table. "Don't let him fool you. He doesn't want your child to warm his heartless chest. One of his mirrors warned him long ago about your daughter. He will try to kill her before she sees the light of…"

The golem reached for Jacob's arm. Someone was coming up the stairs with irregular but determined steps.

Zeta waved them impatiently toward a heavy cabinet. He pushed the Goyl and Jacob between the clothes hanging inside. They were from Jacob's world, shirts and suits, sewn reminders of the world that had given Spieler refuge for eight hundred years.

"Mirror-maker," they heard Zeta's voice through the closed closet doors. "You must have lost your way. This palace is a labyrinth. The wrong staircase, and you find yourself in the wrong tower."

The voice that answered was all too familiar to Jacob.

"Zeta. Witty as always. I've never appreciated that quality in a golem, though." Jacob's torturer was breathing heavily after the many steep steps. He breathed just as fast when he played the torturer. The pain he inflicted excited him. "Spieler and I had many unedifying arguments about the intelligence of the creatures we create. Sometimes I wish he would settle for fathering children with mortal women."

"Without your art, there would be none of us, Master Fabbro." The obsequiousness in Zeta's voice rang false. "Clay, silver, glass… you make even his mirrors breathe. With a little help from my master. I fear he does not show you his gratitude often enough."

The mockery in these words certainly did not escape Fabbro.

"He has seduced me into helping him. Spieler's business has always been the desires we all have—the more hidden and sinister, the better. He promises to fulfill them, and in return, demands what will satisfy his lusts. You have to give him credit that he usually keeps his promise."

Fabbro's irregular footsteps seemed to be approaching. The Bastard gave Jacob an alarmed look through the garments.

"This palace is indeed a labyrinth," they heard him say. "That's how it was designed. I helped Spieler with the floor plans. But how would you know? This palace was built more than four millennia ago, and we made you barely three hundred years ago."

"Yes, our lifespan is woefully short," Zeta returned in a calm voice. "We will never have the wealth of experience our immortal creators have. Yet I find comfort in the thought that this limited lifespan gives our minds, at times, refreshing freedom."

"Freedom?" Jacob's torturer made no effort to hide his disdain for the golem. "Another quality that is anything but desirable for slaves. And you are a slave, Zeta, even if Spieler has made you his First Servant."

"I am well aware of my role, Master Fabbro." The golem's voice remained calm. "And as the First Servant to my master, I must ask you: what are you doing in this tower? I am sure you remember that only I am allowed access to it?"

The mirthless laughter Fabbro emitted brought back bad memories of endless hours of pain and humiliating helplessness. Jacob found it very difficult to stay in his hiding place.

His torturer did not answer Zeta's question.

"Have you heard," he asked instead, "that two prisoners have escaped from the dungeons?"

"Indeed. They talk about it even in the kitchen."

"And?"

"And what, mirror-maker?"

Jacob felt the Bastard beside him groping for his knife.

There was silence for a long time. Then Jacob thought he heard footsteps again. Yes, they were getting closer. He wanted to push open the closet door to get ahead of Fabbro, but Zeta's voice held him back.

"I really must ask you to leave." The golem still sounded calm, but now the clay was firm and hard. "I have precise instructions from my master. No one enters this tower except him."

"And you."

"And me." The clay had turned to stone.

"What is it that makes the ever-suspicious Spieler trust a clay-faced servant?" This time Fabbro sounded unabashedly angry.

"He wrote the recipe you used to make me."

"That goes for the two hundred other golems in this fortress, too."

"Two hundred and twenty-three."

The noise that followed sounded like someone striking against clay. "Watch your tongue, golem. It can be just as easily—"

"I will not repeat it, Master Fabbro," the golem interrupted. "Leave this tower at once!"

"Or what, slave?" It was apparent from Fabbro's voice how much he would have liked to drag Zeta down to the torture room where he'd had his fun with Jacob.

"Well... when I report to my master on the progress of the remodeling, I will also have to inform him that you did not comply with my politely and repeatedly expressed request to respect the privacy of this tower."

The silence that followed lasted a long time.

"The day will come, Zeta..." Fabbro did not have the humor through which Spieler disguised his dangerousness. "Spieler will not protect you forever. I've seen it happen countless times. He grooms a protégé until he is as loyal to him as a dog. He encourages him to become intoxicated with his cleverness, only to enjoy destroying him all the more. But everyone falls for his beautiful faces. I am the only one of my kind who dares to show by my form what an abysmally ugly species we are!"

Jacob heard footsteps again, but this time they moved away. Finally, the sound of Spieler's tower room door opening penetrated the wood of the closet.

"Lock this door well when you leave, slave," said the mirror maker. "I don't want to learn someday that the two mortals your lot let get away had found refuge in this tower."

The door swung again. Then, silence followed.

Jacob felt as if he had been listening to his own breathing for an eternity when the closet finally opened. The golem waved them out as if nothing had happened and pointed to the window where he had opened the shutters.

"The walls of this tower are covered with silver roses. My lord intended them to express his admiration for the Fairy curse that brings Eternal Sleep through the sting of a rose.

The leaves and thorns are sharp as knife blades, but if you want to escape the guards, the descent is your only chance."

"This is the escape route you wanted to show us?" The Bastard stepped to the window and looked out. Then he let out an incredulous laugh. "Even my skin won't withstand the descent unscathed! And how are we going to get across the lake? Show us where the highest tower is, and we'll climb up from there to the cave ceiling and shimmy along the stalactites until we find an old Goyl tunnel. I'm sure there are several in this cave."

"Ah yes, the old tunnels." Zeta shook his head in amusement. "There were a few of those, in fact, close by. My master had them sealed. The descent is your only chance." The golem pulled a pair of gray gloves from a drawer and tossed them to Jacob. "The stone man will survive the roses. My master uses these when he cuts a bouquet of silver roses for a mistress."

Jacob pulled the gloves over his fingers. They were very tight. Spieler had smaller hands than he did. The sixth finger remained empty.

"How can I protect the child from him?"

Zeta eyed Jacob thoughtfully as if weighing how far he wanted to take his betrayal of his master. He did not attempt to explain or justify it, as traitors often do eloquently. "You will have to kill him."

He rubbed his hand, which had only two fingers left.

"My master ordered me to break the mirror that cost me my fingers. He believed Fabbro could see his true face in it. It hurt a lot. We feel pain. We feel many things. My lord knows that, and yet he shatters us like old dishes when he feels like it. I have twice witnessed him kill another Elf. He had a wax likeness made of his enemy's true face and melted it in a fire of Alder wood. But the likeness must be perfect."

His true face. The face that Spieler never showed.

Zeta took the two glass daggers from the dresser on which they lay. "He had himself painted three centuries ago," he said casually. "In your world. I think that was the only time he showed who he really was. He felt very safe there. He was the king of your world, even though no one knew him."

The Bastard listened to the golem as intently as Jacob.

The golem held out the daggers to them. "Use these to cut the thorns from the vines. It will make climbing easier."

The Bastard went to the window and tried the blade on the vines under the window sill. The golem watched him as if he had thought about climbing down the tower a thousand times.

"Does the picture still exist that Spieler had painted?"

"No. My master had it burned." Zeta was still looking at the window. "But the painter was foolish enough to make a copy. He paid for it with a death that did not come easy."

"Where is this copy?"

"My master never found out. Now go. I have already told you and given you enough."

Yes, he had. How many fingers would the betrayal cost him?

The Bastard swung himself out of the window. "You can't tell us how to get across the lake, too?"

"You will have much more dangerous obstacles to overcome if you declare war on my lord."

Jacob looked out the window. It was a long way down, and the roses which covered the tower wall were like a tapestry of silver knives.

"Come with us," he said to the golem as he swung his legs over the parapet.

But Zeta only wordlessly closed the window behind him.

28

Wings

The glass daggers helped with the thorns, even though it took some time to scrape them off the vines. Yet, despite the gloves, Jacob's skin was soon riddled with cuts. The greatest danger was that they would be spotted from one of the bridges, but no one showed themselves behind their glass walls. The windows they passed remained shuttered, and all they heard were the cries of birds searching for prey in the vapors above the lake or the scurrying of bats that silently flitted past them. And so, like two beetles, they continued to climb down Spieler's silver roses toward the sulfur-shrouded waters that surrounded his palace. At some point, even the Bastard cursed as he closed his onyx hands around the vines, and the gloves on Jacob's hands were so drenched in blood that he tried to distract himself from the sharp-edged roses by remembering another descent: down the Goyl's royal palace to free Fox. Fox... How would she react to what Zeta had confided in him? *One of his mirrors warned him long ago about your daughter. He will try to kill her...* He had already kept many things from Fox—to protect her or because he couldn't find the right words. *Or because it was more convenient for you if I didn't know something, Jacob Reckless*, he heard Fox mock him. Yes, that too. But not this time. This time she had to know what he knew because it meant danger for her. He was sure that the daughter the golem had spoken of would have Fox as her mother, and Spieler would hunt Fox, not him, as soon as he suspected she was pregnant. A rose petal cut deep into his forearm. No, these were thoughts better kept for a safer place.

He had to escape to warn her. And she was right. There was no point in running. Spieler would find them wherever. *He had a wax likeness made of his enemy's true face and melted it in a fire of Alder wood.* Was it really possible to kill him?

The Goyl was far ahead. He had already reached the roof that connected the tower to the palace. From there, it was still more than a dozen yards to the water, but even the Bastard seemed to need a break. Jacob watched through the vapor wafting up from the water as the Goyl dropped exhausted onto the silver shingles. His own fingers barely wanted to bend anymore, and above him, Spieler's towers shimmered in the dim light that came from the cave ceiling... but he finally made it down to the roof where the Bastard was lying.

He had his eyes closed when Jacob stretched out beside him, his skin numb with pain and so exhausted he almost threw up.

"I wasn't sure you were going to make it. You were as slow as a snail crawling over broken glass." The Goyl opened his eyes. "Oh no, you look even worse than that."

Had anyone ever been so insane as to climb down Spieler's roses? Probably not. The shutters looking down on them were still closed, and all they could hear was the water slapping against the walls deep below them.

The Bastard got to his feet first. Jacob felt how much blood he had lost as he followed suit. And they still had no idea how to get across the lake. The only living things to be seen were the birds and bats that hovered in dense flocks over the water. Apparently, fish lived in the brew — or whatever else it was they hunted.

"Is it possible to swim through it, perhaps?"

The Bastard gave him a pitying look. "If you're not attached to the flesh on your bones. They'd be pleased up there."

Two massive birds circled between the stalactites on the cave ceiling. Even from a distance, they looked huge.

"They're cave owls. Their sense of smell is better than a hunting dog's. They were probably attracted by our cut skin and all that fresh blood. But hopefully, we're too big for them. We should be more worried about those."

The Goyl pointed downward. Shimmering insects that looked like a cross between wasps and dragonflies swarmed in the sulfur steam that drifted over the lake.

"Silver stingers. This place gives a whole new ring to their name." The Bastard spat contemptuously into the depths. "They sting the back of the neck where Goyl skin is thinnest. Damn. I probably shouldn't have blabbed about that in front of a snail skin."

"Don't worry. Everyone knows that." Jacob pulled the blood-soaked gloves off his fingers. They had kept the roses from cutting to the bone, but his hands still looked awful.

"Sucked dry by silver stabbers or boiled in sulfur soup..." The Bastard sighed. "Why are there even guards in this palace? And that's the end for the best and the second-best treasure hunters in this world."

"You'll be the best for exactly ten minutes."

That's how much longer his skin was going to keep him alive in the broth down there. Jacob glanced up at the owls. One was slowly drifting lower. The other followed its lead.

"You're sure we're too big a prey for them?"

They began to fly their circles above the roof.

"All I know is that they're not Goyl eaters." The Bastard gave him a dirty smile. "I guess your snail skin looks so tasty that the sight of you excites them, despite your size."

Probably.

Jacob looked down at the sulfurous water — and began rubbing the blood from his gloves onto his clothes.

"I was once carried by a griffin. It almost cost me a leg, but without its help, it probably would have been my head." He handed the Goyl the other glove. "Or do you have a better idea?"

The Goyl cast an incredulous look up at the owls. "You're even crazier than I thought! I take back what I said about the beasts. They'll eat us on the spot!"

"Not if they have young. We just have to jump off before they feed us to them."

"And if they don't have young? A crispy Goyl, some snail skin for dessert... Heck, all they'll find around here otherwise are golems!"

"We should be safe in the feather fluff between their legs. And if they try to pluck us out of there, we'll defend ourselves with the daggers."

The Bastard shuddered and stared across the swath of murky water. "I once swam through a lake that was laced with mercury. It can't be much worse down there. How does the Elf get into his palace?"

"Through one of his mirrors, I suppose. You can go back and try to find the right one. I haven't seen a single mirror. He must keep them in one of the other towers."

The Bastard cursed. "Even if the beasts carry us across the lake—how are you going to get them to fly low enough for us to jump off before they feed us to their brood?"

"I don't know. I admit it's not a fully fleshed-out plan."

The larger of the two owls was already so close that Jacob could make out the pale gray mottling of its breast feathers. It had a wingspan of at least eight feet.

"I hate birds. Birds, bats, anything that flies." The Bastard stepped to the ledge of the roof and looked down. "The only thing I find more loathsome are fish."

He sighed and squeezed some of his colorless blood from the cuts on his forearm.

Above them, the winged predators spread their claws. Their flight was as silent as any owl's as they swooped down on them. Good, they didn't seem to intend to use their beaks for the time being. Their beaks were terrifying.

"Jump off over a tree!" cried the Goyl. "The ground will be rocky. But beware of the ones that look like coral!"

He's right, Jacob thought, as the massive claws plucked him from Spieler's roof. *It's an idiotic plan.* And what was most abhorrent about it—Fox would never know what

193

had become of him. At least there wouldn't be the daughter Spieler would have hunted her down for. *I wonder if she would have looked like her.*

Fortunately, none of the arm-long claws dug into his body, but the owl gripped him so tightly that he probably broke a rib or two. Then it silently glided like a ghost out onto the open water, casting its shadow on the acrid vapors that floated below them. The owl's scent seemed to keep away the biting insects the Goyl had warned him about. The vast wings beat steadily and serenely, and as the massive bird carried Jacob away from Spieler's rose-studded palace, he felt the enchantment and terror of the world he called home more clearly than ever before. Soon, the fog surrounding him was so thick that neither the distant shore nor Spieler's palace could be seen. All that existed was the owl, and in the haunting silence, Jacob kept repeating what he had learned from the golem. *He had a wax likeness made of his enemy's true face and melted it in a fire of Alder wood.* Again and again. If only the golem could have also told him where the copy of the portrait was that Spieler had commissioned. *He had himself painted three centuries ago. In your world. I think that was the only time he showed who he really was. He felt very safe there. He was the king of your world, even though no one knew him.*

The shore that emerged from the vapor was lined with tall, densely crowned trees, but most of them actually looked like coral and had disturbingly pointy thorns. Beyond them, the cave seemed to narrow. Jacob saw sharp-edged rocks and a ragged ceiling lost in the twilight that seemed to be coming from luminescent insects and phosphorescent plants.

As the owl glided over the trees, Jacob saw a couple of huge nests in the rocks beyond. No. The beaks of young owls were certainly more dangerous than prickly twigs. He drew the glass dagger. The owl that had grabbed the Bastard flew just behind his, and he thought he saw him getting ready to pounce, too.

Jacob began to squirm like a worm until he managed to free one leg. He barely had the strength of an old man, but when he kicked the sinewy bird's leg, the owl actually opened its talon for a split second, and...

Jacob fell.

Toward a tree with black-green leaves.

29

Gray Goose Feathers

The old ship that carried Fox and Hideo away from Nihon was not even a steamer. But it was the only one heading out west. Most of the passengers stayed below deck at night, and Fox called the fur, hoping that her heart would hurt less in her fox form. But this time, the fur didn't help much, and soon she was sitting on deck in human form, staring sleeplessly at the star-lined horizon and the black waves, while above her the sails caught the wind and carried her westward. She thought she could feel the child already, though she knew it was too soon for that, and it only made the fear worse that she couldn't tell Jacob about it. *About her, Fox.*

She missed the yarn on her wrist and feeling that it protected her and her love for Jacob. Now she carried something with her that needed her protection. Knowing that a child was growing inside of her, a child that would only bind her and Jacob more, threw her into a storm of feelings she had never known. Was she rejoicing? Yes. Was she terrified? Oh yes, so very much so. It wasn't merely the fear of Spieler and the certainty that he considered her child his property. She and Jacob were still so young. With their restless lives, how could they care for a child even if they found a way to protect it from the Alderelf?

Sometimes he gives them to the dark witches, but most of them he has taken to his palace.

They had all been gone when Hideo had returned to the inn in Kakeya for them: Will, Sixteen, and the litter bearers, as well as Jacob and the Bastard. Without a trace. The innkeeper had seen or heard nothing. They had simply disappeared. That could only be Spieler's doing. Hideo had paid the landlady for the ill-fated night anyway, and she had confided in him that there were no more midnight duels at the Fortress of Moons. The new lord had gone out with all his samurai to search for a cursed tree. Fox had crept up to the fortress anyway, but she had discovered no trace of the missing even there. And it had been little consolation that Hideo had not found their names on any of the graves. Her heart said that Jacob was still alive. But what did that mean? It said what she wished to be true. Her worst fears had come true, and she had to try hard not to take out her helpless anger at Chithira on Hideo. He had even left his beloved islands for her!

'Kitsune!' he had said as they had made their way to Hodogaya, the port city from which many ships sailed west. 'The Alderelf would have found you had we not taken you away! And he would have taken the yarn and killed you all! But this way, he will let Reckless-san live because he hopes to use him as bait for you! And you must now think of your safety and that of the child you are carrying. Reckless-san would want that, too, wouldn't he? I won't leave your side until we find him.'

Fox had to admit that she was very grateful for his company. Yanagita Hideo had grown on her, even though he had helped Chithira. He was a steady companion who knew when to be silent and when to offer comfort, and it was good not to be alone when her heart was so heavy. It seemed to her at times as if Hideo had always been by her side. Kitsune... His islands had given the vixen a name—and given her a child.

The cabins for the crossing had been expensive, despite the old planks and sails, but since their pockets had been filled with Toshiró's silver, they were suddenly among the rich of this world. Hideo had sold a few of the trinkets in Hodogaya and gotten so much money for them that it was only then that they realized how great a fortune Toshiró had given them. Hideo did not come from a wealthy family, as Fox knew by now, and she and Jacob had never been made rich by even the most successful treasure hunts.

'Parsia? What do you hope to find there, Kitsune?' Hideo had asked when she had told him where the ship was headed.

He had decided to continue wearing the costume of his homeland, even if it earned him disconcerted looks from their few fellow passengers, all of whom were from the West. Fox had bought a few dresses for herself since it might have been brought to the attention of Spieler that Fox liked to travel in men's clothes. She didn't want to make it too easy for those he would send out to find her—even though a skirt certainly wouldn't throw them off her trail for long. Would they be Mirrorlings like Sixteen, or would Spieler have the ginger-bread baker that the Bastard had told her about looking for her? Ever since his report, she had looked suspiciously at every black bird.

'I hope to find a good friend of mine in Parsia,' she had replied to Hideo's question. 'If anyone can help me find Jacob, he can.'

The friend's name was Orlando Tennant, and he knew many of the secrets of this world that most people knew nothing about, for Orlando was a spy, and secrets were his profession. When Fox had first met him—at a ball at the Czar's court that she was sure she would never forget—he had still been a spy for Albion. But now, he worked for Mehmed the Magnificent, Sultan of Parsia, and the entire Suleiman Empire. Jacob could never entirely suppress his jealousy when Fox spoke of Orlando, for Orlando Tennant was not only an old friend. He had also been her lover for a while.

Probably that's why it wasn't until the sixth sleepless night that she had brought herself to use the gray goose feather he had given her as a parting gift. *Stroke the keel, and I'll feel it wherever I am...* Fox always carried the feather with her, in a pouch embroidered with birds, but she had vowed never to use it, remembering all too well the pain on Orlando's face when he had caught her and Jacob in a kiss. It had been their very first kiss.

The sea was so choppy that one of the other passengers threw up over the railing, but Fox was a fisherman's daughter and more seaworthy than the officers who stood above her on the bridge in their blue uniforms.

Stroke the keel...

How would Orlando react when she told him she was asking for his help because of Jacob? And how would he

199

find her, even if he was in Parsia, as she hoped because his last letter had come from there? Months had passed since he had written it, and her telegram from Hodogaya had gone without reply. What if he was just spying on some enemy of Mehmed the Magnificent in some distant kingdom?

Fox was alone on deck when she finally ran her finger gingerly over the slender quill.

She had decided to go ashore in Jahoon. From there, it was only a day's journey to the city from where Orlando had sent his letter. Jahoon was famous for its markets and for the magical things that could be bought there. Perhaps there was one among them that would tell her how to find Jacob?

It was a muggy evening when the ship pulled into the harbor of the ancient city. Its buildings heralded wealth and power, even if some bore the scars of past wars. They rented two rooms in a hotel where the walls whispered a thousand stories. Fox was especially grateful for the garden within the hotel's walls. Its fountains and flowers let them forget the heat and dust of the surrounding arid landscape. The treeless desert made Fox melancholy, and there was already enough to make her heart heavy.

Hideo couldn't hide how eager he was to explore the narrow streets surrounding the hotel like a maze after all those days at sea. But he only set off when Fox assured him that she would not budge. She had visited many towns like Jahoon with Jacob, where the past was as vivid as the present, and a forgotten secret waited at every corner. But after the long sea voyage, Fox longed for leaves and trees. So Fox sat down by one of the fountains in the hotel's garden, picked white rose petals out of the cool water, and lost herself in the elaborate mosaics that adorned the fountain. The world seemed so safe and peaceful between the high walls, and Nihon's damp forests already seemed so far away, as if the vixen had only dreamed of them. A dream to which she had lost Jacob.

She ran her hands over her body. What if Toshiró was wrong? What if she wasn't pregnant? No, she sensed he was right. When would she first feel the kicks she had felt when her mother had been pregnant with her youngest brother? She hadn't grown tired of pressing her hand to her mother's belly until she felt something stir beneath the taut skin. She had hoped that maybe this brother would be nicer than the other two if she just paid enough attention to him. And yes, her youngest brother was the only one she loved.

A large tulip tree cast its shadow over the fountain. In its branches hung three golden cages. In them, tiny birds, yellow as lemons, sang their hearts out. The vixen detested cages, and finally, Fox climbed onto the well's edge to release the feathered singers. The birds were so surprised that only one dared to flutter out of the cage.

"I'm not sure you're doing them any favors. They only know life in a cage. The hawks will eat them."

Fox slipped off the damp well wall when she heard the familiar voice behind her.

Orlando helped her up. The Parsian men's clothes he wore were certainly more comfortable than the suits he had worn at the Czar's court. And they looked just as good on him, if not better.

"How did you find me so quickly?" Fox wiped the dust off her dress. Silly how flustered she was by the sight of him. The Barsoi. That had been his nickname at the Czar's court. Did he have another one by now? Orlando Tennant

201

still made her heart beat a little faster. That much was true. But his presence also gave her a sense of comforting familiarity.

"How did I find you so quickly? How do migratory birds find their way halfway around the world?" He plucked a gray feather from his sleeve, and Fox remembered the carriage ride where he had confided in her that he, too, was a skilled shapeshifter. Orlando Tennant transformed into a gray goose when needed. The bird that had ventured out of its cage settled on his shoulder as if sensing this. But it fluttered away when Orlando tried to coax it onto his hand.

"The vixen travels alone?"

"No. With a friend. But you're right — Jacob's not here."

Orlando's eyebrows rose like the wings he sometimes had. The gesture was so familiar that Fox had to smile.

"He ran away from you? Jacob Reckless is an even bigger fool than I thought!" He sat down beside her on the edge of the fountain. The tip of his shoe traced the pattern of the mosaic at his feet.

"It's a long story."

"That was to be expected."

It turned out to be a very long story. After a few sentences, Fox felt as if she had gotten lost in the Bluebeard's labyrinth where Jacob had made the fatal deal with Spieler. For when had this story really begun? How much had been masterminded and determined by Spieler long before they had met him? What did she know about Will's part of the story? And how could she expect Orlando to help her find the man she had chosen over him?

It wasn't easy to tell him enough without mentioning the mirrors and Jacob's world. But only Jacob had the right to reveal that secret. She pretended that Spieler had escaped the Fairy curse underground, and Orlando seemed to accept that as an explanation.

He held her with his gaze as she mentioned the Bluebeard. And said and asked nothing until she ended her report on Toshiró. Then he was silent for a while as if he had to find the right words first.

"You are pregnant?"

"Probably."

"*The next, I'll have the young Queen's firstborn child.*" Orlando looked up at the golden cages. "Even I know such a bargain only from fairy tales. What about the modern times that even the Sultan I serve celebrates? Alderelves, heavens!" He shook his head. "Of course, I've heard rumors, but you're the first I can believe to have actually met one of them. Just a few weeks ago in Albion, I suspected that I had encountered one, but since, as you say, they change faces more effortlessly than their clothes, I'm not likely to find him again. The Fairies are gone. I have seen two of their dead lakes. If this is really the work of those Alderelves, then they are taking thorough revenge, and I don't like it at all that you have made an enemy of one of them."

He was glad to see her. He did not try to hide it. But Orlando's eyes were watchful. *It did me good to be far away from you*, his gaze said. *And now you bring the heartache back to me, to save the man you left me for?* He was right. She had hurt him, and it didn't make it any better that she had done it for someone she had loved long before him.

"I'm sorry. I shouldn't have called you."

Orlando's fingers were light as feathers as he put them to her lips. "Don't talk nonsense. I'll ask around. Jacob

Reckless is by no means an unknown figure in many parts of this world..."

Fox was relieved to see no pain on his face, but she still found love there. Orlando had never hidden from her, although his profession was to be invisible behind a thousand false facades. Fox knew only his true face. There was no greater proof of his friendship.

"So... have you ever heard of an underground palace made of silver? Or of a place called Grunico?" She had told Orlando what Toshiró had told her about the Elf who had known Spieler and his palace.

"I don't know anything about an underground palace. I was sure down there you just had to watch out for the Goyl fortresses. But in Tyrol there is actually a town called Grunico. It has a sinister past."

Tyrol. This was a stretch of land in northern Lombardia that was much more familiar to Fox than the lands she had been traveling over the past few months. She and Jacob had once visited the dwarf there—the one who had since put a bounty on Jacob's head. Valiant had sold the castle he had inhabited there shortly after their visit, supposedly because he'd had to share it with too many ghosts. It was not hard to believe that. The castles of Tyrol were ancient. Ancient enough for an Elf?

"Grunico still doesn't have a good name. Dark magic casts sinister shadows even centuries later, as you know. Is that where you're headed next, by any chance?"

Was it? Where else would she turn? Toshiró's words about the Elf who knew Spieler's palace were the only clue she had. But it was such a vague hope—and a very long journey, without any certainty that it would help her find Jacob.

"I admit, I would be very grateful if you could find out something that would give me a less indefinite objective," she said.

Orlando no doubt heard in her voice how much she needed some hope.

"Good." He stood up. "I'll do my best. Stay at the hotel. Enjoy the garden, and don't roam the alleys! Jahoon is not as dangerous as a Bluebeard's maze, but it's easy to get lost in this city. It will be a few days before I hear from my contacts. You have to be patient. I know—that's not your strong suit."

No. It certainly wasn't. And here they came, the damn tears. Fox averted her face and pretended to wipe a fly away. She should have reported to Orlando as a vixen. It would have been so much easier to hide how lost she felt.

Orlando held out a handkerchief to her. It was embroidered with flowers and lined with black lace.

"This looks like a gift from a woman." Fox wiped tears from her face with the delicate fabric.

"You caught me. But she only has one shape. It gets boring in the long run." Orlando joined her again on the fountain's edge, and Fox leaned her head against his shoulder. Tears began to flow as if they were trying to make the fountain overflow behind her. The birds she had set free bathed in the top bowl. Freedom tasted too sweet despite the danger it brought.

"Stop worrying," Orlando said. "Jacob Reckless can survive anything. Who knows that better than you? I'm sure you don't have the fingers to count how many times he should have been dead by now. What about the story that Hentzau, Kami'en's right-hand man, put a bullet in his heart? I suppose that's a bit of an exaggeration?"

Fox shook her head. "The bullet went right through his heart."

"Through his heart? How do you survive that?"

Fox sensed her lips form a smile. "The Red Fairy brought him back."

"Ah. His old mistress. So that story is true, too. I am filled with envy! What about the one about the Bastard firing Guismund's crossbow at him?"

"I thought nobody knew about that one."

"You're talking to the best spy who ever worked for the rulers of this world."

It felt so good to laugh.

"An arrow in the chest, a bullet in the heart? That really doesn't sound like anything or anyone could kill him."

Fox had forgotten how many times he had made her laugh. With Orlando, life was as light as the feather of the gray goose he transformed into with the help of a witch's comb. Maybe she could have loved him as much as Jacob if she had met him first. Maybe.

"Does he make you happy?" Orlando looked up at the empty cages.

"We haven't had much time to find out."

"Time enough. Does he make you happy?"

Fox knew he wouldn't like her answer. But she owed him the truth. "Very. Very happy and sometimes very unhappy. But the good days more than make up for the bad."

Orlando sighed. "Yes, I feared as much. You're one of those couples you think may have met in many lifetimes." Above him, one of the birds returned to its cage. "I admit, I was hoping you'd get tired of him in this one."

He looked around.

Hideo stood among the columns that surrounded the garden. It often seemed to Fox that Hideo, despite his size, could withdraw into himself so much that he was barely noticeable. He stepped toward them hesitantly, and only when Fox called his name.

"Let me introduce you, Orlando. Yanagita Hideo, a friend from Nihon who is traveling with me."

Hideo gave her a grateful look at the word *friend*.

Orlando straightened up and bowed in the formal manner with which one greets those one considers one's equal in Nihon. "Are you one of the Holy Wrestlers of Nihon? Forgive me for asking. I watched a match in Kyōto a few years ago, and I noticed a young wrestler who looked very much like you."

"I was one of them. But now," Hideo bowed to Fox, "I am in the service of Auger-san."

"Oh yes," Orlando said, smiling at Fox. "She easily inspires the desire to serve her."

30

CHILDREN'S TALES

The tree on to which Nerron had dropped was a sponge stone tree. The name was deceptive. The branches were nowhere near as soft as the name suggested, and his whole body ached from the impact, not to mention that he could still feel the owl's claws. And the stench! As if it had rolled him in bird droppings to make him more palatable to its young.

Thousands of stalactites shone from the cave ceiling above him. Their crystal caught the dull green light shed by the glimmer-moss that grew on the rocks all around. The Goyl also called this kind of stalactite 'Hanging Candles'. Petrified trees, bat flowers, glimmer-moss... The lake was no longer to be seen. The owls had carried them further than planned.

Nerron looked for support among the branches while he made sure that his hands did not reach into the tree's prickly fruit. In ancient times, sponge stone fruits had been highly sought-after projectiles.

Where had Reckless landed?

He had been less fortunate. Why had the idiot jumped over a lance tree, of all things? *Because their lances are hidden under giant leaves, Bastard.* Damn, he should have given Reckless a lesson in subterranean botany before leaving him to the owl. The way he hung limply in the branches didn't bode well. There that went, his attempt to save the Jade Goyl. Damn, damn, damn!

Nerron leaped from the tree, sinking to his knees in sharp-edged grass, but his legs still carried him. That was something. Above Reckless, a flock of white crows was already gathering—they could peck the flesh from a man's bones in less than an hour. They fluttered away, screeching as Nerron threw a stone at them, and Reckless raised his head.

Ah, all was not lost after all.

The fool groaned as he tried to sit up in the branches. One of the lance-like spines had pierced his shoulder.

"Be careful it doesn't break off in your flesh!" Nerron called up to him. "The resin in it is toxic."

Reckless actually managed to free his shoulder with a jerk. No, he was not squeamish. Nerron was impressed that the pain didn't make him lose his grip. He even managed to climb out of the tree without his help, but Reckless's legs gave out only a few steps after he reached the bottom. The snail skin wasn't breathing heavily just because of the wound. The heat in these depths was even getting to Nerron.

"All right," Reckless gasped as he got to his knees. "I do realize I can't make it to the surface on my own. What's your price? And don't give me that line again about helping me because of my brother."

Well, it was less far from the truth than he thought. Nerron glanced around. No, it wasn't going to be easy to get the snail skin out of here alive.

"All right," he said. "I admit my help will not be free. If we make it to the surface in one piece, you'll accompany me to Vena. To Kami'en's court. That's my price."

"Kami'en's court?"

Nerron wanted to smash his soft face for the way he pronounced his king's name.

"Kami'en. That's right — the king who plants terror in the hearts of your kings and emperors. I must warn him about the Elves. You will tell him what the vixen overheard, I will tell him about the Mirrorlings, and together we will describe what we saw in the palace. All this will hopefully convince him that he has new enemies."

"The Mirrorlings?" Reckless glared at him. "Are you insane? Are you going to tell Kami'en about the mirrors, too? And about the other world? I won't have it! Besides, I have to find Fox."

"All the more reason to come with me to Vena! Kami'en's network of spies is everywhere. He can help you find Fox! And no, I don't plan on telling him about the mirrors. He has more than enough to do with this world, and have you forgotten that I only know about the mirror in Nihon? You've known what I think of that one since I saw the witch crawl out of it! No, thanks."

Reckless was already elsewhere with his thoughts anyway. The prospect that Kami'en might be able to find his beloved appealed to him.

210

"All right," he muttered. "You get us out of here, and I'll come with you to Vena. If the Goyl turn on the Elves, maybe that will give me time to find the painting the golem was talking about."

Ah yes, the painting. Who cared if Spieler stole the child from the vixen and Reckless? No Alderelf could be a threat to the Goyl if their king was invincible. *And don't give me that line again about helping me because of my brother.* His cluelessness was genuinely touching.

The white crows had settled in the trees. They did not give up easily. Reckless cut a strip of cloth from his shirt to bandage his shoulder, and Nerron made sure to also dress the wound with leaves from the sponge stone tree. Oh yes, he would make sure he stayed alive.

So… which way was up?

Nerron could detect no signs of Goyl settlements, no tunnel entrances, no carvings on the rock walls, or the ruins of forgotten temples often found in caves of this size. *Not at this depth, Nerron!* This was Elf World, so hot he could feel the burning heart of the earth beneath his boots. They had to get away from here. As quickly as possible. Otherwise, even his skin would soon melt.

He thought he had spotted a swarm of candleflies among the rocks on the other side of the cave. If they were lucky, that meant a tunnel entrance. Good. Whatever got them higher!

Reckless got to his feet. At least he could stand.

Steam billowed from a crack in the ground to their left, and Nerron felt the rock tremble beneath his boots. Every Goyl knew the stories of burning rivers in the depths, lakes of lava, and geysers that spewed glowing rocks. He would

211

have to warn the little man about many things — and unfortunately, even he didn't know much himself about these realms.

The insects that soon swarmed them stung effortlessly through Goyl skin in their hunger for fresh blood and the heat made you feel like you were swimming through hot water. It wasn't long before Reckless was leaning against a tree — only to stumble back, cursing, as two snakes, eyeless as many creatures so deep underground, descended from the branches onto his shoulders at once. Even Nerron was surprised at how much life there was in the stifling hell. Bats as pale as moonstone, lizards colored like molten lava, fire toads, herds of wild boar that were almost as red as the lizards... and the damn insects! At least Reckless wasn't constantly tripping over every root and rock in the light given off by the glimmer-moss. Still, it was getting dimmer the deeper they advanced into the cave, and the steam coming off the floor and the rock walls soon made even Nerron short of breath and almost as blind as the human.

By all the lava devils, who were probably cooking their soup right under his boots. Higher. They had to get higher.

The candleflies he had seen were indeed swarming by a tunnel entrance, but the passage beyond had collapsed after only a few meters. The next tunnel they encountered merely led deeper down, exhaling a heat that seemed to melt Nerron's skin like wax.

Onward. From cave to cave, and still, no way led up. All the rustling, screeching, hissing, and flapping of wings that drifted through the darkness put them on constant alert, and Reckless's heavy breathing filled Nerron's ears. Every now and then, the cry of something being eaten rang out among

212

the rocks, or a crashing stalactite splintered in front of them, forcing them to look for another way. Stumbling through this environment was no fun, even if he had dreamed of exploring the fiery womb of the earth as a child. Well, he used to have many idiotic dreams. What had he known about life? One thing above all — that he wanted to run away! From his own father, who had his bastard offspring drowned, from his own skin, which would always mark him out as inferior, from fear, which often leaped at him like an animal from the dark, without him knowing where it came from... The snail skins fantasized about heaven and a paradise in the clouds. For him, paradise had always been in the depths, deeper than the onyx and his father dared to descend, a realm of freedom... *Ha! Look around you, Nerron. Paradise is a boiling hell in which only fire toads can be happy.*

"Do you smell that?" Reckless had stopped.

"What?"

"Flowers. Blindness indeed sharpens the other senses."

Flowers... Nerron looked around. A bush full of bats that barely made it to the size of beetles, a waterfall frozen in veils of amethyst... and yes, it smelled like flowers. But where were they?

A thicket of stalactites made it almost impossible to follow the scent. The rock wall to their left was studded with alabaster beads, each worth a fortune, but Nerron was not in a treasure-hunting mood. The scent grew heavier, it was sweet and peppery at the same time, and the breeze it rode on was definitely cooler than the hot air that had surrounded them for hours, or was it days?

The cave floor began to rise, steeper and steeper until they had to hold on to the stalactites, and the gap that finally opened up in front of them in the rock wall was so large that they could push their way through without effort.

Beyond lay a cavern that was as bright as if it had been waiting for human eyes. The light came from phosphorescent flowers; pale blue bees were busily gathering pearly pollen from their fringed petals. The flowers were everywhere, a sea of blossoms with wide veins of crystal running between them through the cavern floor. As Nerron bent over one, he saw a stream of lava flowing in the depths. The beauty all around made him almost forget the brutal heat. Nerron had never seen a cave like this, but he recognized it from the stories his mother had told him as a child, of subterranean kingdoms, deeper underground than the cities of the Goyl, lit by blossoms, crisscrossed by streams of crystal and rivers of lava. 'Look for them, Nerron,' she had whispered before she died. 'The Deep Kingdoms. I know my son can find them. Only him.'

He stood there staring down at the flowing fire. He missed her. He missed her as if he were missing an arm or a leg. That, too, had connected him to the Pup from the beginning—that they had both loved their mothers. And had hated watching them die. Had the Pup ever told his older brother how resentful he was that he hadn't been there with her?

Reckless breathed so hard, it was as if he had to filter the oxygen out of the hot air with every breath. His snail skin offered little protection against the heat, and they had barely encountered any drinkable water so far. There. He fell to his knees and struggled to get back to his feet. Nerron heard him laugh.

"Heavens! Fox would have her fun seeing me like this."

Hardly. Fox would have seen that her sweetheart was about to die. The beauty that had made Nerron dream of the Deep Kingdoms certainly wouldn't keep him alive.

But there. Nerron felt a breeze. It came from above, from a few boulders covered with citrine yellow flowers. Above them gaped a fissure that looked promising. However, the steep rock face below offered so little support that the climb would not be easy, even for a Goyl. The shattered rocks at the base of the wall gave Nerron hope that there had once been a ramp under the fissure and that beyond it, they would finally find a tunnel leading upward. But how could he get Reckless up there? The snail skins were miserable climbers compared to the Goyl. He could try to hoist him up with the Rapunzel Hair, but then what? He could hardly drag him along with it.

Damn, he was on his knees again.

"Go on, Goyl!" he gasped. "There's little point in dying down here together. Give this to Fox from me!" He unfastened an amulet from his neck. "Tell her to give you my wishing table as a reward. It's a protection spell." He laughed at himself as he barely found the strength to throw it to Nerron. Then he fell on his stomach like a squashed bug.

He was right. *Get the hell out of here, Bastard!* He shoved the amulet into his pocket. He was wasting precious time. He had to warn Kami'en about the Mirrorlings. And stop him from executing the Pup. Even if he couldn't bring him his brother.

Nerron took one last look at Reckless's slumped body. The blind monitor lizards would find him soon. Nerron had seen their dung all over the cave. He missed the Pup. And being among his own kind.

215

He clambered over the flower-covered scree until he stood before the rock wall where the crevice gaped high above him. The climb was even steeper than he had estimated from a distance, but for a Goyl, the smooth stone offered enough grip.

He was clutching the rock with his fingers when he heard the hissing below him.

His mother had imitated it with relish. Why did he have to keep thinking about her down here? 'It sounds like hot air pushing out from between the rocks, son.' She had put her tongue between her teeth and closed her eyes. She had had beautiful eyes, gleaming to old age, golden to her death. 'And their teeth, oh heart of my heart, sharp as the blades the onyx forge in their black palaces, and wet with the blood of their victims.'

Nerron hid behind a rock and looked to where Reckless lay. Oh yes, there they were. Two jade-green monitor lizards more than ten feet long, their eye sockets white as if they were filled with milk. When they were young, they supposedly saw better than a Goyl, but the darkness took their sight. One nosed Reckless. The other was already licking its teeth. Their jaws were indeed very impressive.

'Oh, they are terrible. So terrible, heart of my heart.' His mother would lower her voice when she got to the part of the story where the blind monitor lizards appeared. 'Run as fast as you can if you ever hear their hiss in a cave, even if it's filled with gems.' She'd had a deep voice for such a small woman. She had barely reached his shoulder even on his eighth birthday.

The monitor lizards began to quarrel over the prey. The larger one bit a hand-sized piece of lizard meat out of the other's shoulder and, in return, caught a nasty wound on its back. Then they clutched each other like wrestlers and began to fight over Reckless's motionless body. They were going to trample him before they ate him. That was probably a little more pleasant than being picked apart alive.

Lucky to the end. He was going to suggest that line for Jacob Reckless's obituary.

The smaller lizard had had enough. It dragged itself away, limping, while the victor bent over its prey and sniffed at it.

Oh, blast it.

He heard the Mirrorling boast how they were going to choke the Goyl in their cities. And the Pup glared at him reproachfully. *Bastard*, he heard him say. *You've got to save me. I am your king's bodyguard. I am the salvation of the Goyl in dark times.* Of course, the Pup would never have said such a thing. Not to mention that he certainly wouldn't have been amused that Nerron was about to sacrifice his older brother for him. But still.

The monitor bit into Reckless's jacket, ripping it off his body as if it were unwrapping chocolate from its paper.

Damn. It had been a good plan. Well, not really good, but a plan nonetheless.

"Hey!" Nerron stepped out from behind the rock. After all, he had wanted to fight one of the beasts for as long as he could remember.

For the Jade Goyl.

The lizard had lifted its ugly snout and was sniffing in his direction with blind eyes. Yes, its hearing was as excellent as they said. Nerron drew the Elf's glass dagger. If the fairy tale he remembered did indeed tell of the beast he was facing, then its pale green scales were more impenetrable than chain mail. But the fairy tale said something else about this scaly coat. Nerron heard his mother's voice as he walked slowly toward the lizard, 'The blind monitors have only one weakness. There is a spot right between their eyes where they are vulnerable.' Splendid. Now he was staking his life on a story told to children. *Why not, Nerron? You make your living from treasures that are only spoken of in fairy tales.*

The monitor was visibly irritated that he had to pay attention to something other than its prey. It let out the hiss again that Nerron had heard so often from his mother's lips. Then it opened its mouth menacingly, in which its long garishly yellow tongue danced between double rows of razor-sharp teeth. Ah yes, it did indeed have four tips. The scaly beast moved as jerkily as all lizards — unpredictable for a warm-blooded creature with their unforeseeable change from rigidity to attack. Only the tail twitched, while the rest of the powerful body remained as immobile as only reptiles could manage. The attack came with such lightning speed that the monitor almost tore off Nerron's hand. He plunged his dagger into its flank. The glass blade actually pierced through the scales, but the monitor rammed its head into his face in pain. When Nerron found himself on his back, he was weaponless, and the dagger was still stuck in his opponent.

What now, Bastard?

Nerron rolled behind Reckless and hid behind his motionless body while pulling the other dagger from his belt. The monitor dragged him out of cover by his boots, but when it bent over him to tear him apart, Nerron thrust the glass blade right between its eyes where the scales turned a little darker.

The dagger went into the ugly head to the hilt, and the monitor collapsed so abruptly that it almost buried Nerron under it. The blood that gushed out when he pulled the two daggers from the dead body resembled liquid gold. The glass blades hadn't even a scratch on them, and Nerron shoved them both into his belt before bending over Reckless. Yes, he was still alive. So at least the effort hadn't been in vain. However, the monitor's tail lay across his chest and was so heavy that Nerron had to separate it from the torso to free his atonement gift to Kami'en. The glass daggers did that effortlessly, too.

Reckless did not move. Had his soft human heart melted after all? Nerron felt for a pulse. No, it was beating surprisingly strongly, and Nerron knelt beside the dead lizard and cut open its scaled mantle with the Elf knife. So far, his mother's fairy tale had proven right, but what he was about to attempt, he would never tell anyone.

The monitor's heart was surprisingly small, barely larger than a plum. It tasted bitter and sweet at the same time, and after the first bite, Nerron almost threw up. But he ate the whole hideous thing, like the hero in his mother's story. Had he had a name? He could not remember.

The water that had collected in a stone basin between the stalactites could not wash away the disgusting taste. If he remembered correctly, the tale said that the effect was immediate. Nerron listened inward, but he could detect no change.

He stepped toward the dead monitor and lifted it up as effortlessly as if it were a dead chicken. His laughter filled the cave to the furthest dark corner, rousing at least ten thousand bats. Had he ever felt so good? No. It apparently paid to play savior to the Goyl.

He tossed the monitor lizard between the rocks, where it fell like an offering to the goddess before whom his mother had so often prostrated herself. When he threw Reckless over his shoulder, he barely felt the weight. Strong as a giant. What if his mother had never told him the fairy tale?

"You're a lucky man," he told Reckless. "But soon, they'll be saying that about the Bastard, too."

Climbing up the rock face was a walk in the park. And the tunnel that waited beyond the crevice led steeply upward. Now the fairy tale only had to be right about one more thing: that the power given by a blind monitor's heart lasted forever.

It lasted barely two hours.

31

The Apple

The mirror Spieler most liked to gaze into was not very large but perfectly rounded and framed with a plain band of silver. It was still relatively new. He'd had it made in the other world. A few drops of his own blood had been added to the liquid glass. Not that it was necessary, but the romance of the gesture had pleased him then as it did now.

"He really does look a lot like you."

The glass clouded over, and there she was. A few years younger than the day she had died. Spieler still wondered if she had died from him stealing not only her face but also a few of her life sparks to make the mirror.

"How is he?" It was her voice, even more than the familiar face, that at times made Spieler believe that she was actually alive—and had chosen him instead of the mortal

221

impostor who had betrayed her. Granted, he had seduced John Reckless into abandoning his wife and sons by helping him discover the secret of the mirror. Just as he had arranged for John to find the mirror in the basement of the apartment house Rosamund's ancestors had built. How the mirror had gotten there was a long story. John Reckless had never known it. He was a hopelessly mediocre man, even by mortal standards, and Spieler would never understand why Rosamund's heart had remained so true to him and had not chosen the handsome stranger who she had encountered in the elevator one day, as if by chance. For eight years, he had tried to make her his. He had tried different faces, but even when he had finally succeeded in seducing her, he had seen John Reckless in her eyes every time he had woken up next to her. *He had given her a son.* How many times had he tried to explain it to himself that way? But so had he — well, he had fooled her into thinking she was sleeping with her husband. Nonetheless! And she had always loved Will more than Jacob.

"How is he?" She was still waiting for his answer. The real Rosamund had been almost as patient.

"Good, he has a girlfriend who reminds me a lot of you."

She smiled. No one smiled like she did. There was always a touch of melancholy as if she couldn't forget how fleeting her existence was, and with it all her happiness. Well, he had made her immortal with that mirror. Just a few sparks of life… What did her eternally young likeness know of the Rosamund who had withered like a flower and died years ago? Nothing. He had also had some forgetyourself mixed into the glass. Mainly to make sure her reflection wouldn't think of John Reckless, too.

"I must go, my heart. But I'll be back soon."

She never protested. And she was always there when he needed her.

He'd had the gray velvet he used to cover the mirror embroidered with tears of Grass-Elves. Rosamund had loved books, so wherever he was, Spieler had the mirror hung in his library. The one in the other world had been much nicer, and he had had most of his books moved to his underground palace, where they filled two towers. The room which the merchant who had sold him the plantation had called a library hardly deserved the name, but at least the shelves were of rare tropical wood. They had contained a very sad collection of insignificant writers and words. He had replaced them all with his own or newly acquired books. The poppy red volumes were from his collection of magic books. Only Letterman owned more titles on the subject, but Letterman was, after all, obsessed with anything that saved words from oblivion, whether on papyrus, parchment, or paper. His library filled every wall in his hideously cold castle deep beneath the barren mountains of Caledonia. He had even had the floors and ceilings, every column and door inscribed with quotations… and there were very credible rumors that Letterman collected not only books but also poets and kept them imprisoned in his towers.

Spieler eyed the old-fashioned wood paneling behind the shelves and sighed. Ah, how he missed Rosamund's world. He would return someday, but not until he could be sure that Krieger or one of the others would not dispute his hold on this world.

The Fairies had been proud of their sisterhood. On the other hand, every Elf lived in undying competition with his

223

fellow Elves—for what, probably none of them could have said. Spieler had only once met another Elf whose friendship he had cherished but whose hopeless nobility had quickly turned them into enemies. No, he didn't even want to think his name, even though it had been whispering in him incessantly ever since his nine-tailed messenger had bitten off his finger. It would not grow back. Of course not. Toshiró was thorough in everything he did, whether in love or hate.

Theta entered with a respectful bow and set down another box of books next to the shelves. He had chosen the titles especially for Clara. *The Botany of Death. The Abolition of Mortality. Back from the Land of No Return. On the Road with Ghosts…* Few mortals believed in the usefulness of death. Who could blame them?

"Miss Pencrest sends word that the guest you are expecting has arrived at her establishment."

"Good, then bring my son to me."

He was officially calling Will that now, but only when he talked about him to his servants. Where were the cigarettes? Spieler pulled one out of the silver case that was a gift from Rosamund, but even the tobacco laced with pixie dust didn't change the tension he felt. Unbelievable. He actually wanted to please his son. *Don't make a fool of yourself, Spieler. You're about to steal his girlfriend away.* He usually paid no attention to the children he fathered. After all, immortality made offspring completely superfluous. But with this son it had always been different, even if Will had never known how present his real father had been in his life. Yes. It had to be because he looked so much like Rosamund.

He didn't return Spieler's smile as the golem led him into the library. The jade still hadn't shown itself, but Spieler had

224

given instructions to stop using the herb that weakened the Fairy spell.

He really is a lot like you, Rosamund. Her son and his. At home in two worlds, even if his blood was mostly from this one. Had that killed his mother, too? That she had never known that part of her was at home behind the mirrors, and perhaps that was why she had often felt so alien on the other side? Oh, Rosamund, poor, lost Rosamund...

"Sixteen is almost cured. You see, I keep my promises."

"Yes, she is better. Thank you." He still did not look at him but eyed the books. He was ashamed of being grateful to him. Just as he was ashamed of cheating on Clara and coveting Sixteen. Spieler's son wanted to be noble and good, unselfish, a protector of those he loved or admired. Had he ever been like that himself? No. Will must have gotten all that from his mother. Like her, and unlike his half-brother, he took everything very seriously. But he had betrayed his noble ideals by falling in love with the wrong girl and killing the Fairy. That's how it always started. You had to get them to betray their values, and then you could seduce them into just about anything. *I'll show you who you are.* Hadn't he promised him that when they first met? Another promise he would keep.

There. His gaze lingered on the shrouded mirror. *Go ahead, pull down the velvet.* He was such a good boy. His brother would have peeked under the cloth long ago. No, Spieler didn't want to think about him now. It was enough that he kept thinking about the vixen and the child she was carrying. He'd sent out a few of his Mirrorlings and instructed the gingerbread baker to forget about the Fairy spell and just find Celeste Auger. He could live with the itchy skin

225

for a while, and he would probably only find Toshiró with the help of the others. There were a few powerful spells they could cast together. But the vixen's daughter would only be dangerous to him. Why hadn't Giovanna found her yet? Toshiró must have given her some kind of Elf spell that made her invisible. But fortunately, such spells wore off quickly.

"Why did you tell Clara that Sixteen is a Fairy?"

Now he actually looked at him. What an interesting mixture of distrust and desire to trust emanated from that gaze.

"To protect Sixteen, of course. Mortals don't like to hear that life can be created at all. They instantly worry that you're trying to compete with their god. And you have to admit that the lie is harmless."

No, he would never admit that. His son didn't believe in lies, but Spieler would teach him how necessary they were.

"You're never going to let Sixteen go, are you? You consider her your possession."

"Well, I made her. Maybe you could argue that's why she's mine? But if you want her, she's yours! You have done me a great favor. I'll be in your debt for all time, and the gift I want to give you today will just be a token of my gratitude."

Oh, how they battled on Will's face — curiosity and vigilance, suspicion and the desire to make peace with himself and Spieler.

Spieler nodded to the golem waiting beside the door. He was one of the new specimens Fabbro had created from the clay of this world. He seemed to make them uglier and uglier on purpose. The silver fruit the golem handed Will was the perfect image of an apple.

"Open it." Spieler nodded at him encouragingly.

He knew the reluctance on Will's face. He had seen it many times on Rosamund, and like her, their son eventually could not resist.

"I gave this mirror the shape of an apple because everything it shows has to do with seduction. I love your story about how sin entered the world."

Will stared into the mirror the apple contained.

"The bed you see is in a brothel I recently purchased, and the man who toils there broke your mother's heart and left her alone with you and your brother."

Pearl Ann Pencrest, the woman who gave herself to John Reckless on the red sheets, was the most talented whore in Spieler's employ. Brothels, in any world, were a very rich source of information that brought power and influence. If Pearl was to be believed, John Reckless was as much an impostor as a lover as he was in his professional life.

"He told your mother that he was going on a business trip while he was using her money to keep his whores out in this world. Do you know that for a while he posed as the famous inventor Isambard Brunel?" The disgust in Spieler's voice was not feigned. He had actually intended to punish his rival for all the pain he had caused Rosamund, not to speak of the agonies of jealousy he owed him personally. But why not leave this satisfaction to his youngest son?

"Where is he?"

Will flipped the apple shut as if he could lock away the pictures it had shown him and held it out to Spieler.

"Keep it. It will teach you a lot about the deceivability of people, even if it will show you some things you don't want to know."

Will hesitated but finally slipped the apple into his jacket pocket. Spieler had had clothes tailored for him, such as befitted the son of an immortal. He had put them on reluctantly, so the golems had told him. His brother paid much more attention to his appearance. Jacob Reckless was always well dressed, even when dusty and bruised from a treasure hunt. He was, without a doubt, John Reckless's son.

"Here. I wrote the address of his hotel on the back for you." He handed him one of his business cards. They had come in handy with his brother, but the magic had proven very unreliable in this world. "He's in Charlestown. That's barely an hour from here."

Will eyed the address. Was he seriously trying to convince himself that he had no desire to get revenge on his father?

They had to be given time to succumb to the temptation. They had to do it all by themselves.

Spieler stepped to the box of books the golem had brought. Of course. They kept mixing up the titles. One of the books most certainly did not belong on an open shelf but in one of his well-locked bookcases. The cover was studded with silver, and its contents turned mortals into magic tongues that could bring printed words to life. Letterman envied him this magic. Spielers had long used books like this to travel to other worlds, but they were all too unpredictable because they liked to take on a life of their own. Mirrors were much less complicated.

Will was still staring at the card.

He actually felt a tinge of tenderness when he looked at him. Could he have bequeathed him his immortality? Immortality coupled with the jade skin... If he handled it right, he could make a god out of him. Just like Apaullo had done with the young Greek back in the day. No, that made them too powerful. It was better if Rosamund's youngest didn't really suspect how unique he was. Had the Dark Fairy ever realized that the boy she had given a jade skin was his son?

"How long will he be at the hotel?" He slid the card into the pocket that already contained the apple. Spieler had finding and protection spells woven into all of Will's clothes.

"All week. He's been meeting with weapons manufacturers, selling them your world's inventions. My coachman has instructions to drive you to Charlestown at any time. If that's what you want."

They had to do it all by themselves.

"What if the jade comes?"

Was he actually asking him for advice? Spieler was surprised at how much this touched him.

Rosamund's son…

Should he show him the mirror he used to keep her alive? No, it was too soon. He had wanted to name him Guillaume, the French variant of William. Interestingly, the name had a meaning: determined protector… Was that his destiny? Would he one day be as devoted to him as to the king he had once served? An appealing thought. Even if it would certainly not be easy to turn him against his brother. Or to get him to kill his brother's child. What a challenge.

"Don't worry. The jade will come," he said. "And you will finally punish John Reckless for what he did to your mother."

They had to be given what they had secretly longed for. And in this case, Spieler granted a wish that was also his own.

Will had the coachman drive him to Charlestown that very evening.

And Spieler put a book of love poems in Clara's room. He had written a few of them himself. He had achieved some fame in the field, under a mortal name, of course. Spieler always found it amusing to rhyme hurt with heart, even though he didn't have one. Even Letterman had some of Spieler's books in his collection. Without suspecting who the author was. One day he would tell him. It would be a somewhat trickier task to reveal to Clara that he was her former lover's father. But there was time for that, too. An opportunity would present itself. He had eternity at his disposal, and yes, one day, he would make her immortal, even though Krieger had warned her against it.

When he had the golems serve him dinner in the evening, they also brought him a black feather. The gingerbread baker had picked up the vixen's trail. There it was. Everything would fall into place — even if Rosamund's eldest had run away from him. The vixen would be dead before Jacob found her, and Rosamund's eldest would never know that he had paid his debt to him and had almost become a father. His daughter would not even be saved by the fact that she was Rosamund's grandchild.

32

SHADOW

For three days, Fox kept her promise not to leave the hotel. But when the fourth idle day dawned, and Orlando still hadn't been able to come up with anything, she decided to search Jahoon's famous street markets for a magical thing Albert Chanute had told her about years ago.

It was an amulet called the Eye of Love. If you wore it around your neck, you always knew where the person you loved most was. Of course, it was doubtful that such a precious magic thing was among all the cheap trinkets on sale in the street bazaars. But she and Jacob had already found other powerful spells in the dusty stalls of ignorant merchants, and the prospect of spending a few hours searching for the Eye of Love was far more enticing than another idle day in the hotel garden.

Hideo only got her men's clothes after she swore to him a dozen times on her fox coat that she would stay close to his side. Hideo couldn't hide the fact that he was looking forward to showing her all the wonders he had discovered during his solitary wanderings through Jahoon. He enjoyed the trip, despite the worry that Spieler would find her, and fortunately, the street vendors had a hard time talking him into anything. Hideo handled all the silver in his pockets like Fox did, as if it were just a loan, a charm that could disappear as quickly as it had come to him.

The alleys were already brimming with the heat of the day as they began their foray. Fox's clothes were soon sticking to her body. Still, the beauty of the old city more than made up for the hot air in the narrow streets, and Hideo already knew his way around the labyrinth of Jahoon's old town surprisingly well. He even swapped words with the merchants in their language.

Fox still hadn't dared to ask him about the profession he had pursued before. The Holy Wrestlers of Nihon. Orlando had told her a little about them: that only boys whose father and mother were from Nihon were accepted, that they were chosen at a very young age, and that it was considered a great honor even if the parents rarely saw their sons again. 'Why holy?' Fox had asked. 'Every match these wrestlers face symbolizes the fight against evil,' Orlando had replied. 'The evil in the world and in ourselves. The wrestlers weaken evil by defeating it, again and again, helping good to triumph one day.' That didn't sound like a guild one left lightly. But since Hideo, even though Orlando had recognized him, would not speak of the reasons that had caused him to abandon this sacred trade, Fox tamed her curiosity. She knew all too well how important it was to leave one's past behind sometimes.

She and Jacob had often thought about traveling to Parsia. Few countries offered more wondrous tales, and the trade in magical objects was not forbidden here. The stalls she passed with Hideo advertised magic lamps and flying carpets, amulets that protected against enemies or brought true love, slippers that brought good luck and wealth when worn, turbans that made one invisible, and spoons that granted immortality when one ate from them.

"If his spoons really do make you immortal," Fox whispered to Hideo as the merchant eloquently praised his wares, "then why does he only want a few silver coins for them?"

Hideo nodded in agreement, but he was looking around so longingly among all the merchandise that Fox was glad when she spotted the blossoms of real memory roses at the next stall. She bought one for herself and one for Hideo. The scent of the almost black flowers for a few seconds restored the most profound feeling of happiness one had encountered in one's life. Fox was surprised at the memory the rose brought back to her. It returned her to her father's grave, to the cold winter evening when she had visited it for the first time with Jacob. And for a few precious moments, the blossom once again made her feel the happiness that had been knowing him by her side in a place where she had so often felt alone and abandoned.

What happiness did the scent of the black rose bring back to Hideo? He stood there as if his heart had run away from his body, staring with tear-veiled eyes into the throng of people surrounding them. Then he smiled gratefully at Fox—for the flower and perhaps for not asking where the happiness on his face came from nor why, as the effect of the fragrance faded, it turned to sadness.

With his strange clothes and bulky body, Hideo drew stares at every booth, while no one seemed to notice that the young man at his side was a woman.

"Kitsune!" he whispered to Fox at the table of a merchant who was trying to sell them an oil lamp as Aladdin's magic lantern. "I'm drawing too much attention to us. I'm putting you in danger instead of protecting you. Let's go back to the hotel!"

But Fox still hoped to discover the Eye of Love among all the amulets that promised wealth and happiness, protection from illness or even death. Spieler seemed so far away, and that morning in Jahoon's alleys, the knowledge that she was carrying Jacob's child just made her happy. No. Spieler would search for the yarn and Toshiró. And she had to find Jacob. That was all that mattered.

"Stop worrying!" she murmured to Hideo as she stopped in front of the stall of a spice merchant whose nutmegs supposedly caused golden hair to sprout. "As long as they stare at you, I'm invisible. What better way to protect me?"

How tempting it was to feel safe. Who wanted to worry all the time? And Jahoon had so many alleys and markets full of never-before-seen wonders. She and Hideo lost themselves more with each passing hour in all the smells and colors, all the beauty and carefree bustle that carried them along with a thousand voices and bodies.

They were in the oldest square in town and already very far from their hotel when Fox suddenly smelled cinnamon. She thought nothing more of it. The air of Jahoon was spiced with many scents. Even when a crow perched on the archway behind the stall, she remained blind. All she saw were the amulets one of the merchants held out to her. The Eye of Love? Surely he had that! The amulets in his hand were all shaped like eyes, and some actually resembled the description Chanute had given her.

It was Hideo who noticed the crow's eyes.

"Kitsune!" he whispered to Fox. "Look! It has the eyes of an old woman, and it is watching you."

But the crow had already soared into the pristine blue sky and was circling overhead, casting a shadow that grew with each flap of her wings. Fox was still staring up at her as the vines snaked around her legs, prickly and black-leaved. Trees sprouted everywhere from the old pavement, thorny bushes shot out from between the market stalls, branches clawing like hands into clothes and human flesh. Spieler had found them.

The people crowding the market began to scream and drag their children away from the dark thicket that swallowed everything. But the children tried to free themselves from the arms of their mothers and fathers. A thousand waxy flowers opened among the leaves, the vines sprouted silver petals, and the scent of cinnamon and baked cake stunned even Fox's senses.

Hideo immediately embraced three children and dragged them back. Fox stumbled after a girl who had broken away from her sobbing mother. She caught up with her just as the shadow of an old woman appeared among the trees. Fox reached for the small hand, but the girl tried to break away, and Fox desperately pushed back the tendrils that were closing in on the slender body. She felt dizzy from the flowery scent. Cinnamon. The vines smelled like cinnamon, and Fox felt hands, lean and bony, grabbing her from behind.

"Vixen, oh, vixen!" a hoarse voice whispered to her. "The Elf wants only your child. Come with me, and I'll let the others go."

Fox jabbed her elbow at the bony body behind her as she tried to hold the girl.

"Kitsune!" Hideo emerged from the thicket and leaped protectively to her side.

The gingerbread baker had disappeared, but the child was nowhere to be seen either until Fox spotted her dark hair among the leaves. People were screaming all around them, the sky had disappeared under black leaves, and as she and Hideo tried to free the girl, the crow swooped down on them from the dark trees. Hideo jerked his arm up as it pecked at his eyes, and suddenly a sea-green mouth, scaled like the neck that followed it, shot out of his sleeve. The mouth bared golden teeth, and a dragon, barely larger than a bird at first, grew until it split the witch's forest with mighty wings and soared into the sky that was once again visible. The crow managed to escape the dragon's teeth, but her forest began to wither as if she had forgotten it, and Fox finally succeeded in freeing the child. She pushed her towards her mother, who was wandering among the trees, screaming her name. *Take them away!* Fox wanted to cry. *Take them all far away from me!* She still heard the voice of the gingerbread baker. *Vixen, oh, vixen! The Elf only wants your child. Come with me, and I'll let the others go.*

High above her, the crow drew its circles, and the trees once again stretched their withering branches and clawed at the dragon's scales.

"Karasu!" shouted Hideo. "Kanojo o mitsukemasu!"

An orange-red paw stretched out from Hideo's torn smock, and from between the flowers on his exposed chest sprang a lion. He grew like the dragon, gobbling up the sinister thicket as the dragon broke free from the branches above them, spewing golden fire into the dark trees. The cry the crow uttered as the sparks set its feathers ablaze was that of a woman, and it was the gingerbread baker who plunged from the sky, spreading her emaciated limbs as if they could stop her fall. But she hit the pavement and, like everything she had brought with her, became dirty smoke; the dragon sent its fire after the dark plumes as the wind carried them away.

Hideo's clothes hung in tatters around his body, and the lion, by now so large that its red mane brushed the roofs of the surrounding houses, prowled among the overturned stalls while the dragon, folding its massive wings, landed in the center of the square.

"Nigero!" shouted Hideo to the men, women, and children ducking among the broken tables. "Nigero!"

He seemed to have forgotten that he was no longer in Nihon, but the terrified residents of Jahoon understood. They stumbled to their feet and fled into the surrounding alleys.

"Yamete!" Hideo's voice was firm, but his hand trembled as he pointed first at the lion and then at the dragon. "Yamete!"

Whatever he had said, the dragon began to fade like ink running on wet paper. The lion, too, dissolved until there were merely a few orange-red blossoms on the stones where it had stood. And then... there was silence among the ancient walls of Jahoon.

Hideo pulled his tattered clothes over his tattooed skin as best he could. He looked down at himself as if he had turned into a stranger, and Fox saw on his face the same fear that the darkness of the crow had left in her heart. The world still smelled of cinnamon.

"Wakarimasen, Kitsune. I don't understand. I don't understand what happened."

Fox hugged Hideo as tightly as one hugs one's savior. She saw blossoms through the tears of his smock, scales, foaming waves.

"She would have taken me with her, Hideo!" she said, "You saved me. You saved everyone, and I put them all in danger. We have to get away from here. As fast as we can."

33

HIDEO'S PICTURES

It was a long walk back to their hotel. But the alleys were deserted as if all the residents of Jahoon had heard the screams.

Fox asked Hideo to lock himself in his room while she let Orlando know through a messenger that she urgently needed to speak to him. There would soon be a thousand rumors about what had happened, and not everyone would see Hideo as a savior. What if they condemned him as a pagan sorcerer and cut off his innocent head? And how were they going to shake off the gingerbread baker? They had to leave Jahoon, that much was certain. Fox was convinced the witch was not dead. Spieler would give her a new body. Maybe she could even do it herself.

But one memory erased all others when she looked back on what had happened: that of the girl's tiny hand and the fear she had felt for the child. If Fox had still doubted that

239

she was pregnant before — what she had felt in those seconds had made the child she was carrying an oppressive reality.

Vixen, oh, vixen! The Elf only wants your child. Come with me, and I'll let the others go.

Hideo was wearing fresh clothes when she knocked on his door, but bloody scratches ran across his face and neck. He had assured her countless times on the way back that the images on his skin had never awakened before. Why had it happened now?

His room was furnished lavishly like hers, with a canopy over the bed and a divan whose legs were shaped like lion's paws. They were mouse paws compared to the paws of the fire-maned lion that had leaped from Hideo's chest.

"Orlando will get us out of the city."

Hideo just nodded.

"Have the images on your skin stirred since we got back?"

He shook his head.

"Do you have any idea what woke them?"

He shook his head again and stroked the sleeve from which the dragon had slipped. Fox reached out and ran her hand over the mark Toshiró had left there. "What does it mean?"

"Hogo-sha — protector. Do you think that is what made them come to life?" He looked at her in alarm.

"Possibly. It could be the help you asked Toshiró for."

Hideo didn't seem sure what to make of such help. What did it feel like to have one's own skin come to life? Fox saw it on Hideo's face. It scared him.

Who else was there on his skin? Fox didn't dare ask, worried about embarrassing him. But Hideo read the question off her face.

"I can show them to you, Kitsune. And explain to you who they are?"

Fox was so glad he finally used the more familiar 'you'.

He disappeared behind the screen, which was embroidered with landscapes that reminded Fox very much of Hideo's islands. When he emerged again, he looked as if the illustration Orlando had shown Fox of the Holy Wrestlers of Nihon had come to life. Hideo wore merely the white apron around his loins in which they fought their matches. But he still seemed clothed. Every inch of his body was covered with tattoos, except for his neck, face, hands, and feet. Fox saw faces among waves and flowers, writhing snakes, snarling dragons, and the red-maned lion again ducking on his chest among white flowers.

"This is the dragon that watches with a thousand eyes." Hideo's unpictured hand pointed to a dragon whose blue-green body wrapped around his left leg. "I admit, I'm glad he didn't wake up. The same goes for her," he raised his left arm, "the serpent of Toyotama-hime, the Jewel Princess."

The snake that uncoiled a seemingly endless body on his arm had pale blue scales.

"This one," Hideo pointed to his chest, "you met today. He is one of the divine guardian lions of Zhonggua. And this," he stroked his right arm, where the sea-green dragon that had pursued the crow spread its wings between golden flaming flowers, "is the dragon that serves Yama no Kami, the goddess of the forest worshipped in Nihon."

Hideo smiled at Fox as if looking forward to who he would show her next.

"Last but not least," he said, turning so she could see his back, "let me introduce you to the great hero Kintarō, the

241

Golden Child, as we also call him, and his mount, the Black Koi."

A huge fish leaped through a waterfall on Hideo's back, carrying a boy as a rider, who had his arms stretched out exuberantly. Thousands of pinpricks had imprinted all this on his skin. Hideo wore clothes made of pain, but they were beautiful.

"These are powerful protectors," Fox said. "What enemies were they supposed to save you from before they had to save me?"

Hideo had stepped behind the screen.

"The world is cruel, don't you think, Kitsune?" Fox heard him reply. His images had once again disappeared under his loose clothes as he stepped out from behind the embroidered fabric.

Yes. Yes, that it was. So beautiful and so cruel.

"We all need protection from it," Hideo said. "You have the fur. I have my pictures."

And Toshiró had brought them to life. If the forest goddess dragon had caught the crow — she could have told her where Jacob was. *Stop it, Fox!* she heard him say. *It is you who is in danger, you and our child. Get yourself to safety!* But she had to keep looking for him. Her daughter would not grow up without a father like her.

"I am very grateful that your images will protect me too from now on, Hideo," she said. "No spell could have given me a better helper."

He bowed his head. "My images are as honored as I am to protect you, Kitsune."

"I think I know which one is dearest to you," Fox said. "Kintarō."

Hideo looked over his shoulder with a smile. "Oh yes. When I was a child, I imagined being like him. It was because of him that I started wrestling. I got him tattooed on my back so I can hear him laugh when I'm sad—and he warns me when someone attacks me from behind."

"Maybe someday I'll run into him," Fox said. "Although I suppose I'd better not wish it, because it would mean we're in great danger."

Hideo frowned. "No. I hope you won't run into Kintarō or any of the others again, Kitsune," he said.

But Fox could tell by looking at him that he thought that was as unlikely as she did.

34

Brother's Debt

When Jacob came to, he wasn't sure at first if some fever dream was fooling him into believing what he was seeing. Glassy lizard eyes, frozen in death, gazed down at him from heads that hung from scaly necks from a ceiling of black stone. The spikes that studded the long necks evoked hazy memories. Of what?

Goyl.

His hands immediately wanted to go to his belt, but the instant pain made it unmistakably clear that they were tied tightly behind his back. Ah, it was one of those awakenings he'd experienced decidedly too often in his life: in a place he had no idea how he had gotten to and in shackles that portended a very awkward predicament. But at least the dead lizards gave away who had captured him. Their spines usually adorned Goyl helmets. The Bastard had sold him out. What else had he expected?

Damn, damn, damn!

If only he hadn't been so angry with himself! He had trotted after Nerron like a lamb after its butcher!

The door opened as if the Bastard had heard him swear. The Goyl stepped toward him with a smile that must have tasted like honey to his lipless mouth. Malachite-mottled son of a bitch!

"Is the joy on your ugly face just about me, or are you going to sell my brother next?" *My brother.* Yes, Will was still his brother. To hell with Spieler! After all, they had the same mother.

"I hope you at least negotiated a good price?"

Jacob did manage to sit up. Which only made the situation marginally less humiliating.

"A good price?" The Bastard pulled the cork out of one of the stone jugs and sniffed the wide neck. "What do you think your going rate is? We're in a guard station that supplies the troops moving west. All you can squeeze out of a snail-skinned treasure hunter in this place is a few jugs of booze."

Jacob closed his eyes to avoid looking at his smug onyx face.

"The Dwarf who still has people looking for you... what was his name?" The triumph in the croaky voice was no less difficult to bear. "Valiant. That's right. He's got a very handsome reward out for you, but it must be collected in Terpevas, and I get claustrophobic in Dwarf towns because of the idiotically narrow streets."

Jacob never thought he would one day wish to be Evenaugh Valiant's prisoner, but the dwarf would at least have been trumpeting all over the place that he had caught Jacob, and Fox would have learned where he was. Now he would probably rot unsung in some Goyl pit, and he would never know if she was all right either.

A Goyl soldier appeared behind the Bastard in the open doorway. He wore none of the precious stones on his uniform collar by which one could tell the rank of their officers, only the granite gray uniform in which Will had protected their king. His skin resembled topaz. There was a dead Goyl with the same skin as an exhibit in the Chambers of Miracles of the Austryn emperors—if Kami'en had not had it removed. The ancestors of the princess he had married had been very proud of their collection of dead Goyl in all colors.

"I talked to one of the officers." The soldier nodded in Jacob's direction. "The next transport can take him. The train leaves tomorrow morning."

Damn them all, even if his brother was one of them by now. He could have saved himself a lot of trouble if he had realized earlier how much Will liked the jade skin. How did Spieler like it that his son turned into a Goyl when he was angry? Was this another surprise the Dark Fairy had left the Elf, like the itch in his skin? What did it all matter anymore? All he wanted to know was where Fox was.

"How long does the train take to get to Vena?" The Bastard took a sip from the jug he held in his hand.

"Three days." The topaz Goyl clenched his fist over his heart, proof that he had great respect for the Bastard despite his grained onyx skin. Then he left them alone. The respect was certainly not for his treasure hunting skills but for the fact that he was Kami'en's spy. Or that he had caught them a silly snail skin.

Vena.

So the Bastard was still going to Kami'en.

"Yes, our destination hasn't changed." He winked at him. "But I lied about the reason for our visit. You're going to pay off your brother's debt. Oh, half-brother. Not that that changes anything. Brother is brother."

The Bastard took another sip. "Kami'en wants the Pup executed. I was an idiot not to foresee that. I really believed he had written off the Dark Fairy when she left him. But Kami'en needs the Jade Goyl, or those damned Elves will silver us all or make golems out of us. So I'll bring Kami'en his brother. I'm sure you won't know anything about ancient Goyl laws. According to our customs, you can pay with your life for your little brother's. Isn't that convenient?"

Very convenient. And hadn't he had plenty of practice paying for Will's skin with his own by now? How had he thought those days were over?

"Do you still believe, in all seriousness, in the fairy tale that the Jade Goyl makes Kami'en invincible?"

"Don't pretend! We both believe in fairy tales. It's our profession. Here!" The Bastard held the jug to Jacob's lips. "Drink. It's going to be a long train ride, and I hear the food in Goyl cells isn't the best."

He poured the liquor on the floor as Jacob turned his head away. "Do you know how long it took me to drag you here? You'd be dead by now without me! Just look at it this way, I've managed to squeeze out a few extra days of life for you."

He rammed the cork into the jug and placed it between the others. "They're going to load you into one of the wagons that are taking supplies to Vena for Kami'en's troops. I'll travel a little more comfortably in the officers' carriage." He headed for the door. "The guards here were very impressed with my Royal Jade Seal. Hentzau took the original from me when I didn't bring him the crossbow, but I had two duplicates made as a precaution. If you wonder where all the useful things are that you collected in the Elf's palace — I took them. After all, they will be of no use to you when you are dead. Jacob Reckless gives his life for his brother's. That will make you even more of a legend. I could almost be jealous."

And with those words, he pulled the door shut behind him, leaving Jacob alone with the dead lizards. The Bastard probably enjoyed imagining how their empty eyes prepared Jacob for the fate he had in store for him.

35

NEVER

When Elf dust was dissolved in hot water at a ratio of 1:10 and a pinch of moonroot powder was added, the brew reliably drove away the most severe pain. However, it was addictive after only five days. The gardener who had taught Clara this and much more since her arrival at Spieler's plantation called himself Never. 'I christened myself that,' he had replied with an expressionless face. 'The name protects me from illusions and sums up the essence of my existence quite accurately.'

Clara had not dared to ask what exactly was the essence of his existence. There were no slaves on Spieler's plantation, but his servants and gardeners behaved almost as submissively. And then there were Sixteen and a few others who seemed as perfect as if they were a species all of their own.

Never supervised the twenty greenhouses that were on the plantation. Some were larger than the house Clara had grown up in, and many housed plants not only from this world but also from hers. There were many medicinal plants among them, but most, Never explained to her, Spieler grew for their magical properties.

Clara spent most of her days in the greenhouses. Only there could she be sure she wouldn't stumble into Will and Sixteen and catch them in a passionate kiss. Sixteen did everything she could to make sure Clara caught them kissing as often as possible. Yes, Clara was sure that was her plan. The thought alone filled her with such burning jealousy that she didn't recognize herself. She felt so foolish — all the longing she had had for Will! How naively she had believed in their love. Yet she had lost him to the jade so long ago. But no, she hadn't wanted to see it. All those months, they had lived together in the apartment where he had grown up with Jacob. Clara had felt that Will was still behind the mirrors, and yet she had dreamed of a future together, of marriage and children...

She was grateful that the place Spieler had brought her to was once again very different from the places where her old life had played out, even if the continent was the same as the one she called home in the other world. The same and yet so different — like everything beyond the mirrors.

The air was hot and humid even in the morning, and there were moments when she felt like a caterpillar, intoxicated by camellias and night jasmine, spinning a cocoon in which a new Clara was maturing. Spieler often took her on excursions into the surrounding countryside. The carriage he had brought around was beautiful like the one

Cinderella had taken to the ball, with its matte silver body, black top, and two moon-white horses. The next town, with its wooden porches and tree-shaded streets, also looked as if one were walking through a storybook. Still, the soldiers they encountered everywhere disturbed the idyll. Clara felt sick with indignation every time she saw women in velvet and silk with black slaves carrying the groceries after them. 'Yes, it is absurdly barbaric!' Spieler had replied when she had asked him how he lived with these conditions. 'There are better ways to have devoted servants. An old acquaintance of mine sometimes has the fun of offering himself for sale at slave markets. Usually, he turns his buyers into hyenas. Apaullo can be quite amusing. Quite the opposite of Krieger.'

He often said such puzzling things, but Clara never got to ask for explanations because Spieler had long since moved on to the next and invariably more interesting topic. By now, she was so used to his company, his laughter and the endless conversations that made all her heartache seem almost unreal. However, since he had hurt his hand, she saw shadows in his handsome face that she had not seen there before. 'It's nothing. I got too close to a young alligator. There are all too many in the ponds behind the house.' Then he had smiled at her and shown her a plant in one of the greenhouses that cured blindness.

'What about an herb that brings back betrayed love?' she had wanted to ask. But her pride forbade her to ask the question, and she didn't want Will's love back if she had to bewitch him to get it. At night, while the camellias outside glowed ghostly in the moonlight and a thousand cicadas filled the darkness with their courtship, she dreamed of Sixteen caressing Will with her white hands. When she asked Never

251

for an herb that would give her dreamless nights, he brought her a handful of fuzzy leaves, as silvery-green as if they had frost clinging to them.

"Snow in summer—the name is very appropriate, isn't it?" He slipped the leaves into a pouch and handed it to her. "Keep them in a cool place and drink the brew only every other night. Even the most medicinal herb can become a poison."

Yes, she had learned that herself in the other world.

"Do you also grow the plants that the witches have in their gardens?"

"Which witches? The dark ones or the light ones?" Never asked back.

"Oh, no. The light ones. Of course."

"Of course." Never looked at her thoughtfully. "We grow them both."

Clara glanced at the carefully tended planter boxes—and remembered overgrown beds behind an abandoned house. "I was in a gingerbread witch's garden once. We were looking for a medicine for the stone flesh. But I hear even the child-eaters can't cure it."

"No." Never shooed away a moth that was settling on one of the planter boxes. "But the gingerbread bakers aren't interested in healing anyway. They kill plants and animals with no gratitude, let alone reverence for what they give them. They brew juices that give them power over others or prolong their life and youth, potions that seduce and intoxicate the senses until the mind is lost in darkness, bringing bloodlust and madness. They have become so lost in their own darkness that they see nothing but darkness in everything."

"Why do they lure the children into their homes?" Clara had always had to ask about the things she was afraid of.

"To kill the compassion in their hearts. Compassion can be very troublesome. It can get in the way of knowledge and power. It makes it hard to cut open the belly of a live toad to find out the secret of its poison. One does not lightly brew a juice that kills unloved neighbors just because it sells well or indulge in the heart of an unborn calf. With the first child that a gingerbread baker kills, she exorcises pity for all time. But she pays a heavy price for it."

Clara thought she smelled the cinnamon on the door through which she had stepped with Will to spend the night in the abandoned house of a witch. While Jacob had protected them from other horrors.

"What price?"

Clara, she thought she heard her mother sigh. *Why can't you stop asking? You can't tell children everything.* But how could they be safe from the dark witches if they didn't know about them?

"An insatiable hunger. It consumes them from the day they kill the first child." Never plucked a withered leaf from a young plant that had opened its first blossom. "It steals their sleep and pursues them by day and by night until they consist only of this hunger. But as often as they murder to satisfy it, it only grows larger and larger until it devours all they once were and finally kills them."

"Your master has promised the gingerbread baker who serves him that he will rid her of her hunger." Sixteen stood among the planter boxes. She always appeared as if from nowhere.

"That would be a foolhardy promise." Never eyed Sixteen with undisguised distaste. "You're actually almost as flawless as you used to be. I'm still surprised he bothered to heal you."

Spieler's servants and gardeners loathed Sixteen and others of her ilk, as Clara had been quick to notice.

"Perhaps he prefers us to you and your kind after all." Sixteen smiled. Her smile could cut and sting as if it were of silver. The face she wore was so beautiful that Clara instantly felt as colorless as a meadow weed next to a camellia blossom. She owed it to Spieler's attention that she hadn't wilted with jealousy. The flowers he had put in her room said he thought she was beautiful, too. His smile assured her every day how much he liked her. Only he gave her solid ground under her feet in all the pain of love that Sixteen caused her.

She looked at her as if studying the face she had once worn. "Will's gone."

Gone? What did she mean by that? Gone where?

Never walked wordlessly over to the two gardeners planting young seedlings at the far end of the greenhouse.

"Our lord told him where to find his father."

Our lord. She always called Spieler that. Who was she? What was she? Another question she wanted to ask Spieler, but she was worried that it would sound too much like jealousy.

Our Lord told him where to find his father. How many times had she listened to Will when he had imagined taking his father to task for the pain he had caused his mother.

"My lord is very quick to find out from your kind what your most secret desires are."

How Sixteen's smile mocked her. For what? For still loving Will? Or for liking Spieler?

"Then he knows mine, too?"

"Of course." The scorn was unveiled. Mockery. Contempt... and jealousy. Of what?

254

"You want to be able to cure death."

Clara felt as if Sixteen had reached into her chest and read her heart like a book.

"He'll show you. Who knows? He might even make you immortal."

If he offers to make you immortal, say no.

Krieger had been joking. Of course. And Sixteen was playing with her. Like a cat with a mouse.

But Clara! whispered Spieler's smile. *She is the mouse. Don't let her make you the cat. You are a flower. A flower that can heal the pain of the world.*

She heard the words as clearly as if he were standing behind her. She even looked around involuntarily, but all she saw were the camellia bushes surrounding the greenhouse.

"Why are you still here?" Sixteen glanced over at the gardeners as if she had asked something forbidden. "Why don't you go back? To your old world. You don't belong here. He made you fall in love with him! But it's not real."

Never turned and looked over at them. When Sixteen noticed his gaze, she backed away from Clara.

"Made to fall in love? Him? Are you talking about Spieler?"

"Who else? But I don't call him that. He would shatter me if I did. Into splinters so small that there'd be nothing left of me."

Clara thought she felt her heart fill with darkness. "What do you call him?"

"Creator. Those," Sixteen pointed to the servants, "me, the golems in the house, he made us all. We belong to him. That's why I had to stay when Will left. He won't let me go."

Creator, golems… She was trying to scare her. Nothing

255

more. Maybe she should finally ask Spieler what kind of creature Sixteen was.

"What if I ask Spieler to let you go? With…" Her tongue wouldn't say it. *With Will. Say it. It feels good to have him gone, doesn't it, Clara?* She didn't want to see either of them again. Ever again.

"You would do that? Why?" Sixteen eyed her as if she feared a trap. But at the same time, hope spread across her beautiful face, as helpless as that of a young child. "He'd know right away that I was talking to you." So much fear.

Clara wanted to ask where Sixteen's fear came from, but her heart didn't want to hear the answer. Spieler was so good to her. So wise, so gentle, so endlessly patient, even when he saw her jealousy of Sixteen—and that she couldn't forget Will, even though the very thought of the jade made her shudder. Spieler was like a beautifully bound book that held the answers to every question she'd ever asked.

"He'll never let me go. And Will will come back. My maker has beguiled you both." Sixteen looked back at Never with renewed concern. He was also still looking over at them. Sixteen backed away from Clara and turned. Her fingers left a trail of silver as she stroked the young plants she passed.

Never stepped up to the planter boxes and plucked the metallic leaves from the stems when she was gone. Then he approached Clara and placed them in her hand.

"It would be interesting to find out what properties a brew of these leaves has. Perhaps it turns the heart and all the pain it so easily causes into silver."

The leaves cut Clara's skin as she closed her fingers around them.

"In what hothouse do the light witches' plants grow?"
Perhaps there was an herb there that cast out jealousy—light
against the darkness.

Never pointed to one of the greenhouses at the back.

"The one behind that houses the plants of the dark
witches."

Clara shook her head.

"I'm a healer, Never. That's all I care about."

"Good," Never replied. "As long as you only want to heal
what can be healed."

36

EAVESDROPPERS IN THE DESERT

It was on the fourth morning after their hasty departure from Jahoon that the ruins appeared on the horizon: crumbled towers, mighty gates, walls that stretched endlessly across the desert... Orlando smiled when he saw Fox's look of disbelief. The ruins of Arshan... Jacob always carried a newspaper illustration showing the ruined city. There wasn't a treasure hunter who didn't dream of one day searching for the lost spells of Arshan.

'Do you mind if we take a short detour into the desert along the way?' That was all Orlando had said after smuggling her and Hideo out of Jahoon in a caravan. His contacts had been unable to find out anything about Jacob's whereabouts. So the only hope left was to find the Elf who had given his name to a town in the mountains of Tyrol. And since the ship Fox intended to take didn't leave for a few days, Orlando had suggested the detour. 'There is someone who might be able to help, even if he gathers news in a somewhat more unorthodox way than my scouts.' He had left unsaid that this mysterious someone lived in one of the most legendary places in their world. Yes, he loved his mysteries.

More than three millennia ago, Arshan had been one of the most influential cities beyond the mirrors, with granite and sandstone palaces, artificial lakes, blossoming gardens, and a wealth that had eventually led to the city's downfall. The inhabitants had been sold into slavery, and the conquerors who had come from the south had even chipped the mosaics off the facades for which the city had been so famous. Still, it was said that the real treasures of Arshan were still hiding under the desert sands, though countless treasure hunters had searched in vain for the gate that rained gold, the stone that gave eternal youth, or the chest that never emptied. Fox had suggested a few times that they try their luck in the famous ruins as well. However, there had always been other treasures they were looking for, and since Jacob didn't love the desert any more than she did, they had never ventured there.

The dilapidated walls grew out of the stony earth as if the desert itself had shaped them — along with the sun, whose glaring light dappled the bleached stones with shadows.

"Don't you think it's time you told me who we're meeting here?" asked Fox as she rode after Orlando through one of the massive gates.

"Patience, vixen," he replied with a smile.

Even when she wore the red fur, Orlando's smile would have looked more fitting on the face of Reynard the Fox. She

259

had whispered that in his ear when they had slept together in Moskva. 'And your neck goes much better with the wild goose than mine,' he had whispered back. 'What a perfect pair we make. Too bad the gander doesn't stand a chance because the vixen lost her heart to a stray dog.' Fox remembered that she had pondered for many days afterward whether a dog was indeed the animal Jacob would turn into—if he ever desired or dared to change shape. She still wasn't sure of the answer. A dog is a vixen's fiercest enemy... Did that mean that they would have torn each other apart in animal form? She had to smile. The gander felt safe in her company, even though they were enemies in animal form.

"I'm not going to ask who you're thinking about right now," Orlando said as he tethered his horse next to hers. "I'm glad the thought of him doesn't bring tears to your eyes for a change."

Fox didn't correct him. It was better that Orlando didn't know with how much affection she thought of him, too. She had no intention of hurting him again.

The walls he approached had probably been part of a temple or palace. The outlines the stones still drew in the sand were so spacious—weathered reminders of halls, corridors, and courtyards. Beyond a forest of crumbling columns, they came upon an archway that, Fox surmised from its central location, had once led to a sacred or forbidden space.

Hideo strode under the arch first as if to make sure that Spieler's crow or other unforeseen dangers did not lurk beyond. The images on his skin had not stirred since the events in Jahoon, but Hideo hid them even more carefully than before, and Fox often caught him stroking his chest and arms as if to reassure those hiding beneath his dusty clothes.

Orlando had climbed the broken steps to an altar that now offered to the sun nothing but the sand that had accumulated on it. He spoke softly to something or someone she could not see, in a language Fox had never heard from his lips. As she followed him up the steps, she saw a lizard sitting on the altar stone, with scales so grayish-yellow that it was almost invisible.

Orlando pulled Fox with him as he respectfully backed away from the altar. "I explained to him that, like him, we have two guises, and he can trust us," he murmured to her.

He... The lizard's shadow began to stretch. Many shape-shifters betrayed themselves first by doing this. The shadow changed before the body did—as if it were a little closer to the soul.

The naked boy standing in the middle of the altar was no longer a child, but not yet an adult either. He was skinny and sunburned, with tangled black hair and eyes that seemed too big for his narrow face. They were human eyes, but the pupils were those of a lizard, and there was a knowledge nesting in them that, as was so often the case with shapeshifters, was much older than the body. Animals grew up quickly. Their lives were too dangerous for the luxury of an extended youth.

Hideo had retreated under the archway as soon as the lizard transformed. At first Fox thought the gesture was the same timidity with which he had met Toshiró, but then she saw that something like colored smoke was seeping through his clothes. It was not the dragon that had protected her in Jahoon, but the one whose image adorned Hideo's left leg. Its scales were covered with a thousand eyes, and its golden pupils were drowned in wrath-reddened white. It grew until its shadow fell on the altar—and on the boy standing on it.

261

The lizard boy looked up at the dragon as calmly as if an impetuous pup were panting at him. Then he shouted something, and all the scaly anger turned into nothing but a sigh in the hot air, a green veil settling around the desert boy's narrow shoulders. From Hideo's clothes, however, fluttered blue butterflies. He watched them with incredulous wonder—and laughed delightedly as blossoms rained from his sleeves and gathered on the ancient stones at his feet. *Look, Kitsune!* said the look he gave Fox. *My pictures are not just angry!* No, Toshiró's magic gave shape to both his anger and his joy, and while Fox delighted in the joy on Hideo's face, she felt deep gratitude that the lizard boy had shown him.

What would he show her?

With a movement that was as abrupt as a lizard's, he looked over at her as if he had heard her question.

His voice was throaty and bright.

"You're looking for someone," Orlando translated.

Someone... Fox nodded.

"Are you carrying something that belongs to him?"

Fox didn't ask how he knew she was looking for a man. The coin she pulled from her pocket had been bought for her by Jacob in Zhonggua. The merchant had told him that the characters on it meant LOVE. The fingers with which the boy grasped the coin were reminiscent of lizard toes, and the tongue with which he licked the copper was forked, proof that he rarely took human form.

Hideo watched all this with great disbelief, but Orlando gave Fox a knowing look. Yes, sometimes the vixen also used her tongue to discover the secrets of an object. What senses did the gander use?

The boy closed his eyes for a moment. Even his eyelids resembled those of a lizard. Then he jumped off the altar and nimbly climbed the crumbling walls that surrounded them until he reached the highest point. The vixen immediately understood whom he was calling when he raised his hands and began to sing in a throaty voice.

The wind was not long in coming.

The hot air began to breathe. It drove into the boy's long black hair until the strands danced like the serpents on Medusa's head.

"He's the best of all the wind readers," Orlando murmured to Fox. "But so far, my appeals for his help have been in vain. He never believed that my questions were for personal reasons, but I figured he would have no such doubts about your request."

The boy stood as motionless as if he had become part of the wall, listening. What was the wind telling him? *Please*, thought Fox, *please tell him where Jacob is*.

Hideo placed one of the flowers that had rained from his clothes in her hand. "You'll see, we'll find him!" he whispered to her.

Fox smiled at him and closed her fingers around the soft petals. It was so easy to hope for others and so much harder to do the same for herself. There was the same confidence in Orlando's gaze as in Hideo's words, *You'll see, we'll find him!* But when the lizard boy got off the wall, his face said something different as he walked toward Fox. He stopped in front of her and grabbed her hand as if to add comfort to words without solace.

"The wind knows nothing of him."

She felt Orlando's hand on her shoulder.

"Are there other winds you can ask?" he asked.

The lizard boy looked at Fox as if searching her eyes for Jacob's image.

"No, the wind is all winds," Orlando translated. "He blows everywhere. Those he knows nothing of do not walk on this earth."

Not on this earth... Fox looked at the flower in her hand. She had always found comfort in the thought that if death found Jacob, she would be at his side and die with him. *Stop it, he's not dead, Fox!* she snapped at herself. She tried to speak to herself very firmly, but her heart was empty, and she could feel no echo of Jacob's heartbeat there. Nothing could be worse than this: that he was simply gone.

"You need to change more often," she said to the boy. He barely reached up to her shoulder. "Believe me. It's better."

She turned her back on them all and shifted even as she walked toward the archway. Hideo wanted to follow her, but Orlando held him back. He knew her well.

The sand burned the vixen's paws, but she ran until the pain in her heart drove the fur away, and she fell to the sand on her human knees.

Not on this earth.

How she cursed the wind. Even now, she felt his hot breath on her skin. What if he served the Elf? After all, air and fire were his elements. *Fox!* she thought she heard Jacob say. *Stop it! What happened, happened. There was a Before me, there will be an After me.* He had said something like that in many dangerous situations, and often enough, she had only answered him with silence. Jacob liked to fool himself that his heart could be controlled in that way. His heart, his destiny... nonsense.

She raised her head and wiped the dust and tears from her face.

Fine. So the wind couldn't find Jacob. What if she could prove that the vixen knew more about this world than the wind? She defiantly held out her face to him, even as he pushed sand through her hair. A treasure hunt only ended when the treasure was found, and what had she ever sought that was more precious?

She bent over the scorched earth with a groan until her forehead touched the sand, and she let the pain become a scream.

The rush of wings mingled with it.

The gander landed beside her in the hot sand. He certainly liked it even less than the vixen.

"He doesn't walk on this earth?" He ran his beak over his gray feathers. "So he's under it. And no, that doesn't mean what you think. Love is clouding your mind."

He spread his wings, so wide, so light, carrying the sky within.

"Grunico. A hideously long and arduous journey. Lots of water, dark mountains. Just as you and I like it. And in the end... hopefully..."

An underground palace.

Fox sat up and brushed the sand from her clothes.

The wind never lied. She just hadn't listened properly. The gander knew the wind better.

37

UNBELIEVABLE

The whole world was talking about the palace the Goyl had built deep under the old imperial castle of Vena. The newspapers had already declared it a wonder of the world. But Nerron, on the long train ride to Vena, merely wondered if he would be able to convince Kami'en in his new palace to forgive the Jade Goyl and avenge the Dark Fairy with his brother's blood.

> *The Bastard asks for an audience with the King. He brings a gift that will avenge the Dark Fairy and pay the debt of the Jade Goyl.*

The guard station guards had promised to pass his message directly to Kami'en's new aide. Yes, she was a she, and Nerron had always gotten along worse with women than with men, his mother excepted. What if this aide despised him as much as Kami'en's old watchdog Hentzau? What if he was on Kami'en's blacklist because he hadn't delivered a single piece of valuable information in months but had disappeared after the Fairy's death, along with the Pup?

What if? with every switch the train rumbled over. Nerron blamed the lizard meat they served in the officers' car as he vomited from the drafty platform. But of course, it was once again the fear of failing or making a fool of himself. What if Kami'en construed what he was about to do as treason? Damn, how he despised himself for his bad nerves! Reckless was probably fast asleep in the supply wagon, even though he was headed toward his execution.

The treasures they had stolen from the Alderelf's palace provided less distraction than he had hoped. They had both taken only small things, a magnifying glass, a few combs, keys, tiny boxes… Every treasure hunter knew that the most potent spells often came in small objects. But none of those damned silver things could be coaxed into doing anything magical. Did Elf magic work only in the right hands? Hardly. After all, Reckless had used their mirrors. Nerron had no idea what Reckless had done with the casket containing the vials of Spieler's love elixir. It had suddenly disappeared from the table. Had he dissolved it into thin air to spite Spieler? Whatever. The spyglass he had taken from the snail skin was incredible. Nerron aimed it at the underground landscape that slid past the train windows, but the next tunnel plunged everything into darkness, even for his Goyl eyes. What if this was the future? A black hole into which these Elves shoveled them all with a spade of silver.

He shoved the spyglass into his belt.

Would they send armies of clay-faces and Mirrorlings swarming from their underground palaces? Or infiltrate human fortresses like the Elf in Nihon? And how did one convince a king to fear enemies who were masters at keeping themselves hidden?

Yes, it was a long train ride.

✳

The underground station where the train stopped in Vena was as new as Kami'en's palace. The Goyl, after conquering the city, had built their own settlement under the old town, which now had more than fifty thousand inhabitants. It was utterly self-sufficient in transportation and supplies, with dozens of above- and below-ground entrances, all heavily guarded.

Nerron had asked the officers on the train for an escort for Reckless, but he didn't need them. At the platform, Kami'en's new adjutant was waiting for him with a delegation of ten soldiers.

Lieutenant Nesser, as she had been allowed to call herself since her promotion three months ago, had so far only been known to Nerron as Hentzau's shadow. Supposedly, the old bloodhound had a soft spot for the young soldier. Nerron, however, instead believed the rumor that Hentzau had not vacated his post voluntarily and that he had been as surprised by the king's choice as had all those who had hoped to succeed him.

"Are you the Bastard?"

She was as arrogant as she looked, and Nerron was sorely tempted to ask whom she had had to make eyes at to rise to be the king's right hand at her age.

268

"The same," he said. "Do you wish to see my seal?"

"Are you talking about the fake seal you've been showing around everywhere?" She was almost as tall as he was and, according to rumors, had killed more than a dozen men in saber duels. "In my eyes, that should land you in the dungeon, but I have orders not to treat you as a prisoner for the time being."

The instruction could only have come from Kami'en, surely?

"I brought a prisoner with me. He's in the third transport car."

"I was informed of that."

She pointed over Nerron's shoulder. Four Goyl soldiers were leading Reckless down the platform. You could see the last week on him, the torture, the wound in his shoulder. He was gray as granite from exhaustion. The sight did not displease Nerron. As long as he was still alive.

Reckless did not dignify him with a glance, but he addressed Nesser as his guards stopped beside her.

"Congratulations on your promotion. I hope the bullet wound I gave you doesn't cause you any discomfort?"

In reply, Kami'en's new aide slapped him so hard across the face that blood gushed from his nose.

"You bring the wrong brother," she snapped at Nerron as Reckless wiped the blood from his face with his bound hands. "What does this one have to do with your message to the king?"

"I will answer that question to Kami'en only."

"If he receives you. I merely have instructions to take you to the palace."

She was a miserable Hentzau imitation. The arrogance just didn't work without the latter's scarred jasper face! Her soldiers nevertheless had respect, if not fear, for her. They took Nerron in the middle along with Reckless, Nesser's way of demonstrating that she would have been only too happy to treat the Bastard as a prisoner as well.

"You should watch out for her." Reckless kept pace with the guards despite his exhaustion. "She tortured me once. She's almost as good at it as the Elf. I'm also pretty sure," he added in a lowered voice, "that she has a soft spot for my brother."

Nerron wasn't sure if that made him more sympathetic toward Lieutenant Nesser.

"You have to admire how many enemies you've made," he murmured back. "Elves, Fairies, Dwarves, Goyl... I don't think you've left out any species."

He really couldn't make out if his prisoner was afraid. *He's confident he'll get away, Nerron. Jacob Reckless always gets away.*

They loaded them into two metal-covered wagons that ran without horses. Automobiles. Nerron had heard of them but had never seen them. They were loud and fast, and he worried all the time that they would explode. Through the barely hand-sized windows he saw a wide, underground street running alongside military barracks, then an avenue lined with the kind of stone trees he had climbed as a child, and finally a windowless building covered with mosaics representing all the skin colors of the Goyl. Inside was a long row of barred metal elevators, like those the Goyl used in their gem mines. The elevator they stepped into was as spacious as a train car.

If what one read in the newspapers was true, Kami'en's new palace was another half mile deeper underground than the Goyl settlement. The hardliners took this as proof that

270

the Goyl king had left his weakness for human things behind. There was just one reason that Kami'en had had his palace built under the castle where his human wife had grown up, on that the Goyl and human newspapers were agreed: the son, in whose favor Kami'en had disinherited the two sons of his Goyl wives, was too young to be separated from his human mother. The mother was considered by the Goyl to be much more important than the father.

Reckless was visibly struggling to breathe as there seemed to be no end to the shaft down which the elevator was plunging, and Nesser and her soldiers exchanged the usual look the Goyl had for all snail-skinned people: *Wimps*, it said. Destined to be subject to those who they had persecuted and despised for so long.

When the elevator finally stopped, they were greeted by the kind of darkness their golden eyes cherished and by the view of a vast plaza, the splendor and grandeur of which captured the confidence Kami'ens's rule had given the Goyl.

Reckless could see none of it.

"Describe to the snail-skin what escapes him," Nerron said to one of the soldiers. It was a jasper Goyl like Nesser, and he gave her an uncertain look before opening his mouth, but when she nodded at him, he complied with Nerron's request.

"This is the Square of the Bloody Wedding. The walls surrounding it are made of the skulls of all those who fell in the cathedral and in the later fighting caused by the plot of the Human Empress. The skulls of the bodyguards who gave their lives for the king were silvered."

Of course, Reckless had to comment. "It was the Jade Goyl that saved your king. I was there."

271

"Next time you open your mouth without being asked, it'll cost you a strip of your soft flesh, Reckless." Nesser made this announcement so casually, it only made it sound more believable. Reckless actually remained silent for quite a while after that.

The seemingly infinite wall at the end of the square fore-shadowed the size of the new palace. Its massive carnelian gate could probably be seen even by human eyes in the darkness. Nerron counted more than forty guards in front of the gate. There were almost as many behind it, and they passed through two more gates before coming to the main palace. The guardsman who awaited them in the courtyard was, like all of Kami'en's personal bodyguards, a carnelian Goyl. The Dark Fairy had instituted it that way. There was hardly a more coveted position, though it came with a short life expectancy.

The courtyard surrounding the main palace was tiled with onyx, an unmistakable message to the old ruling clan that the new king was trampling on their pretensions. The artificial sky above was of lapis lazuli, and the palace itself mimicked the craggy stone formations found underground, with a thousand crystal windows in a facade of carnelian. The interior also resembled the caves in which the Goyl were raised. Artificial stalactites hung from the ceilings, and between the halls, lined with amethyst, ruby, or moonstone, crystal flowers bloomed in gardens of malachite. Swarms of fireflies made all this visible even to Reckless. Kami'en sought to impress even his enemies with the splendor of his new seat of government.

"How many attacks in the last few months?" Nerron asked the guardsman as they passed even more guard posts.

"We don't count them," the guardsman replied. "We take every attack as proof of the greatness of our king."

That was one way of looking at it. But Nerron couldn't help but imagine Sixteen's kind suddenly appearing in the corridors. Goyl skin was not as easily silvered as human skin — Sixteen had tried it on Nerron, but the experience had been anything but pleasant. And as they walked down a wide corridor lined with mirrors, Nerron resolved to advise Kami'en against such decoration.

In human palaces, the king's quarters were usually found high up. Spieler's towers proved that the Elves had similar preferences. But for the Goyl, the most important things were always low down, and this palace was no exception. Lower and lower they went, down wide staircases of moonstone until suddenly everything became carnelian. Walls, doors, ceilings, and floors, every visible surface was covered with the stone that resembled Kami'en's skin. Except for one portal. It was gray, like the uniforms of the Goyl, like the rock in which they built their cities, like the stone womb of the earth that was their sky. Five guards stood to the left of it, five to the right, two in front. Twelve. Kami'en's lucky number, if his servants were to be believed.

Nesser instructed Nerron to wait with Reckless and her soldiers. She was still talking to the guards when the portal suddenly opened. It was so high that not even a giantling would have had to duck, and two of them actually stepped through it now — with a child between them, making their size even more impressive.

"On your knees!" murmured the soldier who stood behind Nerron. He rudely assisted when the Bastard did not immediately comply. Nesser was already demonstrating what was expected: one knee on the carnelian tiles, the other bent so that one could press one's forehead against it in awe.

Kochany.

The name Kami'en had given to his youngest son denoted in their language all that was loved.

The prince gave Nerron a smile as he walked past him, and that smile explained without words why not only the human inhabitants of Vena, but also every Goyl was at the boy's feet. Nerron did not believe in angels like his mother, who had always sworn that the goddess she prayed to regularly sent her winged helpers. But if they existed, they were sure to look like Kami'en's son. Even the giantlings who guarded him looked down on the child with a tenderness their coarse faces were not really meant to express.

The crown prince of the Goyl Empire would celebrate his second birthday in a week, but he already resembled an eight-year-old human boy. His hair was neither that of a Goyl nor as golden blonde as his mother's. It curled auburn, and the alert eyes in the perfect face were green. Not only the Goyl, but also all the human newspapers never tired of speculating why he grew up so fast. The Dark Fairy is his real mother — that was the most popular explanation, despite the midwife who swore that she helped Amalie of Austry deliver him. The boy's skin was the same color as his father's, but otherwise it had little in common with Goyl skin. Nor did it resemble Sixteen's. No, the skin of Kami'en's son was reminiscent of a lake's smooth surface, the color of molten lava, holding a thousand secrets.

One of the giantlings lifted the child onto his shoulder before he and the other disappeared with heavy steps into the velvety darkness. Nesser rose from her knees only after the footsteps had faded. She had held Hentzau's post since Kami'en had assigned his old comrade-in-arms to protect his son. The cantankerous old jasper hound as the bodyguard of a child, and one that his king had fathered with a human woman... Nerron was sure that Hentzau considered the task a punishment, not an honor.

"The audience is granted, but it will be short. The king is organizing birthday celebrations for his son." The look Nesser gave Reckless didn't hide how much she enjoyed seeing him as a prisoner. "I remember your brother," she said. "He wasn't an assassin. That he changed must be because of you. I hope Kami'en feeds you to his blind monitor lizards."

She gave Nerron no opportunity to mention that Reckless had narrowly escaped that fate just a few days ago. She turned her back on his prisoner as abruptly as she had addressed him and strode away, accompanied by her soldiers... without turning around again.

The audience hall was vast, as befitted a king who brought an entire world to its knees. The walls were of bare, roughly hewn rock, and the stalactites, hundreds of which hung from the ceiling, dappled the carnelian tiles with shadows and light. The Goyl had over centuries mastered a technique that made stalactites grow as fast as grass. Their crystal reflected the flicker of thousands of fireflies, just bright enough for human eyes and dark enough not to hurt Goyl eyes. On the back wall of the hall, a globe close to fifty meters in diameter bulged out of the rock. Only one half was visible. The other disappeared into the wall. The visible half showed the two Albericas: places, tribes, colonizers, battle lines, naturally imitated mountains, plains, and rivers. But Nerron's eyes wandered to the larger-than-life statue that stood to the left

275

of him in front of the rough-hewn walls. It was a statue of the Dark Fairy. Her skin was of alabaster, her dress of apatite, her hair of coral stone, but even the most precious stone could only capture an imitation of her beauty. No, Kami'en had not forgotten her.

"Well, well, the Bastard... I was sure you had finally defected to the onyx so long have you not shown your ugly face in Vena." Hentzau, as always, stood just a few respectful steps away from his king, close enough to shield him with his body at all times.

Nerron had not expected to see Hentzau here. That would not make the task he had set for himself any easier. He counted twenty other bodyguards in the shadows.

He bowed, even though he felt more like spitting in Hentzau's craggy face. The jasper Goyl was proud of his lowly origins and liked to make Nerron feel how much he despised him for the noble onyx blood in his veins. He tried not to hide his contempt even now.

"What was that nebulous message?" The gold of Hentzau's eyes was dull from all the battles he had fought for his king above the earth. "*The Bastard requests an audience with the King. He brings a gift that will avenge the Dark Fairy and pay the debt of the Jade Goyl.* Seems to me you've once again made promises you can't keep." He pointed to Reckless. "That's the wrong brother."

"That's not what the Bastard thinks." Reckless caught a rude shove from the guardsman at his side.

"Let him talk," Hentzau barked. "Jacob Reckless always gets chatty when he's in trouble."

"And I think he's telling the truth. The Bastard certainly did not confuse the brothers." Kami'en wasn't wearing the gray uniform he usually showed up in, but pants made of lizard leather and a tunic that changed color like an opal with every movement. It was the costume the Goyl princes had worn in previous centuries. The underground palace, the traditional dresses — Kami'en did indeed seem to have shed his love for human things as thoroughly as he had shed his love for his human wife.

The Bastard certainly did not confuse the brothers.

Reckless looked around the hall as if Nerron had brought him here for sightseeing. Many treasure hunters claimed that Jacob Reckless was afraid of nothing solely because of a spell cast by his Red Fairy lover, but Nerron knew better. The idiot was just good at pretending.

"The globe rotates and is hollow and walkable because it maps our major cave systems inside. My best stonemasons have outdone themselves with this." Kami'en leaned against the round table, which was the only piece of furniture in the center of the hall. It was cut from a single piece of rock. "As you can see, we are currently preoccupied with the political situation in the Albericas. Fortunately, the conflicts there are weakening some of our opponents. But such things can easily change. Have you ever been there, Bastard?"

Nerron shook his head.

"No Goyl has ever been there. The locals have turned armies from Lorraine and Albion into bugs. Interesting, isn't it?"

He turned to Nerron.

"So why are you bringing me the wrong brother, Bastard?"

"You owe both brothers your lives." Of course, Reckless couldn't keep his mouth shut. "Has the Goyl King forgotten his debt?"

The guardsman raised his fist, but Kami'en stopped him with a wave of his hand. He stroked the rock table he was leaning against.

"My wedding would have been a peaceful affair without you, Jacob Reckless." He had a voice that filled halls, even when he spoke softly. "The Fairy would have been at my side, and the Empress would never have dared to act against her. She had forgiven you for that, but your brother killed her anyway."

"The Jade Goyl was the victim of a diabolical plot, my king! Someone made him his tool." Nerron loathed the obsequiousness in his voice. Kami'en had that effect. He had too much strength and determination for one man, too much aggressiveness, too much cleverness, too much of everything.

Reckless looked over at him. *Are you also going to tell Kami'en that this someone is Will's real father?* Yes, the Pup truly didn't make it easy to be on his side.

"Sounds to me like the Jade Goyl is serving a new master." Kami'en unsheathed Hentzau's saber. "He killed what was precious to me. Very precious."

He walked slowly toward Reckless.

"Where is he?" He pressed the saber blade against Jacob's throat. "Where is your brother, treasure hunter?"

"I don't know."

"As you wish." Kami'en lowered the saber. "Let's leave the questioning to the torturers."

"Majesty…" Nerron's tongue grew heavy. He was no friend of words, but they were all he had. "I come to you straight from one of those underground palaces that every Goyl mother warns her children about. They exist! And so do the immortals who built them! They tricked the Jade Goyl

278

into destroying the Fairies, and they loathe us even more than the snail skins do, because we, like them, are not afraid of the depths of this world. They are preparing a great war. This world is nothing but a toy for them and only you can save us from these new enemies! With the Jade Goyl at your side! That's why I brought you his brother. Avenge the Fairy with his blood, as our ancient laws permit, and pardon the Jade Goyl so that he may make you invincible for all time."

How hastily he stammered all this! Damn, he wouldn't have believed a word himself.

Kami'en just looked at him.

"Our ancient laws?" barked Hentzau. "It's a damned onyx law!"

Kami'en had not taken his eyes off Nerron. The King of the Goyl was said to see through every lie. Against the Elf, that too would prove very useful.

"The underground palaces. I tried to find them as a child." Kami'en turned and slid Hentzau's saber back into its scabbard. "I have met the blind monitor lizards and seen the veins of crystal with rivers of lava flowing beneath them. But I have not found the palaces. Are you sure you didn't just indulge in the wrong witch's potion, Bastard?"

Help came from an unexpected quarter.

"The walls of the cells there are made of silver. They show you your own face and the fear on it. They remember every expression you use to betray your despair until it stares back at you a thousand times." In his voice, Reckless let Kami'en hear the pain he had endured in the dungeons of the Elf. "The Bastard is right. You will need my brother soon. Perhaps even the human world will need you to defeat these new enemies."

Even Hentzau seemed to be touched by Reckless's words. Kami'en exchanged a glance with him.

"Of course, I have heard rumors of immortals who were enemies of the Fairies. Where have they been all this time if they are so powerful?"

Reckless gave Nerron a warning look. But what better way to convince Kami'en of how dangerous the silver ones were?

"They have mirrors. Mirrors they used to escape to another world." He pointed to Reckless. "The world he came from."

Reckless just looked at him. He had certainly cursed him many times before, but never as passionately as at that moment.

"Another world?" Kami'en exchanged another glance with Hentzau. "What kind of world?"

He looked at Reckless. "Tell me about it."

Reckless shook his head. "The Bastard's a liar. The mirrors he's talking about make you believe in mirages. Very convincing, but as unreal as your reflection. The Elves haven't moved for so long because the Fairies enchanted them, but they've always been here. In the Alders to which the people make offerings of silver."

Oh, why did the words roll off Reckless's lips so much more convincingly than they did off his?

"It is he who lies, my king! To protect his world! The mirrors exist, as do the Elves who made them. And they will declare war on us! You must believe me!"

Kami'en stared at the sculpture that represented his dead lover. "The Fairies had enchanted them? Well, then they're only back because the Jade Goyl killed the most powerful of the Fairies."

He turned to the guards.

"Take the treasure hunter to the old imperial dungeons."

Four guards immediately complied with the order. They clearly expected resistance from the famous Jacob Reckless, but this time he did not resist.

"The Bastard is right about one thing!" he shouted to Kami'en as they led him away. "You're going to need my brother! The Goyl have never had an enemy like Spieler!"

The portal closed behind him, and Nerron stood before his king, certain that he had made a hallucinating fool of himself in Kami'en's eyes.

But his king gave him a smile.

"One brother for the other..." Kami'en stepped toward him. "Oh, Bastard, you still believe in fairy tales. Be glad your king doesn't. The guilt of the Jade Goyl is unforgivable. The blood of a thousand brothers could not wipe it out. But you brought me a good bait for the Jade Goyl. And now," he stopped in front of Nerron, "you will tell me more about these mirrors. And describe to me where the palace with the silver cells is."

38

His Mother's Face

Another dinner at an expensive restaurant. Will thought the men John Reckless dined with looked a lot alike. Arms dealers, politicians, plantation owners — they were all treasure hunters, except they weren't chasing lost magic like his brother, but power and money. The cut of their suits was more old-fashioned in this world, but the scent was the same. Greed, as the jade had taught Will, smelled like metal.

Will ordered another glass of wine while his father, at the next table, sold another world's ideas to warmongers and slavers. Metal? He also smelled of blood, more so than the steaks on his gold-rimmed plate.

Will had been following the man who had broken his mother's heart for three days. He missed Sixteen, but he missed having the Bastard by his side almost more by now. *Alberica?* he thought he heard him mock. *Too much water around it. You'll never meet a Goyl there.*

282

He lowered his head behind the newspaper he had brought with him. But John Reckless's gaze grazed him without interest or recognition. Of course. Will had been a child when his father had snuck away.

NEW HOLLAND NEGOTIATIONS BREAK DOWN

The articles that filled the newspaper made Will feel like he was lost in one of his history books, and yet everything was a little different. There were two independent states on the East Coast. The New York of this world was called New Holland. The Midwest consisted of six colonies that paid taxes to the kings of Albion and Lorraine. The rest of the continent was controlled by Indian tribes that used magic to stem the tide of poor farmers, fur trappers, and prospectors.

THE KING OF THE GOYL CONTINUES TRIUMPHANT

Will could hardly take his eyes off the illustration next to the article. Kami'en was well captured. The longing to stand by his side set in immediately. 'You protect him with your life.' Hentzau's voice was not easily forgotten. 'Do you hear me, Jade Goyl? With your blood, your flesh, the beat of your heart, and the sacred stone in your skin. Your life has no purpose but this.'

He forced himself to read on—three victories in four months. No, Kami'en did not need him. The Goyl King was invincible even without the Jade Goyl. The Bastard was convinced that, despite everything, Will's place was at Kami'en's side, and if Will was honest, something inside him believed it. But how was he ever going to look Kami'en in the eye again? He had still loved the Fairy, even after she had left him. How could anyone stop loving her? But the Bastard had made him promise to return to Kami'en because his belief in the fairy tale of the Jade Goyl and the Invincible King was strong enough for both of them. Oh, he missed his grained face and husky voice. He especially missed him among all these soft-skinned white faces.

He lowered the newspaper.

His father gazed after a waitress, and Will was grateful for the dimness of the gas lamps. He felt the jade every time the man who had tossed his mother away like an old toy leered after a woman who passed his table. Age had stained tired shadows on the dazzling looks that had filled his mother with such helpless desire, and the resemblance to Jacob was not as strong as she had often sworn it to be. Whenever she had been angry with Jacob, she would reproach his brother for this resemblance.

One of his father's guests called for the check, and Will signaled the waitress as well. Spieler had had a purse of silver brought to his room. Will had refused the gift, but the purse had been waiting for him again in the carriage.

He paid with Spieler's silver and left the restaurant to wait among the hackney carriages parked in front. As he stepped out into the street, John Reckless's face displayed the satisfaction brought by self-indulgence and success. Business was clearly going well. One of the waitresses had revealed to Will that the two men his father had entertained that evening were gun manufacturers whose shotguns civilized the wilds of the West.

John Reckless decided to take a stroll back to his hotel. Had Rosamund Semmelweis fallen in love with him because he had in abundance all that she did not possess? All the selfishness, the lack of conscience and responsibility... had that appealed to her? Will thought he sensed his mother by his side as he followed the man who had abandoned her through the nighttime streets of another world, past lighted windows that made you imagine there was happiness and peace beyond. As a child, Will had often imagined what it must be like to live behind such windows, in rooms filled with laughter, with parents who loved him as much as they loved each other. When Jacob began bringing him things from his travels, Will had sometimes put them under his mother's bed, hoping they were one of the magic things his brother so often told him about that would bring back the man whose absence made her so unhappy. And then, one night — Will remembered very clearly, as the gaslight before him drew the silhouette of John Reckless into the foreign night — his helpless desire to bring his father back had turned into something else, dark and unmanageable, like an animal to whom his mother's nightly sobs gave tearing teeth. 'I hope he's dead! Dead!' How surprised Jacob had looked when his gentle little brother had stammered that... To Jacob, their mother had been to blame for his growing up without a father. Still, Will had wished only one thing from that night on: that their father would never come back and that his mother would finally forget him.

John Reckless had stopped. The cigarette he lit in the glow of a lantern smelled of pixie dust.

Will looked down the street. It was deserted except for him and the man whose last name he bore, though he had always wished for another. If only Jacob was here — it was the first time he'd caught himself wishing that since their argument in Kakeya. What had his brother done when he hadn't returned from the fortress? What had Nerron been thinking?

He crossed the street.

The lantern under which his father stood drew a bright circle on the sidewalk, and the cigarette he drew on with relish filled the night with the smell of burnt tobacco and pixie dust. Will stopped at the edge of the circle, one with the shadows of the night, as Nerron had taught him. He felt the jade coming.

John Reckless raised his head in surprise.

No, he did not recognize him. He had long since ceased to be the boy he had left in another world, along with his mother.

Although...

The shoulders in the tailored jacket tightened. The eyes, dull with pixie dust, found the resemblance to his mother. So her unfaithful husband at least still remembered her face. But memory did not bring back love. Guilt... Will saw it spread across John Reckless's face like a rash, and he thought he understood for the first time what his father had been running from.

From too much love. Love he didn't deserve...

It sounded awfully familiar, and Will knew when he threw the punch that he was striking himself as well as the man he'd wanted to see bleed ever since he'd first heard his mother cry at night.

John Reckless was not a fighter. He tried to run. Not a good decision. Will's heart was made of jade, and it felt so good to smash the face that had smiled at him from the photos in his mother's room, full of mockery for the helpless adoration her youngest son gave her. *She loves me more, you little fool*, the photos had whispered. *All your puppy love can't replace me.*

Will lowered his fists. The man at his feet curled up like an embryo instead of fighting back. It was too easy. Will stepped back and wiped the blood from his hands onto his jacket as he waited in vain for the feeling of redemption he had so often imagined. Would someone someday beat him up for the pain he had caused Clara?

Finally, John Reckless mustered the courage to get to his feet. Acceptance of his own cowardice was written on his forehead like a bad joke he lived with.

"At last," he groaned, breathing heavily as he wiped the blood from his mouth and nose with a pristine white handkerchief. "I'm surprised which one of my sons took the assignment, but I'm glad it finally happened. You can't imagine how many times I wished your mother would raise her hand or at least throw something at me." He spat a tooth into his hand and laughed softly. "I should have known! I was sure it would be Jacob waiting for me one night somewhere. But you're the perfect avenging angel. An angel with Rosamund's face and the skin of my enemies."

He slid the tooth into his pocket. "What kind of stone is it? I had no idea you were infected with the Fairy's curse!"

Will still wanted to hit him.

A man with a dog stepped out of one of the houses across the street. Normal people… That's what he had called all the others in his childhood. Normal and happy. 'There are no normal people, Will,' Clara had said when he'd confessed to her that as a child, he'd wished he could be like her. His father took advantage of the stranger's appearance to get away from him.

Will let him go.

John Reckless glanced around a few more times as he limped away, but he was soon gone into the night, and Will leaned against the lamppost, watching the jade on the back of his hand turn to human skin once again.

Across the street, Spieler's carriage pulled up. The driver nodded to him. He got down from the coach seat and opened the door for him.

Will crossed the street and got in.

39

SILVER TRACKS

Lombardia was at war with its western neighbors.

Villages were burning barely a hundred miles away, but there was no sign of it in the sleepy port where Fox and Hideo disembarked with Orlando. Orlando's sources claimed that the Goyl supported Lombardia with Man-Goyl troops to win the country as an ally.

'And how will you explain to Mehmed the Magnificent that his best spy is traveling to a forgotten ancient city in Tyrol, known merely for its dark past?' Fox had asked when Orlando had announced that he was traveling with them to Grunico.

'Oh, I won't even have to lie,' he had replied. 'The Sultan had a run-in a few weeks ago with a prince who calls himself Apaullo and is gaining more and more influence in Alkebulan.

He is said to have six fingers on each hand and a suspiciously comprehensive knowledge of an ancestor of Mehmed who ruled parts of Alkebulan more than a thousand years ago. I have a suspicion that all the spies of this world will very soon be tasked with finding out more about Alderelves.'

It was pouring with rain as they squeezed into the coach headed to Grunico with two other passengers. The two women eyed Hideo as if a demon had joined them. He tried his best not to take up too much space, but with his build, that was a futile endeavor, so he finally just closed his eyes in resignation, so at least he wouldn't see the hostile stares anymore.

"Do you think he's homesick?" Fox murmured to Orlando as Hideo's snores mingled in harmony with those of the two women.

"Hideo's an adult, Fox," Orlando murmured back. "He can decide for himself. And I think he likes being your protector."

Yes, that was probably true.

"Did he tell you why he gave up wrestling?" she whispered. She thought she could once again detect the sadness on Hideo's sleeping face that the black rose at the market in Jahoon had left there.

Orlando was silent for a long moment as if he wasn't sure whether he should give away a secret that belonged to Hideo.

"He didn't have to," he finally said. "I don't just remember his fight. A few months later, a very talented young wrestler in Nihon was banned from continuing to practice his art because he had a moon butterfly tattooed on his chest."

Fox looked at him uncomprehendingly.

"Hideo had fallen in love with one of the other wrestlers," Orlando whispered to her. "In Nihon, the moon butterfly is the symbol of love between two men or two women. The Holy Wrestlers are not allowed such love, so he was cast out in shame. That he nevertheless had the butterfly tattooed on his skin probably proves how much this love meant to him."

Orlando was silent when one of the women opened her eyes and eyed him warily as if she knew he sometimes turned into a gander.

Fox had noticed the butterfly but had not asked Hideo about it. She couldn't take her eyes off his sleeping face as the carriage bumped along the dirt roads, shaking them all worse than the heaviest swell on a ship. *The world is cruel, don't you think, Kitsune?* Sometimes it even punished you for loving. His dragons had not been able to protect him from this, but perhaps they had given him the courage to have the butterfly tattooed on his skin as well. Was love stronger than fear in the end? Years ago, Fox and Jacob had searched for a cloak that a prince had ordered from a magical seamstress so that he could transform himself into a woman and marry the man he loved. In India, there was supposedly even a lake in which two lovers could merge into one figure. Fox stroked her belly. *The world is cruel, don't you think, Kitsune?* There was so much to protect a child from.

The two women alighted in a village where the poor houses crouched into a dark valley. The road, which continued along the densely fir-covered mountain flanks, was barely visible in the darkness, and Fox was just wondering how the horses found their way when lights and the outlines of high, old walls emerged from the night. The marketplace where the coachman reined in his tired animals was surrounded by houses that certainly had not been built by poor peasants. Yet, as she stepped off the carriage, Fox felt the melancholy she had encountered in many places that had fallen into oblivion.

Orlando exchanged a few lively phrases with the coachman. Italian. Parsi, Varangian, Mongol… with Hideo, he conversed fluently in Nihon! No. All these languages could not fit into one head. Except…

"Orlando Tennant!" Fox murmured to him while the coachman threw them the bags from the roof. "Is that ring on your little finger a Babel ring, by any chance?"

Orlando shouted a few parting words to the coachman and took the bag from her hand. "It's too bad you're a treasure hunter. You can see that I owe all my talents to magic objects!"

Hideo stood shivering beside the carriage. He eyed the houses that surrounded the sparsely lit marketplace. It was a cold night, and above the rooftops, the light from the two moons fell on snow-capped peaks that surrounded the city like the waves of a petrified ocean. The mountains were also represented in faded paintings on the facades and archways that lined the square and streets.

"Really beautiful," Hideo murmured. "So beautiful and so different." He glanced up at the square tower that rose into the dark sky just beside the hotel. He then looked at the pavement at his feet and his shadow cast on the gray stones by a lantern.

"My shadow falls on the stones of foreign lands," he murmured. "The teacher who taught me to wrestle claimed that it robs you of your soul."

"That doesn't sound like a wise teacher, my friend." Orlando put an arm around his broad shoulders. "In my experience, each new place explains to us a new region of our heart. It's as if we carry the whole world inside us and just need to discover it."

Hideo nodded gravely, as he always did when he thought something worth considering. "That teacher was very good at making stupidity sound like wisdom, Tennant-san."

Fox almost asked him about the moon butterfly, but the place had a darkness that made her alert and reminded her why she had come to Grunico.

The long carriage ride had exhausted them all so much that she had no trouble convincing Orlando and Hideo that she wanted to wait until morning to find the Elf to whom Grunico owed its name. Orlando and Hideo had the rooms to her left and right, and Fox didn't have to wait long for it to get quiet there.

The young man who had handed them the room keys with a scowl, as if it were the height of recklessness to arrive after dark, was asleep with his head on the guest book when Fox crept past him.

The alleys were deserted, but she transformed only at the cemetery of an old church, where the high walls offered protection from prying eyes. Protective symbols against dark magic were carved into many tombstones, and dried flowers lay on quite a few graves to protect against the child-eaters. Everyone knew that they collected some ingredients for their potions from graveyards, and even the dead were not safe from them. *Vixen, oh, vixen! The Elf only wants your child. Come with me, and I'll let the others go.*

Two crows flew up from a wall as the vixen stole back into the alleys. But they had bird shadows.

Yes, Grunico was a dark place. The vixen could smell evil

in every shadow cast by the houses and under every tree that ducked before the cold winds. She roamed courtyards and alleys for hours, never catching the silvery scent that was by now so familiar to the vixen. Finally, however, she came upon a building that seemed old enough to predate the Fairy curse. The stone carvings that adorned the facade spoke of great wealth, even if they were weathered. Sculpted roses twined around the windows, traces of silver still clinging to their blossoms. The closed shutters were also silver, even if time had blackened them. On the wall surrounding the adjacent garden, Fox found a rotten board into which someone had hammered the outline of a tree with silver nails. The path it pointed to led toward the tall fir trees that grew on the hillsides all around, winding further and further into the increasingly dense forest. It didn't take long for the vixen to scent the silver. It was only a pale whiff compared to the scent she had caught in Krieger's fortress or near Toshiró, but it was unmistakably the same.

How will you pay the Elf if he's still stuck in the tree, Fox? Why hadn't she asked herself that earlier? Grunico didn't sound like someone who would tell her the way to Spieler's palace without asking a price. What if, like Toshiró, he sensed she was pregnant and demanded the same price as Spieler? No. Those were the wrong thoughts. She had his scent. That was all that mattered. She was just surprised that the scent she was following remained so faint, despite all the treasures piling up among the silver beads. Fox understood why as soon as she reached the clearing where the Fairy curse had frozen Grunico.

Did the spell fuse their immortal flesh to the tree, or did it cause the Alder to grow around them? She would have to ask Toshiró that question. Grunico would not answer it for her.

The Alder had been enormous, much taller and wider than the tree Toshiró had escaped from. The crown had made a deep breach in the forest. The charred stump that stretched its roots into the night was surrounded by the remains of the mighty trunk, which had not only been burned but additionally sawed into pieces. Whoever had felled the tree had taken great pains to ensure that the Elf did not survive.

A few lost silver coins still lay around the stump. Fox changed shape and picked them out of the charred moss with human fingers. The stump was hollow. As Fox stroked the wood inside, silver became visible beneath the soot, and her fingers smelled of death.

She wasn't sure if the angry despair she felt was her own or that of the Elf still lingering among the trees.

She sat beside the dead tree for hours as if Grunico might yet be able to tell her how to find Spieler's palace. After that, she wandered aimlessly through the forest, first in human form, then in fox form, haunted by her own thoughts. Had the Golden Yarn, which she had left to Toshiró, been her only chance to get Jacob back? Had Spieler already killed Jacob because she had taken it to his enemy?

It was getting light when she returned to the hotel. Orlando was sitting in the tiny dining room eating breakfast. Fox joined him at the table, and the sullen young man wordlessly brought another plate.

"I take it you found the tree? Or what's left of it?" Orlando pushed the bread basket toward her. "The baker at the store next door says it happened less than a week ago. No one can explain why the fire didn't spread. There are rumors of men made of clay and one who changes faces. They apparently appeared out of nowhere."

The bread was as good as the cheese. Fox was surprised at how hastily she gulped down both. Orlando ordered another coffee from the boy. Fox understood that much Italian. He was served it with a smile. Orlando could make anyone smile if he wanted to.

"It looked like a slaughterhouse. Whoever was in that tree… is no longer there."

Orlando pushed her coffee toward her. "The tree had a bad reputation. Supposedly, it could grant even the darkest wishes and was very popular with the child-eaters who dwell in these mountains. I think I'm glad you didn't encounter its inhabitant."

The coffee was as good as the bread and cheese. Perhaps the women in the carriage had been child-eaters. The tree gave her dark thoughts.

"Hideo has gone in search of you. I told him that there was no forest where the vixen would get lost, but he could not be stopped, nor did he want my help. He was in great distress when he heard about the fate of the tree and that you set out to find it last night."

Ah. The boy had noticed her after all. Had he also seen her change shape? In some places, that could be dangerous. Fox caught herself liking the thought. The vixen wanted to bare her teeth and bite. And if they killed her or set the dogs on her—that wasn't a bad ending. Did Orlando wish Jacob was dead? Heavens, yes, the tree gave her dark thoughts! Maybe it really was a good thing she hadn't met Grunico.

"There's news." Orlando leaned back. "I'm afraid you will get some very foolish thoughts from it."

News. Was she getting hot or cold? Fox couldn't tell.

"Jacob is dead. Spieler killed him." It was almost a relief to say it.

Orlando shook his head. "Sometimes you can be awfully hasty indeed. No, Jacob's alive. Of course, he's alive. I always told you he was. But he's—how do I put this best—not in the most agreeable position."

"What do you mean?"

Orlando was all too accustomed to handling bad news diplomatically.

"Oh, good, you're back, Kitsune!" Hideo stood in the doorway. "Aren't these woods incredible?" He looked as happy as if he had found one of his islands out there in the mountains. "They—"

"Not now, Hideo." Fox was ashamed of the sharpness in her voice. It even drew the dragon out of his sleeve. Hideo hastily shooed him back.

"Sit down," Orlando said as he pushed a chair toward him. "I have something to report that you had better hear as well."

Hideo obeyed, but you could tell he would much rather have gone to his room.

"So…" Orlando pushed the empty coffee cup away from him as if it were to blame for what he had to say. "The lizard boy was right. Jacob doesn't walk on this earth. The Goyl have him."

Fox took a deep breath. The Goyl! That was harmless compared to Spieler, wasn't it? This wasn't Jacob's first time in Goyl captivity—and so far, they had never held him for long.

297

Orlando, of course, saw the relief on her face. "That's not all, Fox." His voice was disturbingly serious. "The Bastard is believed to have turned Jacob over to Kami'en. Maybe that's how he hoped to earn the bounty on the Jade Goyl's head. Kami'en is probably planning to lure Will to Vena by holding his brother captive indefinitely. Jacob will have the honor of being one of the first prisoners in the Goyl's new dungeons. They have built them so deep underground that even they are said to find it difficult to breathe there. That sounds pretty escape-proof."

Yes.

He's alive, Fox. That's all you need to be thinking about.

"Is he there yet?"

"No. Kami'en is celebrating his son's second birthday in a week. The new prison will be inaugurated with Jacob and two leaders of the rebellious Man-Goyl armies moving in."

A week! It would take them days to get from here to Vena!

"The first northbound carriage will come through here tonight." Orlando reached for her hand. "It's a heinous way to travel, but in this case, faster than horses or the train lines through the mountains. If we're lucky, we'll be there in two days."

"And then?" Hideo looked at them both quizzically.

She'll risk her neck for him, Orlando's look said. *And I'll try to keep her from breaking it for his sake.*

"Kami'en cares about a good relationship with the Sultan," he said. "Perhaps he will grant me an audience. However, I doubt that will do us any good unless we bring Jacob's brother to him."

Orlando looked at her. *Do you know where Will is, Fox?*

"No," she answered his unspoken question. "No, I don't. And even if I did… do you think I would sell Will to the Goyl for Jacob?"

Orlando was silent, as if unsure of the answer. And wasn't he right?

Fox was glad she didn't know where Jacob's brother was.

40

VISITORS

Orlando had booked the same hotel for them all, where Fox had always stayed with Jacob when they had come to Vena on an assignment from the Empress. The Grand Hotel had been considered the best hotel in town for more than a century, and after countless nights out in the open, Jacob had loved sleeping behind gold-embroidered curtains for a few days. The Austryn Empress's insatiable hunger for beauty spells and other magical things had paid for the luxury. But Therese of Austry was dead, captured and executed by the Goyl after organizing her grandson's kidnapping from the dungeon. Her daughter was still Kami'en's wife, even if it meant that she was only allowed to leave her rooms on official occasions. Less than a year ago, that rumor and her mother's execution would have caused riots in Vena. But since Amalie's confession that she had helped kidnap her child, her subjects' sympathies had shifted to her son.

Even the entrance hall of the Grand Hotel demonstrated how much Vena loved the prince. Behind the reception desk, there no longer hung a life-size portrait of Amalie but one of her son Kochany. Orlando had told Fox that the places where the prince liked to go had become places of pilgrimage, whether it was the park by the river where he spent hours feeding ducks and swans, surrounded by guards, or the café house where he loved the ice cream. Humans and Goyl brought their sick there, and a fountain into which the prince had once thrown a handful of flowers was surrounded by women dipping their hands in the water in hopes of giving birth to an equally magical child. Not even the rumor that a spell cast by the dead Fairy made Kochany irresistible changed the reverence shown to the child.

Elise, the maid who had mended Jacob's and her clothes after many treasure hunts, fell around Fox's neck when she saw her in the corridor, asking about Jacob with tears in her eyes. It seemed that all of Vena had heard of his capture by now. Alois, the page who carried Fox's bag ahead to her room, assured her that they all hoped his brother would soon turn himself in. He showed her the magic coin Jacob had once given him, along with a detailed description of the man-eater's cave where they had found the coin, of course. The page confessed to Fox that they all approved of Will's deed because they had feared the Dark Fairy, but of course, he had no idea who had made Will her executioner.

When he unlocked the door for Fox, she at first wanted to ask for another room. It was the same one where Jacob had left her, guarded by a soldier, to meet the Dark Fairy and break into the Empress's Magic Collection. He had survived the night, but he had come back half dead, paralyzed by the slime with which he had made himself invisible. A bite from the vixen had expelled the poison. Memories... That same night Jacob had finally realized that she had become a woman at his side, and Fox did not ask for another room. She only covered the mirror next to the door because its silver frame reminded her too much of other mirrors.

Orlando set out for Kami'en's new palace as soon as they were settled. He had been granted an audience without any trouble, but he had been warned that it could take all day before he would be allowed to see Kami'en. It was a mild October day, and the windows of her room looked out on Vena's oldest park. The sight of the autumn-gold trees was very enticing, but Fox was worried that Orlando would return while she strolled along the park paths. So she tried to persuade at least Hideo to take a look around the city, but he only shook his head very determinedly, even as he gazed out the window with barely concealed curiosity. They both remembered the crow. "I'll be next door if you need me, Kitsune," he said—and, before leaving her alone, shook a flower from his sleeve, which he placed on the table by the window where Fox had so often seen Jacob sitting.

How she hated waiting! At some point, she caught herself looking at every little girl who passed under her window. Some pulled so impetuously at their mothers' hands that they walked faster, laughing. Others were dragged down the street so impatiently that their little feet began to stumble. Would she be patient? She hadn't been as a child. Everything her mother did had been too slow for her. And she had despised her for the fear she had seen constantly on her face — of her stepfather, of her own sons, of the whole world. 'Celeste, don't climb the tree. Celeste, don't run so fast. Celeste, don't go into the woods alone.' What if she called out the same nervous warnings to her daughter, fearing that Spieler was waiting for her in the woods?

So many forgotten days…

Each child she looked after brought back a different memory. Had she liked being so small? No! She had wanted to be an adult. Had she ever wanted children of her own? Not that she could remember. Her mother had had two by the time she was her age, and she hated to think about her older brothers. No. She had never played with dolls or dreamed of getting married and having a family of her own. If she had, they had been nightmares. But then the day had come when Jacob had told her about his deal with Spieler. And suddenly, it had been there: the desire for the child that wasn't allowed to be. In her dreams, she would hold it in her arms, only to feel someone snatch it from her, and when she had woken up, she had felt a pain she had not known before.

The dreams had disappeared with the happiness she had found with Jacob. She had held him in her arms and forgotten how the promise he'd had to make to Spieler over-shadowed their future.

One of the children on the street had red hair.

No.

She would not let Spieler find the daughter growing inside her. Their child would be the greatest treasure she and Jacob had ever found. Magic like no other. And they

303

would raise her together, teaching her all that two worlds had taught them.

It was getting close to noon, and Orlando wasn't back yet. Fox tried to sleep, but she dreamed of Krieger's garden, and when she woke up, she thought she saw a crow in the tree outside the window. The branch was empty when she stepped to the window, but the crows were everywhere, down on the pavement among the waiting cabs, in the park trees across the street. Had the gingerbread baker taken on a different shape after crashing on the old stones of Jahoon? Would the air soon smell of cinnamon again and her shadow smother Fox under its leaves? *Don't do that, Fox!* She drew the curtains and lay down on the bed, listening to see if she could find another heartbeat inside her yet. But she heard only her own.

The nearby church bell was already counting the full hour for the fourth time when there was finally a knock at her door. It didn't even occur to her that someone other than Orlando could be at the door.

But out in the hotel corridor, the Bastard was waiting.

He was through the door before Fox could shake off the numbness caused by the sight of him. Her limbs were still numb as he closed the door behind him, eyeing her with a smile she remembered all too well.

She was so tempted to transform and tear his stony skin. But the Bastard had his hand on his knife and wouldn't take his eyes off her.

"The fur still hasn't taught you to hide your feelings, vixen. Thanks for the blackout." He glanced at the drawn curtains. "My eyes really appreciate it. I thought it would be safer to find you before you paid me a visit."

304

"Safer? You'll never be safe from me again." Red mist. Her anger filled her heart and brain with it.

"It is a lie; I did not deliver your beloved to Kami'en! We were picked up by a Goyl patrol shortly after I helped him escape the Elf. I risked my skin for him! How can I help it that Kami'en now wants to use him as bait?" He raised his hands defensively. "I'm here to help! Kami'en knows about the mirrors. Don't look at me like that! I had to tell him about them! To make him realize how dangerous Spieler is! But now, of course, he wants to see such a mirror, and I'm sure you know where to find one around here. I'm sure Kami'en will be willing to trade if we offer him a whole world in exchange for your beloved. And I will promise to find him the Jade Goyl, even without your sweetheart acting as bait."

Kami'en knew about the mirrors.

No.

"Now come on, vixen!" The Goyl smiled slyly at her. "Doesn't that sound like a good deal?"

An entire world, as the price for Jacob's life. Jacob's world.

"Why do you come to me? Was Jacob's answer to tell you to go to hell?"

The Bastard shrugged. "You know how stubborn he is. I thought it would be a better idea to come to you first."

"Kitsune?" Hideo's voice came through the door. "Is Tennant-san back?"

Fox opened the door for him. Hideo eyed the Bastard as incredulously as if Spieler himself were standing in their hotel room.

"The Traitor Goyl!"

"Traitor Goyl! Uhhh, I like that nickname," the Bastard

305

sneered. But he stumbled back with a disgusted expression as a pale blue head popped out of Hideo's sleeve. The snake of Toyotama-hime was the color of the sky and seemed to have no end as it slithered from Hideo's arm down to the floor of the room.

"Well, well..." The Goyl tried hard to sound composed. "Is that your new pet? Or did you bring it back from Nihon as a souvenir?"

Hideo thrust his fist at the Goyl's chest so hard that Nerron stumbled against the bed and fell backward into the soft down. The snake coiled up the bedposts and silently lowered itself onto the Bastard's chest. The Goyl gasped like a fish on an angler's hook as the snake coiled tighter and tighter around him.

"Call it off, meatloaf!" he gagged. "Call the stinking beast back!"

"I think she smells very good." Fox sat down in the armchair by the window. It was better to keep her distance if the vixen felt like biting. "She smells like the sea of his home. Ask her to give him just enough air to talk, Hideo."

Hideo called out in his native tongue. It sounded more like a caress than a command, but the pale blue snake loosened its grip.

"The Elf would have had your sweetheart tortured to death without me!" The Goyl's golden eyes were cloudy with rage. "The blind monitor lizards would have eaten him, and you would never have known what became of him! How about some gratitude!"

The snake ran its forked tongue down his face as it wrapped its body around him one more time.

"You just have to show me one of those damn mirrors!" the Goyl gasped. "Is that really too much to ask? Are you going to wait for Kami'en to torture your lover to get the information out of him? The Elf hurt him badly. He may not survive another interrogation! But you just sit there and watch that stinking snake eat me, along with the souvenir Reckless slipped me for you!"

"If you have something for her, give it to her!" A growl rose from beneath Hideo's clothes, widening the Bastard's eyes.

"He's a damn demon!" he gasped. "A fat, baby-faced demon! Of course! His cursed islands are teeming with them!!!"

The description didn't seem to offend Hideo.

"What kind of souvenir?" Fox nodded at Hideo.

The snake loosened its grip and slowly detached itself from the Goyl's body. He didn't dare move until it crawled up the bedpost again, and his hands trembled as he detached a deception pouch from his belt and pulled out an amulet.

"He told me to tell you that it was a protective spell. I'll admit, he could use one of these himself right now."

He tossed the pendant to Fox.

She caught it and closed her fingers around it. No. She wouldn't show the Bastard any tears.

"I want to see him. Make sure I can visit him!"

"Tell me where to find one of those mirrors, and I'm sure Kami'en will allow it."

No, Fox! she heard Jacob's voice. *No man is worth saving by dragging an entire world into war.*

Yes. Kami'en would send armies through the mirror. And not only him. Soon others would follow him, and then troops from Jacob's world would come into this one.

"I need time," she said, "I need to think. But I want a promise that Kami'en won't touch Jacob!"

The Bastard shrugged. "Sure. A few days can be arranged.

But as soon as the birthday celebrations for his son are over, he'll demand an answer, and either you give it to him, or the torturers will elicit it from your lover."

"Jacob will sooner die. I'm your only chance."

The Bastard looked at her thoughtfully. He knew she was telling the truth. Yes. Jacob would rather die than show Kami'en his world.

Footsteps approached outside in the corridor. Then there were three knocks. Orlando was back.

Hideo opened the door for him.

Orlando eyed the Bastard and the snake as if they were part of the room's furnishings. Spies are used to stumbling into unexpected situations.

"What's he doing here?" He pointed at the Goyl. "Was he trying to sell you the story that's being put out by Kami'en's court? The one with the noble Bastard and the Goyl patrol that appeared out of nowhere?"

"Yes, and he made me an offer."

Fox hung the amulet around her neck.

She knew Orlando well enough to see that he wasn't bringing good news either.

"Tell Kami'en that I want three days to think it over," she told the Bastard. "And that Jacob remains untouchable until he has my answer. If anything happens to him in the dungeon, you'll pay for it, Bastard. We'll find you, count on it, me, Hideo, and the snake."

She nodded to Hideo, and the snake slithered off the post and coiled toward Hideo, where it turned to pale blue smoke at his feet.

"Go!" Fox snapped at the Goyl. "Before I change my mind. You'll hear from me in three days."

Nerron walked pointedly slowly to the door.

"Should you change your mind sooner—I've rented a room in the Goyl settlement. Close to the new palace."

Fox had to take a deep breath when he was gone.

Orlando sat down on the bed and picked a few blue scales from the quilt.

"Kami'en won't let Jacob go?"

"No. But I don't think any of us are surprised. He's assured me he cares a lot about good relations with Mehmed the Magnificent, but not enough to pardon the Jade Goyl's brother. I fear he will execute them both if Will turns himself in. After all, Jacob prevented the Fairy from accompanying Kami'en to his wedding at the time. With fatal consequences."

And he could show him a new world... Fox stepped to the window. She had never told Orlando about the mirrors. She was sure he had no idea where Jacob really came from. *It's better this way*, she thought she heard Jacob warn. Was it? Even the Bastard knew about the mirrors. Why not Orlando? *And then what?* the voice whispered inside her. *Will he tell Mehmed the Magnificent about it? And the King of Albion, whom he once served?*

"I'm tired," she said, "I think I'll lie down for a bit."

"There's something else." Orlando sounded as if he wasn't sure if it was good or bad. "There was a man seen in Charlestown with jade skin."

"Charlestown?"

"Carolina. One of the colonies in northern Alberica that won their independence from Albion a few years ago."

Alberica? How had Will gotten there? And would he ever learn there that his brother was in Kami'en's dungeons?

She was too tired to think about it. Three days.

41

THE RAT

After Orlando and Hideo left, Fox tried to sleep. But she soon gave it up. What was she supposed to do? The same question again and again. And she found only one answer.

She had to help Jacob escape.

Together they would find a way to hide from the Goyl and the Elf. They would find a spell that would make them invisible. Or ask Toshirō for help. Maybe Jacob's world was the safest place after all, and they could use the mirror in Schwanstein one last time and then smash it? Oh, she was so tired of thinking about all this alone.

Yes. There was only one way.

Fox knew the prison where Kami'en was holding Jacob very well. Jacob had served time there on several occasions for upsetting the Empress. They had gone through a dozen

310

escapes each time, and her chance of freeing Jacob was certainly greater there than in the new prison where the Goyl were moving him after the birthday festivities.

Orlando had gone to the Suleiman Embassy. Even if the Goyl had not threatened the Suleiman Empire so far, their troops were getting closer and closer to the borders of Mehmed the Magnificent, and Orlando intended to convince the Sultan that he had to stay in Vena to find out more about Kami'en's plans. He was really doing everything he could to help her. But if he helped her in what she had to do now, it would make Orlando an enemy of the Goyl as well, and she could not do that to him or to Hideo.

She stroked her body. She thought she could already feel a slight bump. "I'll do it for you, too!" she whispered. "Believe me, you'd really miss not having a father."

She still missed hers. She put on her coat and slipped the bag of silver the kitsune had given her into her pocket.

When the knock came, she feared for a moment that Orlando was back. But it was Hideo who was at her door. Of course, he noticed the coat. He pushed her back into her room and closed the door.

"You were going to leave without me, Kitsune! I'm coming with you!"

"To where?"

"You're going to free Reckless-san." He said it as if he had never had any doubt that she would try to do that. Oh, what a wonderful treasure she had found in Nihon.

Hideo pulled up his right pant leg. "There's someone I want you to meet. I forgot all about her when I showed you the others. And I've already apologized to her for that."

Just above his ankle, a rat peeked out from behind a flower.

311

"On my islands, the rat is a revered animal. It is a symbol of prosperity and good living, but it is also admired for another talent that could be of greater use in this situation."

Hideo smiled conspiratorially at Fox as he slid his pant leg over the rat again.

"She can make herself invisible, Kitsune. Herself—and others."

Oh, Yanagita Hideo! Fox remembered how Jacob had strode along the line of guides who had loudly offered their services when they arrived in Nihon. Hideo had remained silent—and Jacob, of course, had known who he was going to choose.

"You are such a good friend, Hideo," she said. He bowed his head, but Fox saw his smile. "I know three methods of making yourself invisible. All three have hideous side effects. Is that the case with your rat, too?"

Hideo shrugged his shoulders. "Shall we find out together?"

Yes. Outside, the sun was still high over the rooftops, but Fox was tired of waiting, and if Hideo's rat did indeed make them invisible, they wouldn't need the protection of night.

"Nezumi!" whispered Hideo. "Tasukete!"

His body disappeared as soon as the rat jumped up his body. It was as if it wiped him away like a chalk drawing, but when it jumped on Fox's shoulder as well, she could see Hideo again—although the mirror outside in the corridor proved that they were indeed both invisible. Now all that remained to be seen was whether the rat's spell would last long enough to free Jacob.

42

THE KOI

The rat proved to be a very reliable helper. Her magic made Fox feel not only invisible but also as light as a feather.

"I'll have its sister tattooed on my ankle when I come to visit you in Nihon!" she whispered to Hideo as they made their way through the less crowded streets of Vena to the prison of the Austryn emperors.

"I'm afraid that tattoo is only allowed on men, Kitsune!" returned Hideo.

"So, some rules have to be broken because they're stupid." Fox was very tempted to finally ask Hideo for whom he had broken the rules of his sacred craft, but she still hoped he would tell her his story all by himself one day. Besides, they had reached the square in front of the imperial prison — not the time for a long conversation about love and the rules it broke.

They didn't have to wait long before the heavy gates opened for a prisoner transport. Fox counted twenty guards, all jasper and carnelian Goyl, as they followed the metal-barred cart into the courtyard. None of the guards looked back at them, though this was quite common with other invisibility spells. Not even the hounds, who had already kept watch here under Therese, sniffed them out. Fox felt the confidence make her walk faster. *Too soon!* she warned herself. Yes, the rat would hopefully make Jacob as invisible as she was, but the guards could still sense her if they stumbled into her in the narrow corridors, and not even the rat's magic could protect her from bullets.

There were more than three hundred cells in the Austryn emperors' prison, and for each cell block, there was a guard room staffed by one or two wardens. Fox slipped into one of them to find out Jacob's cell number. To her disappointment, the list on the wall contained mere numbers without names, with notes in Goyl that neither she nor Hideo could read. But four numbers were written in red ink, so they decided to search those cells first, hoping Jacob was considered a special prisoner. If Fox remembered correctly, the red cell numbers were all in the underground vaults where the death row inmates and lifers were held. She had never been in that part of the prison, but she knew it dated back to very ancient times.

The stairs leading down were so steep and well-worn that they listened for a long time to make sure they didn't meet a guard halfway down, and even then, Hideo insisted that he go ahead and Fox wait for his signal before she followed. As Hideo's footsteps receded, the fear and despair that lurked below in the darkness could be felt even by her human senses, and she felt sick at the idea of Jacob trapped in the foul-smelling darkness below.

Hideo did a surprisingly good job of mimicking the shrill whine of a rat. This was their all-clear signal, and as Fox followed him down the dark steps, she remembered all the stories about the forgotten enemies of the Austryn emperors that they told in Vena. Some family members of the current Empress had even starved to death in the windowless cells, while their relatives gave balls and receptions a stone's throw away. The Austryn dynasty was notorious for its intrigue and political assassinations. Amalie of Austry had continued that tradition when she had allowed her mother and uncle, notorious for his cruelty, to kidnap her son. *You will have a daughter, Fox!* No, she had to forget that now. This was not the time to tell Jacob about her pregnancy. He had to be safe first. The hope that she would see him soon caused her to stumble on the dark steps. Someone screamed in the darkness below her. No, that wasn't Jacob's voice. Was it?

Hideo was waiting at the foot of the stairs, barely more than an outline in the darkness that reigned down here. Behind the pillars that supported the vaulted ceiling, two corridors opened. Hideo beckoned her to the one that faced the stairs. There were a few rusty lanterns on the walls, but the candlesticks were empty. Vena's new masters had no need for light. Fortunately, the same was true for the vixen, and Hideo had coaxed a few glowing moths from his skin. They crept along roughly hewn walls. The cells were barred holes, and the rats that scurried toward them certainly wouldn't make anyone invisible. It was hard to believe that the imperial palace was only a short stroll away.

"Jacob?" She couldn't contain herself any longer.

"Have you forgotten he can't hear you, Kitsune?" came Hideo's gentle reminder from the darkness. "But as soon as we find him, I'll let the rat into his cell, and he'll be able to see and hear you." He said it patiently as if he hadn't explained it to her a dozen times already.

Four red numbers... The prisoner in 419 was asleep, indeed the wisest thing to do down here. It was a young Goyl, and Fox wondered what had brought him to these dark cells. That was quickly answered with the next prisoners. 423 and 440 housed Man-Goyl. Probably the leaders of the rebel armies Kami'en had captured. One paced back and forth, the other clutched the bars that closed the cell to the corridor, staring so grimly into the darkness that Fox could feel his gaze even as she passed the cell. His right eye was golden, the left was brown, and the emerald stone skin was interspersed with remnants of human skin, as it was in many of them.

One cell number was left.

457 was empty, and for a terrible moment, Fox thought she sensed that Jacob had died here, but then she saw Hideo turn to her with a smile. And there he was. Safe and sound, as far as she could tell in the darkness. He was lying on the cot, staring at the ceiling above him.

Fox stepped toward the cell door.

She had found him. But it was such a strange feeling that he could neither see nor hear her. She had barely thought the thought when Jacob sat up, and Fox was already hoping he at least sensed her presence when Hideo reached for her arm.

Footsteps. From the direction of the stairs.

Jacob stood up and stepped toward the cell bars. Fox reached out to touch him, but Hideo dragged her behind one of the pillars that supported the vault.

The voice that echoed down the corridor was one that Fox knew all too well. It brought back terrible memories of Jacob with a bruised chest and of a fresh grave.

"Your Highness. This is the third visit in two days! Your father will not approve."

Hentzau. Kami'en's bloodhound had grown old if that could be said about a Goyl. Stone skin did not wrinkle, and their bodies remained vigorous even in old age. Hentzau's left eye, however, was as dull as a blind man's — too much daylight on too many battlefields — and he dragged his right leg, a lasting reminder of his king's Bloody Wedding. Fox pressed herself against the cool pillar, grateful for the cover it provided, even as her mind assured her she was still invisible.

The portrait in the hotel lobby had captured the boy at Hentzau's side very well. Kochany... The prince resembled his father merely in skin color. He had neither Kami'en's strong stature nor the stony hair of a Goyl, and he resembled his mother just as little. Amalie's son had the chestnut hair and beauty of the Dark Fairy. Children of humans and Goyl were born without skin and usually survived their birth for only a few painful hours. But the Fairy had given her faithless lover's son not only a skin but also her own beauty.

Hentzau held a lantern in his hand. Kochany's eyes were not golden but green. Like the Fairy's.

"On your knees, Reckless!" barked Hentzau as the prince stopped in front of Jacob's cell. "Even his father's generals may not look down on him."

Fox expected Jacob to scoff at the instruction. But to her surprise, he dropped to one knee without protest, bringing

317

him to eye level with the prince, who gave him a wide smile in return.

"Your jasper-skinned bodyguard looks even grumpier than usual, my prince." Oh, how she had missed his voice. The light from the lantern revealed that he'd had a bad few weeks.

"Yes, he really doesn't like you." Kochany stepped so close to the grate that Jacob could have touched him. Hentzau tried to pull the child back, but the prince gently but firmly pushed the jasper hand back.

"Tell me how you stole the Czar's flying carpet."

Hentzau growled like a bored old court dog.

"Your bodyguard doesn't like treasure hunter stories, my prince," Jacob said. "Why don't you send him away, and I'll tell you as many as you want to hear."

Hentzau drew his saber and pushed the blade through the bars until it found Jacob's chest. "Don't make your captivity harder than it has to be, Reckless. And don't think he'll come to see you, either, once you're buried alive in Kami'en's new prison. All your stories won't change your fate." He withdrew the saber but kept it drawn. "Bait for your own brother. And this after all the trouble you went through to keep him from becoming a Goyl. Tell him what your father will do with the Jade Goyl when he comes to save his brother, my prince."

"My father will have him cast in amber. Alive, actually. And watch the murderer's eyes go out."

"My brother is no murderer, my prince. You would like him. I hope to introduce him to you one day. Without your father casting him in amber."

"Oh, Kami'en has other requests for you in the meantime,"

318

Hentzau said. "You will show us the mirror the Bastard told us about, or you will never again see the daylight your kind so cherishes, even if your brother should show himself here. Another world… Kami'en can't wait to see it."

Jacob looked at Kochany as if he imagined for a moment showing him his world. Without his father's armies.

Then he shook his head with a scornful smile.

"I admit the Bastard is an imaginative liar," he said. "But I know nothing of mirrors or another world. He wants to make himself important to your king, that's all. Kami'en didn't really fall for his fairy tale, did he?"

Hentzau eyed him with the irritation of someone who wasn't sure what to believe.

"I know you're a gifted liar," he growled. "And I promise you—if the mirrors exist, you will show them to us. Come, my prince. The story hour is over."

But Kochany had turned.

He looked toward the pillar behind which Fox and Hideo were hiding.

"Is this the vixen you speak of so often, treasure hunter?"

How could he see her? Even if he saw through the invisibility spell, she was ducked behind a pillar. How could he see her through the stone?

"And the man has picture skin!" she heard Kami'en's son say. "You haven't told me about him yet. I have pictures on my skin sometimes, too, but they come and go."

"I must have described the vixen too vividly to you, Your Highness." That was Jacob's voice. "Sometimes she can be very reckless, but I only became such a famous treasure hunter because of her. Unfortunately, I haven't seen her in a long time. I miss her very much."

Oh, he knew she was there. And yes, she had heard the warning. But wouldn't he have done the same? Of course. She pushed herself forward just enough to see Jacob again. He was still kneeling, and he was trying hard not to look toward the pillar.

"As for men with image skin, my prince," Jacob's voice sounded calm, but Fox could hear his fear for her, "do you know that in Nihon there is a tattoo art that covers your skin so densely with images that they look like clothes? It is called Irezumi…"

"Ire-zu-mi?" For a moment, it looked like Kochany might actually be distracted from what he shouldn't be seeing. His eyes lingered on Jacob's lips as if he couldn't get enough of his words. "Do these images appear on their own, too?"

"No, you draw them into the skin with a needle. It's excruciating."

That was the wrong information. The prince turned again and looked with undisguised admiration to where Hideo was barely daring to breathe behind the pillar.

"Ah, then he must be courageous, the picture man!" he said.

Hentzau raised his saber and pointed the tip at the pillar while reaching for his pistol with his other hand. "What exactly do you see there, my prince? Do the picture man and the vixen have weapons?"

He cocked the pistol and aimed at what he didn't see.

"Take her away, Hideo!" Jacob had grabbed Kochany through the bars and was pulling him against them. "Forgive me, my prince! Hentzau!" He had his hand on the boy's neck. "Let her go or…"

"Or what?" Hentzau slashed into the darkness with his saber. "Jacob Reckless breaks a child's neck? No. You wouldn't do something like that, not even for the vixen."

No, he wouldn't. Jacob hesitated but finally let go of the prince and backed away from the bars, defeated.

"Show yourselves! Go!" Hentzau aimed his pistol at the pillar. But then he reconsidered and pointed it at Jacob. "Out with you, vixen! And I want to see the picture man, too, or your sweetheart will have a hole in his forehead. And this time he will — !"

The snake, which had already entwined the Bastard, coiled around Hentzau before he could finish the sentence. The rat had made it as invisible as Hideo, and the Goyl struggled in horror against what he could not see as the pale blue body looped around him again and again.

Now.

Fox jumped out from behind the pillar before Hideo could grab hold of her. She just had to get the lock on the cell door open.

"Are you really a vixen?" Kochany smiled at her.

"Yes," Jacob replied. "Yes, she is."

He still couldn't see her, but when Fox slid her hand through the bars, he felt her fingers, and for a precious moment, they both forgot where they were and that the guards had surely heard Hentzau's cries for help by now.

Jacob, however, did not forget for long.

"No!" he snapped at Fox as if he could see that she had knelt in front of the cell door to break the lock. He found her body with his hands and pushed her back. "Get out of here. The guards will be here in a minute! You're no good to me dead, Fox!"

But she wasn't going to be reasonable. She only needed a minute, maybe two. Kochany watched in fascination as she slid her knife into the lock. He really could see her without difficulty.

"The treasure hunter is right," he said. "They will shoot you all."

Fox stared at the boy as if he had taken the knife from her hand. Hideo dragged her to her feet. His hand was wet, and when Fox turned to face him, she saw that the waterfall which usually ran silently down his back was pouring from his clothes. The floodwaters washed Hentzau and the prince against Jacob's cell's bars, sinking the boy up to his chest in the foaming water. Fox struggled as Hideo grabbed her and threw her over his shoulder, but he was too strong, and the water swept them away from the cell. Four soldiers had come down the stairs, alarmed by Hentzau's screams. They stared in disbelief at the floodwaters and stumbled back up the steps in horror as the back of an enormous, black-scaled fish emerged from them. Hideo, however, clung to the fish's fin crest and, no matter how desperately Fox tried to free herself from his grip, allowed himself to be carried away with it. The last thing she saw was Jacob and Hentzau helping the prince climb up the bars of the cell. Then Hentzau's lantern went out, and there was only the water, flowing as if Hideo had carried all the rivers of Nihon on his skin. The carp carried them on its back through forgotten passages and sewers until Fox found herself in the open air with soaked clothes. Hideo lay beside her on his knees, gasping for breath, his damp clothes covered with scales. The carp and the snake were gone, once again nothing but tattooed images on Hideo's skin, and above them, a bridge spanned across the Danube, the river that ran through Vena.

"I'm so sorry, Kitsune!" stammered Hideo. "So infinitely sorry! I assure you, I did not call the water or the carp! It came all by itself!"

Fox was too exhausted and distraught to reply.

She closed her eyes and tried to recall Jacob's face. But he was looking through bars and could not see her.

43

The Woman in the Mirror

Spieler was not there when the coachman dropped Will back at the plantation.

"Our master had to go away," said the golem, taking his luggage from him. "The young mistress went with him."

Was he talking about Clara? There was an envelope on his bed when he got to his room.

FOR WILL

The letters were more expansive and set on the paper with greater decisiveness than he had known from Clara, but the letter he pulled from the envelope was undoubtedly written by her.

Dear Will,

    Spieler has asked me to accompany him to Austry. I think it will do us both good if we don't see each other for a while. I hope the meeting with your father went as you wished.
    With love,
        Clara

He actually felt something like jealousy. Spieler and Clara… It was better this way, wasn't it?

He sat on his bed for a while, Clara's letter in his hand, numb from all that had happened, unsure what or if he felt anything at all. Maybe he really was like his father—more than Jacob.

He found Sixteen in her room. She was asleep on her bed, in the clothes under which she still hid her healing skin, though she was nearly perfect now. What if they just left? Before Spieler returned with Clara? To the west, as he had always wanted to do in his world and had never done?

Will glanced at Sixteen's sleeping form. Yes. They had to go away. In Spieler's presence, he felt as if he were lost in the fog. In a silver fog that made you think all your wishes had come true. He missed the Bastard. He was pretty sure he wouldn't have gotten lost in the fog. Maybe Will would even dare to go and see Kami'en. Didn't the heroes in fairy tales always take a few detours? Weren't they often clueless fools who performed deeds they were later ashamed of? *What about your brother, Will?* No. He and Jacob were now going their separate ways. He would never feel quite grown up as long as his brother was around. The Jade Goyl belonged in another story.

"Young master." One of the golems stood behind him. Theta. They were not at all as similar as he had initially believed.

"I have been instructed to show you something upon your return."

The golem led him to the library. For a moment, Will wondered if Clara had stayed after all. But there was no one waiting among all the books. On the wall hung a mirror that he had not noticed before. It was plain and round.

The golem left him alone without explaining why he had brought him here. He was gone before Will could ask.

Something stirred in the mirror. At first, Will thought it was only his own reflection, but then he saw that the glass showed a woman's figure. She had her back to him, but when he stepped closer, she turned.

His mother smiled at him as if they had last seen each other only hours ago. She looked young, healthy. Happy.

"He promised me you'd come," she said. "He says you're all right?"

There was no pain in her voice, no fear of death, not even the melancholy Will had heard so often that he had thought it a natural part of her.

He had never seen the room she was in. *It's not real, Will. Nothing you see is real. Your mother is dead! It's nothing but a mirror. An enchanted mirror.*

"Come closer!" She smiled at him.

He obeyed. It could not be. He had seen her die.

"I hope you get along with your father?"

Get along? He had nearly beaten him to death.

"I mean your real father." She stepped toward him.

So close. Will reached out and touched her reflection. It

didn't feel like glass. His fingers thought they were touching fabric, warm skin. He pulled his hand back, startled.

"My real father? He was never my real father. All I ever had was you."

"I'm talking about Spieler!" She laughed. "He hasn't told you yet?"

Will backed away.

"Don't be afraid." She brushed her hair back. The gesture was so familiar. "I'm sure he wanted me to tell you. Aren't you glad? After all, you never liked John. It's like you always knew he wasn't your father."

She held out her hand to him.

"Take my hand, Will. It's going to be all right. It's all going to be the way it's supposed to be."

No. Everything in him said no. *Don't do it, Will. She's dead.* But he stepped toward the mirror and reached for the hand that stretched out to him in the glass.

He felt her fingers around his, so familiar. Like her perfume, as she cradled him in her arms.

He didn't know where he was. But he didn't want to be anywhere else.

44

ENDED

Everything will be as it should be. Spieler tugged at the velvet that hid the mirror that now guarded them both: the woman he couldn't forget and her son. And where could they be safer than behind his glass? The day would come when he would have them both by his side, but now it was time to live a new love. And to be at home in this world again.

It was Theta who brought Sixteen in. He did it with obvious reluctance. They didn't like each other, his creatures, but the golem actually seemed to feel something like compassion. Did Sixteen know why her creator had summoned her to him? Perhaps.

"I will travel with Clara to Austry."

"Are you going to take Will with you, too? He's back, isn't he? Where is he? I haven't seen him yet."

No, she knew nothing. All she could think about was the love nesting in her silver heart. It surprised him that they could love like that.

"Will is with his mother. He won't be back for a while. Which means I'm no longer in need of your services."

Now she understood.

Desperation. Yes, they felt it, too. He had seen it often enough on their faces.

Spieler clapped his hands, and Sixteen shattered into a thousand pieces.

They covered the carpet like splintered ice. Among the shards lay a silver pearl. Spieler picked it up and slipped it into his pocket. He had made Sixteen with a life spark from Krieger. That was one more reason why her story had had to end here and now.

He called Theta to pick up the splinters. He had them ground up and mixed into the soil where the plants were grown in the greenhouses. This strengthened their magic.

45

Buried Alive

The cell smelled of fresh cement, and its walls were still immaculately gray—no desperate tallies counting empty days and nights, no names testifying to previous inmates and their fear of being forgotten. The Goyl had moved him as soon as they had fished him out of the flooded dungeons of the old prison, along with Hentzau and the prince. Jacob had tried to count the cells when they had brought him in, but he had quickly given up. They stretched like wells along the jasper-paved walkways, seemingly endless rows of stone holes with only a grate closing them off at the top. It was a very effective way to keep prisoners—and isolated from each other.

Jacob still had no idea how Fox and Hideo had brought a flood into the imperial dungeons, but it had forced the Goyl to clear all the cells in the lowest vault. Jacob estimated that they had moved close to fifty prisoners — though the dungeon holes made it feel like he was the only living thing down here. Even the Goyl wardens who lowered food through the ceiling grate were mere silhouettes in the darkness, faceless as the voices he sometimes heard in the distance.

He had tried to get the wardens to talk, but neither insults nor the lie that he had important information about the events that had led to his transfer elicited any response. Even Spieler's golems had been more communicative. And so Jacob filled the silence in his open stone grave with the sound of his own footsteps as he imagined what Fox must have looked like when she had stood outside his cell, invisible to his useless eyes, voiceless and untouchable except for the few fleeting moments when he had felt her fingers, and his hand had touched her body.

She had been there, hadn't she? *Yes, Jacob. As real as the water that suddenly soaked your clothes and the anger on Hentzau's face.*

Fox. He reached his hands into the empty air as if he might thus find her warmth once more, but she was not there, and he was nothing but bait for his own brother, kept in a stone hole like a worm in a fisherman's rusty tin can. And perhaps he would soon tell the Goyl how they could conquer another world, for they knew even more about torture than the ugly Elf. Would it help to remember that his father had never told the Goyl about the mirrors, though John Reckless could be called a coward for many reasons?

Jacob kicked at the immaculate gray wall, even though it only made him feel more like a helpless idiot. *Just like back then, Jacob.* The same useless rage as the night when, barely twelve years old, he had trashed his father's abandoned study.

331

But then, through his aimless frenzy, he had at least found the note that had opened the mirror for him. No prospect of similar miracles in this tomb. Yes, that was the appropriate name for Kami'en's new prison.

"What do you think? Is your jade brother on his way here yet, Reckless?"

The voice came from a cell hole to his left. He had heard it before, in the other dungeon where there had still been faces. But even without a face, you could tell it belonged to a Man-Goyl. Their voices were lighter than Goyls', but harsher than humans'. Will had sounded like that since he had grown the jade.

"I don't think the treasure hunter talks to our kind, Mars."

Ah, a name at last. Jacob had heard of Mars. The leaders of the rebellious Man-Goyl liked to give themselves the names of old gods. Mars was the leader of an army nearly five thousand strong that had been marauding through the Goyl's northern territories. There were now a dozen of these bands, all more than a thousand strong and notorious for their ferocity. The complete fearlessness and enormous physical strength that the Fairy's curse gave them made them dangerous. Jacob remembered all too well the battle with Will in the imperial palace of Vena. He had not stood a chance. But Kami'en was a brilliant strategist and fought them successfully with their own kind. The Goyl had integrated the Man-Goyl into their armies from the beginning, while the Humans mercilessly hunted down the new species the Fairy Curse had created and burned alive those who tried to return to their old lives.

"What have you got against us, Reckless?" You could tell Mars was used to being answered. "Your brother is one of us."

His brother. What would they have said if he had told them that Will had an immortal father and was from another world? Why didn't he tell the Man-Goyl about the mirror as well? That would give his old world even more exciting visitors.

"I still can't stand you, Mars!" he called up to the grate. "I can't stand your kind any more than I can stand the Goyl."

The laughter that answered him was well deserved. Fox had overcome her dislike of the Goyl through Will, but to him, they were still the Others, and the Bastard hadn't made it any better. 'They scare you,' Fox had once said to him when he'd tried to explain his aversion. 'The Goyl are like you, but they are stronger and more persistent, and you can't see through them as easily as you can most humans. Secretly you admire them, but you'd never admit it.' She was probably right about all that. She was right most of the time.

Jacob squatted on the floor and leaned his back against the wall. The cells were as stuffy and hot as the child-eaters' ovens, but the stone surrounding them at least provided some coolness.

"We're looking for your brother, too, Reckless!" shouted Mars. "And even if you make a splendid decoy... we will find him before Kami'en. We will make the Jade Goyl our king, and he will unite all our armies and chase humans and Goyl before him like locusts."

Well, fine. Will would undoubtedly like that.

"Of course he'll free you then, too!" the other shouted. "If Kami'en doesn't execute you first. But there are whispers that you're stewing down here for another reason. You're supposed to be keeping some big secret."

Stewing... That described it pretty well. How had he been able to compare cell holes to wells? Wells were cool and damp. These were cauldrons, and breathing was almost as hard as in the caves through which he and the Goyl had escaped from Spieler. Too hard to converse with two invisible voices. *Some big secret...*

"Yes, we will have our own kingdom!" Mars started daydreaming. His voice took on a ridiculously prophetic tone. "The future belongs to the Man-Goyl. You and the Goyl will soon exist only in fairy tales!"

Now it was Jacob's turn to laugh. "The future belongs to you? Is there even one female Man-Goyl? The Fairy played a wicked trick on you there."

The silence that followed his words was black and heavy.

"And as for my brother..." *Hold your tongue, Jacob, or soon there will be someone else who will want to lynch you.* But of course, he couldn't hold it. "He'll throw your crown at your feet!" he shouted up to the grate. "My brother doesn't feel like ruling. He loves to serve — a cause, a king, a woman..."

A woman made of glass, made by Jacob's worst enemy. Where was Will? Had he found Spieler? And Clara? *I don't need an older brother to fight my battles for me anymore.* No, he was probably right about that. *Most certainly*, he thought he heard Fox whisper.

Fox... He closed his eyes — and saw her dancing with Orlando in the Czar's palace. Hentzau had enjoyed telling him that she was staying with her old friend in the same hotel where he had so often stayed with her.

One of the Man-Goyl began to sing. They apparently even had an anthem now. His brother was in it.

MIRROR IMAGES

The mausoleum, where Orlando waited for Fox between large columns, guarded the alchemist prince's mortal remains, a member of the Austryn imperial family. The tomb was considered cursed since a grave robber had been found between the columns with a gilded chest. That is why they had agreed on the mausoleum as a meeting place if one of them had to go into hiding. Jacob dismissed the story as a fairy tale. But even the cemetery groundskeepers, who were used to ghosts, shied away from the marble-white tomb. By now it was so thickly overgrown with brambles and hawthorn that even the vixen was grateful for the path Orlando had cut through the thicket with his saber.

The black sheep of the Austryn imperial family had designed his final resting place himself, including the silver portal and the phoenixes that guarded it with amber eyes. The stairs leading up were covered with wilted leaves. Orlando sat on the top step.

Fox had expected him to be very upset and to make her promise to leave it to his diplomacy from now on to free Jacob. But when she pushed her way out of the thicket in fox form, he welcomed her with a smile.

"Where's your illustrated bodyguard?" he asked as he stood up and plucked the wilted leaves from the black tailcoat that was so often his work attire.

"There are a few graves here of immigrants who came to Austry from Nihon. Hideo was very touched by the inscriptions, and I could tell he longed to sit among the graves for a while and indulge his own thoughts." Fox sensed the child she carried more clearly than ever as she took on human form. Her daughter might not need a fur dress. The children of shapeshifters were often born with the gift. "I often did the same thing at my father's grave," she added, "and Hideo knows that meeting you is not one of my most dangerous undertakings."

Orlando smiled. Sometimes that smile was like an open book, and sometimes it reminded Fox of all the secrets he kept. This time, it was the latter.

"They're still pumping the water out of the vaults of the imperial dungeons. And fifty-one inmates have been moved to Kami'en's new prison. Apparently, it's completed to the point where it's considered escape-proof."

"No dungeon is escape-proof." Fox tried to decipher the inscription above the mausoleum entrance, but the letters were too mossy. Fox sensed no restless spirits behind the silver-studded door, but something troubled her. Fox could not discover what. She looked around and listened into the night. A barn owl called in the trees, and a rabbit darted out from behind a forgotten gravestone sticking out of the brambles. Perhaps his scent had made the vixen uneasy. At this time of night, she was the huntress.

"What are you going to do now?" asked Orlando. "Let me guess. Alberica is far away, so you probably won't go looking for Will. You're going to try one more time to free Jacob. Hideo's dragon is still around, and the lion that helped you in Jahoon. If all that fails, what then? Will you tell the Goyl where the mirror is? The one through which Jacob enters this world?"

The mirror... who had told Orlando about the mirror?

"Yes, you'd probably tell them." There was something in his eyes... it didn't match his face. "You'd show the Goyl the mirror, and Kami'en would be enraptured by all the weapons he can bring here from Jacob's world. What a mess. We probably wouldn't have as easy a time with Kami'en as Krieger thinks. But all that is unimportant compared to the problems the child you carry can cause me. Yes, prophecies rarely come true, but why should I take the risk? For a little girl with red hair and the eyes of her troublesome father?"

Orlando's hair started curling up, and his face changed from the one Fox had loved since the ball in Moskva.

Spieler showed himself to her as she had seen him in the garden of Krieger's fortress.

"Where's Orlando?"

Her heart raced for two. *Yes, Fox, your carelessness has put him and Jacob in danger.* And she hadn't even been able to tell Jacob about his daughter. She would lose her before he even knew about her.

"Orlando?" Spieler turned and eyed the mausoleum as if he were a tourist following the footsteps of the Austryn imperial family. "Oh, he's fine. He's at a reception for the newly crowned Albian queen. I expected him to stay with you at the Grand Hotel. After all, it's the best hotel in Vena, and Orlando Tennant loves living the life of the rich and powerful, even if it means playing the spy. He comes from a very poor family. Did he ever tell you that? I bought the Grand Hotel a few weeks ago and had all the rooms fitted with new mirrors. We have perfected the process so that Orlando Tennant will pay for his stolen face with merely a slight headache. You covered up the mirror in your room and only used the one in the bathroom. Clever vixen."

Clever? No. Fear of him had made her cautious. But not cautious enough.

"You will not have my child."

Spieler gave her a pitying smile. "It's been mine for a long time, vixen. Though I had hoped you would give me a few more years. This world has changed during our exile, and there is so much to do! You really shouldn't have come so close to me in Krieger's fortress."

No. There was a lot she shouldn't have done.

"Toshiró will bring back the Dark Fairy, and this time you won't escape her to another world!"

Spieler stroked his hand. It was missing a finger.

"Ah yes, Toshiró. You shouldn't have gotten involved with my enemies, vixen." His voice cut her with silver and glass. "Perhaps I would have merely taken your child if you had not delivered the yarn to Toshiró. But now you will die with him. It is better, anyway, if she is not born at all."

A croak shattered the silence between the graves. Of

course, he had brought the gingerbread baker. Hideo. Fox looked around searchingly. Would the witch take revenge on him for Jahoon?

Someone made his way through the brush surrounding the mausoleum, panting.

"Kitsune! She's here! I—"

Hideo stopped abruptly when he saw Spieler.

"Go, Hideo!" said Fox. "Find Orlando. See if he's all right."

Of course, he paid not the slightest attention to her words. All the things we say, even though we know they will go unheard…

"This is him?" The snake's head slid over the hand Hideo was pointing at Spieler with. "I admit, I imagined him to be more imposing. More like Toshiró."

Spieler didn't like the comparison at all.

"Ah yes… mortals easily mistake bluster for real power. Toshiró appreciates dramatic appearances much more than I do. But you shouldn't let that fool you, Yanagita Hideo."

Hideo shifted protectively in front of Fox. Usually, she did not allow others to make themselves her shield, but Jahoon had taught her that she could not protect the child she was carrying alone. Hideo's images were her only hope. The dragon with a thousand eyes slipped out of his clothes, and the protectors who had saved her in Jahoon's market took shape at Hideo's side. They grew until they towered over the mausoleum. The lion's mane was a fire in the night.

"I will not let you harm the kitsune, Elf." Hideo's voice did not sound quite as gentle as usual. "Not her, nor the child she carries."

"Oh no?" Spieler was still standing in front of the steps of the tomb. "You overestimate the power of your images, you tattooed fool. The child's story ends tonight, along with her mother's."

Fox clenched her hands over her body as if she could protect the daughter growing inside.

What would her name have been?

"Joie. That's what you would have called her, vixen. Joy." Spieler climbed the steps. "The innocent little thing. I saw her long before the treasure hunter freed you from the trap. At first, I wanted to kill him to prevent the child. But I was really attached to his mother."

Hideo took the stance with which the Holy Wrestlers began their battles, feet planted firmly on the ground.

"Kōgeki!"

Spieler let out a soft laugh.

"The lion came, I take it, from there?"

Hideo stared at the silver hoarfrost spreading across his chest. It ate away at the flowers covering his skin, and the lion at his side turned to smoke. The dragons dissolved even as Hideo tore off his silvered clothes. The images they had hidden were gone.

"I know who weaponized your skin," Spieler said, as the serpent that had been slithering toward him disintegrated into silver dust. "Tell Toshirō that he must have listened too long to the rustling of his leaves and forgotten who his opponent is."

Fox stepped to Hideo's side. She would no longer hide behind him. She had to protect herself now. Hideo stroked his bare skin and looked at her in despair.

"Your story is told, vixen." Spieler smiled at her. "And so is your daughter's. I hear the treasure hunter won't be around much longer, either."

The Witch Crow landed on his shoulder. Its feathers were tarnished silver. Yes, Spieler had given his helper a new body.

"Spare her fur dress," he said to her, "it's a very rare magic thing."

The crow soared into the air, and her forest began to grow, nourished by her darkness, interspersed with Spieler's silver. The blossoms that opened among the dark trees poisoned the night with their scent. The tendrils that reached for Fox clawed into her skin even as she transformed, and above her the leaves began to whisper.

"Come, vixen. Get lost in my dark forest with your daughter. Let her taste the cinnamon and the sweet cakes. Where better to end your life?"

Fox fought off the branches that poked at her and the twigs that reached for her with prickly claws, but there were too many. Hideo tried to come to her aid, but the trees pushed him back.

"Yes, come, tear me apart!" cried Fox desperately into the thicket. "At least that way, he won't get my fur coat!"

Spieler was still standing on the steps. He was enjoying himself. He was enjoying himself very much.

If only she could have saved the child like she did the vixen's pups back then. Now they would both die in the fur the vixen had given her. Hideo pushed back the branches and twigs as if fending off a dozen other wrestlers. Oh, Hideo. She felt so sorry that he had lost all his pictures because of her. And now probably his life, too.

The vixen bit around, but her teeth found only leaves and thorny plant flesh. A tree that sprouted from the ground behind her poked at her with its branches. She dodged two of them, but the third pierced her body like a lance. Oh, the pain. *Joie. That's what you would have called her, vixen. Joy.* She fell to her knees.

"I'm so sorry," she whispered, "so sorry."

"Tasukete!" she heard Hideo cry desperately. "Toshiró, Tasukete!"

Fox thought she saw him bending over her protectively. Was the pain clouding her vision? How had he broken free? The thicket around them began to wilt, and cranes swarmed from Hideo's chest. Their slender bodies became fire, and the witch's forest began to burn as the birds flew toward Spieler. The Elf's face contorted in pain — or was it anger? — as they plunged their burning beaks into his immortal flesh, and Fox heard a scream of silver as his form dissolved before their eyes. He vanished as if the night had swallowed him, while fresh green drifted from the witch's darkness and silver pollen rose in veils from Hideo's skin. Wherever it fell, blossoms opened like fragrant snow, and the night no longer smelled of cinnamon and death.

Fox tried to sit up, but the pain of her wounds threw the vixen whimpering into the grass. She searched among the stars for the crow, but the gingerbread baker was gone as well as Spieler, and the silver pollen from Hideo's skin trickled down on her, covering her fur with flowers.

Like a shroud, it whispered inside her. How could there still be life in all that pain? Joie. She had lost her. What was she going to tell Jacob? She had not been able to protect his daughter.

A few steps away, Hideo lay on his knees, panting. On his chest, fiery cranes flew through a rain of silver flowers, but they were only colored ink on his pale skin. His entire body was once again covered with images, but the pain blurred them all before Fox's eyes.

"Kitsune!" Hideo got to his feet with difficulty and stumbled toward her.

She felt blood, blood everywhere, in her fur, in the damp grass.

"Failed!" stammered Hideo as he tried to stop it with his clothes. "Oh, I'm the worst of protectors!"

Fox was too weak to disagree. The fact that the fur had not left her made it easy for Hideo to carry her.

47

A World as Prize

Jacob woke up to something crawling across his forehead. The rats had not yet discovered Kami'en's new dungeon, but the insects were everywhere: ants, rock mosquitoes, spiders. He swatted at the nocturnal visitor, even though he knew the next one wasn't far away. Was it night? One lost all sense of time in the subterranean darkness. Only sleep gave escape, and Jacob was about to roll onto his side to find his way back to the dream from which the insect had snatched him when he saw the will-o'-the-wisps above him.

This was new.

They swarmed into his dark dungeon hole in such numbers that their flickering briefly transported him to another place, a palace in Venetia where, surrounded by will-o'-the-wisps,

344

he had searched for a carousel that turned children into adults and adults into children.

"I thought your human eyes would appreciate some light." The Bastard's voice quickly chased away the illusion.

Too bad. He wasn't in Venetia, he was still in a dungeon. This was happening decidedly too often by now.

"The wardens were very obliging. After all, the Bastard is in and out of their king's chambers." The Goyl was just a black outline above the grate that was Jacob's new sky, but he could hear how much the Bastard enjoyed looking down on him like at a trapped bug. "Kami'en is fascinated by the idea of another world. You'll see. The mirrors will make him forget his anger at the Jade Goyl, and once he sees how dangerous the Silverlings are, he'll call him back to his side himself! How did I manage that? I think you should applaud me. And maybe fall to your knees in gratitude? The Bastard saves Jacob Reckless's little brother..."

"To make the Goyl invincible. Perfect." Jacob remained lying on his cot. At least that way, he didn't have to crane his neck when he talked. Outplayed. He still wanted to slap himself for actually believing he could trust his old enemy. And now the Goyl knew about the mirrors.

"Come on!" The Bastard leaned over the grate. "Tell me where the mirror is that usually brings you to this world. It's certainly not the one in Nihon. I'd bet my grained skin you've got it hidden not too far from here. How does the name Schwanstein sound?"

Easy, Jacob.

"Fantastic. Did you get that from a fairy tale?"

Damn. Of course, the Bastard knew he'd had a room in Schwanstein for years. Any kid could have figured that out.

Jacob sat up. "All right, all kidding aside. You seriously think I'm stupid enough to live in the same place where I hide the mirror?"

That gave him second thoughts, at least. But eventually, the Bastard would search the ruin. And then? *You have to get out of here and smash the mirror, Jacob.*

"If you don't tell me, the vixen will. Her pitiful attempt to free you will probably have convinced her that this is her only hope of getting you back. That is if she's still alive. The floods that washed her away could have drowned more than one vixen."

Nonsense, Jacob. She's a fisherman's daughter. She was all right. She definitely was. But now she had to hide not only from Spieler, but from Kami'en's soldiers, and he wasn't by her side.

Damn!

He turned to the wall. "Get out of here! Or I'll tell the guards that your precious seal is a fake."

The Bastard laughed. Oh yes, he was having the time of his life. "Kami'en gave me a new one. Come on! Tell me where the mirror is. She's all alone out there. What if the Elf finds her while you're in this cell?"

Yes, what if? The Bastard had learned too much about his problems with the Elf in Spieler's castle. What if he just pretended to show them the mirror? Tempting. It was better than playing bait for his brother while Fox was probably already planning the next insanity to free him.

"You know what the maid who mends your clothes at the Grand Hotel told me?" The Bastard let every word roll off his tongue. "Your vixen wanted to know if she'd ever been pregnant. Interesting, isn't it?"

Jacob stared at the cell floor. The Goyl read every emotion from humans' foreheads.

Don't be an idiot, Jacob! he snapped at himself. *Of course, that's a lie. Fox has assured you a thousand times that the witchcraft remedies she uses are safer than any contraceptive available in your world.*

"The child is yours, I take it? Although… the last time I saw her, she was with that Albian spy, Orlando Tennant. The two of them seemed very familiar with each other." Oh, the Goyl was having so much fun.

Orlando. Yes… Why was Orlando with Fox? *Stop it, Jacob! Are you going to play the jealous fool now, too?* It was good that Orlando was with her. And Hideo. She wasn't alone. That was all that mattered.

Pregnant… What if the Bastard wasn't lying? And Spieler found out about it? He wanted to smash his head against the wall.

"I'll say it again. Get out of here!" he snapped at the Goyl. "Show your king where Spieler's palace is. After all, it's underground. That's Goyl territory, isn't it?"

The wisps had settled on the Goyl's clothes. They drew his figure in the darkness as if it were made of stars.

"Oh, don't worry. We're already drawing the map that will record the exact location of the palace. And all the caves and tunnels I dragged you through. But fine, I'll leave." The Bastard spat through the grate and straightened up. "I'll go in search of the vixen. If Kami'en threatens her with torture, I'm sure you'll show us the mirror. What do you say? Does that prospect frighten even the intrepid Jacob Reckless?"

He wheeled around.

The voice shouting something gruffly at the Bastard in Goyl was familiar to Jacob, even without his seeing the one shouting. Hentzau. The wisps swarmed as he appeared beside the Bastard.

"What are you doing here? Trying to prove once again that the Bastard is smarter than all of us? Mirrors to other worlds, the Jade Goyl who makes Kami'en invincible... You're the only one who still believes in the fairy tale. You've been looking for magic things too long, Bastard. The Jade Goyl killed the Fairy. That's the most useful thing he'll ever do. Now all he has to do is die so Kami'en will finally forget about her!"

Hentzau unlocked the grate over Jacob's cell hole and lifted it.

"Don't do anything stupid, even though I know how hard that must be for you!" he shouted down to him. Hentzau had a heavy accent when he spoke Albian. He pushed a rope over the edge of the hole with his boot. "Start climbing, treasure hunter."

Jacob hesitated but finally obeyed. Anything was better than being down here thinking about whether Spieler had found Fox yet.

"Do I get to know where we're going?"

"You'll find out soon enough!" Hentzau barked at him. The three Goyl soldiers standing behind him were royal guards.

"And you," Hentzau pushed the Bastard back from the dungeon hole. "What are you still doing here?"

"I was close to extracting from him where we could find one of the mirrors!"

"Damn fool!" Hentzau now barked at Nerron. "You should never have told Kami'en about the mirrors. He has more than enough on his hands in this world. Find the Jade Goyl if you want to be useful. The rebellious Man-Goyl are blathering about making him their leader. The sooner Kami'en executes him, the better."

The Bastard stared down at Jacob. *Do you believe me now?* his gaze asked. *Show Kami'en your world if you want your brother to live.*

He was gone when Jacob pulled himself over the edge of the dungeon hole. Only the wisps still swarmed in the darkness.

48

FLOWERS

Who wove the threads that inextricably bound one's own destiny to that of others? Kami'en held his son in his arms and heard the child murmur the same words over and over again:

"Jacob Reckless! Find Apaullo and the one who makes wax breathe."

One of the nannies had begged the guards to wake him because the crown prince was unresponsive and kept whispering those words. Kami'en had been grateful that they had roused him from sleep, for he had been plagued for weeks by the same dream: he was searching for Kochany in a maze of mirrors, but each time he thought he had found him, his hands bumped into glass, and he touched only his son's reflection.

Kami'en had never been a particularly caring father, even if he had tried to play the role better than his own maker, and it disturbed him that this son held his heart in his small hands like a bird. The love he felt for him both frightened him and gave him joy he had never known.

"Jacob Reckless! Find Apaullo and the one who makes wax breathe."

The words, meanwhile, were just a sleepy flow. The eyes under the long lashes were shut tight, and the Fairy lilies stood out on his son's skin as if looking at their white blossoms through frosted red glass. They were everywhere, on the little hands, arms, legs, and narrow chest. The nannies had at first mistaken the blossoms for a rash, but Kochany's skin was as smooth and warm as ever, and Kami'en had only had to glance at him to know what the lilies and the words meant: his lost lover was not extinguished like her sisters, whose dead lakes he had seen for himself. She spoke to him through the child whose true mother she was. But what was she trying to tell him?

"Jacob Reckless! Find Apaullo and the one who makes wax breathe."

It was still dark when Hentzau took the treasure hunter to the pavilion where the Dark Fairy had lived after Kami'en's wedding. A few weeks ago, Hentzau had found Kochany there after he had disappeared from his bed at night, sleeping among the shards of the collapsed roof. The child had insisted on sleeping in the pavilion every night since. So Kami'en had it restored and spent many hours there himself—with his son and the memories of a past that seemed so much more powerful than the present.

"Here he is, Your Highness." Hentzau made no secret of how reluctantly he had carried out his order. "Jacob Reckless."

Who was weaving the threads? Why was his fate so inextricably linked to that of two human brothers? The Fairy probably could have explained it to him, but he had chosen a human woman over her.

Hentzau looked with an expressionless face at the sleeping child in his king's arms. Kami'en knew that his old comrade-in-arms felt, at best, jealousy and distrust for his youngest son. Hentzau thought Kochany was just another of the Fairy's devilish spells and hated playing his bodyguard. Still, no one would defend him better and more selflessly. And Kami'en had, of course, not explained to Hentzau that he had also given the task to him because he feared for his health. His jasper dog was getting too old for the rigors of a warrior's life. The sunlight had nearly blinded him, and the child he had to guard, like his true mother, preferred night to day.

"Unshackle him."

Hentzau did not like that command either. He could not resist making it clear by a brief hesitation. But finally, he nodded to the guards.

Jacob Reckless eyed the child in Kami'en's arms with much more benevolence than Hentzau. His face showed curiosity, surprise, and, yes, affection. Human faces...

Their soft features were shaped by their feelings as if by the fingers of a potter. Kami'en, of course, knew of the visits his son had paid to the treasure hunter—and of Reckless's help when the child nearly drowned in the floods that still filled the vaults of the old prison.

"I suppose the blossoms on his skin are familiar to you." The Dark Fairy had told Kami'en how much her red sister had been in love with Jacob Reckless.

"Indeed."

Kami'en kissed his son's forehead. "Moje serce, wake up! Tell the treasure hunter what you told me."

Kochany's eyes were cloudy from sleep, but they cleared when he saw Reckless. The flowers on his skin opened wide, and his lips formed the same words Kami'en had been listening to for hours:

"Jacob Reckless! Find Apaullo and the one who makes wax breathe."

He smiled at the treasure hunter with as much contentment as someone who has finally delivered an important message to the right person. Then he closed his eyes again. The lips fell silent, the flowers faded, and Kami'en left his son to the nannies. They were all Goyl women, even if Amalie had protested.

"Can you explain what the words mean, treasure hunter?"

Jacob hesitated. But finally, he shook his head. "No. I don't know what they mean. But I can find out. If you let me go."

He knew more than he was saying. Jacob Reckless had many secrets. But Kami'en decided to let him have them for now. The Fairy had chosen him. Even the other world would have to wait now. Eventually, he would lead him to the mirror anyway. And the Bastard would have to find the Jade Goyl without his big brother playing bait.

Jacob Reckless. Find Apaullo and the one who makes wax breathe.

Why was that her wish? Whatever the reason, he trusted her. Just as he always had.

"You can't let him go, Your Highness! The Dark Fairy no longer exists! The words did not come from her!" Only Hentzau was allowed to speak so bluntly to the King of the Goyl. "And even if they did, why should you trust her? She abandoned you! The child has a fever, nothing more. And the treasure hunter is our best chance to catch his brother. Before the rebellious Man-Goyl find him and make the Jade Goyl their king!"

Kami'en looked to the treasure hunter. He could tell by looking at Reckless that he thought Hentzau's prophecy was ridiculous.

"Have you made your peace with your brother having a skin of stone?"

The question surprised him.

"He likes it," he finally returned. "And he would still serve you. If you forgive him."

"And make me invincible? I am invincible, treasure hunter."

He took his time picking an answer. Kami'en could tell he was discarding some.

"Do you believe in fairy tales?" he finally asked. "The one about the Jade Goyl promises you a good ending. Why would you want to thwart that by killing the one who brings it to you? My brother is not destined to be the king of a rebel army. My brother is destined to make you invincible. If you believe in fairy tales. In this world, it is wise to do so."

"And in yours?"

He weighed his words carefully. He was a wise treasure hunter.

"The Bastard has fallen for the delusions of a mirror. There is only this world. But in my experience, it contains thousands of worlds to be discovered. Above and below the surface."

Kami'en did not believe him. Even if he was a convincing liar. But it was better to pretend that he had deceived him. That was the only way he would show him the mirror one day. Jacob Reckless was not a man you could force. He had to be tricked.

Kami'en caught himself missing Jacob's brother.

He nodded to Hentzau, "Give him what he needs. Provisions, horses, weapons... what else?" He looked questioningly at the treasure hunter.

"A few magic things from the Empress's Chambers of Miracles."

"Your Highness!" Hentzau almost choked on his anger. It had always been that way with the Fairy. One more proof that the words came from her.

"How many men?" Kami'en asked the treasure hunter.

Jacob rubbed his wrists as if he still couldn't believe that the shackles were gone.

"The vixen," he said. "The vixen is all I need."

Kami'en looked questioningly at the guardsman standing just beside Hentzau.

"The spy has brought her to the Suleiman Embassy, Your Highness. The Sultan's doctors are treating her. Something attacked her last night and mauled her badly. By the cursed tomb."

Kami'en saw fear on Jacob Reckless's face for the first time. Fear. And love. So they were indeed a couple, the shapeshifter and the treasure hunter. *Make sure she stays by your side*, he wanted to tell him. *Or the void in your heart will never be filled again.*

"How bad?"

Reckless had forgotten where he was—not to mention the assignment he had been given.

Kami'en ignored Hentzau's angry glare and nodded to the guardsman. "Take him to her! Offer to have my doctors treat her as well. And you, treasure hunter, will find out what the words my son spoke mean."

"Not until she can come with me. I will not go without her."

"He lets you go, and you set conditions?" It would have made his old jasper dog so happy if he had let him teach Jacob Reckless some respect. But it was that very disrespect that made him so successful at what he did. His jasper dog should have understood that.

"Open our archives to him, too. The ones about the missing Elves and about magic."

Hentzau opened his mouth—and closed it again. "As you command, Your Highness." No one else could utter those words with such disdain. And no one knew him better. Except the Fairy.

She was not gone. Was that possible?

Jacob Reckless! Find Apaullo and the one who makes wax breathe.

Hopefully, he was as good as they said.

49

At Home

Fox dreamed that someone was kissing her. No, not someone. Jacob. He was kissing her as gently as if she had a skin of glass, like the prince she had seen outside his cell. She didn't want to wake up in the aching, bruised body, but Hideo's voice was so loud and angry, and suddenly Jacob's lips were gone, and his hand, which she had felt cool on her forehead.

She snapped her eyes open, lids still heavy with fever and neck so unwilling to turn to see who Hideo was shaking like a young dog.

"Show it!" he shouted. "Show it already, Elf! You can't outsmart us this time! Show your true colors!"

"Let go of me, Hideo! I only have the one face, you idiot!" Jacob.

Fox tried to sit up. But the wound in her side hurt too much and she fell back into the pillows with an annoyed groan.

"Kitsune!" Hideo dropped Jacob like a rag doll and hurried to her side.

Jacob got to his feet and wiped the blood from his lips.

"You won't escape this time!" Hideo insisted. "This palace is full of guards. And wizards. Tennant-san!"

He pointed to Jacob as Orlando stepped into the room with one of the doctors who had patched them up. "The Elf is here!"

Orlando eyed Jacob for a moment as if unsure whether Hideo might be right.

"No," he finally said. "No, I think he's real, Hideo. Don't you think your pictures would get excited if he wasn't? I was about to report to Fox that Kami'en had let the treasure hunter go. But he beat me to it again."

"I appreciate Hideo's caution," Jacob said. "I hear she's only alive because of him. He's welcome to knock out a few of my teeth for that."

"I'm sorry, Reckless-san," Hideo stammered. "The Elf has too many faces."

"Indeed. And too many servants." He looked back at Orlando. "Are you sure she is safe from him here?"

"No. There is no such place. But the Sultan I serve asked me to give you this. So that at least you won't lose sight of her in the future." He pulled a locket from his pocket and placed it in Jacob's hand.

"The Eye of Love!" Jacob looked at Orlando in disbelief.

"It's on loan. Mehmed the Magnificent has many magical things in his treasuries. And he gets very sentimental when he hears of separated lovers."

Jacob sat in the chair Orlando had spent many hours in since he and Hideo had brought her here. Seeing Jacob sitting there now was so surreal that Fox wondered if she was just caught in one of the endless fever dreams the crow had given her. Jacob reached for her hand as if to prove her wrong. His fingers cooled her burning skin, and her heart opened as if it were coming home after a long, long time.

What if Hideo was right to be cautious? What if Spieler would one day deceive her like he had deceived Jacob's mother? He had succeeded with Orlando. *No*, whispered the vixen. *I will always smell the silver. Spieler knows and that's why he didn't get too close.* Hopefully, she was right. Because Spieler would find them again. Fox had no doubt about that.

Jacob brushed the hair from her damp forehead and gave the doctor a questioning look.

"No," Orlando said in his place. "It's a miracle, but she didn't lose it."

Fox groped for Jacob's hand. Who had told him?

"The Bastard," he whispered to her. "He got it from the maid at the hotel. He had tremendous fun telling me."

"One wound, in particular, was very deep," Orlando said. "But your child already seems very attached to life. Like its mother."

Fox saw so much on Jacob's face. Relief, fear, bewilderment… yes, that too. She saw everything she felt herself.

"It's a daughter," she whispered to him. "And I couldn't protect her." She felt tears streaming down her face. It had been a terrible feeling, more terrible than anything she had ever felt.

"But you were protecting her."

Fox shook her head. Even that hurt. "No, that was Hideo."

"And I will continue to protect her, Kitsune," Hideo said. "Both of you."

The doctor said something in Suleiman to Orlando. Then he left the room with a bow.

"He thinks you'll be back on your feet in three weeks." Orlando stepped to Jacob's side. "And yes, you couldn't ask for a better bodyguard for her. Show him the dragon, Hideo. He loves dragons."

Hideo coaxed a long-tailed blue dragon from his sleeve with a low hum. "I just spotted him behind some flowers." He hastily shooed it back before it began to grow. "There are so many, Kitsune! Many more than before."

Fox saw Jacob struggling to get used to the idea of traveling not only with her from now on, but with her bodyguard as well. And with his magical creatures...

"I can see I've missed a lot," he said. "I have a thousand questions, but I will ask Orlando. You need to sleep. And get well."

Yes, she had to. But it would be so much easier now. Without all the worry about him.

"Why are you free?" Even those few words were a tremendous effort.

"That's a long story, too. I'll tell it to you when you're feeling better."

"I want to hear it now," Fox managed to say.

Jacob exchanged a knowing look with Orlando. "She's not going to back down."

"No." Orlando again had a trace of sadness in his eyes. Fox feared that sadness, because she was the reason. Was it possible to love two men?

"I can tell you that Kami'en's son played a crucial role," Jacob said. "And that his father let me go so we could find something for him. Sound familiar?"

Fox closed her fingers tightly around his hand. Yes, he was indeed there. "My fur dress is torn."

"Not for the first time. We'll have it mended."

"It's bad this time."

"I'll take it to the maid at the Grand Hotel, even if she's been chatting with the Bastard." He kissed her. "You'll see, it'll be like new by the time you're well enough to wear it again."

She hadn't lost him. And she was still carrying his child.

She closed her eyes, but that's where the questions waited. How badly had Hideo's cranes hurt Spieler? Had the crow escaped their fire? The fever made Fox feel like it was still burning inside her. But Toshiró had given Hideo new pictures and all was well.

"What shall we find for Kami'en?" she brought to her lips.

"Later." Orlando sounded very firm.

Jacob leaned over her.

"Whatever it is," he whispered to her, "you know we'll find it."

50

THE SHRINE

On the northernmost island of Nihon, there once stood a shrine dedicated to the sea goddess Toyotama-hime. It was a very modest shrine, hidden in a mountain forest near the coast.

One night an old man came there pleading for help for his sick daughter. He stole into the inner chamber, although this was forbidden to supplicants, because he believed he could hear the voice of the goddess there. But he did not find Toyotama-hime, only a robe lying on a large stone that had surely once been washed by the sea. The robe consisted of only one golden thread and it wove itself. The old man could not take his eyes off the yarn, which added row after row to the shimmering fabric. And as the moonlight stole into the shrine, as if it had caught him, he thought he saw the body of a woman beneath the fabric. Fearing that he had angered the goddess and that she would not heal his daughter, he fled outside. But there three guards were waiting for him: a dead man, pale as the silver moon, an enormous stallion the color of night, and a kitsune with nine tails. They made him promise not to tell anyone about the robe. The old man swore it on his daughter's life and the next morning she was cured.

TEEN AND YA FICTION

*Available and coming soon
from Pushkin Press*

BEARMOUTH
Liz Hyder

GIFTEN
Leyla Suzan

THE DISAPPEARANCES
SPLINTERS OF SCARLET
Emily Bain Murphy

THE BEAST PLAYER
THE BEAST WARRIOR
Nahoko Uehashi

GLASS TOWN WARS
Celia Rees

THE MURDERER'S APE
THE FALSE ROSE
Jakob Wegelius

THE BEGINNING WOODS
Malcolm McNeill